'This is a wonderful book; it has the air of absolute truth. Funny, tragic, horrifying and ultimately noble, it succeeds in its aim of depicting the agony of a whole great country and at the same time telling us something about human nature in all its richness.'

– *British Book News*

'One of a very few Indian novels in which portraits of both male and female characters are equally well drawn.'

– Barbara Harrison in *Learning about India*

'Told with a confident realism lost to English fiction.'

– *Observer,* London

'This is a warm and optimistic book because it believes in people.'

– *Birmingham Post*

'There have been many books written on India from various aspects and various points of view. But I have not read anything with this depth of understanding or concern for a long time.'

– *Business Times,* Kuala Lumpur

'This is a book very well worth reading.'

– *Times of India*

'Chaman Nahal brilliantly draws a portrait of a war-torn land and of one family trying to bring order and safety to their lives... A memorable journey and one related so dramatically and realistically that it is likely to live forever in our minds and our hearts.'

– *Chicago Sun-Times*

'Sparked by humour, wise, calm...this fine book illuminates not only a bad time in history, the lot of the Hindu and the Muslim, but the human condition.'

– *Sunday Telegraph*

'No one...has dramatized this terrible episode in our recent history with such sweeping power and authenticity.'

– Bhabani Bhattacharya

AZADI

Chaman Nahal, formerly Professor of English at Delhi University and Fellow, Churchill College, Cambridge University, was the author of nine novels, four of which constitute *The Gandhi Quartet*. For *Azadi*, which has been translated into ten languages, he received the Sahitya Akademi Award as well as the Federation of Indian Publishers Award. His other publications include a collection of short stories, three children's novels and several other literary books. He was a Fulbright visiting scholar at Princeton University from 1967 to 1970 and was a visiting professor at various universities in the US, Europe, Asia and Australia. He ran a column, 'Talking about Books' in the *Indian Express* from 1966 to 1973. Chaman Nahal also held the Dai Ho Chun Distinguished Chair at the University of Hawaii, 1998-99, where he taught creative writing. Mr Nahal passed away in 2013.

PRAISE FOR THE BOOK

'A classic.'

– Diana Athill

'Nahal's work will take its place as one of the rare tragic narratives in Indian fiction...intensely felt and poignant.'

– Mulk Raj Anand

'A poignant and moving narrative...full of lessons that will never be learnt.'

– *New York Times*

'Moving, dignified, and enthralling.'

– *Sunday Times*

'Nahal's impressive and elegantly written novel...tells more of the truth about Partition than any historical study.'

– *Times*

'As long as novels like *Azadi* are written in the language, there is strength and continuity in the English novel.'

– *New Society*

'Mr Nahal, with detailed description of the daily lives of seven families... shows how they were swept along by events. Hindus and Muslims spoke and wrote one Punjabi language, implicitly respected each other's religion, intermarried, shared business interests, attended mixed classes in schools, joined a mixed police force and mixed arms regiments—but in 1947 it all disappeared. Mr Nahal's simple and moving story brings out each of these points.'

– *Times Literary Supplement*

'Here is India. India colourfully, penetratingly, amusingly and agonizingly. No one but an Indian could have written this book, and not many Indians would do it as well as Chaman Nahal.'

– *Seattle Times*

'Done most convincingly, revealing the contradictions, the illusions, the smallness of outlook and occasional acts of kindness and humanity in the face of common disaster.'

– *Sunday Standard*

'A wonderfully deep and interesting story that is full of the flavour of India, the Punjab, and the time.'

– John Kenneth Galbraith

'Chaman Nahal, an Indian writer of unusual ability, has come close to answering the question of the slaughter of the innocents in the compelling novel *Azadi*.'

– *Philadelphia Inquirer*

'Mr Nahal's achievement is to show through the eyes of his main character, Lala Kanshi Ram, a Hindu, how people insist on the same patterns of behaviour for themselves whatever their circumstances, whether "free" or not.'

– *Guardian*

'This novel depicts in graphic detail the catastrophic incidents that took place immediately after the announcement in June 1947 of the British intention to quit India after partitioning it.'

– *The Hindu*

'Hope and renewal are mingled with terror. The reader is moved but heartened, terrified but uplifted. Therein lies the unique quality of the novel.'

– *All India Radio*

'*A Passage to India* written by an Indian...with a lyrical, loving tone.'

– *Chicago Tribune*

'The power Nahal displays is his sympathetic human involvement, his ability to show that in spite of wide differences in social mores between India and the West, man is man wherever you find him.'

– Carlos Baker

'A magnificent work of fiction... It should be required reading at our universities.'

– *Hindustan Times*

'In *Azadi* Chaman Nahal describes this disaster and this tragedy with brilliancy, compassion, and great humanity.'

– Maxwell Geismar

'Chaman Nahal is a brilliant writer. The book is a good illustration of painstaking and painful documentation.'

– *The Tribune*

'Novels such as *Azadi* can help us to know and understand other peoples, to find some meaningful sense of our common humanity.'

– *Kansas City Star*

AZADI

Chaman Nahal

hachette
INDIA

First published in the United States in 1975 by Houghton Mifflin
First published in India in 1975 by Orient Longman

This edition published in India in 2023 by Hachette India
(Registered name: Hachette Book Publishing India Pvt. Ltd)
An Hachette UK company
www.hachetteindia.com

SRD

Map illustration by Neelima P Aryan (adapted from the original by K.B. Kumar)

The introduction has been excerpted from the original version that appeared in the 2001 edition of the book.

ISBN 978-93-93701-86-2

Hachette Book Publishing India Pvt. Ltd
4th & 5th Floors, Corporate Centre,
Plot No. 94, Sector 44, Gurgaon - 122003, India

Printed and bound in India
by Manipal Technologies Limited

TO THE MEMORY OF
KARTAR DEVI

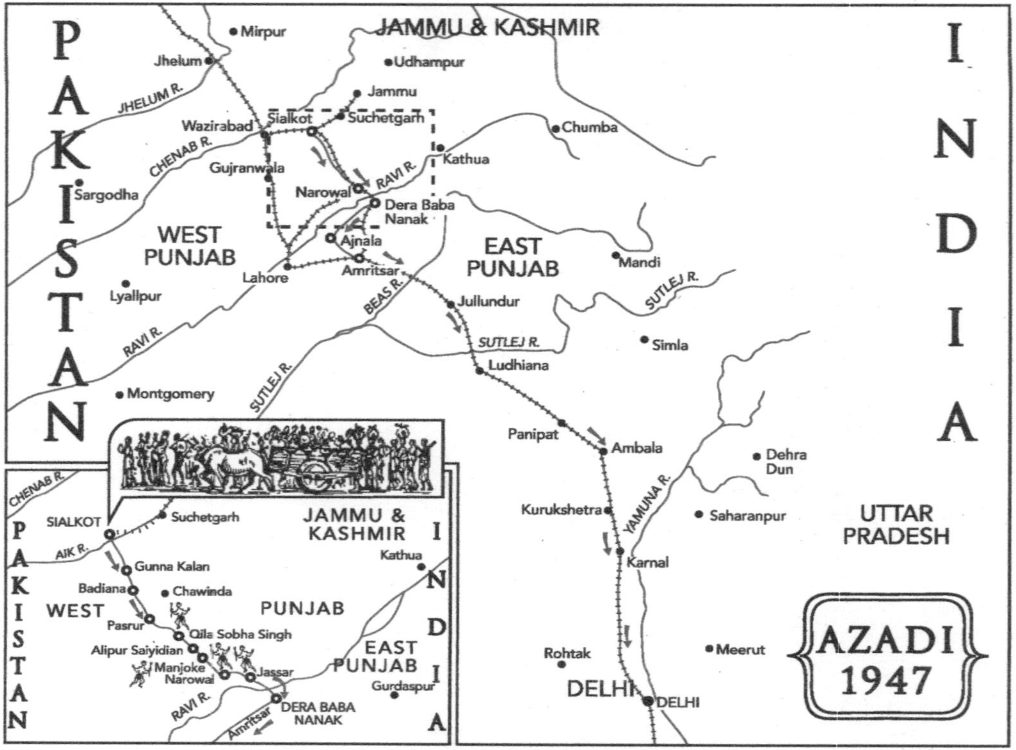

This map is a pictorial representation and not to scale. It is for general illustration only. Neither boundaries nor locations depicted above are accurate or precise and should not be used for reference purposes.

Where the mind is without fear and
the head is held high;
Where knowledge is free;
Where the world has not been broken
up into fragments by narrow domestic walls;
Where words come out from the
depth of truth...
Where the clear stream of reason has
not lost its way into the dreary desert
sand of dead habit...
Into that heaven of freedom, my
Father, let my country awake.

– Rabindranath Tagore

CONTENTS

INTRODUCTION

At the time of Partition, I was in college and like many others was completely taken aback by the decision to divide the country into two separate states. More than fifty years after that event the scars still show, in my reaction to ethnic violence, ethnic insults and ethnic demands which surface every now and then in the same divisive, unwholesome vein. What have we learnt from that monumental event in our history, if we persist in confrontation instead of dialogue?

Azadi was published many years after Partition. In the meantime I mulled over the vagaries of history which like fate I came to regard as an adversary of man: it also heaped unrelieved misery on him. One can perhaps explain away fate; faith in reincarnation and karma allows us to rationalize these impositions. History is made by man here and now and its disasters are avoidable.

Though history can be a bane for humanity, it can also be a boon. New ideas are discovered in its course, new notions floated, new horizons make their appearance. Even Mahatma Gandhi is part of history and what could be a greater blessing for us than to have had him as our leader? While analyzing and assessing history then, we have to be extremely objective.

For the professional historian, historical developments constitute so many events. He categorizes and catalogues them in a sequential manner, trying to find a justification for what happened; he is not concerned with emotions and feelings. For the historical novelist, human suffering of the moment has greater significance. Calamities like Partition will in all probability occur in the future as well. But their blows can be somewhat deflected if we remain aware of the traumas we have been through.

That was the core of this novel, though as a novelist it was not my business to be pedagogic. I wanted to tell a story, not write an essay on the subject. So I take up an average Indian family living in a small town and show how their entire lifestyle and attitudes are changed by Partition. As in every novel, there are some autobiographical bits in this one as well—the fact that I was born and raised in Sialkot, the town still closest to my heart, and that I had a sister who was assassinated during Partition, a sister I loved most dearly and who was the very epitome of personal dignity in the face of tragedy.

In *Azadi* I was largely concerned with showing how the partition of India in 1947 destroyed an existing harmony which had prevailed for centuries. India is known for its cultural synthesis, and never once when I was growing up did it strike me that I belonged to one particular sect and had to act according to its norms. The norms by which we lived were Indian norms, accepted and acknowledged all over the country and practised as such.

The first section of the novel, 'The Lull', establishes the harmony that kept the various communities in Sialkot together. Lala Kanshi Ram or Chaudhri Barkat Ali and their families never make religion the basis of their day-to-day decisions, nor does anyone else. Choices are made on the basis of economics, expedience, necessity and above all friendship. But these choices don't bring about a rift amongst them at any point. The greatest harm political decisions such as Partition do is that they polarize ethnic groups and place them in their own narrow confines and compartments; they force them to act their ethnicity out. Chaudhri Barkat Ali remains affable and friendly towards Lala Kanshi Ram till the end but the link between the communities in general is temporarily smashed.

To register further the cultural collapse of the time, I decided to show how the emotional damage caused by Partition occurred within each family itself, no matter what their ethnic identity. Lala Kanshi Ram, Prabha Rani and Arun feel altogether isolated and can hardly communicate with each other when they reach Delhi towards the end of the novel.

In the vast drama that unfolded after Partition, thousands were on the move at any given time, thousands were living in refugee camps, thousands were looking for new homes, thousands had turned destitute overnight. In all, ten million people were involved in the horror.

Kartar Devi, my remarkable sister, who perished in the riots and to whose sacred memory this novel is most humbly and respectfully dedicated, was twenty-seven when she died. When the communal riots aggravated just after Partition, she considered Wazirabad, the village where she lived, unsafe and along with her husband tried to reach us in Sialkot. But the train in which they were travelling was stopped along the way by a hostile mob and they were both cruelly murdered, as were hundreds of others on the train.

She was the most vivacious, the most provocative, the most engaging individual I have ever known; nothing could put her down for long. Her spirit has always been with me, in all the work I have done as a novelist, in whatever stories I have written. She continues to be the motivating force of all my faith, all my beliefs. For tragic and disturbing though her short life was, it raises a couple of even more disturbing questions.

Are wars and conflicts, which kill so many, which inflict unimaginable pain, which eventually resolve nothing, which bring out only the animal in us, necessary? Can't they be somehow avoided? More importantly, what do the lives of ordinary people like myself and my sister, amount to? The chronicles of the world are studded with luminaries alone—those who make it to the top. What about millions upon millions of us who happen to be just ordinary, making do with whatever comes our way? What is our reward? Who will ever remember us?

And this sister of mine perches next to me and mocks me and makes fun of my fits of depression. All lives have a meaning in a vaster context we cannot see. Not a single life is wasted away. Carry yourself with dignity, with uprightness, with firmness, no matter what. That's its own reward.

The character of Madhu in *Azadi* is partly based on her; she figures in some of my short stories and articles as well. Only very imperfectly, very imprecisely. My writing has failed to come up to the excellences of her life.

I'm aware that countless other sisters of mine were also done to death, raped, or whisked away in a similar fashion. And not only in Pakistan but here in India as well—my sisters from other faiths. The novel is a tribute to them all.

Even though there was distress of the same magnitude and horror in Bengal at the time of Partition, I refrain from covering that region; I was afraid of making a factual error somewhere. I stay firmly close to the Punjabi character and scene.

Indian towns are built on the guild system. A large number of communities belonging to a particular trade or profession live together in specific parts of the city and form a certain web. For a novelist to know his characters, he has to know his city. He has to know the connection between each mohalla and its residents: the jewellers, the ironsmiths, the carpenters, the hookah manufacturers, the watch makers, the rickshaw pullers, the weavers, the barbers, the butchers, the sweetmeat sellers, the cobblers, the temple priests, and many others.

Such people ever float at the back of my mind though I may not directly bring them into the story. The shuffle of their feet, their wide-open, white eyes, their slim but firm, dark chests, their unkempt hair, their panther-like agility and swiftness, their broad smiles constitute my never-ending reveries. As a writer, I look upon myself too as an artisan. I too work with my hands, when I'm chiselling away at words, sharpening pencils or pounding on my keyboard. The voice in me remains dormant until I have rubbed shoulders with these people. I'm only one of a crowd.

The sublime for me thus exists in the mundane and the ordinary. Prabha Rani packing her trunk while leaving Sialkot, Nur's reaction to the death of Madhu, Lala Kanshi Ram looking for a house in Delhi, Sunanda running her sewing machine in her room, are more momentous moments for me than the regalia and fanfare of aristocracy.

It is worth recording that there are two versions of *Azadi* now extant. The first one was published in 1975 and was lucky to get the attention of several highly reputed international critics. I realized then that there was a lot of strength in our freedom movement and perhaps the whole story could be retold by a novelist. Even though Partition itself was a disaster, the country did win its freedom from the British, a unique achievement by any account. Indeed, whatever power and momentum we have today as a nation stems from that period, and I decided to write a series of novels about it, a task on which I spent nearly a quarter of a century. I create another family in those novels, living in Amritsar, many members of which come under the sway of Gandhi. Through marriage I establish a relation between them and Lala Kanshi Ram, and the second version of *Azadi* has a fifty-page Epilogue to carry that connection to a conclusion. It was published in 1993 as the final volume of *The Gandhi Quartet*. The version appearing here is the original one of 1975.

Whenever I am present at a seminar, conference or classroom where the novel is discussed, I am invariably asked one question: why was there violence when people were willing to leave and migrate? There is no clear answer to this except that humanity at such moments stoops to its lowest. No religion, no sect, no mode of worship will sanction or condone organized aggression against the innocent. Yet, such aggression has occurred repeatedly in the story of mankind, much to its shame.

The 1975 edition has been translated into many languages, but the one that has given me the greatest satisfaction is the Urdu translation. It was done by my learned friend and colleague, Shujaud-din Siddiqui. That a Muslim scholar living in the heart of Delhi should accept and approve of my generalizations was immensely gratifying for me. He was also in agreement with me about the overall bonds that continue to survive amongst ethnic communities in India, occasional clashes or lapses notwithstanding.

I shall not offer an explanation or justification for writing in English. With the world-wide acclaim Indian English has received, any such clarification is superfluous. I will say this much about the mother tongue myth, though. The mother tongue gives no special edge to a creative writer; you are lost for words there as well when you are trying to balance the language and your narrative.

Using his skill, an artist creates vast, congenial spaces for us all. This is where his inspiration comes in: in expansion into the unknown and unfamiliar. The refurbished world he brings into existence has to be a more enjoyable place to live in, and he might well succeed if he is lucky. It is right over there, inviting us to test it out. We have only to take a step ahead.

New Delhi
May 2001

Chaman Nahal

PRINCIPAL CHARACTERS

Lala Kanshi Ram: a grain merchant of Sialkot, West Punjab (now in Pakistan), and Bibi Amar Vati's chief tenant
Prabha Rani: his wife
Madhu Bala: their daughter
Arun Kumar: their son
Bibi Amar Vati: a landlady of Sialkot
Gangu Mull: her husband
Suraj Prakash: their son
Sunanda Bala: Suraj Prakash's wife
Sardar Jodha Singh: a dry-fruit merchant of Sialkot, and another tenant of Bibi Amar Vati
Sardar Teja Singh: his son
Isher Kaur: Teja Singh's daughter
Niranjan Singh: Isher Kaur's husband
Padmini: a charwoman, also a tenant of Bibi Amar Vati
Chandni: her daughter

Lala Bihari Lal Phool Chand Bhagwan Devi Mangat Ram Ram Kali Mukanda's mother	other tenant families of Bibi Amar Vati

Chaudhri Barkat Ali: a sports-goods dealer of Sialkot, and a bosom friend of Lala Kanshi Ram
Begum Barkat Ali: his wife
Munir Ahmad: their son
Nurul-Nisar: their daughter
Dr Chander Bhan: a medical practitioner of Sialkot
Abdul Ghani: a hookah manufacturer of Sialkot
Pran Nath Chaddha: Deputy Commissioner
Asghar Ahmad Siddiqui: Superintendent of Police
Inayat-Ulla Khan: Inspector of Police
Sergeant William Davidson: a British army officer
Captain Rahmat-Ullah Khan: a Pakistani army officer
Major Jang Bahadur Singh: an Indian army officer

PART I
The Lull

CHAPTER 1

IT was the third of June, 1947. This evening, the Viceroy was to make an important announcement. That's what Lala Kanshi Ram told his wife Prabha Rani, whose education had become his task. Lala Kanshi Ram was not too literate himself—it is doubtful if he ever finished high school. But life had rolled him around, misfortunes had come and gone, and this had given an edge to his intelligence. And then he at least knew fairly well one local language, Urdu, which was the first language he had learned to read and write. His own language was Hindi, or so it was supposed to be. For over twenty years he had been an ardent member of the district Arya Samaj, and one thing that the Samaj had done was to give status to the low and the humble. Was he the son of a rich man or poor? Did he inherit landed property or did he not? These were the questions the Arya Samaj did not care one bit for. So long as you could tie a white turban on your head in a becoming manner, and so long as you boasted of an upright moral character, you were a khandani, a worthwhile citizen. And the Samaj taught him in no uncertain terms that the true heritage of an Indian was the Vedic heritage, and the true language of an Indian, Sanskrit—the language of the Vedas. Since Sanskrit was an ancient language, its modern derivative Hindi would do if you were unable to get that far back. So when the census was taken by the government every tenth year, Lala Kanshi Ram dutifully entered against the column for mother tongue, the word 'Hindi'. But he neither spoke Hindi nor ever wrote it on paper.

When he opened his mouth he spoke Punjabi, the rich and virile language of the province to which he belonged. And when it came to writing, whether the entries in his shop ledger or a note to the vendor down the road, he wrote in Urdu. Who said it was the language of the Muslims? He had learned it from his father and from the primary teacher in his village a few miles out of Sialkot, and neither of the two was a Muslim. The upshot was that every morning, after his breakfast, he spent at least a half hour reading through the Urdu newspaper he took. No one in the house was allowed as much as to whisper during this sacred half hour. 'Don't you see your father is looking through the paper?' Prabha Rani would tell Arun sternly, if he made the slightest sound. And in that rebuke was the pride of select ownership. For wasn't her Lalaji the most learned man in the whole neighbourhood? Wasn't he an avatar of Vishnu, so far as she was concerned?

Lala Kanshi Ram at such moments was propped up on his bed. Having finished his bath and his morning prayers, he would be ready for his nashta. 'Nashta' was one of the Urdu words Lala Kanshi Ram liked particularly, it gave him the feeling of status. What he in fact took in the morning was a glass of milk. A heavy breakfast did not agree with his system. And Prabha Rani would boil *pure* cow's milk, let it cool a little, and serve it to him in a long, brass tumbler. She no doubt knew how important his health was to her and the entire family. Who else was there to take care of her if he was gone? Who else had she in the entire wide world? Her eyes brimming with sentimental tears, she poured a lot of thick cream on top of the milk—cream that she made at home by boiling up the leftover milk of yesterday. She also threw a handful of peeled almonds into the brass tumbler, before she took the milk to him. These almonds she soaked in water, last thing at night before she went to bed. In the morning she had only to press them lightly from one side and out came the white, smooth nuts slipping on to her hand.

This hot stew of milk, patchy cream and white almonds, with at least four spoons of sugar in the mixture to give it the right flavour, Prabha Rani carried to Lala Kanshi Ram, sitting on the bed. Each man's bed in this house was his divan, so to say. It was a middle-class home, and they did not have a separate living room. There were tables and a few chairs, but they were only used when a guest arrived. The family sat down and relaxed on beds—except for Lala Kanshi Ram who used an antique, sprawling easy chair in the evenings. Lala Kanshi Ram had his bed in the chaurus room (it so happened it was square—chaurus), Prabha Rani in the next room, and Arun in the very last room, at the back of the house. At night the arrangement was somewhat altered, depending on the number of guests in the house, but no one dared intrude into the chaurus room, at least not during the day. It was the citadel of the Head of the Family, as the data processing forms of the government would have him called. He sat there alone and undisturbed.

Lala Kanshi Ram took the long, brass tumbler of milk from Prabha Rani, and wrapping himself in a chader, leaned back against the round, tightly stuffed pillow. It was then he opened the morning paper and, adjusting his glasses, resumed his own and his wife's education. And while he rolled the milk in his mouth with infinite pleasure, taking time to crunch-crunch the almonds and break up and swallow the thick cream, his eyes roved on the page with their own hunger. And from time to time he spoke up aloud.

'Arun's mother, you know what? Germany has turned round and attacked Roos.' (Coming as it did from a mouth filled with milk, 'Roos' sounded far more impressive and terrible than Russia.)

'They've dropped an atom bomb on Japan!'

'Today Gandhiji goes on a fast unto death.'

'We have a new Viceroy now—Lord Mountbatten. He is related to His Majesty the King.'

Very often he stopped in the middle of his exclamations, and looking up from the page peered at his wife from above the rim of his glasses. Patiently he asked: 'You know what a fast unto death means, don't you?' Prabha Rani nodded her head in slow appreciation, but Lala Kanshi Ram went on in a liberal mood: 'It means a fast until a person *dies.*' He took on a tearful tone: 'Gandhiji might now die—he might pass away!' Prabha Rani uttered a desperate 'Hai Rama!' and satisfied he had created the right dramatic tension, he passed on to other subjects. Or he asked: 'You know what an atom bomb is?' And when his wife doubtfully shook her head and said, no, she did not, Lala Kanshi Ram had the time of his life. Pontifically he lurched forward and took hold of the opportunity (with both hands, as it were) of revealing the mysteries of the universe to this peasant woman, whom he had married when she was only thirteen and who could not tell an 'alif' from a 'bai'—who till this day thought they lived on a flat earth and not a round one. He had since taught her many things, including how to sign her name, though she still could not read and write. He would teach her more, he said to himself complacently.

'So you don't know what an atom bomb is!' And he chuckled to himself, while Prabha Rani stood with her eyes on the ground, looking guilty.

'An atom bomb, Arun's mother, is a bomb filled with liquid fire,' he said slowly, rolling the milk in his mouth. He had a slight doubt—wasn't that what it was? He went on with confidence: 'Millions of people perish when you drop such a bomb.' There was no problem about *that*—it was all in the paper. But what really *was* the bomb? What was the principle behind it?

'You remember the Mahabharata, don't you?'—and he looked at his wife with a little annoyance at her slow grasp of things. 'Remember the last days of the epic battle?'—his wife was now vigorously nodding her head, and saying, yes, yes, yes. 'The fire darts they threw at each other, the Kauravas and the Pandavas?' After a pause: 'Well, it is like that, the atom bomb. You throw a dart or a bomb at your enemy, and that burns him up!'

'Then it is nothing new these Angrez loge have made?'

That line of reasoning was to Lala Kanshi Ram's taste. It prevented serious thinking, and it satisfied some deep national urge in him.

'New?' he said with obvious relief. 'What are you talking about? No other nation in the world can ever touch the glory of the Vedic civilization, can ever invent anything we haven't already found out. And these English particularly, they're a race of monkeys, who till a few hundred years back used to live in jungles. Why, you ought to read *Satyarth Prakash*. The entire Europe was a piece of swamp, while great kingdoms flourished in the land of Bharata.'

'Did many people die in Japan?' asked Prabha Rani eagerly, to convince him how much she valued his discourse, while in her mind she was thinking of the food which would soon burn in the pan.

'Millions!' whispered Lala Kanshi Ram in sorrow for his suffering brother, secretly relieved it was the brother who was the victim.

His finest moments of elation came when the news pertained to the British royal family. Like any other Indian he had a prejudice against the British (he spoke of them as the Angrez—the English). He hated them for what they had done to his country and wanted azadi. Throughout the Second World War, he had prayed they be defeated by the Germans. The news of German victories, at front after front, had pleased him beyond measure, and when eventually they were held and contained by the British, Lala Kanshi Ram did not give up. With the coming of flying bombs in 1944, with hundreds of V-2s falling on London every day, and the chance of a British defeat again becoming pronounced, he loudly proclaimed he had known all along that one day the Germans would defeat this bunder race, the monkey race.

But deeper down, he also admired the British—in any case he enjoyed the safety of the British Raj and hugged it lovingly. All said and done, the British had brought some kind of peace to this torn land. Think of the Sikhs after Maharaja Ranjit Singh—or the Marathas. Think of the Muslims in Delhi or in the Deccan. When had this country ever been united? Who let down warriors like Porus or Prithvi Raj Chauhan? For that matter, who let down the Moguls in their fight against the British? Always our own men, our own kith and kin!

And the British had somehow made a nation of us. Or was it Gandhiji who had done that? Lala Kanshi Ram was confused about this point, but he did not let that interfere with the drift of his argument. There had been less bloodshed in India in the two hundred years of British Raj than in any similar period in the past. No one could deny that. Even Gandhiji or Jawaharlalji would have to concede that. The British had brought peace to the land and they had brought justice. They no doubt were pagans, they had no religion worth the name ('no awareness of the atman, I tell you'), and he knew all their church services were a fraud. Their hymn singing and the stupid smile with which their padres moved about were merely snares for the unwary, to make a few more converts to Christianity. Lala Kanshi Ram knew all that, thanks to Swami Dayanand. But he also knew that in impartiality they were miles ahead of any Indian he knew of. He could get his way with any of his countrymen—a few rupees into the man's pocket and the deed was done. But try and bribe an Englishman! Lala Kanshi Ram quaked at the mere thought of it.

What sent him into raptures over the British was his schoolboyish passion for pageantry: their bands and their parades and the colour of their uniforms. Baljit Raizada, the nationalist editor of the paper he took, said in his columns men like him were simpletons. The British, he said, were not as just as they were made out to be. It cost you nothing to be just with people when you were not a party to their petty disputes. What of the injustice the British had visited on the entire land? The British in India were paid their wages not in paper money but in gold. Each year tons of that gold were shipped back to the bunder motherland, where ruled those bunder kings and queens. 'And where does the money they take away come from?' asked the theatrical Raizada of the Urdu daily *Inqlab*. 'It comes from the pocket of each one of you!'

Lala Kanshi Ram invariably felt at his pockets every time he read this favourite phrase of Raizada. The first time he read the *Inqlab*, he took out his money and counted it paisa by paisa. Now he confined himself to feeling the weight of it from the outside. But it was always all there, every paisa of it. Raizada said the British King was not a king but an Ali Baba. And England was really a robbers' den, filled with the loot of the world. Ah, the things Raizada said! Lala Kanshi Ram did not quite approve of many of them, but he enjoyed reading them all the same. After all, he too wanted to belong to the times; he too wanted to claim for himself the role of a revolutionary. 'I've even been to prison,' he would boast before his listeners, real ones or imaginary. It mattered little if the only night he had spent in prison was in connection with a Sales Tax strike, where along with the merchants of his trade he had taken part in a hartal (much against his wishes) and in a procession (even more so), when some of the merchants including himself were taken into custody ('Oh,

God! Now what will become of my family!') and forced to pass the night in the district lock-up. The point was, he had been inside the four walls of a prison, and with the passage of time he had convinced himself it was because of his part in the freedom movement. It was in similar prisons that Gandhi and Jawaharlal lay and wasted their lives away. With his own experience to back him up, he could quite see the privations they had gone through (this on the verge of tears). Some heroes, like Bhagat Singh, paid for their courage with their lives—as indeed he too was very near to doing that night; he, Lala Kanshi Ram, the 'registered' grain merchant of Sialkot (ah, the risks he took that night!). But then what was one's life compared to the honour of one's country, anyway?

Carried away by the emotion of the moment and the last article of Raizada he had read, he would shout: 'Oh, they're kutai, they're dogs—these Angrez.' And to continue for a while in that state of self-induced indignation he kept repeating, 'Kutai! Kutai! Kutai!' He couldn't agree with Raizada, though, that the shows and the parades the British put on periodically were meant to keep the average citizens befooled, while they plundered them behind their back. Now *he* was not an average citizen and even he liked those shows. And he liked the British for doing them for him.

There were many such pageants in his mind and he went fondly over his memories. The most recent one was the Victory Parade in 1945. So the British had won once again; so the Germans had in the end lost and the Japanese too. 'Eh, behan chode!' said Lala Kanshi Ram slowly, not making it clear whether the abuse was meant for the British or the Germans. That was a subtlety of the Punjabi language he enjoyed immensely. Abuse could mean a thousand different things, depending on the way you said it. Behan chode and maan chode were the most commonly used words, but they touched only the fringe of Punjabi ingenuity in the matter of obscenities. Pedigreed Punjabis went much further; they fabricated compound swear words, where a little arithmetic was necessary before you could see through the insult. Lala Kanshi Ram knew exactly how it was done, but like a good Arya Samaji he stayed away from too hurtful phrases. Behan chode meant, you seducer of your sister. Maan chode meant, you seducer of your mother. That was simple. A compound obscenity ran something like—you seducer of your mother's father's daughter. Or, you fucker of your father's mother. The second one was not too complicated, the genealogy was easy to follow, but the first was a tough nut. For your mother's father's daughter need not necessarily be your mother. It might as well be your aunt. The aunt again might be from the same wife as your mother, or another wife. So Lala Kanshi Ram was being polite when he said only behan chode.

But the very same abuse could be used in *praise* too. The Ganges water, behan chode, cold! meant positively the speaker was in a state of bliss over it. Who indeed would dare abuse mother Ganges? Wasn't that a novelty, though? Could you think of any other language in the world where you might try that kind of a poetic experiment? All right, all right, Hindi is my language, if you say so. But it is a senile drivel compared to Punjabi, if you ask me. Even Urdu comes nowhere near the vigour and plasticity of Punjabi. You are too damned concerned with nafasat, with gentility, to be able to say anything effective. But Hindi, my God, Hindi was a joke. Look at the swear words they have in Hindi. Dusht, moorakh, papi, atyachari...You call those swear words? So soft, so weak, so impotent! And what is a language if you cannot have a manly explosion in it to your entire satisfaction?

That's how Lala Kanshi Ram reasoned with himself, when he was compelled again and again to state his mother tongue as Hindi. Maan chode, he said quietly on such occasions. Those who stood next to him in the Victory Parade that day had the impression he used the obscenity not for the Germans but for the British. They also had the impression he used it in admiration. For he was smiling when he raised his eyes to the British Superintendent of Police who had passed by on a bay stallion, and he placed his stress on the first word of the abuse, thus showing his praise for these 'eh's', that is the British.

And that precisely was what he was saying to himself, as he watched the Tommies march through the street, their tanks rolling ahead of them. They are a nation which cannot be easily beaten, he thought. A handful of them have kept us under their feet for over two hundred years. And now that Hitler too has met the same fate at their hands. An absolutely invincible race—eh, behan chode!

Another parade that often came to his mind was the one celebrating the enthronement of King Edward VIII. The glorious King—for wasn't he a friend of Nehru, and wouldn't India stand to gain at his hands?—the glorious King was forced to abdicate soon afterwards, but the parade was a great success. Beginning from the Cantonment grounds outside of the city, the horse cavalry and the men on foot had marched through the entire city and one of the bands had stopped right in front of Lala Kanshi Ram's store, playing the pipes and the drums for a full fifteen minutes, while Lala Kanshi Ram stood outside on the platform of his store, and with the crowd all gathered around in the chowk, and women and children looking down from every balcony, and his the only store at the crossing and him standing erect on the platform—it looked as though the whole show was being staged in his exclusive honour. At least that's what Lala Kanshi Ram imagined when he stood there and took his bow.

But the parade that happened annually and which Lala Kanshi Ram never missed was the New Year's Day Parade. It was held each year on the first of January, and the population of the town referred to it as the Hurrah Parade. It took place at a ground about five miles out of the main city at eight in the morning, but Lala Kanshi Ram was always there on time. When Arun reached his sixth year, he began taking him along too. For shouldn't the boy witness the magnificence and grandeur of the British Raj from an early age? And as the sun broke on the distant hills near Jammu, and as the gora sahibs of the army and the police shouted 'Attention!' or 'By the right—*quick march!*', Lala Kanshi Ram explained to the sleepy child how every word of command being used there had been approved personally by His Majesty himself, sitting bolt upright five thousand miles away in London on the Peacock Throne and wearing the Kohinoor Diamond.

Lala Kanshi Ram was a wholesale grain merchant in the city of Sialkot, and one of his many customers happened to be the present English Superintendent of Police. Lala Kanshi Ram had, on occasions like Diwali or Dussehra, tried to send dalis to him—baskets of fruit and bottles of Scotch whisky (much against his Arya Samaj training, for he did not drink himself). But he could never get his gifts past the Muslim City Inspector, who accepted them in the name of the Superintendent and consumed them himself. One day the Superintendent in person arrived at his store, looking for a high quality wheat. Lala Kanshi Ram was at once electrified. He was not only able to provide the right stock, he was willing to provide it without charge. And when the Superintendent remonstrated with him, he folded his hands and entreated: 'I am only your servant, sir. I'm running this business only in your name.' Lala Kanshi Ram would not make out the bill and the Superintendent would not take the goods gratis. Ultimately the Superintendent left a reasonable amount of money on the counter, which the Muslim City Inspector, who always accompanied the Superintendent on his rounds of the city, quickly pocketed. For Lala Kanshi Ram it was all the same, whether the bribe went into the pockets of the Superintendent or the City Inspector. He was satisfied: at least the lower hazoor sahib (as he called the Inspector) accepted his favours.

But that episode won Lala Kanshi Ram the acquaintanceship of the Superintendent. It became simply impossible for the Superintendent to ignore him at public functions. While he walked around, swishing his cane and curling his thin mustache, he would all at once become aware of a small figure in the crowd who was pining to do his obeisance. Even when he casually glanced in that direction, he would observe the man fold his hands and get ready to bend forward in supplication. He tried to ignore him, but with a starched turban tied neatly on his head, the Lala was present at every gathering. In the end the Superintendent gave in, it was too much for him to keep up the fight. Whenever he saw Lala Kanshi Ram now, he went over to him, and after the man had bent forward from his waist and almost touched the ground, he said a word or so of politeness to him.

The bands came marching at the Hurrah Parade—drum, drum,—drum, drum—and the stern white Tommy faces with blue eyes looked straight ahead. Lala Kanshi Ram said to Arun: 'See, the way the sahibs march!' Arun would be too sleepy and he said, unhunh, unhunh, and Lala Kanshi Ram jerked him awake and roared: 'I'll give you a slap on your face if you don't look at the sahibs. Don't you see how lucky you are! There are Indian children in villages who never see the face of a white man. They come and go'—and he gave himself the luxury of a moan— 'they come and go as flies. Arun, beta, you were brought by me into the world in a big city. Make the best of the opportunity I've given you.' He saw the child's head still drooping and pulled him hard by the hand. 'You listen to me, you haram zadai, you son of a bastard. I'm telling you, look at the gora sahibs!'

The Superintendent of Police was not obliged to march with the troops in the Hurrah Parade. Being a senior officer, he was allowed his liberty, and he sauntered up and down as the columns marched past a central Union Jack. Spotting Lala Kanshi Ram, or seeing that he had been spotted by Lala Kanshi Ram, he walked up to him and perfunctorily asked:

'Lalaji, thik hai?'

Lala Kanshi Ram only hoped everyone in the crowd had heard the question. He of course was all right—what was wrong with him? He was hale and hearty and only last night had emptied his water into Prabha Rani. But he expanded with the concern of the white Superintendent for him, and grinning from ear to ear replied, as much to the crowd around him as to the Superintendent:

'Han sahib, thik hun. Bilkul thik hun, sahib.'

The Superintendent would have liked to move on, but Lala Kanshi Ram pushed Arun in front of him.

'Is this your son?' the Superintendent asked reluctantly.

'No, sir, no. He is your son only,' Lala Kanshi Ram replied, folding his hands and going into additional raptures.

The Superintendent knew the Punjabi terminology and did not show alarm at the fatherhood attributed to him. He only smiled benignly and somewhat confusedly at the little child.

'Sir, he is quite good in his studies.'

'Now is he really?'

'Yes, sir, very good. He knows all the causes why Henry VIII broke up with the Pope.' Addressing Arun: 'Come on, Arun, tell the sahib what you know about Reformation in England. Begin by numbers...' In a whisper, 'Now wake up, you behan chode. I'll skin you alive, if you cannot mention the causes.'

The Superintendent passed on, but Lala Kanshi Ram had his day. If he was disappointed in Arun, he recovered his composure after he had boxed his ears and the child had started crying.

After having marched around and displayed their regimental flags and scarlet uniforms, the Tommies gathered near a Union Jack in the centre and hollered three times—hip, hip, hurrah!

hip, hip, hurrah! hip, hip, hurrah! The natives did not know a thing about what was happening, but they joined their masters in shouting out aloud, some saying hup, hup, and some hoorah, hoorah, in place of the right words. Another year had been formally ushered in for a people whose New Year really began in April, on the Baisakhi day. And the entire parade marched back to barracks, and the crowd broke up.

The seasoned spectator did not leave the parade ground. For now was the time when the stray dogs were shot by the gora sahibs. The sahibs were cut to the quick to see these shaggy creatures with ulcerated skins and flies buzzing in their ears roaming around the place, while the soldiers were smartly presenting arms and standing to attention to the tune of *God Save the King.* They took all human precautions to exclude these sickly brutes in advance from the parade ground. But what was an Indian dog if it could not sneak past *any* barrier? And while the RSM was shouting, 'Atten—*shion!*' several of these lowly creatures would be running at top speed from one end of the cleanly swept parade ground to another. A few orderlies ran after the dogs to shoo them away, but the dogs, though wobbly on their thin legs, were too fast for them. And then the crowd drove them back into the centre of the ground the moment they reached the periphery. The soldiers on parade were certainly fun for the crowd, but the dogs were a greater fun, and they drove them back with stones, doubling up with laughter and cheers. Soon the orderlies would be running in the other direction, until they caught up with the dogs and cornered them and took them out. But do you think they had finished with them? No, sir, they did not know what creatures they had taken on. For surely as the Adjutant rode past on his white horse, his sword held upright in front of him, the brass of his uniform and the steel of his sword dazzling in the early morning sun, there would be a small stray dog only a few steps away from the horse, marching almost in step with the horse, its skinny tail wagging, its shaggy, lean mouth turned towards the ferocious looking man on the horse, just unable to contain its curiosity about what the horse and the man were doing there. It must be stressed that not once did any of these Indian dogs break the decorum of the parade. There is no record that any of them defiled the ground with its feces (a remarkable display of fortitude, considering this precisely was the hour when they usually emptied what the humans call their bowels), nor that any of them ever used a motionless soldier as a prop for lifting its leg and emptying its bladder. If the itch on the shaggy skin became too much, the dog momentarily stopped and with one nimble foot gave a vigorous scratching to a part of its belly. But it did this in absolute taste, quickly and smartly, and in another moment it was back again in step with the Adjutant on his charger.

As soon as the parade was over, three or four sergeants came back on bicycles, with guns in their hands. No one had dared flout the authority of the King Emperor for the last several centuries. The geography books and the huge wall maps in school rooms proclaimed in bold letters the sun never set on the British Empire. But during the parade it did briefly set here because of the sacrilege committed by these filthy beasts of a filthy race. Left to themselves the sergeants would have made men pay for that crime—as they did as recently as in 1919, when they shot hundreds of them out of hand with machine guns at Jallianwala Bagh. But times had changed for that kind of revenge, so now they only went after the dogs.

The sergeants held the cycles with one hand, leaving the other free to carry the gun. They appeared to be cool, they even whistled an old British tune, but the crowd knew the storm brewing inside their minds. And obligingly, they made room for them, gathering themselves into several small circles. This was quite an effort for these people, to adjust themselves so abruptly to another type of formation. The Indian mind, immersed as it is most of the time in such lofty subjects as the Brahman and the atman and the ultimate end of man, is not a very fast-moving mind; it takes care of earthly, wordly things rather slowly. But knowing the agony of their foreign masters, these men, with the proverbial generosity of the soul each Indian possesses for the entire created universe, willingly obliged. It was not for nothing their history spoke of their ancestors feeding snakes with milk, or carrying food for tigers into their dens. All created matter was one, man and beast and bird, and the flowers and the trees to boot. And these Angrez were another aspect of the same Brahman who constituted total reality. Today they governed the Indians, tomorrow maybe the Indians would rule over them. At the moment they needed their help. Their Hurrah Parade had been ruined by these nasty dogs, which no one owned and which were a nuisance to the entire community. They must help them to corner these scavengers and destroy them.

The crowd had not only split up into several small arenas, but in each arena they had cornered one dog for the ultimate arrival of the sahibs. It went against Lala Kanshi Ram's grain to see a dog being killed before his eyes, for he was a vegetarian. Yet there was another grain in him, in common with the rest of his countrymen, much deeper than religious or ethnic conditioning. And that was the acute need for thrilling spectacles in his otherwise drab life. Mornings he went to his store, evenings he came back home. This had been the routine, without a break, for the last thirty-five years of his married life. No movies, no books to read, no other recreation; his puritan upbringing kept him away from such pastimes. Meetings, yes, plenty of them. Spiritual meetings, satsangs, political meetings, meetings of the Arya Samaj. But they too had a pattern which seldom varied. Somebody got up and spoke on for maybe sixty minutes without a break. Or someone started a chant and the same chant went on for several hours. In the Arya Samaj meetings, you might be asked to fill in an entire evening by looking fixedly at a picture of Swami Dayanand without batting an eyelid. Political meetings he enjoyed, they were like a merry-go-round, someone would get up on a platform and start abusing the British and there was always variety in the quality and the content of the abuse. But Lala Kanshi Ram worried about the possibility of police interference at such meetings, and even there he did not fully relax.

A spectacle like a stray dog being shot by a stray Tommy was different. It was fun, he said to himself—quietly, so that no one should overhear him. The arena was formed, the dog cornered, and the sahib had finally arrived. Getting off his cycle, the sergeant with the three stripes placed the cycle on its stand, and taking deliberate aim, without more ado, shot the dog dead. Somehow the poor thing would suspect the end was near. Tucking its tail between its legs, it started moaning dolefully the moment it saw the man with the gun. But the sahib paid no attention, this bastard had ruined the entire decorum of the parade and deserved instant death. So he lifted the gun, took aim and fired, and the dog went straight up into the air six feet high, eight feet high, at times ten feet high, with the impact of the bullet, and then dropped lifeless with its neck broken and curled up hopelessly on its chest.

What struck Lala Kanshi Ram was the deftness of the sergeant. Only a few feet away from the dog stood the ring of people and there was not an instant's hesitation on the part of the Tommy lest he might miss the dog and hit them. Up went the rifle—and bang!—and that was the end of the dog. And how elegant the sergeant looked when, soon as the dog had stopped shivering, he went forward in his spotlessly polished shoes and cut off its tail. To this day Lala Kanshi Ram did not know what they did that for. Maybe they stuffed them and hung them on their walls back home as trophies. Or maybe they got a reward from the company commander and had to carry the tail in as evidence. What mattered to Lala Kanshi Ram was the precision of the

British Raj, which was seen in as small an act as the killing of a stray dog. No wonder they ruled the world over, no wonder, he said to himself. There indeed was no Raj like the Angrez Raj!

The respect for the Raj was implicit in his voice, when he declared to his wife in the morning: 'Tonight Lord Mountbatten is to make an announcement from the All India Radio.' He had fallen in love with the new Viceroy the day he saw his picture in the newspaper. If the British were going to lose India, it was not because of Gandhi or the awakening amongst the masses; it was because of the tactical error they made in sending out an ugly Viceroy in the crucial days of their Raj. This, according to Lala Kanshi Ram, was the root cause of the tide turning against them. Wavell's bulky frame looked so ungainly in baggy trousers—and then he had only one eye! Having spent centuries here, didn't the great sahibs in Walayet know that Indians have an ingrained superstition against a one-eyed man? Thanks to the Arya Samaj he had got rid of his prejudices, he said Om-Bhur-Bhawa-Swaha ten times when he saw a one-eyed man and walked on. But there were men in this land who would return home if such a calamity befell them, would have a bath, change their clothes, and refuse to stir out for the rest of the day. It is true Maharaja Ranjit Singh was one-eyed too, but then he had many virtues to make up for that. He tied such a beautiful turban and he supported a hawk so superbly on his hand as he rode. At least he looked so handsome whereas Wavell only blinked like an owl. Why of all the persons at their command, did the big sahibs have to send *him?* They had taken themselves very close to ruin in 1857, by issuing cartridges greased with cow's fat. And now they had done a worse thing—even the Muslims mistrusted a one-eyed man.

The arrival of Lord Mountbatten in March seemed to restore a semblance of the earlier dignity. How tall he was, how slim! That's how a Viceroy should look—majestic! The derby on his head and the sleek robes on his body sat perfectly, to say nothing of the beautiful wife by his side. And Lala Kanshi Ram confided to Prabha Rani, he was also related to His Majesty the King. He used the Urdu expression Badshah Slamat for the King, and the chewability of the words in his mouth sent a thrill through his entire body. Even if all the millions of Indians were to turn hostile to the King, he would find at least one person ready to fall at his feet if he were ever to visit India in the future. For he was the great English King, direct descendent of the great Malika Victoria, on the sight of whose fat statues in Indian cities Lala Kanshi Ram had grown into manhood.

This morning when Lala Kanshi Ram told Prabha Rani of the coming broadcast, he was in a reflective mood. He was not jubilant and gay; he looked timid. As usual, he was sitting on his bed propped up against the round pillow, and Prabha Rani was standing in the doorway, dividing her attention between her learning and her kitchen.

Lala Kanshi Ram said, 'Arun's mother, come and sit near me on the bed.'

Prabha Rani was surprised at these words. Company was what Lala Kanshi Ram wanted least when he was reading the paper. And he seemed so scared. Nothing had happened in the house for several days to upset him; nor anything special in the store, either. What then?

She slowly walked over to the bed and sat down beside him. Lala Kanshi Ram gazed at her. Her dark brown face had grown weary through anxious years, but she was beautiful still. What big eyes she had—almond shaped and so wide! He gazed at her hands, and the skin on her fingertips was cut and broken at many places. How many household chores did that mean? Her haunches had grown big with time, but that was not her fault. That happened to every Punjabi woman after giving birth to one child—and she had to many. In any case big haunches were not a blemish in a good woman, *nothing* was a blemish in a good woman. And she had been a good woman to him, he could say that for her.

He looked around and there was silence and peace in the rooms. From where he sat, he could see all the three rooms that constituted their home. There were connecting doors all the way through. At the end, by the side of the last room, was the kitchen, which was not visible from here. He could see the three main rooms, and in each things were so neatly arranged and stacked. The room next to his was a very large room, almost like a funnel, connecting his room with that of Arun at the end, and there were two beds in that large room, one in each corner. Printed sheets were spread neatly on both the beds, and in addition to the usual flat pillow, a round pillow was placed on top of the flat one. In the large room there were also several spare beds, stood up against the wall on one side, the legs of one bed going through the string nets of the others, so that they did not take up much space. And, artist that Prabha Rani was, on top of these standing beds too she had spread a printed sheet, so that the sight did not hurt the eye. No one could tell at first glance there were beds hidden behind the sheet; it looked more like a curtain, a decorative curtain.

The clothes of the house were kept in small trunks. Things like sheets and quilts and bed pads, and pillow cases, both flat and round, were placed in big steel chests, which were about as big as a twin bed. Each house had one or two of these chests, called paities locally. Lala Kanshi Ram and Prabha Rani had two of them and they were placed on the left side of the big room. On top of them rose the other trunks of the house. The smaller trunks could be opened any time of the day by any of the children, but the big chests were the job of the mother or the father alone. Not only did it mean lifting heavy steel lids, it meant there were things in those chests which parents alone could see. Their contents remained a matter of endless mystery and the never ceasing subject of discussion for children. The privilege of opening them was never claimed by any of them, nor was this right ever allowed to them however big they might grow. The utmost they were permitted was to stand by the side of the chest, while it was being opened by one of the parents. And if their eyes were dazzled by the gold ornaments or the currency bills tied into bundles, they were not supposed to have seen anything.

Lala Kanshi Ram looked through the door to the far end, where Arun's windows opened out at the back, and the peace of the house came to him with something of pain. He had got so used to it he did not know how gracious it was. For about three decades had he been living there, and what he saw today had all been put together by him and Prabha Rani bit by bit through their own efforts. How loaded with goodness it was—everything! There were eight small trunks stacked on top of the two steel chests. On each one of the chests and the trunks, there was spread a separate cloth cover. Prabha Rani had whole sets of them in different colours; some days she used green, on others yellow, on others pink. Today the covers on the trunks were lemon yellow.

In yet another corner, she had hung a thick line and over the line lay blankets and towels and spare sheets. Behind, on the ground, were arranged the shoes, in one long row. There were no wardrobes in the house, but would that deter a strong woman like Prabha Rani in her will to live? She had even fixed up a temple in one of the small alcoves in a corner.

In his own room, Lala Kanshi Ram saw every picture on the wall had been wiped afresh. In Arun's room, the table cloth on his reading table matched the printed bedspread, and she had also given the boy curtains for the windows, a luxury which Arun alone enjoyed. None of these things was expensive, but they were durable and they looked strong. And they looked clean—and they *smelled* clean. There was not only peace and goodness in the house, there was the smell of goodness—a faint smell of soap and water and clothes recently pressed with a hot heavy iron.

Lala Kanshi Ram took Prabha Rani's hand in his hands and felt unutterably nostalgic. And the house had proved otherwise good to him too. It was here he had received the best at the hands of fate. He was now fifty and Prabha Rani forty-eight. The seven years of their married life before they moved to Sialkot had been a tremendous grind. Sambrhial was too small a village to provide a living for the clan of brothers and cousins, which constituted the joint family they lived in. And then God would not bless them with a child there. Not that Prabha Rani did not conceive. She gave birth to many, but none survived. Prabha Rani knew for certain it was because of the evil spells cast on her by the wives of Kanshi Ram's brothers, who were ever busy mixing charms and going to fakirs. She even believed they went to the cremation ground at night to feast on half-burned dead bodies—they were dains, all of them! It was only after they had moved into the present house that they had these children, a daughter and a son, who grew into healthy adult life. It was in this house again that Lala Kanshi Ram had acquired a social status for himself. His business as a wholesale dealer in grain was of firm standing now. His reputation as a learned Arya Samaji was known to every child of his mohalla.

As he held Prabha Rani's hand, Lala Kanshi Ram was filled with his old longing for her. Now who had given her this name—Prabha Rani? That was no name for a peasant woman, that was a name for a modern, Angrezi girl. There must have been an artist in her blessed family, he laughed to himself, though he knew they were only landless agriculturists, her people. But Lala Kanshi Ram liked the name and was sorry that everyone, including himself, now just called her 'Arun's mother'.

They had not known each other as man and wife for years. Lala Kanshi Ram wondered if she still removed the hair from her vulva. There was a time when she kept its surface smoother than his chin. Every other week she went down to the bazaar, and came back with a new cake of hair-removing soap. And when she came to him in the night and he mounted her, it was like riding on velvet.

When Arun was born, she had suffered badly. It was the seventh or the eighth child, and she should have had no difficulty. Somehow the child refused to emerge, though she pushed and pushed. And she shouted and begged of Lord Krishna to come and help her in person, she cried and shouted hard. Lala Kanshi Ram knew it was a punishment from the gods—for continuing to mate, when they were as old as that (he was thirty and she was twenty-eight). And then and there he took a vow that if she was spared further pain, he would refrain from such filthy matters in the future. Prabha Rani was of healthy, rural stock, and today, at the age of forty-eight, she was fit as a horse, had all her thirty two teeth in her mouth, and menstruated regularly like a girl of eighteen. Lala Kanshi Ram did not quite stay with his vow, he continued to climb on her, but since he had to be extra careful about not giving her a child (that's how he interpreted his vow, to make peace with his conscience), in the end he left coupling altogether out of his life.

Today Lala Kanshi Ram was filled with desire once again and even had a weak erection. He at once controlled himself by saying, Om, Om, Om, but it was unmistakable, the sense of security Prabha Rani gave him. Sitting there in that house, padded with clothes all around, he felt comforted. A few more clothes on a certain body, a few more layers, folds of a sari and a laced petticoat, and *there* in the centre lay the pearl of his life. He liked the metaphor of a pearl in the centre of layers and layers of multi-coloured clothes for Prabha Rani's genitals. They were all a cushioning—these clothes—a shell, for that one bright gem which shone on her being. The sheets on the beds were rough, but the closer you got to her body, the finer and finer became the quality of the fabric. The sari she was wearing was of the finest

Banarsi muslin, so thin you could see through all the folds of its six yards length. There was one more layer below the folds, and he knew the petticoat must be of the softest poplin imaginable. She was a connoisseur, this peasant woman, and she knew the value of what she carried on herself. And the prints on the sheets and the sari were matching too. They sprang up like branches, and they rose like fruits, at places mango-shaped, green and oblong, at places orange-like with the pulp spread open. On the sari the prints were smaller and of a violet hue, and though she accepted factory printed sheets for beds, she would not touch a sari that was not hand printed. It was like walking through a garden, thought Lala Kanshi Ram—approaching her. The nearer you got to her the foliage and the fruits became more scented and denser. Uncover the last layer, gently traverse the last labyrinth of the shell, part the last petals, and *there* shone the pearl, soft and silvery and incandescent.

He took hold of himself, and said to her:

'Arun's mother, I'm worried about the announcement the Viceroy might make.'

Prabha Rani heaved a sigh of relief. She had given him his milk, adjusted his pillow behind him, placed the newspaper in his hand, and he was still summoning her, asking her to come and sit on the bed, and was trying to hold her hand in those clumsy paws of his with that queer look on his face. Now, didn't she know that look! She knew they were alone in the house, Arun had left for college. But surely he did not want *that* after all these years. As he looked at her and seemed to struggle with himself, seemingly trying hard to put thoughts into words, she was not sure what pose to strike. Like a dutiful Hindu wife, she could instantly summon her theatrical skill and rise to the occasion to meet any requirement. She could cry, she could laugh, she could purr like a cat and curl up near him, she could open her eyes wide in surprise or fear, she could get angry too, if that's what he wanted, to give him the ground for getting angrier and feeling in command, and as far as 'Hai Rama!' or 'Accha' (this in many shades) were concerned, those she carried by the dozen in her mouth for handy use. What was it he wanted today from her?—what kind of reassurance?

When he gave out what sounded like a whimper and looked at her longingly, she felt certain her end had come (as the Punjabis say). She could see that this husband of hers, who had passed his fiftieth year, was thinking of ravishing her again—after all these years, when he had turned a deaf ear to her entreaties and when she had just learned to control herself. She might have shouted a lot when she gave birth to Arun, but that was not her fault, if the pain became too unbearable. But Kanshi Ram was a faddist, and since that day had slowly removed himself from his husbandly functions, first by learning to withdraw when she would be at the height of her excitement, and then by discontinuing to come to her entirely. She couldn't say she liked that, but what could she do? And now that after repeated prayers God had given her burning limbs some peace, did the old man want to set that ball of fire rolling yet again?

She sat near him in alarm, feeling uncertain of herself. For if he pressed her enough, she knew she would yield. But at *this* time?—early in the morning?

She was somewhat disappointed, when all he said was: 'Arun's mother, I'm worried about the announcement the Viceroy might make.'

'Why should you be worried?' she said, striking no pose.

'What if the English agree to give Pakistan to Jinnah?'

'You know that won't happen. Gandhi would never agree to a division of the country—you've told that to me all along.'

'That's true. But what if there is no other way out? And you know these English, they would rather divide than leave behind a united India.'

That was too abstract for Prabha Rani.

'I've taken more than quarter of a century to make all this'—and he made a vague gesture towards the rooms. 'Everything will be ruined if Pakistan is created.'

Prabha Rani felt a sinking of the heart.

'Why talk like this?'

Lala Kanshi Ram pursed his lips and let out his breath with a hiss. He saw his wife was frightened and he tried to stifle his anxiety. He had his fears since February, when the British set up a time limit for independence. They had clearly committed themselves; they had said that not later than June 1948, India would have its azadi. They also said if the Indian political parties did not agree on a solution by then, the British would hand power over to any constituted authority or authorities of the moment; but they must quit. It was this that disturbed Lala Kanshi Ram. Good, India would be free. But why were they in a hurry to leave? And why this reference to freedom in the plural? Didn't that mean they were thinking of Pakistan? And the Congress leaders—what trust could you put in them? Didn't Gandhiji and Rajaji themselves as much as offer Pakistan to Jinnah in 1944? They were the ones who put the idea in his head, if you ask me. Take a section in the East of India and a section in the West, they said. Only let's have a common defence and foreign policy. Until then Jinnah had talked of Pakistan, but he did not quite know what he meant by it. Gandhi, by going to him, not only gave Pakistan a name, he gave Jinnah a name too. Who took Jinnah seriously before September 1944? It was doubtful if he took himself seriously, either. Ever since then he had been sharpening his teeth and becoming more and more menacing. If the Congress would give this much, why not go for complete separation? Gandhi had meanwhile asserted he would never accept *that*. Over our dead bodies alone, the Congress leaders said. We would shed the last drop of our blood, but we would not allow India to be partitioned. And now the English, Lala Kanshi Ram's last hope of peace on the sub-continent, seemed to be giving in too.

Maybe he was exaggerating. Mountbatten Sahib had so far said he would hold by the Cabinet Mission plan, and that did not suggest a division. What had passed in the meetings the Viceroy had been having last month in Delhi with the Indian leaders? Those leaders too were speaking this evening over the radio, weren't they? What formula had they cooked up between themselves?

Lala Kanshi Ram scanned the newspaper. Yes, they were all there, Nehru and Jinnah and Baldev Singh, speaking one after the other, once the Viceroy had finished. What accord had they reached on the fate of four hundred million people? What accord had they reached on Pakistan, on the future of the Punjab and Bengal? That's what concerned him, in the main.

'If Pakistan is created, we'll have to leave. That is, if the Muslims spare our lives!'

'There will be much killing, you think?'

'Don't you know the Muslims? There has been much killing going on for the past many months. Imagine what will happen once they're in power!'

'Listen—' said Prabha Rani, showing more calm than her husband— 'you know destiny. What has to happen will happen. Put your trust in God, and don't worry too much.'

He was the lord and the master, but in disasters it was she who took charge and steered the ship. He was too restless, he demanded too quick an answer to a problem and wore himself out too fast. She was a woman of the soil who believed in rhythms, in things happening in their own order. She had perforce to move in and take charge each time he felt too upset in the soul. She had her own fears, though. They had just come into that maturity of age when they could sit back and relax. Madhu Bala was married;

Arun was preparing for a job. They had almost everything, as things go. They had even bought land and were thinking of building a house. And now to be pushed out of that safe little nest, in the name of freedom. But—she must take care of him.

'You've read for enough. Put the newspaper away and go to the store.' She said this very gently, as if he were her son.

She pulled his chader aside, and helped him to get into his shoes. She then went into the big room and brought out his stick and his cap, and handed these to him, first the cap, and then, after he had adjusted it on his head (looking into a mirror on one of the walls), the stick.

But then she said: 'It's too hot outside. You better take the umbrella instead of the stick.' And gently, touching his hand very softly, she took the stick away and going into the next room, returned with the big, black umbrella.

'Please don't think too much,' she said to him, as he was leaving. 'And come home early!'

'I'll have to,' said Lala Kanshi Ram. 'I have to listen to the broadcast.'

CHAPTER 2

PRABHA RANI had almost finished cooking. It was early, but the broadcast was to be at seven, and she wanted to be done before Lala Kanshi Ram came home.

It was a very hot evening. She was squatting in the smoke-filled kitchen and was wiping the sweat off her face with a towel. She removed the lid of the large pan, in which was boiling the main meal of the day. Taking a big spoon she stirred the stew, and lifting some of the green beans she was cooking she pressed them with her fingers to see if they were soft enough for her husband's mouth. Lala Kanshi Ram got wild with her unless she served him tender stuff. He had bad teeth and as the molars failed to crush the vegetables, he jumped with pain and his hands shot towards his face in defence of his shattered root canals. And since the food was still in the hollow of his mouth, he couldn't exactly shout at Prabha Rani. But hadn't she done him a bad turn again! The moment he had finished swallowing, going through all kind of grimaces, he took off after her. And it was hours before he was calm again.

Prabha Rani could see the beans were really soft, and giving the stew one final boil, she removed the pan from the stove and placed it on one side. Hurriedly she now started rolling the chapatis.

She heard movements in the adjoining kitchen, where Isher Kaur was cooking her meal.

Prabha Rani shouted: 'Ni, Isher Kaurai, what are you making?'

'Nothing much, chachiji. I'm only making bhurta.'

Prabha Rani envied her for the simplicity of her men, who would be satisfied with brinjals as the chief dish.

'You are kismat wali, Isher Kaurai—fortunate. Your chacha won't sit in the kitchen unless I can give him something with gravy. And then there has to be rice with every meal, and a sweet dish too.' At heart she was happy her Lalaji was so sophisticated.

'Yes, I know how fussy chachaji is,' Isher Kaur replied with a laugh, her ringing voice coming clean through the brick partition that separated the two kitchens.

Prabha Rani also laughed and the noise of utensils in the kitchens continued.

There was a difference of about twenty-five years between the two women, Isher Kaur could as well have been Prabha Rani's daughter. That was the reason why Isher Kaur always addressed her respectfully as chachiji, or auntie, and Lala Kanshi Ram as chachaji, the masculine derivative of chachiji (Punjabi again). The two families had been living in this house for many years. The girl had grown into maturity here, was married off here, and here it was she and her husband had come back to live. She had lost her mother when she was only a child. But she had a grandfather still alive, a tall, very handsome Sikh, who at the age of eighty stood straight like an arrow, and who still told you stories about women with a gleam in his eye. Then she had her father, Sardar Teja Singh, who had inherited the good looks of his father—if not his height and manly bearing. After Isher Kaur got married, the family asked her husband, Sardar Niranjan Singh, if he would make a permanent home with them. Niranjan Singh made a living selling odd things as a vendor. He had a small cart which he pushed from street to street. Now he could join his wife's family business of dry fruits and he jumped at the opportunity. What the family wanted was a woman in the house to take care of them.

Prabha Rani came out of the kitchen and stood in the verandah that opened on an inner courtyard. On one side of this quadrangle were the three rooms in which lived Lala Kanshi Ram and his wife and Arun. On the other side were the two rooms in which lived the Sardars.

Not only did they have one room less than Lala Kanshi Ram's family, there were fewer things inside their rooms—it was a more modest household. This in no way prevented a deep bond between the two families. There was not a day when Lala Kanshi Ram did not ask Ishero: 'Are you all right, beti? Are you doing well?' And as far as Prabha Rani was concerned, Isher Kaur was her major confidante, in spite of the difference in their ages.

Prabha Rani stood in the quadrangle and fanned herself with a small hand fan. The fan was beginning to tear, but thrift was worked deep into Prabha Rani's blood, and she had ingeniously saved the little thing by trimming its edges with a piece of cloth. And she had used a beautiful red for that purpose, sewing the cloth gingerly along the edges and also working it into two dainty flowers at the two ends. The fan now not only looked safe and strong, it also looked a thing of beauty, as she stood there and shook it with her healthy peasant hands.

She could not see Isher Kaur from where she stood, but she could hear her movements. Smoke was rising from the ground floor of the house, and she knew Mukanda's mother must be busy cooking too. 'The old witch,' she muttered to herself.

She said aloud: 'Ishero, do you think the Muslims will get their Pakistan?'

Isher Kaur's voice: 'Difficult to say, chachiji. I hope they don't—these badmash!'

'Your chacha thinks there will be much killing.'

'Our kismat!'

Isher Kaur, having completed her work, came out of the kitchen. She was an extremely beautiful woman, with a skin white and crimson. Since she had been close to fire, her cheeks were burning red like apples. She was removing the dough from her fingers, as she stood near Prabha Rani. In the heat of the evening, both of them were wearing light clothing, Prabha Rani a sari and a blouse, Isher Kaur long pyjamas called shalwar and a shirt. Since no men were around, neither of the women was wearing a headdress. Isher Kaur had no dopatta, and Prabha Rani had let the sari slip from her head. And as they stood there, they both shone with that animal health so characteristic of Punjabi women. Prabha Rani was nearing fifty, but her breasts stood out almost as magnificently as those of Isher Kaur. There was a difference, there certainly was. Isher Kaur was soft and delicate and her eyes were what the Punjabis call salty, namkeen, which means they were more liquid and more devastating, for there was so much more sensuality in them. Her hips were also narrower than those of Prabha Rani. But in the strength of their bodies, and in the firmness of their necks and their other joints, their elbows and wrists and fingers, they were more or less identical. There was not a single wrinkle or ring around Prabha Rani's neck, and the skin on her hands sat tight and firm, almost as tight as on Isher Kaur's. And when they spoke or laughed, the older woman's voice had as forceful a ring.

Prabha Rani looked at the abdomen of Ishero and mentally worked out how far gone she was in her pregnancy. It was the fourth month or the fifth. The two women did not talk much about it, otherwise Ishero would have heavy pains at the time of delivery. That's why Prabha Rani had such easy deliveries—she kept the exact day of confinement a secret even from her husband. Somehow the news had leaked at the time of Arun's birth, and sure enough, someone had put a curse on her. It might be the evil eye of Mukanda's mother who lived on the ground floor. Didn't she have pains then, didn't she learn her lesson! And what pains! It almost killed her, that child.

Prabha Rani felt Ishero was doing all right. It was just beginning to show, her swelling. The breasts had started to grow as well, and soon she would have to go in for shirts of a bigger size. Prabha Rani felt like making a dirty joke, there were so many she knew. Let Ishero grow big until she touched the sky, but one thing in her got narrower and narrower all the time because of the pressures around it—tighter. Now how many men knew the secret of *that*—how tight that thing got in pregnancy! She wondered if Niranjan Singh still slept with her. Or was he frightened of her bigness? She made no joke though and let the moment pass. There were other thoughts on her mind.

'Have you finished?' she asked.

'Yes.'

'Clean up then. We have to listen to the radio.'

'Yes, chachiji.'

Isher Kaur had heard of the broadcast from her own men. In each home, on each street corner, this was the only subject discussed that day. As the women stood there, Arun came home. Prabha Rani could hear him lock up his cycle downstairs. Soon he climbed the stairs and came in. It looked as if he had not played much tennis that day, for he was not soaking wet with sweat as he usually was. Holding his racket in his long, bony hands, he went and joined the women.

'Ma, I think they are going to have Pakistan,' he said as soon as he was with them, shaking his head in grave thought.

A flicker of fear passed over the faces of both the women.

'Why do you say that?' asked Prabha Rani.

'Well, that's the general feeling—they all thought that in the playground.'

Arun was a shy, pimply youth of twenty (he celebrated his birthday only yesterday), with very long hair which fell on his forehead. He pushed the hair back with his hand and his mother knew he was too confused, her boy.

'Did you see Munir?'

'I did,' he answered, absorbed in thought.

'What did he say?'

'He too feels Congress will yield this time.'

The women remained quiet.

'It's a betrayal, ma! It's a *betrayal*!'

They did not know what a betrayal was, but they knew he was right.

'I better clean up,' said Isher Kaur and left in a hurry. Arun's arrival had brought up afresh the urgency of the moment, and Prabha Rani too slipped back into the kitchen.

It was at that time Lala Kanshi Ram returned home from the store. Through the day he had fortified himself with assurances and he did not look as gloomy as in the morning. After all, how *could* it happen? The Congress had a promise to keep with the people. For the last thirty years, since that wizard Gandhi came on the scene, it had taken the stand that India was a single nation, not two. And Gandhi was not only a politician, he was a saint. He had his inner voice to satisfy, too. Would that nagging voice of his let him accept the slaughter of so many? That's what it would mean, if Pakistan did come into existence. And Gandhi was shrewd—surely he saw it all. He wouldn't give in to such butchery. If nothing else worked, his fasts unto death always did. Lala Kanshi Ram's business friends in the market were certain that's what Gandhi would do.

Said Lala Radhey Shyam, who true to his name sold pictures of Hindu gods and goddesses a few doors away from Lala Kanshi Ram's store: 'No, ji, Mahatmaji would never let that happen.'

Radhey Shyam had placed many of his teeth on the altar of his gods fairly early in life, and his face had not only a hollow look, it sounded hollow too when a sound came out of the pouch that hung loosely below his nose. It was funny—the droop of his mouth under his nostrils. The nose was fairly straight, at least it started out straight from the forehead, the forehead on which stood the round chandan religious mark, but then on the way the bridge got wobbly and by the time the nostrils showed up, it looked altogether collapsed. At the base of these shaky nostrils spread the expanse of wrinkled flesh that was Lala Radhey Shyam's toothless mouth. It looked as though someone had hit a wall with a sledge hammer and created that ruin. But that was the most pronounced feature of Lala Radhey Shyam's face, his jelly-like wrinkled mouth. And strangely enough—for shouldn't one like to believe in the goodness of the human heart?—strangely enough, whenever anyone picked a quarrel with Radhey Shyam (which was often), like a coward he went straight for his mouth. A prick in your mouth! came the insult. No one ever gave him any other abuse. Never the mother's abuse. Never the sister's abuse. Never the other long complex abuses. Always—a prick in your mouth! They surely saw a sexual symbol in it, for one of his angry customers said once to him: 'Is it a mouth or a cunt?'

But he was a kind soul, Lala Radhey Shyam was, and if the teeth had gone early, it was only the will of his maker. And if these fools abused him vulgarly, that too was the will of his maker. It was the will of his maker again that before the air from his mouth carried the sound of his throat outside, it filled the entire mouth like a balloon and sounded so hollow when it escaped from that dungeon.

He filled the mouth with air, and shaking his head in absolute conviction exploded, 'No, ji, Mahatmaji would never let that happen.'

Lala Banarasi Das, another grain merchant of the community, rubbed his hand over his closely shaved head, and said: 'And the English are afraid of him!'

Lala Shamsher Bahadur, who had such an awe-inspiring name and wore such a downy turban around his thin head, but who only sold material by the yard in a small shop around the corner, said: 'Bapu has a shakti, an inner power, which no one else can dream of.'

A few others said 'Quite so', or 'That's right', but it was not a day for weak interjections, and those speakers were ignored by the assembly. It was a day for passion, for strong, declarative statements, and to win a nod of recognition you had to come out with something like a sword in the hand.

Said Lala Kanshi Ram, in whose store the meeting was being held: 'Mahatmaji is going to save us.'

On that note the merchants parted, each going back to his store convinced the Viceroy's broadcast would say nothing new. The British had all along spoken of a united India; they could not change now. There was nothing to despair about really.

The merchants got quite noisy and melodious, as the meeting went along. The Muslim shopkeeper in the small shop across the road from Lala Kanshi Ram's store remained contemptuous of them. He knew Pakistan was a certainty, and with much relish he kept rolling the gold thread on the stem of the hookah he was manufacturing. By his side burned a small fire, on which he had placed several thin bamboo stems. The temperature was near 109 or 110, but expertly that wiry hookah manufacturer, in his mind the direct descendent of Prophet Muhammad, but in reality the product of many crosses between low-caste Hindu women and Mogul foot soldiers, kept on with his work—ignoring the heat as his ancestors had done, when they took captive this land of kafirs.

Expertly he lifted each bamboo stem when it was hot enough and with one quick motion twisted it into a V-shaped figure, both ends of the stem coming out even. The rest was easy. He had threads of many kinds arranged on a shelf behind him, with many more loose by his side on the mat on which he sat. When Arun was a boy, it fascinated him to go to his father's store and watch Abdul Ghani work. He worked not only with his hands, but with his feet too—at times with three feet and three hands, for he had props enough, nails or wooden pegs pushed into the ground near him, to use as additional limbs. And once the bamboo stem had been twisted into the right shape, his dozens of hands and feet and pegs all came alive. Gold and blue and green threads rolled from them on to the stem, until Ghani was ready to fix an upright stem, a wholly straight one, next to a section of the twisted one, and tying up the two together push the base of the two stems into a metal bowl. These bowls he did not manufacture. He got them from a wholesale dealer in metalware. Yet he displayed them in the shop as if he were the sole genius behind their enamel polish.

Near Abdul Ghani's shop there was a public drinking fountain, which served the needs of the community in diverse ways. Early morning the truckdrivers or people who had no permanent homes had their baths under it. Next came the sweepers, after finishing up the morning sweeping and cleaning. A little later was the turn of the bahishtis, the water sprinklers. Tying the open end of the big leather skin to the mouth of the faucet, they waited around it, chatting, and the moment the skin was filled, the bahishti would heave it up to his back and start sprinkling the water on the street. Then came housewives, who had no taps in their own homes. While their pitchers filled with water, these dusky women sat on the low wall of the tank into which ran the fountain, displaying their rounded ankles and their alta painted feet to anyone who happened to be around.

Much before the shops and the stores opened, they were all gone. For the rest of the day the tap and the tank were deserted, but for the assistants of the store owners around the area who might need a sherbet for themselves or their masters. The assistants ran to the tap—the heat was acute, the sun burning into every patch of the tarred road—and they pushed their silver jugs (they were made of sterling silver, to keep them safe from contamination) under the faucet rushed the water into them, and closing the faucet ran back to the store to add lime and sugar and ice to the water. But no one went near the tap for long periods until the evening, when the process of the morning was repeated, only in a slightly different order—first the water sprinklers and the sweepers, then the men who wanted a bath, and only in the end, when the dusk had fallen, the housewives with their rounded ankles and heavy breasts.

A frequent visitor to the tap during the afternoon lull—and a visitor who stayed there for minutes—was Arun. He was ever on a search for an excuse to make the trip. Father, do you want water? Father, shouldn't we give the Inspector Sahib (who had just come in) a nimbu pani, a glass of fresh lime? Father, I think it is time for lassi, for buttermilk (around three in the afternoon). Father, I'm going to wet my handkerchief to place it on my head; I'm dying of the heat. And since he could have this luxury only on weekends, or when his school was closed for some holiday, he made the best of that freedom. On week days, Lala Kanshi Ram wouldn't let him come near the store except to bring his evening milk (filled with patchy cream and almonds, as in the morning), when already the water sprinklers would have crowded round the tap. The best time was around noon, when everyone was lying flat with exhaustion and to go out of doors was an affliction. And on the days when Arun was free to be at the store around noon, he went and glued himself to the tap. Not to drink water, not to mix drinks for his father or his visitors—he would do *that* too, if that was the gimmick he had played to get there—but to do the one thing he had pined for days. And it was to watch uncle Ghani ply his wizardry with the bamboo stems and the gold threads. Yes, *uncle* Ghani. He had become impudent only in the last three or four years. Hadn't he always greeted Arun with 'Ohai, Arun de puter, how're you?'—a sentence which made Arun feel so grown up. And when he needed a small loan—and when was it that he didn't?—who did Ghani go to except to his father, Lala Kanshi Ram? 'Lala Kanshi Ram, can you lend me two rupees for the night?' 'Sure I can!' With smiles, always with smiles on both sides!

Fortunately the amount of money Ghani wanted to 'lift' or 'catch' (as Punjabi idiom would have it) from Lala Kanshi Ram was always small enough, and fortunately again he returned it soon enough, if not the very next day, still jaldi enough, for Lala Kanshi Ram to continue to indulge in the expansive feeling of compassion for others. So there was utter harmony among them, and the fact that Ghani was a Muslim and Lala Kanshi Ram a high-caste Hindu never entered their heads. They spoke a common tongue, wore identical clothes, and responded to the weather, to the heat and the first rains, in an identical manner. If they worshipped different gods, it was in the privacy of their homes, except when Ghani made a spectacle of himself by joining Tazia marches at the time of Muharram once a year and beating his breast in public. But then, didn't Lala Kanshi Ram make a spectacle of himself too, when he joined other lalas of the bazaar in throwing colour on others during Holi? No, thought Lala Kanshi Ram, they were not Muslims or Hindus, they were Punjabis—or at least they were till the other day.

Arun cupped his hands and after drinking several cupfuls of the water, kept his head under the faucet in the drinking position. That gave him the advantage of observing Ghani on the sly. Ghani knew all the while he was there. 'Come and have a smoke out of my hookah, Arun!' he shouted. And he would laugh, holding the stem of the filthy hookah he smoked and drawing a long, noisy pull of the smoke. For Abdul Ghani knew no one in Arun's family smoked or drank.

'Uncle Ghani, why do you smoke a dirty hookah, when you've such fine ones beside you?'

Arun was now sitting on the mat, close to Abdul Ghani.

Ghani went into peals of laughter at that, twisting his small wiry body as he laughed and in the process cleverly (thought

Arun) transforming his laughter into a cough (now, could you do that?), going houghoon, houghoon, houghoon, houghoon, houghoon, until tears stood out in his eyes.

Recovering himself and taking another pull at the hookah, where the smoke came gurgling through the metal bowl and the water in it, he shouted:

'Lala Kanshi Ram, do you hear what your son says? Do you hear that?'

Lala Kanshi Ram was too busy to answer.

'If I were to use the fine hookahs for myself, how would I make a living, you dim-wit?' Ghani said, turning towards Arun and tapping him on his head. (No logic in that! thought Arun.)

The hookah he was manufacturing was nearly ready. He pushed the two stems, the straight one and the one from the inverted V into the metal bowl, placed a clean earthen chilam, the clay pipe which held the tobacco, on top of one of the stems, the straight one, and put the thing on display on a wooden plank. What Arun liked about a hookah was how one thing was joined up with another—how one thing *led* to the other. One could easily smoke the tobacco straight out of the clay pipe, as some did. But a hookah was a lesson in sophistication! You were miles away from the clay pipe, and the smoke came to you wafting through strange passages and valleys, having been cooled in the process, having been filtered, having been cooled once again. Arun's father did not smoke, but all his uncles back at Sambrhial did. And hadn't Arun seen the look of utter peace on their faces, as they reclined on a round pillow with the stem in their mouths! His father prayed for shantih, for peace of mind, morning and evening, and yet was restless like the devil. But his uncles at Sambrhial and uncle Abdul Ghani had their ultimate peace many times over in a single day. When I grow up, I'll learn myself how to smoke a hookah, said Arun to himself. Even the placing of tobacco in the earthen pipe and lighting the tobacco, the getting ready, the tiari of the chilam as it was called, was an art. You had to do it right or it wouldn't do—you had to do it the way uncle Abdul Ghani was doing it, having finished his work for the day.

Those days had passed and Abdul Ghani was no longer friendly with the Hindu businessmen of the bazaar. Compared to them, his was a small business—it was no business at all, it was only a living from day to day. He made a few hookahs during the day, and by the evening he sold them all, and wrapping up his things he put them on a shelf in the wall and went home. That shelf in the wall was all his store consisted of. Yet his neighbours treated him as an equal, and he had lived in peace with them. But the Muslim League had slowly made him aware of the threat to him in a free Hindu India. It was not a question of his personal views; the League or Jinnah Sahib knew better. They said, view your Hindu neighbour with suspicion, and he did that. They said there should be a Pakistan, and he shouted for Pakistan.

When the businessmen were arguing in Lala Kanshi Ram's store, Abdul Ghani watched them with disdain. No power on earth could now stop Pakistan. He knew the noise they were making would be short lived—they would see this evening when the broadcast was heard.

He finished smoking his hookah, and closing the shutters of his shop, he spat on the ground in contempt and went home. 'Eh, maan chode!' he shouted loud enough for them to hear him. In his mind he knew he had just enough time to go home and rush to the paan shop of Karim Baksh to listen to the wireless.

Lala Kanshi Ram was not shaken by the rude behaviour of Abdul Ghani and when he reached home he looked composed and confident. Handing his cap and the umbrella to Prabha Rani, he washed his face, and summoned Arun to join them in the evening prayer. As an Arya Samaji he was not supposed to pray before personal images, but that was only for export. At home, he liked praying before an image, especially before the image of

Lord Krishna, the naughty god. Carefully he removed the curtain from the niche in the wall, where there was the family shrine. Taking his time he lit the incense, first rolling up the black stuff into a thin little wick. When the wick had burned for a while, he put the flame out with his hand, and as the scented fumes arose, he touched the feet of the picture in the alcove—the feet of Lord Krishna—and carried his hand to his forehead. He then sat down on the jute mat Prabha Rani had spread, and while Arun worried in his mind and Prabha Rani worried too with a vague sense of doom, he led them through all the hymns they usually sang in the evening.

They had agreed to eat their meal only after the broadcast was heard. There was nothing then to do but to climb to the roof of the house, and from there step on to the roof of the adjoining house where lived Bibi Amar Vati. Bibi Amar Vati had a husband and a son, but it was a household run on the matriarchal system—or so it seemed. For everything pertaining to that household was taken care of by Bibi Amar Vati herself. It was she who owned the two buildings which stood side by side in a street off Trunk Bazaar. The rent was paid to her personally, and if you wanted a receipt and were able to write it out for her, it was her thumb impression which went on the paper. Her husband and her son were around, but were inconspicuous. Just as in Lala Kanshi Ram's home, he was the indisputable leader, in their home it was indisputably she.

Lala Kanshi Ram, his wife Prabha Rani, and Arun stepped on to the adjoining house (that was the normal way of going from one house to the other), and climbing down from the roof, went into the living room—the one with mirrors all around—where Bibi Amar Vati had her radio. In the evening Bibi Amar Vati would throw the room open to all her tenants who might want to come and listen to the music or the news. Lala Kanshi Ram was her most respected tenant and he could get the room opened any time in the day. Bibi Amar Vati liked him so much she called him 'brother' and he no doubt called her 'sister' (the simple Arya Samaj training in good manners). They had known each other for years, and what was a radio—it belonged as much to him as to her. Needless to say Lala Kanshi Ram made full use of the liberty, and it was in that living room he had gathered much of his knowledge of the world.

As the three of them entered the living room, they found it packed with tenants. Isher Kaur was already there. So was her husband, Niranjan Singh, and her father, Teja Singh. Every other tenant from both the buildings was also present, including Mukanda's old mother. The room was charged with excitement. Most of the tenants sat on the mat on the floor, but a chair was fetched for Lala Kanshi Ram.

Near the radio sat Bibi Amar Vati's good-for-nothing adopted son, Suraj Prakash, twiddling as usual with the radio knobs and holding a cigarette in his yellowed fingertips. He was twenty-six or so, but the dreamy eyes with which he looked at the audience gave him the look of a small, shrunken lad. He had a gaunt, pointed face. No one knew where Bibi Amar Vati had picked him up. Speaking of that, no one knew where she had picked up her good-for-nothing husband, Gangu Mull, who sat like an archaic relic the whole day long on the parapet at the street entrance of the buildings, smoking a clay pipe. People were not certain whether or not she was properly married to him. All her tenants knew was she was the only child of her parents and had inherited from them the two massive buildings in Fort Street on the rent of which property she now lived. For the rest, it was a mystery which baffled everyone. There sat Bibi Amar Vati in the top storey of her house, smoking a small, dainty hookah. And there sat the whole day long, doing absolutely no work at all, her husband on the parapet below. Occasionally he made brief trips upstairs, when the tenants would hear loud abuse and things being thrown. They heard both voices, Bibi Amar Vati's and her husband's, and they also heard someone giving someone a beating. The general opinion was it was Bibi Amar Vati who thrashed that nincompoop with a bamboo cane, but no one could vouch for it. Come evening the two of them would be completely reconciled, and anyone who went up to the roof and passed their flat would see them bathed and combed and with kohl in their eyes, sitting together like two parakeets, she with her hookah, he with his clay pipe, eyeing each other silently.

They never had a child of their own, and the history of Suraj Prakash's real parents was again shrouded in mystery. Lala Kanshi Ram and Prabha Rani were the oldest tenants in the buildings, and even they did not know how Amar Vati had come by him. They well remembered the day when Amar Vati sent for them and showed them the child, saying with obvious delight: 'Brother Kanshi Ram, I've taken this boy as a son!' 'Where from?' asked the inquisitive Kanshi Ram. 'From the gods,' she answered, looking at him with some displeasure. Lala Kanshi Ram and Prabha Rani asked no more questions.

Bibi Amar Vati had money and the child grew up in luxury. In her excessive love of him she named him Suraj Prakash, which means light of the sun, which further means knowledge, a man of knowledge. And a man of knowledge, was what Suraj Prakash never turned out to be. Unaided he could not pass his middle exams, and when after several years of special coaching at home he did struggle over that hurdle, he got stuck at the high school level and resolutely refused to matriculate. He always got his answers wrong and came home with a big zero in each subject. Making no headway, Bibi Amar Vati took him away from school. It was a day of great rejoicing for Suraj Prakash, the man of knowledge, who celebrated it by distributing sweets to his friends.

Everyone liked the boy, though. Bibi Amar Vati dressed him in silk shirts and poplin pants, and after the debacle at school, she entrusted him with the task of collecting the monthly rent from the tenants. What did it matter if he bungled his exams ? She had enough to live on. She wouldn't leave him destitute!

Not only were there the tenants in the two buildings, there were stores below, shops, which too she rented out and which brought in a regular income. What more did Suraj Prakash need in life? You think Kanshi Ram's Arun would be able to make this much after all his 'education'? Go wash your face! Arun would be lucky if he got the job of a clerk somewhere. Her Suraj would be a thousand times better off still. Bibi Amar Vati smiled with her two-thousand-year-old face, blinking her round, cunning eyes, when she thought of that. And she had fixed him up with such a beautiful wife, too! Let Lala Kanshi Ram try and find a wife so stunning for Arun. Stunning indeed—go wash your face! That fat-nosed Arun will be lucky if he finds a sweeper's daughter to marry him—hunh!

Suraj Prakash had none of his mother's—his foster mother's, that is—arrogance. He was a dullard, but a courteous dullard, a likeable dullard. What could he do if he had no brains? It was not *his* fault! He laughed at his imbecility, and said, let's face it, I'm a budhu. Here he took a puff of the cigarette and holding the smoke for a while let it out with such force the jet travelled a long way before vanishing.

'Not only a budhu, you're a loafer too,' shouted Bibi Amar Vati.

She said that more as a joke, for she loved him so. No wonder Suraj Prakash was the first in this small community to have a radio set. They cost a good six hundred rupees apiece those days (before the tiny transistors came on the scene), and who else could afford that much money?

Suraj Prakash treated his radio as a toy. As he treated everything else very costly, his wife for one, to marry whom he had travelled two hundred miles into the state of Kashmir, in a marriage party occupying four big buses. Not sure whether it was four or five buses he made an effort to count on his fingers, holding one finger apart for each number—but getting confused in the process he would give up. Lala Kanshi Ram's perpetual source of annoyance with Suraj was that he wouldn't let the needle on the dial of the radio rest at one place. The station was all right—everything was coming through fine, music and words—and he had to move in, twiddle with the knob, and ruin the behan chode thing with his fingering. And he made it no better than before, often worse. Nor did he leave it at that. Seconds later he moved in again and taking hold of the knob twiddled the needle to the right, to the left, and bringing in a storm of jumbled noises and whistling wind sounds, took it back to where it was previously.

'Why don't you leave the damn thing alone?' said Lala Kanshi Ram with utmost irritation.

He and his wife Prabha Rani were the only two persons who could speak to Suraj Prakash like that. The others said, Bawa Suraj Prakashji, or Bawaji. For wasn't he the son of Bibi Amar Vati, their landlady? He had to be addressed reverentially, with a title.

Lala Kanshi Ram and Prabha Rani would have no such pampering. Bawa Suraj Prakash indeed! He was a stupid boy who couldn't count straight up to ten—Bawaji! And they had seen him grow up from his earliest days. It was always plain Suraj when they spoke to him. And Suraj, the good boy that he was, replied readily, yes chachaji, or yes chachiji.

'Now why don't you leave that damn thing alone?'

The broadcast was about to begin and Suraj made no reply.

'And don't blow the smoke at me—put the cigarette out!'

'Chachaji, you are getting angry today for no reason.' Suraj crushed the cigarette in an ash tray beside him, and looked at Lala Kanshi Ram with an apologetic smile through his dreamy eyes.

'Sit still. For goodness sake, sit still for a while!'

Suraj shook his head and laughing to himself at some private joke leaned back in his chair. And then he involuntarily shot forward, twiddled with the knob of the brightly lit radio, creating hundreds of crackling sounds, and remembering Lala Kanshi Ram, was immediately sorry and looked at him, in regret and fear, and once again sat back in his chair—not smiling this time, but looking helpless.

'Wah!' said Lala Kanshi Ram, screwing up his lips.

Bibi Amar Vati sat in a corner on a small cot, pulling at her small hookah.

'You better remove him from that chair if you want to listen to the speeches in peace,' she said to Lala Kanshi Ram.

Many of the tenants laughed, for they knew it was meant as a joke. Bawaji did have such restless hands! He could never sit still!

'Promise,' said Suraj Prakash, raising his hand like a boy scout. 'I won't touch it now.'

They all laughed again, but not Lala Kanshi Ram. He was too tense. There was tension in the room, too.

It was at last seven o'clock and the Viceroy, after the preliminary remarks by the announcer, came on the air. The speech was in English, but there was a hush in the room. When Phool Chand's young child began to cry, Lala Kanshi Ram shouted promptly to his wife, 'Bhagwan Devi—take him out of here.' For a second Lala Kanshi Ram was thrilled he should be listening to the voice of an English Viceroy, but he was more concerned with what he was saying and looked at Arun's face for some clue. The Viceroy spoke in a clipped, sharp accent and even this non-English speaking audience could sense the emotion behind what he was saying. He was soon finished and all eyes turned first towards Suraj Prakash (since he was older of the two), who knew *some* English, and when he threw up his hands in despair and shook his head and said, 'Not Viceroy's English!—you don't expect me to understand *that*!' the eyes turned towards Arun, the college boy of the community. Arun had understood it all only too well, and in a shaken voice he said, 'Partition!' and made a gesture with his hands of chopping a thing in two. 'Partition!' many voices shouted out aloud and the mouths remained open. 'Yes, partition!' said Arun.

Soon it was Pandit Nehru's voice coming through the radio, and the audience was quiet again, though restless now, anxiously waiting for the English part of his speech to end so they could listen to him in Hindi. In both versions Nehru spoke with much feeling, and with a sense of exhaustion rather than triumph. He had been acting as Prime Minister of the interim government since September 1946, and his voice had boomed on the air many times in the last nine months. Yet never before had he sounded so tired. He was a brilliant leader, a very proud leader, and in leading the motley millions of his people, people speaking many tongues, living in such diverse climes, having such diverse customs and habits, in leading these millions to a single, united goal, he had a right to be impatient with them, to be abrupt. And his people were indulgent of him, the crowds would laugh at his temper and dismiss his angry words as the pranks of a 'king'. For hours they would wait for his arrival at a gathering, and when he came wearing a snow-white cotton cap and swinging a cane and even hitting some of them in his impatience, trying to make them see the meaning of discipline, of sitting down quietly in a meeting place or making an orderly line and a clear passage for the leader to pass through, the leader who had other things to do for them than to waste his energy in cutting a pathway through their dense bodies, and while he rebuked men and women who jumped forward to touch his feet and threw him off balance (for he would jump back, to take his feet out of their reach), and shouted at them that what freedom meant was not feet-touching but dignity, and that's what he wanted from them, an uprightness, the power to face dangers, he wanted courage and no fear, no fear at all, and no slogans, no shouting, but attention, attention to what he had come here to tell them, to say to them, and he wanted them to abide by him so that they could march forward together, hand in hand, which would never be if they continued to be irresponsible and noisy and ill-mannered as they were today—when he said such abrupt things to them, they bore him no ill will, they accepted that as a rebuke they deserved and they smiled to themselves.

This day he said no abrupt words to them. He sounded meek and gentle, he sounded in sorrow. And in spite of that he could win no sympathy from this group gathered in the mirror-studded living room of Bibi Amar Vati. What stupid things was he talking about? Was he really Nehru? The drawl was the same, the emotion in the words was the same, the disjointed, queer Hindi syntax was his alone, but what had happened to his akal, his mind? Have partition if there is no other way, have it that way—we're willing to make sacrifices. But what nonsense was this of no panic, no violence, full protection from the government, peace the main object! Had he gone mad? Didn't he know his people? Didn't he know the Muslims? And why the partition in the first place? What of your promises to us, you Pandit Nehru?

The feelings of the group exploded as soon as his broadcast was over. They were not interested in what Jinnah or Baldev Singh were to say—what more or different *could* they say?—and the radio was switched off by Suraj on a command from Lala Kanshi Ram. They looked at each other and more than regret, more than fear, on the face of each one of them was disbelief.

Bibi Amar Vati was the first to speak.

'Brother Kanshi Ram, what does this mean?'

The gurh-gurh of her little hookah had long since ceased, and the stem was lying idle in her lips.

'Behan, you heard it as well as I.'

'You mean Pakistan is now coming?'

Several voices together: 'It is coming!'

And then they were all speaking to each other and the room became a Babel. Each family instinctively drew its members together, as a gesture of protection against the danger. In the light of their understanding, each group went over Nehru's speech again. Bibi Amar Vati had gone to sit near Lala Kanshi Ram and Lala Kanshi Ram was raking his mind to find some loophole which might permit a different interpretation. There was none.

Suraj Prakash switched the radio on again and in the sudden crackle of noises, the room went silent. Jinnah was finishing his speech and what they heard, loud and crisp, were his last words: 'Pakistan, zindabad! Long live Pakistan!' Suraj at once turned the radio off. But they had heard the cry of Jinnah and there was no mercy in it, only pride.

'What will happen to us, Lalaji?' said Sardar Teja Singh, giving voice to the fears of them all.

Everyone in the room waited for Lala Kanshi Ram's answer.

'I suppose we'll continue here. Why can't Hindus and Sikhs live in Pakistan? Why should they wish us harm?' he said, without much conviction.

'Be realistic, father,' said Arun.

The middle-class businessman in Lala Kanshi Ram wanted to cling to his hope.

'Well, why can't we live in Pakistan? They certainly would like to have us, have our business. Their whole economy will be ruined if they drive us out.'

'They can have our money without having to keep us!'

'But how has the Congress agreed to the partition? And how have our Sikh leaders, the Akalis?' asked Sardar Niranjan Singh, the young, volatile husband of Isher Kaur. While he spoke, he nervously clutched the hilt of the long sword he carried. He was young and he was strong, and what he wanted to do was to take out his sword and hack Nehru to pieces.

'They've all agreed to it—our Sikh leaders too!' said Sardar Teja Singh, staring hard at his son-in-law.

'It's a betrayal,' shouted Arun.

'Has Gandhi agreed to it?' asked Mukanda's old mother, from one corner of the room. She was very old and her voice was always a little unsteady. Now she could hardly stay coherent.

'He must have!' said many voices in contempt.

'What will happen to my Mukanda?' said the old crone, her hair spread out wildly around her. She was making an attempt to peep at them through her cat-like eyes, and her face looked like the centre of an old, weary cobweb.

In other circumstances they would have laughed at her question. Her middle-aged son Mukanda was one of the most wanted ten men on the police's black list, always in and out of prisons. These days he was in again, serving a term for the latest of his larcenies. Mukanda's mother maintained he was an innocent lad, the *nicest* of the lot, and he was pushed into the jail because of the malice the police Inspector had against him. But no sooner was Mukanda out, he found ways enough to be sent right back to where he had come from. Everyone in the street felt safer that way too—with Mukanda inside—and they laughed at his mother when she stopped them on the way and read out to them a list of points in his favour.

No one laughed at her question, though no one gave her an answer.

The meeting broke up and they went back to their apartments. Lala Kanshi Ram's advice was, let's wait till the morning when the newspapers come out. Maybe there still is a way out.

A gentle breeze had come up and Prabha Rani brought the food to the roof, as did Isher Kaur. The two families sat on cots, on their respective sides of the roof, and ate in silence. In the dusk of the evening, the three Sikhs looked tall and straight. Sardar Jodha Singh, the grandfather, had heard the news and it brought about a slight stoop in the eighty year old back. But he held his head high and and his white turban shone like a distant star in the sky. Arun's nostrils were invaded by the smell of the spices, and the laden thali, the platter before him looked good. With deliberation he poured the beans and the fried cauliflower on the cinnamon-covered rice and ate it up. The soft, fluffy basmati rice went well with the salty tang of the beans. He also put bits of chapati into his mouth. And as the noise of the utensils continued, and as he ate, Arun thought of Nur....

CHAPTER 3

AND as they were eating, they heard the first noise of the fire-crackers.

Muslims in the city were celebrating. From all over the city huge fire-crackers shot up into the sky and exploded into billions and trillions of little lights of red and green. The Muslim mohallas, the neighbourhoods where the Muslims lived in strength, were far off, but they could hear the noise right here and they could see the lights. Food remained unswallowed in the mouth of Prabha Rani, when the first cracker exploded. And they all looked upwards as light after light blazed into the dark sky.

And then came the illuminations. In the distance, they could see the rooftops and the homes being lit with earthen lamps. As time passed, more and more lights came on as if the earth had suddenly errupted in a volcanic explosion, cutting so many holes in the surface of the city.

It was late in the night that the procession came. All shops in the city had closed early—hardly anyone walked abroad. Only the paan shop in Trunk Bazaar was still open and a few men stood there. Arun could hear the noise of their conversation, where he sat and ate his food.

The first indication of a procession was rumbling noise in the distance. It was the sound of drums. Everyone on the roofs raised his head in alarm. When the sound drew nearer and was joined by the sound of men shrieking and shouting slogans, they knew what it was.

Suraj Prakash appeared at the top of his roof:

'Arun, the gate, the gate!'

Niranjan Singh had the same thought, as he sprang up shouting: 'The gate, the gate!'

The three ran downstairs. There were two flights of stairs to the street, and on the way they bumped into Mukanda's mother. She was slowly climbing to the roof.

'Arun, I was coming up to ask you—what do you *think* they could do to my Mukanda?'

'Later, Grandma,' said Arun, and pushing her out of the way they ran on. Once in the street they ran to the junction of the street with Trunk Bazaar (the two buildings stood at the east end of the street, the flank of one of them facing the bazaar proper). Mohinder Lal, the paan walla, hastily pulled down the shutters, and the men who lived in the street ran at a scramble. Many hands moved the heavy wooden gate shut, drawing the bolts and sliding the thick iron bar across the panels.

"The other end!"

They ran the length of the street toward the other end. It was a long, winding street, and half way through they met other youngsters of the mohalla who were coming their way. The two teams assured each other that both the gates were locked. The group consisted of twelve to fifteen young men. And quickly they held an on-the-spot council of war.

'What shall we do?'

Said Niranjan Singh, 'I suggest we stay here and we fight the bastards if they try to enter the street. We should be able to kill a few before we get killed.'

'Their number—their number is against us,' spoke Hare Krishna, the young clerk, who lived on the west side of the street and was one of the leaders of the group.

'That's right. Facing them at this time would be suicidal. I suggest we go up into our homes and wait and see. But if they attack a single house, we all come out regardless,' said Arun.

It was only during the last year they had formed a youth club to face the Muslims. The gates had been set up only three or four months back. Sialkot was a Muslim majority city and many Hindu mohallas had installed gates to protect themselves. Most inhabitants of Fort Street were members of the Congress and they had implicit faith in the assurance of their political leaders. Hare Krishna was among the few who suspected the Congress, and it was at his insistence the youth group in the street was formed, as well as the gates fixed. 'What if we are let down by the Congress?', he asked. 'What if the Muslims come and attack us?' And most young men of the street at his advice had joined the training in self-defence a few Hindu organizations were giving in the town. By now the youngsters in the street were trained in the use of the stick and other guerrilla activities and each house had its store of acid-filled bottles, bricks and heavy sticks. No one in the street possessed a firearm except Shri Kant Bahadur, an affluent lawyer, who had the biggest house in the mohalla. He was generally too drunk in the evening to be trusted; in his peevishness he was capable of firing at you rather than the Muslims. The men depended on their own resources. Or they depended on the help of the police. The headquarters of the city police were situated on the Fort, which was barely four hundred yards away from Fort Street, directly in front of the east end. (They could see the police buildings from their rooftops.) Why need they fear? They were well armed, in their manner. They were well protected.

'Our safest course is to be tactful. Maybe they won't come into the street at all.' This was Suraj Prakash, who seemed of a sudden matured under the threat to survival.

They all agreed and climbed back into their homes.

Arun and Niranjan Singh went up their stairs, bolting the street door behind them. Suraj Prakash went up the other house, bolting that door. Soon every door in the street was shut tight, as if they were fearing a visit from some prehistoric monster.

The procession came down Trunk Bazaar, and stopped outside the eastern entrance to the street. It was a wild sight. The mob was in a transport, which exceeded panic or hysteria. As far as you could see, the bazaar was a sea of heads. They were split up into many small groups, and before each group there were two or three drummers. Also interspersed in the length of the procession were a half dozen brass bands. They all appeared to be on the crest of a private wave. Many groups wielded drumsticks, many indulged in mock sword fights or gatka playing, which was like sword fighting except that the 'sword' was made of a bamboo cane, overlaid with leather. In certain groups they swung the lathi, a thick stick as long as the javelin, which is the staple arm every Punjabi villager carries to protect himself. Many of them were dancing the Bhangra, the Punjabi dance of victory. The drummers hit wildly at the drums with their sticks, and the dancers bent forward and bent backward and swung on their toes. And frequently the drummers and the dancers stopped. And together they shouted, 'Pakistan, zindabad. Long live Pakistan.'

At the entrance to the street the procession stopped and there was a brief discussion amongst the organizers who walked ahead of the procession, wearing red Muhammadan caps with the black tassel on their heads and garlands of jasmine around their necks. It was too hot and they were clad in muslin shirts and long white pyjamas. From the opulent size of them—their heavy paunches, and their strong arms and limbs—they were either professional wrestlers or the meat sellers, the butchers, of their community.

The organizers of the procession were aware of the Hindu heads watching them from atop the houses by the side of Trunk Bazaar, and the sight of the wooden gate leading off the bazaar into the interior of the mohalla seemed to excite them further. They had passed other mohallas on their way, but the presence of the Fort on their right, with the police flags fluttering on top of the Fort, was too dramatic a situation to be missed. They did not want to harm the Hindus—at least not today. Today they were only celebrating the acceptance of Pakistan by the British. But they had to make the meaning of that acceptance apparent enough for these banyas, the traders who had long dominated the business affairs of the city.

And the head of the procession, instead of following along Trunk Bazaar, turned towards the closed gate of Fort Street, and the organizers demanded entrance into the mohalla.

Also at the east end of the street stood the large house of Shri Kant Bahadur, the affluent lawyer. On his roof, his children and servants too were glued to the parapet and were looking down at what was happening in the bazaar below. Shri Kant Bahadur was not there amongst them, nor was his wife. As usual, he was lying drunk in one of the rooms of that vast mansion. His wife, as usual, was crying her eyes out in another.

'Why don't the police urge them to move on ahead?' hissed Lala Kanshi Ram through his teeth.

There were many policemen along with the procession, walking with their turbans held crookedly at an angle on their heads. They stood passively aside as the procession turned in the direction of the closed gate.

'Listen, ohai, lalas! We don't wish to harm you. We only want to take the procession through this street. So come on down and open the gate!'

Everyone on the rooftops heard that. No one moved. Nor did they talk to each other. It was so imminent, the threat, they were frozen where they were. Isher Kaur felt a faintness coming on her, and she stood clutching her abdomen. She knew she should go and sit on a cot, but she found it impossible to leave the parapet.

The men in the bazaar shouted again, this time many of them together:

'We're telling you, *open* the gate!'

And a huge cry of 'Allah-o-Akbar' rose from the head of the procession—a cry which travelled the length of the procession, each group picking up the shout and passing it on to the next. Soon the sky was filled with many echoes of 'Allah-o-Akbar, Allah-o-Akbar, Allah-o-Akbar... Allah-o...'

Padmini came up to Lala Kanshi Ram and said, 'Lalaji, they might dishonour us!'

Padmini was a destitute woman, who lived in the basement of Bibi Amar Vati's building, along with her young daughter, Chandni. They had come along a few years back and rented the single room lying vacant in Bibi Amar Vati's house. The husband of Padmini was long since dead, and she made a living as a charwoman, mostly by washing dishes. Twice a day mother and daughter appeared in several houses in the street, and squatting near the kitchen sink cleaned up the mess the family had made. They worked chiefly for Bibi Amar Vati and Lala Kanshi Ram, but they had three of four other households also to take care of. The daughter was very young, about eighteen, plump and healthy in spite of the poverty, and the mother was in her early forties, a faded beauty of a very delicate type. She went about in rags and had streaks of grey hair which she did not bother to dye. Yet she had a strange poise on her yellow, sallow face, and in the fall of her small, drooping breasts there was the lure of distant sapphires. I may look a poor widow, she seemed to be saying, but really I am a queen!

Lala Kanshi Ram looked up when he heard the voice of Padmini. It was a cloudy night so it was quite dark on the roof. Lala Kanshi Ram knew not what to say to Padmini. Fear took hold of him and he had a severe constriction in his chest.

Arun, Suraj Prakash, Niranjan Singh and Phool Chand, the muscular son of Lala Bihari Lal, the grocer, surrounded him. These men were young and they wanted action. The street gate was locked by the law of the local municipality (any mohalla could lock up the gates after nine at night), and they had no business to be pounding on it. And what were these policemen doing there, who were supposed to prevent rowdyism?

'Why don't you let me throw an acid bottle on them?' said Niranjan Singh, feeling sore to be restrained.

'You know what that might set off?'

The other boys accepted that, but Niranjan Singh walked away disgruntled. These Hindus were too weak. Always thinking of consequences. Guru Maharaj had given him strength for occasions such as this, and they wouldn't let him use it. He loosened his beard, and quickly running his small comb through it a number of times, wound it up into its little knot below his chin. He then adjusted his turban and giving his shoulders a shrug stepped down to his own roof.

'Ohai, Niranjan Singh, Niranjan Singh!—ohai Arun!'

Niranjan Singh did not know who it was, only the wind brought the voice and its anxiety to where Niranjan stood on his roof.

'Now what do *you* want?' he shouted back.

'What's happening up front?' came the voice, carried unevenly by the wind.

Another bloody Hindu. There were many Sikhs too living in the street, but Niranjan Singh knew it must be some Hindu. The Sikhs must be sharpening their swords, as they should be.

'Come and see for yourself,' he shouted back in contempt. Relenting at once, he shouted:

'They're trying to get into the street.'

A sigh arose along the street, showing how on every rooftop anxious faces were amassed awaiting the outcome.

The crowd in the bazaar had become restive and when the gate was not opened, the leaders kicked the gate with their feet and announced:

'We're not moving from here until we pass through the street.'

'You better hear that!' they shouted, to a general cry of 'Allah-o-Akbar' and the brandishing of countless spears the men in the procession carried in their hands.

Also they summoned many of the drummers to the front, and massed them outside of the gate. And they ordered them to beat on the drums with all the force they had in their bodies.

The din that ensued was deafening. There must have been about thirty to thirty-five drummers there, wearing multi-coloured lungis and going crazy in the madness of the sound. They bent backwards in their frenzy, crazily balancing themselves on their feet, and their drums projected in front of them like cancerous growths, something that was a part of the body and was inescapably joined to it. And the two sticks in their hands, one of them strong but bent like a crow's foot, the other straight and flimsier, the two sticks came down on the two sides of the drum like lightning, beating down at them with excitement and centuries-old terrors of Punjabi myths associated with that sharp hollow sound. The general rhythm was daga-dug-dum, daga-dug-dum, daga-dug-dum, daga-dug-dum. The last 'dum' was given by the powerful right hand which held the strong, slightly bent stick. The first 'daga' and the second 'dug' alternated between the left and the right hand, both on a softer note, until the right hand repeated the stroke with a mighty 'dum'. As the frenzy rose, the first and the second beat were repeated many times over, like stretching out a live wire, when in the end came the explosion, the final powerful stroke of the right hand—'dum'. The 'dum' was the full stop of the foot of the rhythm and had the key to your heartbeat, as it were. For when it fell, when the juggler with the sticks had concluded his run, you rose up like a maniac, and along with you, with each fall of the 'dum', rose up other weird spirits which came and stood by your side.

The drummers were in a madness of the purest kind. And why shouldn't they be? Today their Pakistan had been sanctioned—the land of the pure. Today they had become pure, at the last. And they bent their backs, projecting the drums far in front of them, and went daga-dug-dum!

And another cry arose from the procession, louder and more menacing than the daga-dug of drums and which could be heard clearly above their din, and which said, 'Torh do! Torh do!' 'Break it open! Break it open!' They also shouted, 'Pakistan, zindabad!'

Isher Kaur could take no more and started crying, so terrible was the shout, so demoralizing!

Prabha Rani heard her whimpering sobs and said sharply, 'Ishero, go back to your roof and lie down. You want to ruin yourself—with that child in your womb?'

So now they all knew she was pregnant! Why did chachiji have to say it so loud? And Isher Kaur broke down openly, burying her head in her dopatta and sobbing.

'You don't have to worry, beti,' said Lala Kanshi Ram. 'No harm will come to you. We're here to protect you.'

'I think I better take her to her bed,' said her father, Sardar Teja Singh.

At the same time they saw a large posse of policemen descending from the Fort on the run. The Fort was well lit, and the men were clearly visible from the roofs. That's what they had been waiting for. How could a thing like this happen right in front of the City Police Headquarters?

'Patience, boys,' said Lala Kanshi Ram to the youngsters by his side. 'We don't want to lose our heads. We'll let the police handle it for us.'

'The police were already here!'

'Very few of them. Now they're coming in force—look at the line,' Lala Kanshi Ram said, pointing towards the front of the Fort, from which a narrow road ran down to Trunk Bazaar.

Soon on the scene below appeared Inayat-Ullah Khan, the City Inspector, along with a large body of policemen armed with rifles. He had been in the police force for the last thirty years, and knew almost every person in the city by sight and thousands of them by name. It was the policy of the British government not to transfer junior officers from one city to another, unless there were grave charges against a man. Senior police officers, above the rank of inspector, were transferable all over the province, but not inspectors and below. And they're damn right, said Inayat-Ullah Khan to himself. How else can I fight crime, unless I get to know a city inside out? Consequently he had been in Sialkot all his life, had grown rich on the crime in the city, and was feared in the city as no criminal was.

When he arrived at the scene, the men fell back.

Raising his arm in the air, he shouted at the leaders:

'What do you think you're doing?'

'Inspector Sahib, we're doing nothing irregular, we're doing nothing against the law,' one of them replied in a soft tone. They knew of Inayat-Ullah Khan's temper.

Inayat-Ullah Khan waited for the explanation.

'Hazoor, you must have heard the broadcast. The English have agreed to the new state of Pakistan, a state for which all national Muslims like you and us have pined for years—' Cleverly the leader paused here, and raising his hands towards his mouth like a loudspeaker, he turned towards the procession and shouted, 'Pakistan—' and waited for the crowd to reply. They roared back like hundreds of muskets: 'Zindabad!' 'Pakistan—' he said again. 'Zindabad!' they replied. 'Pakistan—' 'Zindabad!'

Facing the Inspector, he continued:

'We are only celebrating the event, sir, and are taking out a procession in that honour. And the Hindus won't let us pass through the street. It's a public street!'

Inayat-Ullah Khan knew of the municipal law which allowed the citizens to close the side lanes and mohallas to general traffic at night. But he too had listened to the broadcast, and things had ceased to have a legal right or wrong for Inayat-Ullah Khan in the past few hours. It was a matter of conscience. For years he had ordered lathi charges on Muslim processions at the command of the British government. He hated doing it, they were his own brethren, but orders were orders. The only consolation he had was that when the lathi charge was to be on a crowd of Congress Muslims, he made it as violent as he could. But on his own Muslims, the Muslim League Muslims—Allah! Allah!

And he had lived with the heavy burden of his conscience, not knowing how to atone for it. He was certain Allah would never forgive him! Today came his chance. Lowering his arm, he said to the leaders:

'You have a point there!'

The crowd yelled in triumph and the drummers went into a long beat of the drums, while one of the leaders went forward and put a garland of jasmine around the Inspector's neck.

Inayat-Ullah Khan could not identify the people on the roof, but he knew who lived there.

He ordered: 'Lala Kanshi Ram, will you open this gate?'

The crowd again yelled in triumph.

'Hazoor, we're afraid. They might set fire to our homes, or loot our property.'

It would be a good thing if they did that, thought Inayat-Ullah Khan. Aloud he said, 'They won't. They only want to take the procession through the street.'

There was dead silence on the roof.

'Do nothing,' they heard a soft voice. It came from Vakil Sahib's house, the affluent lawyer's. Looking up, they saw the profile of the wife of Shri Kant Bahadur.

'I've called the Deputy Commissioner and the Superintendent of Police on the phone. They should be here any minute.'

With these words she disappeared. She had come like an apparition, and like an apparition she was gone. Shri Kant Bahadur's house was the only house in the entire mohalla with a telephone. They knew the conceit of his liquor-filled brain, and no one had thought of seeking his help. He had connections in the city, and they knew no harm would come to him and his family. And then he had a gun too, didn't he? But his wife seemed to be made of a different stuff.

'She is a devi,' announced Lala Kanshi Ram. 'She married a beast, but she herself is a devi!'

Inspector Inayat-Ullah Khan had no response to his order and the gate remained shut. That incensed him immensely.

'Listen, ohai, Kanshi Ram. If the gate is not opened in five minutes, I'll order my men to force it open.'

'How can he do that?' Arun whispered to his father.

Lala Kanshi Ram craned his neck to see if the Deputy Commissioner was coming. Not that he put much faith in him. In the last few years, there had been a rapid Indianization of senior jobs and many posts previously held by Englishmen were passed on to the natives. The Deputy Commissioner of Sialkot these days was a Hindu; the Superintendent of Police a Muslim. They were members of the Indian Civil Service, the highest and the most powerful arm of the British Raj, but they were Indians nonetheless and Lala Kanshi Ram did not put much trust in them. (He had literally burst into tears when the English Superintendent of Police left Sialkot, and though he was not invited, he had gone with a load of garlands to the railway station to see the Superintendent Sahib off!)

Yet such as they were, even they were not in sight.

'All right, if that's what you want,' said Inayat-Ullah Khan, and turning to a group of constables by his side he ordered: 'Break open the gate!'

The crowd shouted: 'Ya Ali! Ya Haider!'

It was a scene of increasing chaos. For the police party consisted of constables drawn from various religious faiths. The Hindus could not be distinguished from the Muslims at first sight, but you couldn't mistake a Sikh—the turban and the beard were clear identification. And in the party with Inayat-Ullah Khan, there were several Sikhs.

When the order to force the gate open came, the Sikh constables to a man refused to budge. No one could say what prompted the stand they took, but they refused to move.

Inayat-Ullah Khan went mad with rage. He was only waiting for an opportunity like this to come into his element. Taking out his revolver, he jumped at them.

'You know what the penalty of indiscipline in the Force is, don't you? Get a move on or I'll shoot you where you stand!'

Other constables had procured a beam, no one knew where from (Lala Kanshi Ram was certain the Muslims had brought it with them), and placing the beam in front of the gate, they were getting ready to ram it.

None of the Sikh constables moved. The crowd cried, 'Pakistan, zindabad!' and some yelled, 'Shoot them!'

Inayat-Ullah Khan did not want to shoot them, he wanted to humiliate them. And he had a better plan—he went after them one at a time, to separate them.

'Banta Singhian!' he roared.

A young Sikh fell out of the line, marched a few steps forward and saluted.

'You want me to shoot you?'

'No, sir.'

'Get on behind the beam.'

The Sikh faltered for a second, when Inayat-Ullah Khan shouted: 'Forward!' and he went ahead and joined those near the beam.

'Daljit Singh!' roared Inayat-Ullah Khan.

A Sikh out of the line, a few steps forward, a salute.

'Sir?'

'You heard me give you an order?'

'Sir!'

'Go and stand behind the beam.'

'Havaldar Nathu Singh!'

This one was in a different group—of drill sergeants.

'Sir!'

'Go and give a hand at the beam.'

The Inspector now turned towards a young Sikh officer. He was the only Sikh officer present there; all other junior officers were either Hindus or Muslims.

'Sub-Inspector Hardit Singh!' said Inspector Inayat-Ullah Khan in a tone only slightly milder than he had used for the other Sikhs.

'Sir!'

'Order these men to push the beam.'

He should have done that in the first instance, thought Inayat-Ullah Khan—watch a Sikh order other Sikhs to their destruction. Only he wanted to handle the whole thing himself.

The Sikh officer remained quiet for a while, and then shouted in a broken voice:

'All right men, get on behind the beam.'

The men obeyed, seeking comfort in the plaintive one of their officer.

Just then the Deputy Commissioner and the Superintendent of Police arrived and the whole operation came to a standstill, like a fifty mile an hour wind suddenly dropping down to zero.

The Inspector had not foreseen the possibility, nor those who were in the procession.

The Deputy Commissioner had been in Sialkot only a few months, as had the Superintendent of Police. They arrived in the same jeep, as if there was unanimity between them in their move. It was the Deputy Commissioner who had suggested that, and had picked up the Superintendent from his home. Behind them came six truck loads of reserve police from the Police Lines outside of the city, troops which were not under the jurisdiction of the City Inspector and which were retained in barracks.

The Deputy Commissioner was a small plump man, round faced, and with heavy, ungainly buttocks—and he belonged to that senile race of Hindus which had been enslaved and ruled over by the Muslims for centuries. But disregarding the odds against him, he jumped off the jeep briskly and marched forward courageously into the middle of the crowd.

The crowd made way for him, they knew who he was. Inspector Inayat-Ullah Khan, and every other officer of the police present, smartly came to attention and saluted.

Along the entire length of the procession, a silence had fallen. Over an hour had passed since the march had halted in Trunk Bazaar and just when things were about to move, had arrived the chief executive of the district. They knew he was a Hindu, but they also knew he represented the government. And they waited in a hush, forgetting to shout their slogans.

'What's going on around here?' asked the Deputy Commissioner with authority.

'Nothing, sir. Nothing, sir,' said the Inspector sheepishly.

Ahead of them stood a number of constables hanging on to a heavy wooden beam.

'What's the meaning of that?' The Deputy Commissioner pointed towards the beam.

'It is like this, sir. These people want to take their procession through the street, but the residents have locked the gate...'

Lowering his voice and coming a little closer in a vulgar gesture of intimacy, as if the Deputy Commissioner were his friend and he was confiding to him something he did not want the others to hear:

'You see, sir, if we resist the demand of the marchers, they might become violent and do much harm.'

The uncouth tone of the Inspector and the crude manner in which he had obviously conducted himself so far, was too much for the well-bred, English-trained civil servant.

He first moved a few steps away from the Inspector, to physically disassociate himself from him, and then ignoring his explanation, asked: 'Do you mean to tell me your men have been forcing that gate open?'

'Sir, there was nothing else I could do,' replied the Inspector, waving his hands. 'The crowd would have become violent and destroyed property in the bazaar!' He gazed at the Superintendent, hoping to find corroboration in a fellow Muslim. The Superintendent did not glance his way.

'And why are you wearing that garland around your neck? Take it off at once,' continued the Deputy Commissioner in the same abrupt manner.

'Yes, sir. Yes, sir. I don't know how it got there!'

The Deputy Commissioner had assessed the situation fairly accurately, though. Taking the Superintendent by the shoulder, he walked aside and whispered: 'I guess it's hopeless, Asghar. We have to let the procession go through.'

'You're right.'

They had been discussing this while they were driving to Trunk Bazaar. Both of them had heard the radio announcement, and both were bewildered by its contents. How do you cut a country in two, where at every level the communities were so deeply mixed? There was a Muslim in every corner of India where there was a Hindu. And then so soon, at such short notice? The broadcast had said nothing at all about the fate of the minorities in the two new countries. If the logic behind the creation of Pakistan was accepted, there was no place for a minority anywhere. Pakistan wouldn't solve the problem of a minority, it was going to create new minorities—minorities which would be hounded out with a vengeance. And what of the civil service to which they belonged? And what of the army? How were they going to cut up the machinery of the government? There were Hindus and Muslims at every level of that machinery!

The Deputy Commissioner and the Superintendent of Police were trained in England, and they were both above the politics of the day. Rather, till the other day they were contemptuous of that politics. They belonged to that grand arm of the imperial power to which very few Indians had been admitted. With freedom on the way they were slowly becoming nationalistic. Yet they were essentially men to whom conduct was a question of aesthetic preferences and not of political involvements. A search for sophistication bound them together more closely than ethnic bonds. And to this search they remained faithful.

'You will perhaps opt to serve in Pakistan?' asked Pran Nath Chaddha, the Deputy Commissioner.

'Will I have a choice?' replied Asghar Ahmad Siddiqui, the Superintendent of Police.

That too was true, thought Pran Nath Chaddha. The announcement had said the services would be divided. But how? No one knew. Maybe they would be herded together and colour dyes put on their heads, as they did with cattle, and some would be sent to one side and some to the other. The country was to be split up down to the last peon, and not even senior officers like them were consulted or informed or forewarned about it.

'I hope I will have your cooperation until the whole thing is sorted out. I mean, we don't want the district to go up in flames, do we?'

'There will be no riots here, Pran, this I can promise you. The police will back you up to the hilt, and we can always send for the military.'

That was in the jeep. They were now reviewing the situation on the spot and it seemed imperative to them that the procession be allowed to go through the street as quickly as possible, before tension built up to a point where it got out of control.

The Deputy Commissioner stepped forward and enquired about the people who lived in the nearby houses. He moved with tremendous courage and self-confidence, making it apparent enough in his clenched, determined visage that his own life was of little consequence to him.

'Lalaji,' he spoke softly, after the Inspector had confided the information to him in a cringing, debasing manner, bending over backward in his effort to ingratiate himself. 'Please come down and open the gate. Superintendent Sahib and I both guarantee that no harm will come to anyone living in the mohalla.'

Asghar Ahmad Siddiqui, to show his support of the Deputy Commissioner, at once said: 'Yes, Lalaji!' He also ordered the constables with the beam to throw that infernal thing away and get back from the gate.

'Yes, get away from there, and fall in at the rear!' shouted Inayat-Ullah Khan, making the best of a bad bargain.

The gate swung open and there stood Lala Kanshi Ram with a group of people from the street. They had seen the Deputy Commissioner handle the situation, and they were impressed.

'Open it wide,' said the Deputy Commissioner. 'Don't be afraid!'

The two panels of the gate were pushed all the way back, and behind the panels lay the street and the houses stretching into the interior, like a painted stage set.

Like a masterful conductor of a musical performance, the Deputy Commissioner did not move when the gate was thrown open. There was a ripple of excitement in the procession, but so dominant was the personality of the Deputy Commissioner, the murmur died down the instant he turned his head and looked at the procession. For several minutes he did not say a word, as though daring them to march forward if they would. So confident did he seem, so firmly rooted in some inner conviction, that not a man in the procession moved a step.

The Deputy Commissioner leisurely walked up and down, going over in his mind the things in his favour and things against him. It was all a bluff, he knew. If these several thousand people really wanted to rush the gate he couldn't do a thing to stop them. But if he had to maintain peace in the city, this was the time to show his strength. Until he was removed, he was the most senior officer of the district and his word must be respected. What he saw from the corner of his eye further reassured him. He saw Asghar Ahmad had taken charge of the police from the Inspector and was busy deploying men of the special police along the street.

He kept the procession waiting for a few more moments, and then went and spoke to the leaders:

'I'll let the procession go through the street provided there is no violence and provided you take the procession back to your own mohallas in an orderly fashion once you have reached the other end of the street.'

'We agree, sir!' said the leaders.

'My men have orders to shoot if there is any violence,' said Asghar Ahmad Siddiqui.

Lala Kanshi Ram and the rest were sent back to their homes and the procession did pass through the street. The drummers and the bands came morbidly alive, and many hearts trembled to hear their deafening noise. They had leaders with each group and on the whole they remained orderly. As they squeezed into the street, it was like a swollen river breaking a small side dyke with all its force. Many gaslights, carried by men shoulder high or on top of their heads, accompanied the procession and the scene was like a marriage party, a baraat, proceeding on its way. Every now and then the groups stopped in the street and indulged in mock fights. The show was stolen by the solo lathi swingers. A man stood in the middle of a group, and while the drummers went up in a crescendo, he swung his stick round and round, making figures of eight in the air in several directions, and attacking an imaginary foe with each swing of his arms. Or the show was stolen by the Bhangra dancers. To the tune of many drums, the dancers danced the classic Punjabi dance, with bright-coloured handkerchiefs on their heads and with bells tied to their ankles. On a truly festive occasion, like Baisakhi, the Bhangra would have been in shiny bright clothes. Today the procession had been organized in a hurry and the men were in their work clothes, sweaty with the day's labour and the heat. They had come straight after hearing the broadcast. But their frenzy was greater than of the Baisakhi dancers. In one of the groups, consisting mostly of petty labourers, danced Abdul Ghani, throwing up his arms, a great joy on his face. And as he passed the house where lived Lala Kanshi Ram, he looked up and shouted, 'Pakistan, zindabad.' All his companions joined in: 'Pakistan, zindabad! Pakistan, zindabad!'

Lala Kanshi Ram was praying on the roof that no fool would throw a brick or something from the houses along the street. In each house sat dozens of women and children, and a mad man could provoke a blood bath. The very last group in the procession was wildest of all and some of them started throwing rocks and a number of glass panes in a few houses were smashed. There was no retaliation from the mohalla.

When the rock throwing began, Siddiqui looked at Pran Chaddha. The Deputy Commissioner shook his head.

'If it doesn't get any worse, we won't act.'

The marchers were too worn out to do much damage, and soon they were at the other end of the street.

The gates were once again closed, and the residents retired to bed. It was two o'clock in the morning.

Niranjan Singh lay awake, thinking. He had passed the evening like a caged lion—they would not let him act. He was certain in his mind he was stronger than all those Muslims put together. He could even dance the Bhangra better than they! At that he smiled, and went to sleep.

CHAPTER 4

It was some days before Arun was able to meet Nur at the college. Their classmates had long known of their romance, but after the announcement of Pakistan they had both become suspect. He was now a 'Hindu' boy carrying on with a 'Muslim' girl. And the Muslim boys in the college stood watching them menacingly.

So far as Arun was concerned, nothing had changed. Sialkot was his city still and he loved it immensely, its sounds and smells and its mosques and temples. The very next day after the radiobroadcast, the Viceroy announced in a press conference that the date of freedom would be advanced from January 1948 to August 1947. He had in the broadcast announced the appointment of a Boundary Commission to decide the precise boundaries of Pakistan and India. Lala Kanshi Ram said there was every hope Sialkot might never go to Pakistan. The Sikhs were demanding the boundary line at the Chenab basin. It meant a clean sweep for India right up to Gujrat, including such important cities as Lahore and Gujranwala. That would include Sialkot too, if the demand was accepted.

Arun knew how flimsy these hopes were. The Sikhs were staking their claim on the ground that they had many religious temples and places of worship in this part of the Punjab. That was not the basis on which the two new states were to be formed. Arun knew the boundary was going to be at the Ravi basin and not at the Chenab.

None of that interfered with his love for the city of his birth. If it became a part of Pakistan, it would continue to be his city still. It will continue to be my city, whether I live here or not, he said to himself.

And he roamed through its streets fearlessly from morning till evening. The entire tenor of living had changed after the Viceroy's broadcast. There were hostilities and tensions, previously under the surface, that had come into the open; hardly a day passed without an untoward happening—a procession, a group quarrel, a gathering. His mother was afraid for him, but he said, 'ma, don't worry, these are not riots, these are local brawls. We've always had things like these—it is the Punjabi temperament. It could happen between a Muslim and a Muslim.'

And taking his bicycle, he went flying through the streets. Whenever he saw a gathering in the distance, he slowed down. There was a slight fear, a vague fear, in the middle of his being. Maybe they were a band of goondas. Taking hold of himself, he cycled on with confidence, only slightly increasing his speed as he neared the group. And he kept up with his routine regardless of the changing mood. He went out for his morning walks. He attended college. He went to play tennis in the evenings. He went up to the Cantonment to see the English movies.

One day he ran into Nur at the college, when there weren't many students around. He had actually been waiting for her under the mango trees near the college chapel, and as she came out of the girls' common room in the corner he went up to her.

'Nur, can't I see you some time?'

Nur briefly looked towards the girls' room.

'Where?'

'Behind the canteen, near the football field. At two!'

A shadow of doubt passed over her beautiful face, her eyes opened and shut quickly in thought, but she said, 'Yes, I'll be there.'

At two, his heart beating in uncertainty, Arun waited for her at the back of the canteen. It was his fifth year at Murray College, and second since Nurul-Nisar and he had spoken of love to each other. And yet every time he approached her, wherever he approached her, he longed for her as if it were the first encounter. There was ever a flutter in his heart. Will she come or won't she? Will an enemy be hiding somewhere to report back on them? Will she be able to make it—or won't she?

He saw her coming and he could have died at the pleasure of seeing her. If only he could be invisible and be near her and watch her unobserved all the while. She was a tall girl, exquisitely formed, and there was an alluring resilience in her shoulders and her torso. As she walked, she seemed to disregard the universe completely. All the precautions were on his side alone, if she was worried as to who saw them together and who did not, she did not show it. She had not spotted him yet but she knew he must be around, and the knowledge that she was wanted and being waited for conferred a strange quietude on her. Her tangerine chiffon dopatta was fluttering in the breeze; she had wrapped it securely around her head and neck like a scarf. She came to the canteen and for a fleeting second looked at the deserted entrance to that ramshackle structure and walked on.

Soon she was in Arun's arms.

'Let's get out of here,' he said.

A few more steps and they were outside the college. In front of them lay the Ramlila ground where every year the Dussehra festival was held. Huge effigies of Ravana and his evil associates were burned on that ground, each year. It was a Hindu festival but the effigies were made by Muslim workmen; the crackers and the fireworks too were supplied by the Muslims.

On one side of the ground ran the railway tracks, one of them going to Jammu and Kashmir, the other to Amritsar. The road on which they stood separated the college from an old Christian cemetery, which was adjacent to the Ramlila ground. To the right, the road ran into the heart of the town. To the left, it went over the railway tracks and continued into the Cantonment.

Arun and Nur knew the area well. The town they avoided, but Arun would put her on the bar of his cycle whenever they were free and take her to the Cantonment. Or they cut across the Ramlila ground and walked by the side of the railway tracks, holding hands. Or they went into the cemetery and lay under the shade of a neem tree.

Arun took her into the cemetery and as soon as they had turned the corner and were behind the trees, he took her in his arms and was kissing her wildly. He held her mouth and almost bit her in his frenzy. And she returned the kiss, without shame.

They were standing in the middle of a path and around them were the quiet graves. Arun held her slender hands and squeezed them hard. He pressed her to himself and felt the weight of her breasts. Putting his lips on her throat he sucked her flesh, until she pulled away from him flustered.

'What will we do?'

It was Arun who spoke.

Nur did not speak. She put her head on his chest and started sobbing. It had been mostly a banter, the love between them; it was a tease. She made fun of his Hindu idols and he of her namaazes. Or she said he looked no good, not at all like what a Punjabi lover should, and he said she was no husn pari, no fairy, either. For days she would refuse to see him, knowing full well that he was pining for her. When he tried to hold her in his arms, she slipped away from his reach and stuck her tongue out at him. And when he said, 'Nur, I love you—will you marry me?' her usual answer was, 'Ja, ja!'

Yet Nur came to college with her lips painted red and her eyes loaded with kohl. And the dancing quivering youth in her, the swift steps she took in her desire, and her ever darting eyes, ever moving restlessly, and the soft, seductive smile that never left her lips, who else was all that for if not for Arun? Except that their separate inhibitions did not quite give them the peace of love, only its tension. They were from different religions, on the face of it they could never marry, there were other areas of discord too.

Today the tensions were dissolved in the burst of emotion. They were both extremely young and inexperienced and they hung on to each other clumsily, clawing at each other.

'It means nothing to us. How can Pakistan stand in our way?' There was no mask now. Nur was intent on what she was saying.

'We may have to go away from here.'

'Go away where?'

'To India. We may have to leave Pakistan.'

'Why?'

Slowly it was coming to Nur, but the unreason of youth and love persisted in her. 'Why can't you keep living here?'

'They won't let us.'

'Who won't? My father would be heartbroken if you left!'

'But the fanatics.'

'They don't count,' she said, throwing her head back.

Her face became shadowed with pain. And then suddenly, holding him tight, she demanded:

'But why must *you* leave—*you?* Let your family go if they have to.'

She said this only faintly. It was the beloved in her speaking, her want of him. Arun knew what she meant and he wished he could have reassured her at once.

Nur saw him falter and separated herself from him.

'Don't tell me you aren't going to stay! You have said so often you would embrace Islam for my sake.'

Embracing Islam for the sake of Nur meant nothing to Arun, embracing *death* for her sake would have meant nothing. What was Islam anyway? Seen as faith it was as good as any. Seen as intellectual enquiry, it was as superstitious and wanting. If by switching a few rituals he could hold Nur next to him in bed every night, that would be a small price for the ecstasy of living.

The issue was no longer as simple as that. The cry of the new state, the name of Pakistan shouted repeatedly before him as insult, had split Arun asunder. He knew the conspiracy of politicians behind the whole move. Jinnah and Liaqat Ali Khan were coming into an estate; as was Nehru. Why else would they rush into azadi at this pace—an azadi which would ruin the land and destroy its unity? For the creation of Pakistan solved *nothing.* One would have to go around with tweezers through all the villages to separate the Muslims from the Hindus. Arun knew this, the game of which he and Nur and millions like them were only victims. But politicians gave ideas legs, even though they were the wrong kind of ideas. And Arun too at the moment was driven by the irrational part of his being.

He saw Nur looking at him, her beauty expanded and made ethereal by her mental anguish.

He heard himself say:

'Why should I become a Muslim?'

He was harsh in his voice, as if it was Nur who had created the new states.

'Why *should't* you? That is, if you love me.'

It sounded like anger, but she was only pleading.

Arun was cruel to her:

'Why shouldn't you become a Hindu?'

For a while Nur was stunned. She looked at him in anger, her passive, pleading eyes lit up with fire. And then she said in a voice mixed with tears:

'Because I'm a girl and am defenceless and cannot force my will on my family and because you're a man, more independent than me, and I expect you to defend me and make sacrifices for me, that's why!'

Nur was weeping, but Arun did not soften towards her.

Turning her back towards him, Nur faced the row of small mounds below which lay the dead, decomposed and putrefied yet in peace. Huddled over in her emotion, she covered her face with her hands and kept weeping. Arun could see her back heave with sobs. Going forward he held her by her shoulders, and said tenderly:

'You know I love you and will do anything for you. But soon it will cease to be a question of personal love. My parents are old, and they'll be hard hit if they are obliged to leave. I'll have to go with them to help resettle them somewhere. But maybe I'll come back and then we can marry the way you wish.'

Nur rounded on him.

'Oh, go and die somewhere. You're a Hindu, after all—a *Hindu*. Too timid!'

'It is not that, and you know it.'

'No, I *don't* know it!'

Saying that, she directly started walking out of the cemetery. Arun ran by her side.

'Don't go back yet.'

'Don't talk to me.'

'I have to.'

'You are only a timid Hindu. Go put your head in your mother's lap!'

There was such vigour in her body that soon, taking rapid strides, she was out of the cemetery and inside the college compound. Briskly she walked on, not waiting for a second for Arun to fall in step beside her. He couldn't have done that anyway, not inside the college compound.

He said: '*Please*!—Nuri, I love you!'

It was no use. There was contention once again between them. Only to the contention was added bitterness, and the playful banter was totally missing from it.

Arun saw a few boys coming out of the canteen and he fell many steps behind Nur. His mouth was full of bile and he was perspiring profusely. The heat was very intense and he could feel his shirt sticking to his back. He gave up and stood under a tree, looking at her receding figure until she was lost behind the mango trees near the girls' common room.

Arun felt miserable and helpless. Wiping his face, he turned towards the canteen and walked in.

Inside he saw Munir sitting alone at a table and he went and joined him.

'It is not safe to meet Nur in the open like this.'

'How long have you been sitting here?'

'All the time, while you were in the cemetery.'

'I didn't think *you* would spy on us.'

'I didn't. I was only concerned about your safety. You know what the temper of the college these days is—the Muslim boys will lynch you if they see you with her.'

'Oh, Munir, I love her so much.'

This was not the first time the subject was mentioned between them. Nurul-Nisar was Munir's sister, two years younger than he in age. Munir and Arun had known each other from early childhood. Chaudhri Barkat Ali, Munir's father, was a bosom friend of Lala Kanshi Ram and came from the same village as he—Sambrhial. Arun had no idea when Chaudhri Barkat Ali moved to Sialkot, but he still had land in Sambrhial which was cultivated for him by tenants. In the city Chaudhri Barkat Ali had a sports factory, where sports goods like hockey sticks and footballs and tennis rackets were manufactured. He lived in Mohalla Mianapura, not an exclusively Muslim mohalla but one which had a mixed population. Many of Arun's early memories were associated with Chaudhri Barkat Ali. He would come and squatting in the kitchen Indian-fashion say to Arun's mother, 'Now sister-in-law, how are you? But first tell me what is there to drink?' Or of him saying to his father: 'Kanshi Ram, the price of everything is shooting up—I don't know how you manage to run the house!'

Arun's memories of Munir were of chasing him up and down the open drain that ran by the side of their schools. Arun went to Arya Samaj School and Munir to Islamia School. The names meant nothing to the boys. There was a Khalsa School in the city, and a Mission School, too. Maybe the English made those parochial distinctions, or maybe the different communities wanted it that way. The children themselves did not think on ethnic lines. Arun could not recall a single fight between the schools on parochial grounds. The fights between the schools were on other grounds. There were rivalries in sports or in debates or in the school results, in academic distinctions. And when one school beat another in any of these fields, the boys worked themselves up into a fight in the streets. Heads were broken and later communal shape was given to these fights. But none of them began as a communal battle.

And he and Munir never fought, of course. Through the heart of Sialkot ran the open drain of the Municipal Committee and in Arun's mind this was a unique feature of the town. In no other town had he seen a drain like this. It was only a narrow drain, but some aesthetic-minded city father had conceived of it in the form of a sunken feature and not an openly exposed one (as drains were in other towns). It was not covered and concealed as you have in some of the ultra modem cities. It was an open drain. Only it ran at the base of a moat, so that you did not see the drain. And it was not a kachcha, a rough moat; the aesthetic-minded municipal father had it lined with bricks.

At the top the moat must be about six feet wide. On both sides ran a low parapet, and then the walls of the moat tapered inward, so that at the bottom the width was no more than two feet. The total depth of the moat was about six feet but since the walls tapered inward, the sides would be perhaps eight. The drain proper ran down the middle of the two-feet-wide bed.

Though it was supposed to be a sewage drain, it was not too dirty. At least, it did not smell as much as some other parts of the city. Every two hours huge quantities of water were flooded through the base by sweepers to clean it up further, and at times the water in the drain was as clear as in a stream.

As it happened, all the boys' schools were located right on this drain. First there was the Government School, then Arya Samaj School, then Islamia, and at the other end Khalsa. The fronts of these schools opened on different roads, but the backs opened on the moat—which ran like a river through the heart of the city. At recess time or immediately before the school began or after it closed, it was not uncommon for boys of one school to wander over to the territory of the other. And the route they took to each other's areas was through the moat.

The moat was the biggest playground of these boys of the city. The ingenuity lay in your sliding down the tapering wall to the bottom and then climbing back up the same side or the other side of the moat in the smallest amount of time. The boys shot down like the wind, and like the wind they climbed back. Because of the constant use to which they were put, the two walls of the moat were marked with innumerable foot and hand holds. The rule of the game was these holds must not be very large. That way any fool could climb those walls. They must be very small.

You could play many games along the drain, but they were all a variation of the mother game Chon Chuai. There was no team work involved in it, it was a game of individual skills. In a way it was a masochistic game. Through a process of elimination the runner or chaser was selected. Then he had to run and touch each one of the other players before he could retire and rest. The fun of the game existed in eluding his grasp and enjoying his discomfort as he chased others up and down the moat. After he had touched each of them, he was supposed to have done his turn. And it became the turn of some other sucker who was selected through yet another counting out (called 'pugai').

Arun was a very fast runner and could finish his turn in no time. Munir on the other hand was slow. That's how the two came rather close to each other. 'Your father is a friend of my father, now help me!' And Arun protected Munir when they were on the run and someone else was chasing them. And when it was Munir's turn, Arun shouted encouraging directions to him. (You could do that according to the rules, though you could also misdirect the boy—to add to your fun.)

That's what Arun's earliest memory of Munir was. Running up and down and along the narrow base of the drain. When they went up to college, the boys retained their comradeship. Only in place of the drain, they now played in the college gym or the college tennis courts. Both of them had taken up the liberal arts, both were hoping to be teachers one day, and in the evenings they were almost always together.

Nurul-Nisar had come to college when Munir and Arun were in their third year. Like the rest of the family, Arun had known her too from early childhood. There was no purdah in Chaudhri Barkat Ali's house, though the location and atmosphere of the female quarters in the house were somewhat different. Arun did not ever see Begum Barkat Ali without her headgear, as he often did his mother. Then the noise and the laughter in there were also more subdued; though Nur was often moving around humming film songs.

"My daughter is a no-good Muslim. The way she sings those film songs!' said Chaudhri Barkat Ali, teasing her.

'I guess you're right, abba.'

Chaudhri Barkat Ali did not believe in what he said. On the contrary, he believed his family represented a fine Muslim household. He and his wife said the namaaz, their prayer, five times a day, and even Munir and Nuri said it though not as regularly. They also visited the mosque nearby, gave alms to the poor, and observed fasts through the entire month of ramadan. More than anything else, he regarded himself and his family as good Muslims because they believed in the unity of all religions. There was not a single ayat, a single verse, in the Quran which preached otherwise. God is great and Muhammad is his prophet. But the same God is the God of the Hindus as well, and if they preferred to worship him in another form that was their business. It was not for Barkat Ali to go round correcting the world. His job was to live the life God had given him in friendship and love. And the Hindu next door was as much his brother, more his brother than an unknown Muslim living elsewhere.

And then he had been fired with the spirit of nationalism the day he had heard Gandhi. That was in 1930, about seventeen years back. Gandhi was touring the Punjab after the 1929 Congress session in Lahore, and he had come to Sialkot in the course of that tour. A public meeting was held at Ramtalai, which is a water reservoir in the middle of the city and where the water has long since dried up and the place is used for holding large gatherings. It was packed with people that day, as were all the houses that overlooked it. Chaudhri Barkat Ali and Lala Kanshi Ram were sitting in the centre, and were only twenty-five to thirty feet away from the rostrum where Gandhi was to speak. Lala Kanshi Ram as usual was a little afraid and uneasily he looked to the top steps of the reservoir to see if a police party was descending on them. But Chaudhri Barkat Ali was curious. Here was a man who in ten years' time had revolutionized the spirit of the country. After the Champaran agitation of 1917, there was not a city in India where Gandhi's name was not known. And he talked of peace in place of war and he talked of non-violence in place of violence, and yet he also talked of fights with the British on his own special terms. The Chaudhri was at heart a rebel; in his family they believed one of his forefathers had taken an active part in the Delhi uprising of 1857 for which he was later executed by the British. So Barkat Ali waited eagerly for this man who said he knew of a new way to azadi.

Gandhi's train was late by four hours, and it was only at three in the afternoon that he managed to reach Ramtalai. The crowds along the road from the railway station were so dense it was considered to be the biggest welcome Sialkot had ever accorded to a visiting dignitary. (Lala Kanshi Ram disputed that statement and held the biggest welcome was to the Prince of Wales in 1921—at least it was the most colourful.)

When Gandhi's frail figure, flanked by Congress volunteers, emerged at the topmost steps of Ramtalai, half the crowd got up on its feet and the air was rent with the cries of 'Mahatma Gandhi ki jai', 'Mahatma Gandhi, zindabad', 'Mahatma Gandhi, zindabad'. From the distance Lala Kanshi Ram and Chaudhri Barkat Ali could only see a pair of spectacles, a bare torso, a loincloth and a long staff. That was Gandhi, the leader of the masses. Even Lala Kanshi Ram was excited and along with the rest he shouted, 'Mahatma Gandhi ki jai'.

Gandhi walked fast through the path cleared for him and reached the rostrum. He was old and frail but he walked like a young soldier, and as soon as he came on the rostrum, facing the crowd he folded his hands in greetings with a most winning smile. The man is honest, thought Barkat Ali. The man has something to say.

Before Gandhi could say a word, before he was even properly introduced, half the gathering at Ramtalai got up to leave. It was the women who were leaving. They had started collecting here since six in the morning and many of them had made special arrangements for the care of their children. Gandhi was supposed to arrive at eleven. Bravely the crowd kept it up. For the women it was particularly hard, used as many of them were to the sheltered life of their homes. When Gandhi showed up and they had seen him, they felt no need to stay there longer. They were not interested in politics, nor in Gandhi's speeches. For them Gandhi was a mahatma, a religious figure, and they had come only to pay homage to a saint.

The volunteers made desperate efforts to make them sit down and not to interrupt the proceedings, but they were undaunted as only Punjabi women can be. Adjusting their shalwars and saris, and placing their hands on their knees for support, they heaved themselves up, bowed towards the rostrum with folded hands and left.

Nothing availing, Gandhi smiled disarmingly and sat down until those who wanted to go had left. There followed a brief speech by a local leader, and then Gandhi got up and stepped to the loudspeakers.

The crowd listened in hushed silence. He had a very soft voice and the Hindi accent was somewhat heavy—in particular he could not say his s's properly, he said them as sh's. But he had disarmed the crowd with his smiles even before he began, and he now disarmed them with his humility. 'Not like the usual leaders at all', Chaudhri Barkat Ali whispered into the left ear of Lala Kanshi Ram. 'You can say that again', whispered back Lala Kanshi Ram in the double nuance of a Punjabi sentence. Comparing him with the English sahibs he had seen, he regretfully reminded himself the man was not even dressed properly for the occasion. Ten thousand persons had assembled here to greet him and he had come half naked!

The rostrum was packed with local leaders, but there was not the least attempt on the part of Gandhi to assert himself. He waited in the back modestly, unobtrusively, until they were ready for him.

After so many years, Chaudhri Barkat Ali did not remember the full text of the speech, but it was that speech which changed the course of his life for him. Gandhi first explained the contents of the new resolution passed by the Indian National Congress at Lahore; explained what the words *puma swaraj* meant—full azadi. He then listed the alternatives a slave nation had to achieve that objective, and discounting each of them one by one, spoke of the non-violent way. It needed even greater preparation than the violent way, he said, and it needed greater self-discipline. India had a long history of self-discipline and self-sacrifice. Only division in the country had made it weak. The British had played the different religious groups against each other to their own advantage. He did not blame the British for that, he said, he had no ill-will against them. But they must now give up the country they had held in bondage for over two centuries. How could they have two sets of moral values, freedom at home and slavery abroad? They had therefore to go. And they must be made to realize the wrong of their rule before they would leave peacefully. For that there was no other way for the Indians except that of self-discipline and self-sacrifice.

As a basis for self-discipline Gandhi spoke of Hindu-Muslim unity, and as a basis for self-sacrifice he spoke of non-violence. Gandhi smiled here and said the Congress was preparing a national plan of action. Till that came about, he would show them a plan of action they could introduce right away. From today, he said, let each Muslim accept one Hindu as his 'brother', and the Hindu that Muslim as his brother. And from today, he said, wear home-made things and not those imported from England.

Of the Hindu-Muslim brotherhood he spoke at some length. India, he said, was divided into geographical not communal entities, and the whole of India was a single nation. Islam came from the outside but later the immigrant Muslims settled here as the English never did. A Muslim in India was more an Indian than anything else. The same was true of a Hindu. His gods came much lower in rank than the motherland which had given him birth.

The claim for Pakistan had not yet been made by the Muslim League and Gandhi did not speak of Hindu-Muslim unity in that context. He spoke of it as the need to put up a united front against the British, the common enemy.

Of home-made things, he very simply and bluntly said any foreign article they bought deprived the Indian workman of his labour and it prolonged the British rule here by that much time. Instead wear home-spun cotton, and if possible do the spinning yourselves, he said.

Immediately after the speech, and before the renewed shouts of 'Mahatma Gandhi ki jai' had died down, Chaudhri Barkat Ali turned towards Lala Kanshi Ram and said seriously: 'You're my brother from today.'

Lala Kanshi Ram chuckled. He had always regarded Chaudhri Barkat Ali as a brother, he did not need a Gandhi to make him aware of that. Yet moved by the intensity of the moment, he took Chaudhri Barkat Ali's extended hand and shook it actively. 'And we are going to wear khadi, the home-spun cotton,' said Chaudhri Barkat Ali. 'Right!' answered Lala Kanshi Ram.

From that day the two friends wore shirts and pyjamas of coarse cotton. For Lala Kanshi Ram the decision was a godsend, for wearing khadi was cheaper and he could enjoy thrift while being patriotic. Chaudhri Barkat Ali took his commitment more seriously. He went ahead and became a member of the Congress and soon rose to be a minor official in its local heirarchy. They could not impose their wills on their wives, nor on their children, in the matter of khadi. Yet Arun and Munir fought many battles—many physical battles too—with those who contended against the Congress. And Nur had arguments with other Muslim girls each day she went to school.

No, Nur was a good Muslim, a pious Muslim, and Chaudhri Barkat Ali was proud of her. What if the girl sang film songs? That had nothing to do with religion, that was her youth! And he smiled to himself when he looked at her budding body and for a while felt sad when he thought how soon he would have to find a husband for her.

Arun became aware of Nur physically only when she joined the college after her high school. She would then be sixteen, yes that's what she was, she had told him so herself. And her breasts were sixteen too and her nose and her eyes and the look in her eyes.

One day Arun was going home after class. As usual, he cycled, going leisurely along the road by the side of the railway tracks. A short distance away, near the Burmah-Shell petrol station, he spotted Nur walking ahead of him. She generally came to college in a tonga, along with a few other girls, and that's how she returned home. Arun was a little surprised to see her on the road, walking briskly, with her books in one hand.

'What happened to the tonga, Nur?'

Nur was taken aback, for Arun had quietly sneaked right up to her and shouted into her ear.

'You gave me a fright!' she said with a giggle, placing a hand on her breast.

Arun got off the cycle, and keeping up the mischievous tone asked: 'But what happened to the tonga?'

'I finished early and didn't want to wait another hour.'

'Come, I'll take you home.'

His tone was non-serious, half playful, but a part of Arun felt excited at the suggestion.

'How?' Nur was laughing.

'On the cycle.'

'You're mad—my father will strangle me!'

'No, he won't. If he knows it is me.'

Somehow it had become very important for Arun she should agree to go with him and he was surprised at his desire, a new kind of desire.

'Come on, I'll take you through the side lanes.'

As the words were being uttered, both became aware of the altered rhythm of their breathing. Nothing explicitly was stated, nothing given, nothing taken, but a gossamer like creeper had suddenly sprung from the womb of the fertile earth and seemed to be twining itself around them, binding them together—and suffocating them.

Nur found she had no will to say no. Arun's cycle had no carrier and she was obliged to sit on the crossbar in front of him. Posing that it was only a dare, and she had to take up the challenge, she gave a toss of her head and went and sat on the bar.

'If anyone sees me like this, I'll be thrown before the dogs,' she said, blushing.

Arun made no answer, only laughed to convince her how ridiculous her fears were. His laughter was hoarse with passion.

Steadying the cycle and the weight of Nur on the bar, Arun started pedalling, and though they kept up casual conversation, neither heard what the other said. Nur's back was touching Arun and her soft brown hair was brushing his chin. And when he lowered his mouth to say something to her, he could almost touch the skin of her face with his lips.

A strange smell exuded from Nur and Arun became aware of it all at once. She herself was having a feeling of well-being, a hypnotic calm, and she relaxed her back which she had kept stiff and went limp in Arun's arms. To Arun that limpness came as an aroma—a mysterious odour her relaxed flesh was giving out. Yes, there she was, so close at hand, the object of his quest. That thought too came to him all at once. She it was he had been seeking in his sleepless nights, in the endless hours he pored over books trying to fathom their meaning, in the exercise he took to tire himself out, in all the prayers he said when everything else failed to calm him. How could he have been so stupid as to have overlooked the possibility!

They both seemed flushed and the conversation came to a complete halt. Moving through the side lanes near the railway station, they were soon in Mianapura.

'You better let me off here,' Nur whispered.

His heart beating fast, Arun stopped and she gently lifted herself from the cycle bar and out of his arms. They looked at each other perplexed, having nothing in their past to which they could compare their present feelings.

'Let me come in with you,' Arun said, so very gently.

'No,' she answered as gently, flushing crimson red.

'I can say I met you outside.'

'No.'

That's how it had started, their awareness of each other; shyly, haltingly. And then it had exploded into a passion which neither of them tried to conceal.

Arun was sure her parents knew of their fondness for each other, though he could not bring himself to discuss the subject with them. It was different with Munir. He talked throughout to him of his future with her.

'I'm going to marry her as soon as I have a job,' said Arun to Munir one day in the college gym.

They were exercising on the parallel bars, and Munir's face was bloated into a distorted pumpkin with the swings he was taking at the bars. He did not speak until he had finished his run of fifty swings, and then coming to a halt, and breathing deep for several seconds, said: 'Why not?'

'I'll become a Muslim, if your father insists.'

'You don't have to. Why can't you keep your separate religions?'

It was something Arun had not thought of.

'How do we solemnize the marriage?'

'A ceremony in a civil court.'

'Are you sure this is permitted?'

'It should be. I'll check on it...'

Today Munir sat quiet in the canteen when after upbraiding him for eavesdropping, Arun said, 'Oh, Munir, I love her so much.'

Munir was a tall young man, with a contemplative face. He had an aquiline nose, and small eyes, which always seemed to be concentrated on some idea in his mind. He was still frail of health, but he was no longer the weakling of his early days. When he walked, he felt self-conscious of his height ('I don't have the weight to go with it') and he cultivated a stoop that added to his scholarly bearing.

'I don't think this can go on.'

'Don't talk like that!'

'You have to be realistic Arun. Stop meeting Nur altogether.'

'Not of my own free will—never!'

'I may have to stop Nur, then.' Seeing Arun writhe in agony, he added: 'Are you so naive as not to see it is a question of your safety? All right—promise one thing: you will see her only in my presence. Preferably at our house. But you must no longer see her in public.'

'There is no need of a promise. I don't think Nur wants to see me any more,' said Arun, remembering their conversation.

'Listen, we'll talk of this later. Let' go and see Bill Davidson. Let's see what he thinks of the partition.'

Munir had switched to Davidson so suddenly it took Arun considerable time to realize they were no longer discussing personal affairs. It also made him sad to see how, Munir too, like him, was torn in his mind between many different emotions.

In the lush, sweaty heat of the evening, the two of them cycled to the Cantonment, where lived Sergeant Davidson. Arun liked the look of the Cantonment. Its cleanly swept roads gave him the feeling of cool—and there was less overcrowding there too. It had only one main bazaar, Sadar Bazaar, and the rest was all barracks and big bungalows and playing fields and parade grounds. In each field, the army men could be seen working at the ropes or playing hockey, the national game of India. Arun liked their neat sports uniforms, as that also made him relax and feel rested after the noise and confusion of the city.

Sergeant Davidson lived in the barracks near the Hurrah Parade ground, and it was by accident Arun and Munir had become his friends. They looked at each white man in uniform with suspicion, and would go out of their way to insult or be rude to him. The white men had changed considerably during the last couple of years, and their attitude to the natives had decidedly softened somewhat. At the English picture house in the Cantonment—the Capital Picture House—after the last reel of the film had run and the hero and the heroine were locked together in the final embrace, the Union Jack would come on the screen and the audience was supposed to stand to attention while the British national anthem was played. For some time now the Indian audience would not stand up. The British had read the writing on the wall and they did not insist. The audience was usually made up of British soldiers and their wives and there were a few odd Indians in the hall, students from Murray College mostly, and the soldiers could afford to ignore their rudeness.

Once at a matinee Arun and Munir wanted to leave right after the film, while the national anthem was still playing. They were stopped at the closed door by a man, who said good-humouredly, 'I'm afraid the doors can't be opened until the anthem is over.' They thought it was an attendant of the cinema house, but on closer inspection saw the man wearing an army uniform.

Soon the anthem was over and the doors were flung open. The hall lights came on, and they saw a huge, bulky sergeant blocking their way. There was a smile on his face, though he looked determined. He stepped aside as the lights came on, leaving the way open for them to go out. He added at the same time, with an infectious smile: 'Why carry the protest so far?'

The Sergeant also left the hall and walked with them towards the cycle stand.

'We don't owe any allegiance to this flag,' said Arun gruffly, when outside.

'All right, then you need not get up! But why leave the hall and upset those who want to sing the anthem?'

It appeared to them a reasonable question and they were at a loss to answer it. Seeing their embarrassment, the man laughed and said:

'I know how you feel.'

'No, you don't,' said Munir.

'Don't I ?'

'No, you don't.'

'All right.' And here again the man laughed like a friend. There was something in his demeanour, a deference, a respect, though he was clearly a good deal older than they and also much stronger physically, that they were touched. It was like a giant bending before two saplings.

'Eh—excuse me, my name is William Davidson. Call me Bill.'

'I am Munir Ahmad.'

'I'm Arun Kumar.'

'Well, can I call you Munir and Arun?'

Rather eagerly, they replied: 'You certainly can!'

'Listen, I'm not far from my barracks. Why don't you come and have a cup of tea with me before you return to the city?'

Again this was unusual for them—the courtesy, the pleasant tone, the respect—and they readily agreed. The three of them cycled over to the barracks, and as they were passing the Hurrah Parade ground, Arun said:

'That's where you shoot our dogs on the New Year's Day.'

'Not me!' said Bill Davidson.

Entering a British barracks was so unusual an experience for Arun and Munir that for a while they forgot Sergeant Davidson was an enemy. They had seen these barracks many times before, but always from a distance, and with envy and resentment. They were the strongholds of the British power, wherein resided the might of the army. Natives were not allowed in and the Tommy on guard would drive them away if they got too near. Outside the British officers' mess, the guards and the display of regimental colours and guns were formidable. But even here, outside of sergeants' quarters, there was a regimental flag and there were two small guns, one on each side of the large gate.

'They're with me,' said Bill Davidson to the guard softly, as they cycled past him.

It was early evening, and from one side of the barracks, where the mess was, smoke was rising in the air. For the rest, it was quite peaceful in there. The roads inside were not paved, but they were neatly cut out and were lined with gravel. Each sergeant had a set of two rooms, into which these barracks were divided. Khaki bush shirts hung from the line in the courtyard of the set into which Bill Davidson took them.

'Won't you sit down?' said Bill Davidson, pointing towards the chairs in his sparsely furnished room.

Munir read philosophy, but Arun was a student of English literature and he had read English novels. Bill Davidson's room resembled the descriptions he had read in some of them, particularly in Scott. It was a soldier's room and there was no lavishness about it.

Clean and neat it was, and there was a picture of King George VI on the wall as it should be. Then there were innumerable family portraits, of old men in knickerbockers and women in long gowns. And to be sure there were the pictures of Bill Davidson's sports teams in which he had played at school.

'Are you a career soldier ?' asked Arun, remembering the word from his recently acquired English vocabulary.

'Well, not really. I used to work in the Boots chemical firm in Nottingham when the war started and I joined up. That was eight years back. I'm waiting for demobilization.'

'Are you married?'

'No.'

'How many brothers and sisters have you?'

Just like a bloody nosey Indian, wanting to know all about your family, a part of Bill Davidson's mind reacted. Then he saw the innocent, absorbed look on the face of Arun and he knew he was only trying to be friendly.

'I'm the only child.' Walking to a picture in a corner, he added: 'That's my mum and dad.'

The two young men folded their hands in greeting, as though the persons in it were actually present in the room.

Much of their awkwardness was gone and they were sitting on chairs.

'Well, give me a minute, and we'll have some tea.'

Bill Davidson disappeared into the next room, and soon they heard the hissing sound of a stove. While he made tea, Arun and Munir did not say much to each other. They were too worried about what to talk about with the Englishman. This was not their first introduction to a white person. They had English teachers at Murray College; the Principal Sahib was white and Dr Linwell, the Head of the English Department, was white too. And their wives also taught at the college, and though they were old and faded, they were white women without doubt, neat and spruce, with their hair done into small buns in the Indian fashion, but otherwise all European in their skirts and nylon stockings. And—and Arun and Munir had often shaken hands with them, too. No, it was not that they were so unfamiliar with white skin, they had certainly touched it before, they sure had. Only this white man was somehow different from the missionary sahibs and memsahibs they had known. In looks he was martial and built big. Otherwise he was gentler, more understanding, than the missionaries. And he seemed to be so concerned about them and their future. Now how did they speak to him and what language did they use?

Bill Davidson emerged smiling and was quick to note the confusion of the youngsters. He remembered his own school days in Nottingham and how shy he used to be. These fellows were growing up in far more difficult conditions.

He had been in India for three years and he knew one subject which would put any Indian at ease

'Do you know where Nottingham is ?' he began.

'We do,' both shouted together.

'The Robin Hood country,' said Arun, with much pride.

And for the next fifteen minutes, while they sipped tea and ate biscuits, they talked of nothing but England. The young men at once forgot their hostility towards the British or the British Raj, and what came out was their enormous fascination for that land from which came their rulers. Yes, how far was Nottingham from London ? How long did it take to get there by train? Was it true you could walk right into the Buckingham Palace and see some of the rooms in which the royal family lived? Why was the underground railway in London called the 'tube'? Was it buried deep under the city? How did you get oxygen there—so far down?

Bill Davidson also talked of the three years he had spent in India and how much he liked the country. It was a great injustice, the continued British rule. He was certain it would end soon. At the school Labour Club, back in England, he and his friends had all been against imperialism and foreign possessions. And he had seen what his people had done in Malaya and Africa, before he was posted to India. Local cultures had been destroyed everywhere. More so in India which had such a long history and tradition.

There were occasional giggles in the room, occasional hand shakes when they all agreed on something, and the group was beginning to relax. Bill Davidson was twenty-nine, ten years or so older than the other two, but he put them completely at ease. They were even getting less self-conscious about their English, and spoke without worrying about their grammar.

'But we're pushing it too fast,' said Bill Davidson in the same casual, friendly mood. 'Too fast—from all sides. That bloody Gandhi wants us to quit at once.'

There was dead silence in the room, absolutely dead silence.

Bill Davidson sensed there was something wrong. Perplexed he looked at Munir, who avoided his glance. Then he looked at Arun, who too refused to meet his eye.

'What's the matter?' Bill Davidson asked.

Munir and Arun looked hard at him, but refused to speak. Then they looked at each other.

'Come on, what's the matter?'

'You abused Gandhiji!' said Munir, going red in his effort to control his anger.

'I did *what?'*

'You abused Gandhiji—you called him a name.'

'When?'

'Just now.'

'Don't be silly!'

To seek support, Bill Davidson looked at Arun. Arun said, 'You did call him a name.'

'Now is this some practical joke or what? When did I abuse him? I've great respect for him!'

'You just now said "bloody" Gandhi.'

'Oh that!' Looking at them through his grey eyes, he said smiling: 'You got me worried!'

'But that's an abuse,' Munir persisted.

'Go on, who told you that ?'

'We know English !' said Arun in hurt pride.

Bill Davidson wouldn't dream of questioning that knowing full well how touchy every Indian was on that subject.

'My dear chaps, "bloody" is good English slang, which is quite often used in endearment.'

'No, it is not.'

'Now listen, you perhaps know English better than I do. But believe me, this word is no abuse in current usage.'

'Still, we want you to withdraw it,' said Arun, and Munir nodded his head.

'Very well, if that'll make you happy.'

Bill Davidson was keen to win their friendship. He knew they were being silly, but his own commitment to freedom and socialism was at stake in the bargain. And one thing he had learned in his local fights in Nottingham was that it hurt no one to say sorry. You could turn right round next minute and kick the man in the shins. If however by saying sorry you could save a situation, why not?

'I'm indeed sorry if I hurt your feelings. What I really meant was the Indian leaders were pushing things too fast. India should first prepare herself for freedom...'

While Arun and Munir jumped up with counter arguments, Bill Davidson realized he had unwittingly offered the old imperialist reason for the slavery of India. According to the British the Indians must arrive at their freedom *slowly*. They must get there by *stages*. They must first *educate* themselves to be free. He knew that line of reasoning smacked of hypocrisy. All the handicaps were nothing compared to the exhilaration of freedom. To be free, to be left alone to sort out their problems, to breathe, exist and function not in fear but in joy—what preparation was necessary for that? And the British used all these arguments only to prolong their stay here—not in the interest of India, but in their own interest.

Munir and Arun were getting worked up. Bill Davidson said: 'Don't get me wrong. I'm not advocating continued British rule. What I mean is haste will lead to fragmentation. In the interest of a united India the delay of a month or a year won't hurt, it would rather strengthen the nation, if the Indian leaders were not too rash...' Finding himself not getting anywhere with them, Davidson laughed and said, 'Hell! Let's talk of something else. But rest assured, I am a friend in the cause of freedom and not a foe.'

Bill Davidson gave them a brief account of his own life. He was born the son of a miner. His father worked in a pit outside of Nottingham, and the family lived in Beeston, a suburb of that midland mining town.

'You should have seen the house I grew up in. Don't imagine there is no poverty in England!' His father did not want him to go down the pit and so he grew up to be a white-collar man, proving good in science at Beeston High School, and later joining the Boots chemical department. 'I wanted to go up to the university—it was across the road from Boots—but I guess I wasn't good enough.' He had been an active member of the Labour Party, and had read the whole of Marx and Lenin. 'I'm not a communist though'—this with a laugh. 'I still sing *God Save the King.*' (All laughed at that.) For the three years he had been in India, he had travelled up and down the land everywhere, and had been posted to Sialkot only recently. 'An absolutely fascinating country, it is.' It was a shame they were not united in their demands. But freedom was their birthright and they should get it soon enough.

'Do your army friends know of your thoughts?' asked Arun.

'Well, the British army is not what it used to be. We have a lot more freedom of expression, within limits. In any case I—and many like me—I'm not a professional soldier. I'll quit the day I can.'

'I am not a rebel, either,' he said after a pause. 'While in the army, I do what the army wants me to do.'

'You kill with kindness, eh?' said Arun, parading his knowledge of English literature with some glee. Bill Davidson had not heard of Heywood nor had Munir and Arun was sorry the joke was lost on them.

Bill Davidson looked at them. They were good lads, both. The tall one, the one called Munir, was the more sober of the two, and the other one was very shy and sensitive. But they looked dependable and Bill Davidson liked them.

'Are you two good friends?' he asked.

Munir and Arun gave no reply, but looked at each other and shook hands with broad smiles.

'How is that? A Hindu and a Muslim?'

'Do you find that so odd?' asked Arun.

'It is not very common, is it?'

'That's what you have been told by the government. You should visit the villages and see for yourself. What you've seen is only towns. In every village you'll find hundreds of others like us.'

Bill Davidson got up, remembering he was getting late for supper. From that day the three became good friends and often met together. Arun and Munir invited him to their functions at Murray College, and he entertained them in his rooms or in the mess canteen. The other Englishmen in the mess ignored them, but they were not rude. Arun and Munir knew they thought of Bill Davidson as a freak, as he was the only one who brought in Indian friends. The young men didn't mind if the others did not speak with them. In a way they were happy—they would have collapsed if they had to exercise their English with so many Englishmen together.

Arun and Munir had first met Davidson in 1945. Gandhi was released from prison in 1944, but Nehru was still inside at that time, and the Quit India resolution of 1942 was very much alive in the mind of every Englishman. Through the following two years, through the arrival of Wavell as the Viceroy, the release of Nehru and the other Congress leaders, the Simla Conference of 1945, the British Parliamentary Mission and the British Cabinet Mission of 1946, the two Indians and their English well-wisher had reviewed all the events, and Bill Davidson maintained all along the Indian leaders were pushing things too fast. 'There's something of a panic in the way they behave, and this will result in tragedy,' he asserted.

When Arun and Munir reached the barracks of Bill Davidson on the evening of that late June day, he had taken off his uniform. He was sitting on an improvised hammock in the small compound of his apartment, wearing only his shorts.

'Come on in,' Davidson shouted.

They had not seen him since the Viceroy's announcement. They wanted to come, but they were preoccupied, and then they could not make a concerted, joint move. Bill Davidson could see they looked very ill at ease.

'Well, aren't you happy? India is going to be free and we're really going to quit.'

'What of the division?'

'Well you'll have *two* free nations instead of one. Numerically speaking, this looks like an improvement—an expansion of the family of free nations of the world!'

'Quit being non-serious,' said Arun.

Bill Davidson did not get off his hammock, and drawing up a couple of chairs they sat down near him. A breeze was blowing, but still the day was very hot. There was not a trace of a cloud in the sky. Arun calculated mentally and knew the monsoon was late this year.

The youngsters sat quiet, not feeling nervous, but tongue-tied, not knowing how to express what filled their hearts.

'Mr Davidson, what do you think of the plan?'

Bill Davidson could see tears in the eyes of Munir, so he stopped fooling.

Without waiting to reflect, as though he had mulled over this carefully during the last two weeks, he said: 'If you must ask me, I think this is the most stupid, most damaging, most negative development in the history of the freedom struggle here. And this time it is *we* who are pushing things. The Cabinet Mission plan of the last year was the best plan that could have been devised for the future of India. Indian leaders unfortunately did not see its merit and foolishly threw it away. But we, the British, should have stood by that plan. Six months more of negotiations and the political parties would have come round...'

'And that plan offered everything. The country was to be grouped in three semi-independent areas, and the right of secession was there too,' intervened Munir.

'Only we would have stayed united,' said Arun

'I believe that Wavell mismanaged things, or at least didn't quite handle them right.' This was Bill Davidson, speaking indignantly.

Arun felt like repeating what his father often said in the house—that he was one-eyed too. Only he didn't want to be regarded as superstitious by Bill Davidson, and kept quiet.

'You may sing songs in honour of Mountbatten, as I believe you've started doing. But he has duped you into a division of the country. Even Gandhi and Nehru failed to hold their balance before him—Jinnah I never counted for much. They have all fallen for a handy prize, not realizing the misery it will heap on the masses.'

Bill Davidson was speaking as if he was hurt inside, as if a dream of his own had miscarried.

Arun asked: 'What do you think we should do, Bill? Do you think we'll be able to live in Pakistan? My father feels we can.'

'Can't answer the question. It depends on how Pakistan treats the Hindus.'

'And also how the new India treats the Muslims,' said Munir, prompted by a spontaneous desire to come out in defence of Islam.

'True enough! True, true. But call on me if you need my help. These are going to be hard months for you. Come and let me know if there is anything I can do.'

The meeting ended abruptly and rather to the dissatisfaction of each of them. The old feeling of easiness was gone. The event had hurt them in ways they couldn't understand, but while the sense of disappointment was common, the localised injury, the convulsive reaction of the myriad of cells that constituted the psyche, was different in each case. Even Munir and Arun felt a tension towards each other. When they left Bill Davidson, they cycled to the city in total silence. It was not rudeness; it was the slow absorption of the unexpected into their systems. When they parted at the Railway Chowk, Munir going home towards Mianapura and Arun cycling on towards Trunk Bazaar, they said only a barely audible good night to each other.

CHAPTER 5

THE first riot took place in Sialkot on the twenty-fourth of June. Many cities of the Punjab had been aflame for months; there were large scale killings and lootings in Lahore, Gujrat, Gujranwala, Amritsar, Ambala, Jullundur, Rawalpindi, Multan, Ludhiana and Sargodha. Sialkot remained quiet all this while, largely because of the vigilant eye of the Deputy Commissioner. Like a tiger, he moved through the city fearlessly. His jeep had become a symbol of law and order. For the Hindus he was a source of much cheer and encouragement. The Muslims resented him, but they knew of his determination to keep the peace. And then he had such an understanding with his junior officers, be they Hindus or Muslims, and the word had gone round of the unity among them.

On the twenty-third of June, the Legislative Assembly of the Punjab formally decided in Lahore to opt for the partition of the province. After the announcement of June the third, which gave a province, or a part of a province, the right to secede from the Union of India, the vote in the Muslim majority Legislative Assembly of the Punjab was a foregone conclusion. But for the common Muslims that vote had a sentimental appeal; for them it was a step further in their goal of Pakistan. And in their excitement, the Muslims of Sialkot broke loose the following day and killed a number of Hindus.

And then it became almost a daily ritual. There were four or five cases of stabbing each day, and at least four or five fires. It was not mass killing or organized killing—not yet. The average rioter was still not certain how far he could trifle with the law, and how determined the government would be in putting down trouble. These were all isolated cases, a Hindu was caught hold of in a deserted part of the city, a large kitchen knife was driven through his stomach, and he was left to die on the road. The police arrived at the scene soon after, in many cases the Deputy Commissioner included, but no one would point out the killers. A little later in the day there would be another stabbing in an entirely different part of the city. Again the police arrived at the scene to pick up the dead man, and again no charges were brought since no one would say who had done the crime.

Though these were acts of stray individuals, or of isolated, small groups of individuals, and though as yet there was no movement behind the violence to annihilate the Hindus *en masse,* there was one thing common to them all: the brutality of the act. In no case was the victim allowed to survive the attack and tell what happened; he was stabbed to *death.* The killing was invariably done with a knife, and often the knife, the large blade driven clean through, was left in the body of the victim. Where the victim survived the first blow, he was repeatedly stabbed in the chest and the abdomen. Faces were not disfigured, but the killers had a macabre fascination for ripping open stomachs. In each case, the intestines of the man would have spilled from the body and would be lying next to him in a pool of his blood.

The fires were started in the night, and the four fire engines the city had were kept rushing from one fire to the next. More than murders, it was the fires that were frightening and demoralizing. You only heard of the murders after they were over, but you saw the fire lighting up the sky with your eyes. It was summer and most people slept out of doors. Suddenly the sky over a certain part of the city would be aglow. If you lived close enough, in addition to seeing the tongues of flame, you heard the noise of the people and you heard the hiss and the crackling of the fire itself. Mostly you heard nothing. You only saw a glow in the distance, a red glow of death, which slowly spread out and became more menacing when the smoke came up. And you went numb with fear. You knew someone was burning out there. Soon you heard the bell of the fire engine rushing through the streets. Ding, ding, ding, ding, ding, ding, ding, ding, ding, ding, ding. The fire was put out, the glow suddenly shut off, as if someone had switched off a light, but the smoke remained for over an hour. And then in a totally different direction another glow in the sky came up, and yet another ding, ding, ding, ding, ding, ding, ding, ding. If the first fire was toward the South East, in Mohalla Dharowal, this one was in Mianapura, in the North West. If that one was in Kanak Mandi, this one was in Trunk Bazaar, two miles away. The way these fires were spread out, it looked as though some planning went behind them, for the fire engines were harrassed to the limit in running from north to south and east to west. But no, the arson too at this stage was only sporadic.

And then one day, late in the evening, a strange howl spread through Trunk Bazaar. The bazaar was the main artery of the city, since it connected the various mohallas in the interior of the town to the railway station at the northern end. The Amritsar train came in at six, and a few tongas, rushing through the bazaar and speeding towards the inner mohallas, told everyone the train had arrived.

It was then that the howl spread. Out of some of those tongas came loud wailing cries. 'Hai—they've killed us!' 'Oh, Allah, may your wrath fall on these Sikhs—they've ruined us.' 'Hai—hai!' 'Allah—Allah!' And there followed whimpering, smouldering, blood-curdling cries of people weeping. 'Oh, Nawab Din, where have you gone! Oh, my son, Nawab Din!' And the unseen weeper broke into incoherent hiccuping sounds overwhelmed by grief. 'My arm, my arm. My arm has been butchered by these kafirs.' 'Oh, God, my head, I think it's going to explode'—this from someone holding tight to a heavily bandaged head.

There were at least nine tongas loaded with people, which passed through Trunk Bazaar. They were not in a procession; they came intermittently. The news soon spread in Trunk Bazaar that these were Muslims arriving from the Eastern part of the Punjab—some from Amritsar, the rest from other towns. It also went round they had been attacked and driven out of their homes by the Hindus and the Sikhs.

'It doesn't augur well for us,' said Lala Kanshi Ram to Prabha Rani. 'Maybe the Muslims started it all, by driving the Hindus from this part of the Punjab,' said his wife. 'I don't care who started it,' said Lala Kanshi Ram, feeling sorry for himself.

And that night occurred the first massive violence in Sialkot, and Mohalla Dharowal was looted and burned down. Around eleven in the night the noise from that part of the city became overpowering. And the sky was lit up with a number of fires, all in the same mohalla. And then streams of people started pouring through Trunk Bazaar on their way out from Mohalla Dharowal, trying to escape from it. There were a few tongas, but mostly the people were on foot. They came in groups, each family staying together. Many in the crowd were weeping hysterically, uncontrollably. A few had bandaged arms and heads, and Lala Kanshi Ram wondered who had rendered them first aid at that hour of the night. Each person carried a bundle on his head or in his arms, a few belongings; many carried their children on their shoulders. The police had also made their appearance, and they were hurrying the crowd along out of the mohalla. Apparently the situation had become unmanageable. 'Come on, get a move on!' came the shouts of the police officers. The people needed no urging. Many of them were running, as though a fiend was after them. Watching them from the rooftop of Bibi Amar Vati's house, Lala Kanshi Ram was not sure where they were headed. To his questions, all he got back from the crowd was: 'Hai—hai! We're ruined.' Lala Kanshi Ram thought maybe they were leaving town. 'Are you going to the railway station?' he shouted. 'No, to camp,' answered some of them. 'What camp?' 'Refugee camp.'

These two words—'refugee camp'—were to become a household name all over India in the next few months, but Lala Kanshi Ram was as yet not familiar with them. No camp of any kind existed in Sialkot. No preparation whatsoever was made by the government to meet large scale disturbances. Every night a police jeep went through the streets announcing over the amplifier there was a curfew on in town and anyone coming out would be shot. People ignored that warning and violence at night had occurred for several weeks. The personality of the Deputy Commissioner alone had been able to maintain the tenuous balance of peace; but the government machinery as such was in no way equipped to handle vast emergencies.

'What is a refugee camp?' asked Lala Kanshi Ram of Arun, who stood beside him.

'It means a camp for people seeking shelter,' said Arun uncertainly.

'I didn't know we had a camp here.'

'They must have set one up overnight.'

The exodus of people from Mohalla Dharowal continued through the night. Around dawn the military moved into the area, and they put those who wanted to leave into trucks and took them to the camp. By mid morning a precarious truce was established. Military vans went announcing the city was quiet and no one was to worry: the army was posted in town and people could move about freely.

Lala Kanshi Ram could not sleep at all that night. It became clear to him how vulnerable the minority community was and that soon he too might have to leave. It hurt him, the thought of it, and he paced his room restively. 'Refugee, refugee, indeed!' he shouted, when he had understood the word. 'I was *born* around here, this is my *home*—how can I be a refugee in my own home?'

'Father, we'll have to leave—' Arun said.

Before he could finish his sentence, Lala Kanshi Ram cut him off. 'Why will we *have* to? Why?'

'Well, the government seems unable to protect us, and we'll have to go to save our lives.'

'Why can't the government protect us? I've seen communal riots before in this country. How were the English able to put them down?'

'Let's say the government is incapable or unwilling to control the situation. What then? Shall we wait here and perish?'

'He is right,' said Prabha Rani, fear gripping her heart.

'Aha! Incapable or unwilling—which precisely?' Lala Kanshi Ram ignored his wife and addressed himself to his son: 'If unwilling, the government is a party to murder. If incapable, we Indians had no right to ask for freedom.'

And in his mind, Lala Kanshi Ram thought how the English Superintendent of Police would have lifted his arm and ordered a lathi charge on the unruly mob and how the furore would have settled down in a matter of minutes. Leave it to the English to handle emergencies, he murmured to himself. And he also saw in his mind the English Superintendent receiving a medal for bravery at a colourful parade afterwards, and though some years had passed since the English Superintendent at Sialkot had been replaced by an Indian, Lala Kanshi Ram distinctly heard his crisp voice coming to him, soon after he had received the medal for valour, 'Lalaji, thik hai?' In addition to personal pride, what protection there was for him in that greeting, what sense of safety! With much bitterness he recollected they had now also withdrawn English army units from active service and confined them to barracks. His eyes filled with tears as he felt so unprotected and forlorn.

'We had no right to ask for freedom,' he repeated.

Lala Kanshi Ram refused to accept his family's suggestion that they pack up and leave. How could he leave? He would rather die here. It was the middle of July; if only they could hold out a little longer. Moving the populations would ruin both the countries. Yes, the leaders said, don't move, stay where you are. But that was half-hearted, that was rather a lie, when they were doing nothing to protect the people—nay, when they were inciting violence. One firm declaration and the whole thing could take a different turn. Didn't he know? The average run of people did not have the courage to play with the might of the government. They ran amuck only as long as they knew the government was weak—or when they knew it was behind them.

But to leave Sialkot? Lala Kanshi Ram ran his hand over the wall of his room and something in him snapped. No, he couldn't just give it *up*. Behind these walls lay years of labour and hope. He was young though, he was only fifty, he could start a business somewhere else, in some town on the other side of the border. But *could* he? Could he, *really*? He looked at his wife and Arun and he knew how tired his arms and shoulders were. You mean, to begin right from *scratch*? Wasn't that asking a little too much—now wasn't that asking a little too much of a middle-aged man? And where precisely would he begin? In what city? How much capital did he have in cash? How early, at how short a notice, could he withdraw it from the bank? What of the shop—the grain stored there? How would he dispose of it? Would anyone give him any price for it in such times?

'Arun's mother, I'm an *old* man and I cannot begin all over again!'

His tone was mournful, though he spoke with dignity.

'I'm here to help you, father,' said Arun.

Arun indeed was there, but with what resources would they begin? He was hoping to leave Arun well-provided. Would the boy have to go through the same mill as he?

No, that was not all—that was nothing; that was only a very small part of the whole story. The pinch was he should have to give up this land, this earth, this air. That's where the hurt lay! He breathed deep, filling his lungs with the air of the town to their utmost capacity, and tears welled up in his eyes. How could he give this earth up?—and again he ran his hand over the wall. Some of his earliest memories, memories of his remote childhood, came back to him as he stood there. He remembered how as an urchin he was very fond of eating earth and how his mother used to beat him for that. He didn't know how he got out of the habit, but he remembered his mother's anger. He very much wanted to scrape a part of that earth and eat it again. 'We aren't leaving yet,' he said aloud. He would become a Muslim to stay here, if need be. To the others he only said, 'We aren't leaving yet.'

Late in the afternoon, Lala Kanshi Ram went to his shop. Schools and colleges were closed for the summer and Arun went with him. In Trunk Bazaar, the Hindus had reopened their stores and they sat uneasily on their seats. A few military men, in khaki uniforms and with rifles in hand, stood in the chowk. Lala Kanshi Ram had no confidence in them. They did not even know how to stand properly. There should have been English military in a situation like this!

Father and son turned the corner of Ghas Mandi and opened up the shutters of the store. Lala Kanshi Ram's store was situated right under the Fort and he derived some comfort from the thought. He could always ring for the police, he said to himself, trying to boost up his morale.

'You have opened rather late, Lala Kanshi Ram,' shouted Abdul Ghani from his seat, where he sat leisurely, not manufacturing a hookah but smoking one. He was leaning against the wall and had one of his feet rested comfortably on top of the other.

Lala Kanshi Ram made no reply, but Arun said: 'We were held up in the house.'

'Oh, you were,' said Ghani, thoroughly enjoying their discomfort.

'I hear the Hindus of Dharowal Mohalla left last night,' he went on, not quite asking them a question, but forcing them by the tone of his voice to give some reply.

'I hear that too,' spoke Lala Kanshi Ram shortly.

Abdul Ghani started laughing, opening his mouth and showing his irregular, dirty teeth. Now what was he laughing for—the idiot? Lala Kanshi Ram stopped cleaning the store and looked at him across the road. And seeing the puzzled look on his face, the laughter of Ghani became uncontrollable and he went hi, hi, hi, hi, hi, hi, hi.

Jumping down from his perch, Ghani crossed the road and walked over to Lala Kanshi Ram's shop. Placing his hands on the wooden platform of the store, he asked:

'When are *you* leaving, Kanshi Rama?'

On the instant, Arun lurched forward to hit Abdul Ghani. No one in his hearing had ever spoken to his father but with respect, and here was this filthy menial calling him 'Kanshi Rama'. Lala Kanshi Ram restrained him and held him by the arm.

'Why do you want me to leave, Abdul Ghani?' said Lala Kanshi Ram. 'We have been good friends—for years we have been such good friends!'

Abdul Ghani was taken aback at this. He had many other nasty things he wanted to say to Lala Kanshi Ram; he couldn't bring one of them out. Deflated, he sat on the wooden platform and looked at the ground.

Remembering he was speaking to a kafir after all, he flared up again.

'I want you to leave because you're a Hindu, and you don't believe in Allah.'

'You know that's not true. I believe in God as much as you do.'

Again Ghani looked timidly at the ground.

But soon enough the mean side of him, fired by political opportunism, returned. Avoiding Lala Kanshi Ram's eye, he said:

'Look, why don't we go into partnership? You sign a deed including me in your business, and then even if you're forced to leave, I will always send you your part of the profit'

It was Lala Kanshi Ram's turn to laugh. Ghani's audacity, his insolence, far exceeded his expectations, and cornered though Lala Kanshi Ram was, he broke into a roaring laugh. Lala Kanshi Ram could see that his neighbour shopkeepers, most of them Hindus, were not ignorant of what was happening at his shop. Would one of them come to his aid now? The other day they were so noisy about their solidarity. Today they only watched. Yet, in spite of the fact that he was isolated and on his own, he laughed aloud in Ghani's face.

'I'll think about it,' said he to Abdul Ghani and turned his back on him. He knew it was useless to talk with him. The decent part of him, the part that made diamond-like hookahs and made a clean living out of them, had been destroyed. Argument couldn't restore his sanity to him; only a calamity could.

Abdul Ghani returned to his shop, shaking his head, telling himself he had given the Lala his chance, but he had not taken it.

During the next week, each night systematically one Hindu mohalla in Sialkot was burned down. Systematically each night around eleven the sky was rent with the cries of 'Nara-e-Takbir, Allah-o-Akbar!' and after that there was the usual tumult of noise and the sky lighting up with red flames and columns of smoke rising, and people trekking to the refugee camp, weeping and wailing pathetically. Newspapers carried hair-raising stories of what was happening in the Punjab and Bengal. Murder, arson, rape. And to confirm this, each day more Muslim refugees, not only from East Punjab but also from many other parts of India, arrived in Sialkot by train or by buses. And each day hundreds of Hindus and Sikhs left Sialkot. Only those who could make no quick arrangements for leaving went to the refugee camp. Their first attempt was to get to India, and fast.

The morale in Lala Kanshi Ram's house and Bibi Amar Vati's house was quite low at this time. They all wanted to leave. But Lala Kanshi Ram said, no, it was irrational, it was madness incarnate, this violence, and it had to stop. And now, on the twenty-second of July, all the leaders, Hindu and Muslims together, had come out with a joint declaration for the protection of minorities. Why go to the refugee camp, when in a few weeks' time they will have to return to their homes?

Lala Kanshi Ram was so convinced of this his rhetoric moved his listeners to tears. No, there was no point in leaving, they all agreed—and secretly they hoped they were right.

One afternoon Lala Kanshi Ram arrived home ashen grey. Prabha Rani and Isher Kaur were sitting in the vestibule, speaking of how they were left pretty much alone in the street. Even Shri Kant Bahadur, the affluent lawyer, had departed last night for Amritsar in a caravan of cars. Though the night defence system still worked in the mohalla—they locked up the big gates on both ends and the young men patrolled the street in three-hour shifts—the number of families had dwindled to less than half.

Arun had gone to the store with his father, but he returned home at noon, leaving his father in the care of two trusted servants who worked at the store.

Lala Kanshi Ram usually walked with heavy steps; his wife said she could identify him out of thousands just by the sound of his feet. Today he came up the stairs stealthily, like a ghost, and surprised the women when he suddenly emerged before them. He looked so crestfallen and pale Isher Kaur clutched her stomach in panic and Prabha Rani was paralyzed into silence—she only stared at him in fear.

'The shop has been looted,' he said, the words hardly coming out of his mouth.

'Hai!' said both the women.

Arun had heard his father and running out of his room, he shouted: 'What?'

'As I said. The shop has been looted.'

'When? How? By whom?'

'Be quiet!' Prabha Rani told Arun.

Lala Kanshi Ram stood transfixed, strange emotions working through him. It was his habit that whenever he came home, he first took off his shoes, and wearing his chappals, went to the tap, washed himself, and then went and bowed before Lord Krishna's image in the alcove. He then went and sat in his easy chair in the square room, and it was then alone that the news of the day was narrated by him to Prabha Rani, or he let her speak to him. He now stood motionless, unable to decide what to do, as though he had come to the wrong house or were not the same man.

'Come, sit on your chair,' said Prabha Rani, holding him by the arm. The fear in her heart was acute.

Arun ran and brought his father's chappals, and kneeling down he took off his shoes and slipped the chappals on. Prabha Rani took him to the chaurus room, and Isher Kaur followed them, still clutching her belly.

They grouped around him.

'Are you sure?' asked his wife.

'Yes.'

'What happened?'

'I saw them coming from Mohalla Dharowal side, looting each Hindu shop that was open.'

'What about the military?'

'They were nowhere to be seen. There was not a single soldier in the chowk.'

'And the police? Didn't you try to ring?' said Arun.

'I did. They said they were sending help down—but none arrived.'

'Was there violence?'

'I don't know. When they were still some distance away, I closed the shutters and ran.'

'But chachaji, then the shop was not looted,' said Isher Kaur, rolling her big eyes that in her pregnancy had acquired a darker colour.

'It was, beti. They were so near, I was not able to put the locks on the shutters. I only closed them and ran.'

They waited.

'At Ghas Mandi, I turned to look. By then they had entered the shop and they were taking sacks of grain out.'

'Hai,' said Prabha Rani and she gave a big sob and started to cry. Tears rolled from her eyes instantly, and seeing her cry in pain, she who was so strong and determined and was the absolute centre of their domestic life, Lala Kanshi Ram forgot his own sorrow.

'Now, now, Arun's mother!'

'Was Abdul Ghani amongst them, father?'

'I don't know. His shop was closed.'

While they were talking, Chaudhri Barkat Ali came up the stairs and entered the room. He had been here many times in these days. They saw he was unusually tense as he went and sat on the bed.

He saw Prabha Rani crying, hiding herself behind the chair on which sat Lala Kanshi Ram, and he asked:

'What's the matter?'

'Chachaji's shop has been looted,' said Isher Kaur.

'Oh yes?' Chaudhri Barkat Ali said, starting up. But he showed no great surprise and asked no further questions, as though he expected this to happen.

'Well, that's what I have come to tell you, brother Kanshi Ram. This street is going to be looted and burned tonight. You must leave at once.'

They looked at Chaudhri Barkat Ali horrified. Prabha Rani forgot to wipe the tears from her cheeks, and as she stared, the salty drops glistened like glass beads on her eyelashes.

'I'm sorry about it,' said Chaudhri Barkat Ali, 'I wish to Allah it was my house to be looted. All my arguments for peace have failed with my brother Muslims; they have ceased to be Muslims and have become shaitans. Tonight is the turn of your street—I have it from the most reliable source. You'd better pack up and leave.'

'You know the Deputy Commissioner Sahib was murdered last night?' he added.

'No!' Lala Kanshi Ram got up from his chair and started pacing the room. He knew the communal element in the government had parted the Deputy Commissioner and the Muslim Superintendent of Police by transferring the Superintendent to another town a few weeks back. But he didn't know they would go that far.

'Remember he used to go round with a Muslim bodyguard—a constable with a loaded rifle? He did this to instil confidence amongst the two communities. That very constable shot him dead last night with his service rifle, while the sahib was in the bathroom.'

'What about the constable?'

'Absconding. That's the story. He will turn up soon enough, and I think the Pakistani government will bestow a medal on him!'

Lala Kanshi Ram, recalled the night when the Deputy Commissioner had so boldly faced the Muslim mob. And now his very defiance had carried him to death. Yet Lala Kanshi Ram's worry was what faced him in his own life. Here was Chaudhri Barkat Ali, the one man in Sialkot he fully trusted and who had vowed to treat him as a brother, telling him in all earnestness he should give up this house, this home, and drift loose. Did this man know what that involved? Was he in his senses?

At the first words from Chaudhri Barkat Ali, Isher Kaur disappeared and spread the news. Soon they all were collected there. Bibi Amar Vati came; so did Suraj Prakash—Bawa Suraj Prakash. Lala Bihari Lal the grocer came. Padmini and Chandni came. Mangat Ram, who was a small revenue official in the city and who lived on the same floor as did the grocer Lala Bihari Lal, came with his wife, Ram Kali. Two of the three Sikhs came. Mukanda's mother came too. There were seven families living in those two buildings, and they were all represented there. Mangat Ram was on long leave from office, and the others had not ventured outside that day.

'Do you mean to tell me,' asked Lala Kanshi Ram, 'the Congress Muslims in the city have become powerless to prevent mass violence?'

Chaudhri Barkat Ali thought for a few seconds.

'Let me put it like this. Either the Congress Muslims were a fraud to begin with, or they have changed sides. I'm afraid there is no organized body of Muslims denouncing what is happening in the city.'

While his audience digested this, he went on: 'We have tried individually. Professor Ghulam Hussain spoke at length at a meeting in the Red Mosque last night. So have, as you know, Chaudhri Imam Baksh and Dr Wazir Khan—on other occasions. I have personally argued and argued. But it is of no avail; the poison has seeped in. Added to that is the fact that every day hundreds of refugees from India continue to arrive with tales of terror and disgust. Whatever is happening here in Sialkot, things very much like that are happening on the other side too—let's make no mistake about it. It is not the collapse of Congress Muslims in Pakistan, apparently it is the collapse of Congress Hindus in India also. When refugees with stories of personal misfortunes land here, the politicians use them to their advantage to fan up further hatred.'

'It is really a failure of man,' said Lala Kanshi Ram reflectively.

'But the Muslims started it first,' said Bibi Amar Vati, looking at Chaudhri Barkat Ali in anger.

'Sister,' said Chaudhri Barkat Ali calmly. 'How can you be sure of that?'

'Then the English have let us down,' said Lala Kanshi Ram, after a brief pause. 'It was their job, their *obligation,* to see that freedom came smoothly. If today the man in the street feels insecure and if the government is powerless to protect his life and property, I hold the English responsible for that crime.'

After a long time, Lala Kanshi Ram felt bitter against the English once again and all that Raizada used to say about them in the *Inqlab* came back to his mind. Yes, they were the real villains; they had let the country down—they had let *him* down, he who put such faith in them.

'Our problem is to get organized and leave,' said Chaudhri Barkat Ali. 'The attack will come around eleven. We have six hours.'

'Where will we go?'

Chaudhri Barkat Ali kept quiet. He very much wanted to take at least Lala Kanshi Ram and his family to his house, but he knew that wouldn't do. There would be no safety for them there, and his Muslim neighbours would plague him for life.

Several alternatives were put forward.

'Let's take the train and go to Jammu. It is only ten miles to the border and we'll be safe in a matter of few hours.'

'There are no trains running to Jammu.'

Trains had been as much victims of violence as individuals. Many of them were stopped on the way and the Hindus butchered. Sialkot was connected by train with three railheads; with Jammu, with Amritsar, and with Wazirabad. In the direction of Wazirabad there was no question of safety; it only led further into the interior of West Pakistan—unless you turned south at Wazirabad and went to Lahore and then on to Amritsar. A train going to Jammu was derailed a few days back and it was still lying on the tracks; no one had bothered to clear the wreck of human flesh and blood.

To Amritsar trains did run, but the last train for the day left at two p.m. And it was anyone's guess whether a train to Amritsar would get through safely or not.

'We have no choice, we've got to go to the refugee camp,' announced Lala Kanshi Ram. 'Those of you who want to go to Amritsar, may leave from the camp tomorrow.'

Secretly Lala Kanshi Ram was glad they were only going up to the refugee camp. It dried his inside up to think of going too far away—like to Amritsar. Amritsar! What a nasty sound it had compared to S-i-a-l-k-o-t, the finest city in the world. If they stayed at the refugee camp, there was always the hope of returning home one day. Who would come back from Amritsar? It was the second of August today. Soon there would be independence. The two governments would have to come to some agreement to stop this madness. No, the refugee camp was the right place for him. He was glad a camp like this was there in Sialkot, and though he could not see Lord Krishna's picture in the alcove from where he sat, he turned in that direction and made a grateful nod.

'What do you say?' shouted Lala Kanshi Ram. 'Shall we leave for the camp then?'

'Yes. Yes.' Many voices. Only Niranjan Singh looked on sullenly. He said nothing.

Here Mukanda's mother got up and strode into the middle of the room.

'Leave?' she asked, viewing Lala Kanshi Ram through her beady eyes. She was a frightening sight, standing there with her white hair streaming on her shoulders. Because of her stoop, she could not stand straight, and like an aged tortoise, she had lifted up her head as she questioned them. 'What do you mean? You know Mukanda is still in prison out there'—and she spread her thin arms in the direction of the Fort where stood the city prison. 'I'm not leaving so long as my boy is there.'

'It will only be for a few days,' said Lala Kanshi Ram, placing a hand on her shoulder. 'We'll come back—we'll all come back.'

She pushed him away.

'I'm not leaving until Mukanda comes with me.'

'They'll kill you, if you stay here,' said Lala Kanshi Ram, raising his voice.

'As though I care. I'm not afraid—like you are. Or like *you,*' she said, turning and pointing at Bibi Amar Vati. 'For years you have sucked the blood of the poor, like my son Mukanda. And now you're afraid!'

'Shut up, you bitch,' said Bibi Amar Vati.

'Bear with her, behan,' said Lala Kanshi Ram.

'You have to leave—with us,' he said authoritatively to the old woman, closing out other options.

'See if I do,' she said, making a face at him, and walking unsteadily out of the room.

Munir arrived at that moment.

'I've been to Davidson Sahib. He has promised to get two army trucks for us by seven.'

He continued: 'He said he couldn't help directly. British troops were not allowed to enter the city. He said he would somehow arrange these trucks through his native friends.'

As he spoke, Munir was trying to catch the eye of Arun, but Arun avoided him.

'All right then,' said Lala Kanshi Ram. Get back to your rooms and pack up. Take only what is absolutely necessary. And be ready by seven. I'll give you a call.'

They scattered and went to their rooms. What was absolutely necessary? How much to take and how much to leave? Two weeks back Lala Kanshi Ram had withdrawn three thousand rupees from the bank, and that was all the money he possessed in cash now. Prabha Rani had said, take the whole amount out; Arun said the same. Lala Kanshi Ram said he wouldn't dream of it. I truly am a poor man today, he mumbled.

But three thousand rupees was a lot. It would last him for six months, even a year, if he was careful—and he would be careful. And there was Prabha's jewellery. There was nothing to worry about. He had ability, he had the know-how. He wouldn't perish.

As Arun and Prabha Rani packed, Lala Kanshi Ram watched them with an immense tightening of the heart. They were stripping the walls bare, and Lala Kanshi Ram felt they were stripping his flesh from his body. The bone was showing—whichever way he turned.

He would offer no advice on what to take and what to leave, and Prabha Rani did not ask him. She emptied one of the smaller steel trunks out, and into that she shoved whatever she thought would be useful. And Lala Kanshi Ram was amazed at the treasures she expertly fished out of the big steel chests. He had known of the gold ornaments. But when did Prabha buy those cashmere shawls, and those soft, hand-embroidered silk blouses and the gold-threaded strings for her pigtails? She took out white silk handkerchiefs, many pairs of meshed, richly beaded bangles, and silver-lined looking glasses, small and round, which one could hold in the palm of one's hand. And she brought out many small glass vials, in many colours and shapes, out of which came different hues and fragrances.

'My perfumes,' she said, blushing a little, when she found her husband looking at her askance.

'Take only what's absolutely necessary,' said Lala Kanshi Ram, repeating the phrase he had used before others, only now he said it mildly, not having the heart to rebuke his wife.

'They are absolutely necessary,' said Prabha Rani, the blush on her face spreading, for she knew Arun also was was watching her. 'These are made from real flowers and woods. Where can you find a genuine perfume these days?'

And with a toss of her head: 'They are all cheats—these attar wallas.'

Lala Kanshi Ram looked the other way in pain. For he knew, he knew for certain—at this hour of renunciation when he was giving up all he had—how much he loved this woman. Indeed, indeed, he said to himself, his face puckering with emotion, if he were asked to take just one article out of this house, just one memento of the blessings of his life here, or one marvel for the future to come—he would take only Prabha. Yes, Prabha alone, and maybe leave Arun behind too.

'Take whatever you like,' he said, touching her with hands which were trembling a little.

Soon they were ready, in a manner of speaking. They had one steel trunk and a bedroll filled with blankets and sheets. The rest they left where it lay—books, and sheets, and clothes. The furniture in their house was so massive, beds so strongly made and tables and chairs with thick, solid legs and tops, that stripped of their coverings they presented a gory sight, as though several giants lay in ruin. Lala Kanshi Ram did not look at that for long. He stood by the side of his bed in the square room, waiting for Chaudhri Barkat Ali and Munir to return with the trucks. He now wanted to get away from here. Yes, the move was inevitable.

All right, all right. Let's finish with it then, run the loop of fate quickly, and get back to here where we belong. It would be only then, on his return, that he would go and have a look at his rooms.

Having locked all the other trunks and suitcases, Prabha Rani put a lock on the one they were taking with them and heavily sat down on the bedroll Arun had tied up in leather straps. She looked exhausted and woeful. She too did not wander from room to room.

And then she suddenly burst into weeping.

'Ma!' said Arun.

With a quick movement, Prabha Rani got up and opening one of the two steel chests took out two of her finest pillows. It had come to her right at the end—she had taken no pillows with her at all. And Lala Kanshi Ram must always have *two* of them before he would go off to sleep.

'Here, Arun, you hold these in your hands,' she said.

There was a knock at the door, and when they opened it there stood before them a tall man in big army boots, but wearing civilian clothes, a light blue bush shirt and grey trousers. His hair was tousled, and his face had black marks of grease on it. He had a very white complexion.

'Bill Davidson,' said Arun in surprise.

The man greeted Lala Kanshi Ram and Prabha Rani with folded hands, Indian-style.

Winking at Arun, he said, 'I had to camouflage myself to look like an Indian. I couldn't have come along with the trucks otherwise.'

'Father,' said Arun. 'This is Bill Davidson Sahib. He's a friend of ours.'

Lala Kanshi Ram knew at once he was English, a white sahib. Normally he would have jumped up to welcome him. An Englishman in his house—he had not thought of the possibility in his wildest dreams. But his excitement was dampened by his immediate predicament.

'I'm indeed lucky,' he began in his loyal way, folding his hands. The voice refused to take on the old resonance.

'Won't you sit down, sir,' he said pushing a chair ahead and dusting the already clean seat with his hand.

'I think we should be leaving. The trucks are in the street,' said Bill Davidson to Arun, while smilingly declining Lala Kanshi Ram's invitation with a shake of his head.

Prabha Rani had covered her head with her sari. In their family, she was the least overawed by spectacle, and the fact that an Englishman was standing before her did not have much significance for her.

No one moved.

'I advised Munir and his father against coming at this time. They would have attracted attention in the street,' said Bill Davidson to Arun.

Again no one spoke or moved.

'Bill Davidson Sahib has been having long discussions with me and Munir,' said Arun to his father, in an effort to break the tension. 'He too disagrees with the partition.'

Lala Kanshi Ram looked at Bill Davidson with belligerent eyes.

'We have been let down by you people,' he said, softly enough, but pointing his finger at Bill Davidson.

Bill Davidson knew a little Urdu, but even without that knowledge he would have had no difficulty in understanding what Lala Kanshi Ram was saying. He stood hunched up in his sorrow, as though his whole body was badly lacerated. And there was a distress in his eyes which was deadly, a distress which needed no language to communicate itself.

'*All* that I had—' Lala Kanshi Ram went on— 'all that I had taken nearly *thirty* years to build is being lost because *you* refuse to protect me!'

'Father, father!'

Bill Davidson lifted a hand and quieted Arun.

'You were our sirkar, our masters, and I and millions like me gave you our *complete* loyalty. While striking a deal with these "leaders", did you ever think of us? Did you for one moment consider what might befall us? Freedom to be sure, we welcome it. But why the violence? It is a denial of what the English stood for during two hundred years in this country! And it is the English who have the biggest hand in this butchery.'

'How? Kaise?' asked Bill Davidson in Urdu, haltingly.

'For you had the power to prevent it and you did not use the power!' His voice was rising by degrees.

If Lala Kanshi Ram could have seen himself from a distance, he would have wondered at himself—he, a humble servant of the English, carrying on a spirited argument with one of his masters. But no, they were his masters no more; they had betrayed his trust and had no right to his loyalty.

'Perhaps you will come back here,' said Bill Davidson gently, forming his words in Urdu slowly.

This softened Lala Kanshi Ram at once. Oh yes, if only he could come back, if only. He would forgive the English and the Muslims all their sins—if only he could return. Return and die here and be cremated by the side of the river Aik! He shivered at the luxury of the thought. To be carried shoulder high on a bier through the streets of Sialkot, through all these streets in each one of which somewhere sat a friend, with the bands playing in front of the bier, and riderless horses, at least six of them—no, he would not have less than six—walking ahead of the bier, and his grandchildren walking behind him, immediately behind and shaven-headed, so that the crowd would know who they were, sons of his only son, and Arun, himself shaven-headed, maybe holding the finger of the youngest of them, and his wife, Prabha, way behind in the cortege, in the group of women, not crying for she would have to respect her age before others, but inwardly sad and thinking of him lying flat on the bier, walking with dignity and with love, and the bier all decorated with buntings and balloons and coloured bamboo sticks and zari and kinari, gold ribbons at least two inches wide, and the ding dong of the brass bell struck by the priest by his side coming faintly into his dead ears but telling the world loudly enough that it was no marriage party, these bands and horses, but a funeral, a dead man's funeral, a man who had died of old age, having done his duty by his family and his clan, and therefore it was not a sad but a solemn and even a happy occasion. 'Who's dead? Who's gone?' 'Lala Kanshi Ram, you know, the great Lala Kanshi Ramji.' And then at the last minute—for didn't the Vedas say you retained a grain of consciousness right till the time when the fire reached and burned up your brain—at the last minute when the brain burst open and he was really gone, for his spirit to look at the Aik and the land of Sialkot from above, from the sky, or to come down and roll in the dust of its fields—that would be the very pinnacle of his delight.

'Sir,' he was very humble and his hands were folded.

No one had said a word while he stood in a trance in the midst of them. Prabha Rani knew her husband was nowhere near them, but she also knew he was a little mad and would soon come back. But Arun was alarmed at the look of vacancy on his father's face, and Bill Davidson, who had seen death and suffering in war, saw Lala Kanshi Ram's bent posture and the raised face and the film of tears on his eyes that were fixed on the wall ahead but actually were centred nowhere, and he held his peace—unwilling to intrude into the old man's world.

'Sir,' Lala Kanshi Ram was very humble. 'Do you really think we could come back?'

'It is possible,' said Bill Davidson briefly but soothingly.

'Please sit down, sir, please forgive me for my harsh words, sir, you know, I'm getting on in years.'

He wanted to push Bill Davidson into the chair, but Bill Davidson said: 'We should be moving.'

'Yes, father, we should be leaving.'

'All right, then. Let's leave,' said Lala Kanshi Ram, swallowing. 'Come Arun's mother, let's go. And don't once look back—and no tears either. Arun will bring the things down.'

Other tenants had already collected in the street, close to the two trucks parked in the lane. The two drivers were helping them with their luggage. They threw the belongings in and then helped them climb up. No one was crying or being hysterical. Bibi Amar Vati was standing with a horrid look on her face, eyeing her two buildings. She was an ugly woman and her sorrow made her uglier, not tragic. She was wearing a shirt and wide Punjabi pyjamas, and the string of her pyjamas was showing. Because of her dark complexion her eyes were looking a little extra white. The furrows on her face ran longitudinally from the base of those eyes to the corners of her mouth. The mouth was thin and the lips were tightly closed, though there was a slight quivering in them.

Her husband, the good-for-nothing Gangu Mull, was being very loving and lavish, trying to mitigate her grief. 'I say ji, now you get up into the truck, don't worry too much. We will build these mansions all over again for you elsewhere,' he spoke, addressing her in the second person plural. And right there, in the middle of that street, with all the tenants watching and the trucks waiting to pull out, they had a quarrel.

'Go away, you dog, don't talk to me in such slippery words. What do you know about building things and making money? Get on with yourself and leave me alone.'

Gangu Mull caught her roughly by the arm and pulled her hard. 'You—' he began. Before he could speak the words, Lala Kanshi Ram moved in and separated them.

Speaking in whispers, he said to Bibi Amar Vati: 'Sister, not at this time, for goodness sake.'

'Get into the truck!' he said to Gangu Mull roughly, who obliged, but biting his lips, and swearing inside and glaring at Bibi Amar Vati as if he could murder her.

The most touching sight at that departure was of Sunanda Bala, the daughter-in-law of Bibi Amar Vati. Sunanda came from Kashmir, and when she was brought into this household as a bride, there was quite a celebration in the whole street. Whosoever came to see her was dazzled by her beauty. She was very small, but very delicately formed, with hands and fingers exquisitely shaped and her nostrils thin like soft tissue. The nails of her hands were a soft pink, and when Munir said to Arun, 'It must be the paint,' that evening Arun had a special look at them. No, they were not painted or coloured; the shine on them was plainly natural—like the shine on her cheeks. In the light of the evening, her whole being, cheeks and nails, all glowed and shimmered. She was not a human being, she was a presence.

During the last seven years that Sunanda had been a daughter-in-law in this house, no one had seen much of her. As though she came of a rare species, she jealously shielded herself from unwanted contacts; she even appeared before the womenfolk of the house only occasionally. She belonged to an aristocratic Brahmin family. Her parents knew Suraj Prakash, the man they were marrying her to, was not much good. But they also knew he was the sole heir to the property of Bibi Amar Vati, and what more could they wish for their daughter than to be an heiress? And she had to act that part, to keep herself aloof and pretend to be the future mistress of the household. Then she had been to high school and read poetry and played on the sitar—factors contributing further to her isolation. The real reason why she couldn't bring herself to mix with others was a very private one, a very dainty one. It was that she was uniquely aware of her beauty. Somehow she had a fear that through touch with others this exquisiteness would be defiled. It was not pride, nor a stupid sense of cleanliness; it was more a matter of sensitivity. Most of the Punjabi women in these two buildings were beautiful and exceptionally well made, particularly Isher Kaur and Chandni. But they were sturdy women, and their beauty lacked grace. And they indulged in such vulgar jokes, such crude jokes—all about the body. And Sunanda kept herself hidden, preserving her wealth for her own comfort and for the comfort of her husband.

Two children were born to Sunanda in these seven years, a boy and a girl. The girl was the first to come and was now almost six. And she was growing to be just like her mother, soft and delicate and very exquisite and reserved. Even though she was so young, Sunanda found a closer companionship with her than with the rest of the women. Very often, on sunny days, when a visitor went up to Bibi Amar Vati's flat, he found the mother and the daughter sunning themselves on a cot, the mother reading out loud from a story book and the girl listening to her with a rapt face—wholly absorbed with each other.

Arun was thirteen when Suraj Prakash got married. He well remembered the day for he was member of the marriage party which had gone from Sialkot to Gulmarg, that sleepy town on the mountain slopes of Kashmir. He had just started growing his pubic hair and had only just discovered how to take pleasure out of his own body, and was dying to see this new woman who, as the boys put it, was coming out to 'do things' with Suraj Prakash.

At Gulmarg he got no chance of being near her—there were so many ceremonies and there was such a rush of people. On the return journey to Sialkot he tried his best to get into the bus in which the bride and the bridegroom were, but the older boys pushed him out of it. But back at Sialkot, it was a field day for him. For when the women of the mohalla came to see the bride, the men and the older boys were driven out of the room but he was allowed to stay on; he was too small to be bothered about. And he sat ahead of them all, looking with unbelieving wonder as the woman from Kashmir bared her face. He paid no attention to the praise the women of the mohalla showered on her. Feeling shy, and not wanting to appear ill-mannered, he kept his eyes on the ground. There was a flutter in his heart and every few seconds he looked directly ahead, dropping his eyes right away. The bride sat on a thick, Persian carpet, and was wearing tight pyjamas and a long shirt, both of red silk. That was not what Arun saw. He saw her hands, and her bare feet, and her thin nose, and he saw her teeth and the glitter in her big brown eyes as they flashed across the room. The feet and the hands were painted scarlet with mehandi, with innumerable patterns on them, and her flesh was white like mother of pearl. Arun flushed inexplicably when he saw the soles of her feet, with their soft wrinkles, so soft and so warm. The women were giving the bride gifts of money and there was a shower of currency notes and Arun had to try hard to see through the shower. And apologetically, guiltily, he looked at her unduly large breasts which were heaving with excitement. And then he looked at her buttocks, a trifle heavy for her size, and thinking of what Suraj Prakash was to do with her that night he became truly embarrassed and hung his head. The girl had watched him for some time, the confused look on his face and his shyness; there was a difference of only five or six years in their ages, but he really was a child, she thought. Looking up, Arun saw her staring at him, and breaking into an unassuming innocent smile, he said, 'Bhabhi! Sister-in-law!' at which, the young woman leaned forward and touched him lightly on the chin.

For years, until he graduated from high school to college and until he was attracted by Nur, Sunanda was Arun's principal love. The boy was crazy about her and would run to Bibi Amar Vati's house on every conceivable occasion. And what a thrill he had running errands for her. 'Eh, Arun, get me a paan from the bazaar!' 'Arun, will you go and buy me a bottle of collyrium?' She was ever so demanding, but Arun's answer was an immediate, 'Yes, bhabhi!' And as he raced down the stairs, his young heart quivered with only one thought. Would she smile or wouldn't she? She was a whimsical woman, so proud and aloof. He would run all the stairs two at a time both ways, down and up, and when he had delivered to her what she wanted, at times she did not as much as give him a nod. Reading her book, she casually dismissed him, no, she would say not a word, and after waiting for a while he was obliged to go away. On other times, she kissed him on his cheeks or held his hand in hers and said, 'What a nice boy you are!' And at certain times she hugged him too, when he could distinctly feel the pressure of her breasts on his thin chest. He was happy if she only smiled. Now would she or wouldn't she smile today?

As Sunanda emerged from her house, holding her children by the hand, a quiet fell on the audience. She walked with majesty even in grief, and floated out into the street like a tableau; her face pensive, her eyes downcast, her shoulders soft and sagging, her fingers firmly gripping her children. In all these years she had not once been exposed to unfamiliar eyes so mercilessly. Yet she walked unconcerned, she walked as though she still owned the world. It was pretty warm, but she had wrapped a peacock blue stole on top of her polka-dotted sari. Both the children were talking endlessly. 'Where *are* we going, mummy?' asked Nava Kant, the son. 'You ask too many questions,' the little girl said. 'We're going for a holiday—aren't we, mummy?' Sunanda stopped for a second and people saw her nod her head to the girl. It was an imperious nod and there was no sorrow in it. With a regal fortitude she urged the children along to the trucks.

There was such dignity in her demeanour, such self-assurance, the men folded their hands and lined up to greet her. Even Bill Davidson took off his hat.

Arun went a few steps forward and took Nava Kant in his arms. He then took them to one of the trucks, where they eagerly made room for them.

It was about seven in the evening and the sun was still there in the sky. There were few people around. But the presence of the trucks was a curiosity, and near the entrance of the lane a few urchins had collected.

After everyone was seated in the trucks, Lala Kanshi Ram proposed a roll call, and it was then they discovered Mukanda's mother was not there with them.

Bibi Amar Vati said: 'Shouldn't you go and see?'

Reluctantly Lala Kanshi Ram got off the front seat, where he had deposited himself by the side of the driver. It was a seat of privilege. In one of the trucks the place was left vacant for Bill Davidson; in the other Lala Kanshi Ram had settled down, claiming it as his right. Folding his long coat under him, he sat on the heavily padded seat, and had only just begun to relax. Life was a misery everywhere, but right now it was cozy and trouble-free in that seat, when Bibi Amar Vati raising her head from the back of the truck shouted to him. He had no alternative but to get out, which he did, grumbling and swearing at Mukanda's mother, but saying aloud to Bibi Amar Vati, 'Yes, sure; yes, sure.'

The room on the ground floor where the old woman lived was the dingiest corner of that building. To be precise, it was not a room, it was a space on which the inner verandah of the first floor opened. Bibi Amar Vati had walled up the space and put a door to it. Inside, it was quite smoky and indistinct. There was no electric light there. Late in the evening the old woman lit a kerosene lamp. The rest of the day the only light the room had was what filtered down from the opening above.

As he stood there, trying to find his bearings in the dark, Lala Kanshi Ram had the distinct feeling he was entering enemy territory—no, territory that was evil itself. Living in the same building, they were poles apart, he and his family and this ghoulish woman. It was only expedience that held them together, and Lala Kanshi Ram had the feeling the mystic balance was going to be upset today. Till today neither had trespassed into the other's realm. If Mukanda's mother came upstairs, she came by request and sat in one corner of a room. So far as they were concerned, they had never stepped into her fortress.

'Grandma!' said Lala Kanshi Ram hoarsely.

That's what everyone called her—grandma. Her hair looked as though a comb had not been through it for years. And it rose like a crop atop her head and fanned out wildly in different directions. She had quite a way of looking at you. Her head slanted downward, aiming at the ground. And out of that lowered head, where everything, the brow, the nose, the chin, pointed at some part of the ground, the eyes shot upward—at you. And she appeared in a way ageless, so fossilized she seemed, throwing her quizzical glance at you. And everyone in the city called her grandma too, which in Punjabi merely meant 'Old Woman'.

'Grandma,' said Lala Kanshi Ram again, this time a little more forcefully.

There was no answer. He could feel her presence in the room. In the farthest corner, where she had collected all kinds of junk, old bottles and cans and newspapers—huge piles of them—in that corner the sense of foreboding the room carried with it, the sense of doom or vague fear, that sense seemed to thicken. Lala Kanshi Ram knew she was there, hiding herself in that corner.

He heard a rustle in that corner.

'You better come out, grandma, I know you're there.'

'What do you want of me?'

'I want you to come with us.'

'You know I'll not come without my son.'

'Mukanda is safe in prison. But they might kill you here tonight.'

'I'm not coming—how often have I to tell you that?'

'Be reasonable, we aren't leaving without you, said Lala Kanshi Ram, losing his temper.

Arun appeared at the door, along with Suraj Prakash.

'I'm not afraid to die.'

'We will have to take you by force, then,' said Lala Kanshi Ram. 'Come on boys, pick up some of the luggage of your grandma.'

There was no luggage to take. It was all garbage, refuse. Suraj Prakash and Arun stood uncertainly. They would either have to take the whole lot or leave it all. So they stood and looked, without making a move.

Lala Kanshi Ram sensed their predicament.

'Come on grandma, I'm giving you the last chance. Tell us what you want to take and the boys will pack it up for you. I'm not going to live the rest of my life with the guilt of your death on my conscience. I'm definitely not leaving you here!'

'And I'm telling you I am *definitely* not going.'

Time was running short, and Lala Kanshi Ram was getting impatient. Stepping back a little, he whispered to Arun and Suraj Prakash. And the two young men jumped forward to catch Mukanda's mother by the arms. She must have been watching them, for she made a lunge at them, and a heavy iron rod she had thrown at them missed its mark and fell on the ground with a loud clang—first hitting the farthest wall with a dull thud.

'You crazy fool,' said Lala Kanshi Ram.

'Leave me. Let me be! Let me be, I'm telling you, you scoundrels, you ruffians, you—' and Lala Kanshi Ram heard those choice Punjabi swear words, coming not out of the mouth of a man, as was customary, but out of the mouth of this shrivelled up gnome. 'Let me be, you sister-fuckers, you mother-fuckers, you...'

Firmly holding her by the arms, the young men dragged her out, and Lala Kanshi Ram followed a few steps behind, silently looking at the spectacle.

By now Mukanda's mother was shrieking at the top of her voice. They carried her across and put her in one of the trucks, where in addition to Arun and Suraj Prakash a few other men also tried to hold her down. But the demon in her was fully risen, and she was out to justify all the stories her neighbours had heard about her. She bit at the hands of the men, she went for their throats. Nothing availing she started beating her breasts and crying.

'Hai, hai, I don't want to leave. They are taking me away from my Mukanda. I don't want to leave. H-a-i! H-a-i!'

'No one is taking you away, we're all coming back—soon,' said Lala Kanshi Ram, much distressed at her plight.

'I don't believe you. I don't believe a word of what you say.'

Bibi Amar Vati came forward and slapped her hard across her face.

'Shut up, you slut. The whole street is watching you. Have some shame.'

Bill Davidson sat in his front seat, looking impatiently at his watch.

The moment Bibi Amar Vati was within her reach, like a trap Mukanda's mother caught her by her hair and started pulling. She clung to her hair and wouldn't let go.

Bibi Amar Vati cried out in pain, and Lala Kanshi Ram shook Mukanda's mother hard. But she had a hellish strength in her grip, and she pulled and shook Bibi Amar Vati from side to side—so much so that soon they started fearing for her life.

'Chachaji, why don't we let her go?' shouted Suraj Prakash. 'Let her remain here!'

'Let go of Bibi Amar Vati, let go of Bibi Amar Vati,' shouted Lala Kanshi Ram.

Mukanda's mother had ceased crying and all her strength was concentrated on destroying Bibi Amar Vati, on pulling at her hair. Bibi Amar Vati was making a wild effort to save herself, and she was flapping her hands and loudly moaning. But there was nothing that would loosen the hold of the other woman, and on her face appeared a curious satisfaction, as though she were paying Bibi Amar Vati back for years of neglect.

And suddenly in this commotion, when the men were concerned about Bibi Amar Vati's safety and had slackened their grip on Mukanda's mother, she let go of Bibi Amar Vati and jumped off the truck and ran back into the house.

It happened like a flash. The moment before she was pulling at Bibi Amar Vati's hair and shaking her from side to side. And the next moment she had jumped off the truck and was sprinting away.

No one made an effort to follow her. With one breath, many voices said: 'Let her go.' And they turned their attention towards Bibi Amar Vati, who had collapsed in a heap on the floor of the truck.

While the women attended to Bibi Amar Vati, the men said to Lala Kanshi Ram: 'Let's leave!' Yes, that's what they should do, thought Lala Kanshi Ram. He said faintly, 'Yes.'

But he made no move and did not return to his seat in the truck.

A silence fell on them all, as following Lala Kanshi Ram's gaze, they looked at the two houses. For there stood the houses already like ruined monuments before them, in which no one seemed to have lived for ages. They looked spectral and forbidding: everything around them, the windows, the doors, the ventilators, was shut tight—Mukanda's mother having sealed the only open entrance, one of the main doors. A few hours before the buildings had hummed with activity, with the laughter of children and the passion of men and women. Now the quiet of the grave seemed to have settled on them, and it seemed the life which had been lived in them was only wasted away. They were not very attractive houses, when you looked at them from afar. They were only two storeys high, the paint on them was uneven and thick. The balcony that ran in front of the second house was collapsing, it certainly was not level with the rest of the floor. The doors were of strong wood, but they were plain doors, heavy and clumsy. No, they were not houses of architectural beauty. And yet every single person in those two trucks was yearning to run back into them and fill them up.

And at that minute, while Lala Kanshi Ram was getting ready to tell Arun to pull out, they heard the loud and fiendish laughter of Mukanda's mother from the roof of the building. They all stared at the roof, but no, she wasn't there. And yet the laughter, unearthly and defiant, more a squeal than a laugh, filled the air. It came in loud spurts, and fell over their heads like a shower of burning fire. And then it died down for a while, and came up again, but now from the other building, from Bibi Amar Vati's roof. But no, soon it was coming from one of the small windows on the first floor. And yet, after a while, again from the roof of the second building. And still a while later, from the floor on which lived Lala Kanshi Ram.

They stood there spellbound. The houses did not have to wait for the evening to be taken over by other forces, a force had already come and dominated them. Starting from the little cell in the basement, where it had lived imprisoned for so many years in the company of old cans and bottles, this force had issued forth like a genie. And like smoke it had spread through the two houses, before taking on the physical appearance of the genie. And having spread itself through each room and each nook and corner, its first word or cry was a demonic, defiant laughter.

Prabha Rani pressed Lala Kanshi Ram's arm.

'Let's leave, for God's sake.'

'Yes,' he whispered. 'We'd better.'

And turning towards Arun, who was sitting close to Bill Davidson in the first truck, Lala Kanshi Ram waved to him. And he returned to his seat in the second truck.

And soon the two trucks rolled out of Fort Street into Trunk Bazaar, and headed for the refugee camp in the Cantonment.

In the dusk of the evening, the uncanny laughter of Mukanda's mother followed them a long way. It seemed to be defying everyone—those who were leaving, and those who were to come there that night.

PART II

The Storm

CHAPTER 1

THE rain had been heavy through the day. Small streams of water flowed through the muddy lanes of the refugee camp and in many cases flooded the tents which stood shoulder to shoulder on both sides of the lanes.

The clouds had parted in the afternoon, and the sun had at last appeared. Groups of men were busy clearing the lanes with shovels and pickaxes. Children and the womenfolk in each tent sorted out the wet things and spread them out on lines, which were hung inside the tents. Most of the women had removed their saris and were working only in petticoats. With brooms in hand, they vigorously pushed the water out of the tents and made little mud dams outside to prevent it from coming in again.

The monsoon was late this year, but it had been raining off and on for many weeks. It had also rained on the fifteenth of August, the independence day. The news of the celebration in Delhi was blocked out by the Pakistani press and no Indian newspapers were available. Most families in the camp sat together on that day and while they were aggrieved at their personal fate they also felt inexplicably proud.

The families from Fort Street were allowed four of the smaller tents. They were tiny army tents. The canvas sloped sideways from two poles in the centre, and the space inside could barely accommodate a single family. Bibi Amar Vati was given a full tent for her family. The Sardars too, because of the special condition of Isher Kaur, got a tent to themselves. Lala Kanshi Ram allowed Padmini and Chandni, the charwoman and her daughter, to move in with his family. The remaining families moved together into the fourth tent.

The afternoon had the peculiar freshness Indian days acquire after rain and Lala Kanshi Ram had gone out for a walk with Arun. The far-off hills of Jammu stood out clear in the clean-washed blue sky. The air smelled of wet earth and made you feel good. The red army barracks in the Cantonment looked redder and thoroughly scrubbed. Lala Kanshi Ram knew the army men would soon come out to clean up the damage caused by the rain. At the moment the fields were deserted, and the trees by their side shook majestically in the wind.

When they returned from their walk, they found Dr Chander Bhan and his wife sitting inside their tent. Dr Chander Bhan had a small medical practice in Trunk Bazaar and the two families occasionally met each other. He too had moved into the camp a few days before independence. Lala Kanshi Ram had seen him around, but had not had the time to talk to him.

'So at last we can sit for a few minutes with each other,' said Lala Kanshi Ram, going forward to meet Dr Chander Bhan with his usual friendliness and a warm smile on his face.

Dr Chander Bhan and his wife were sitting on one of the beds that was spread on the ground. Dr Bhan got up and gripped Lala Kanshi Ram's hands.

'My privilege,' he said.

'How do you like living in a camp?' asked Lala Kanshi Ram of Dr Bhan's wife.

While she smiled noncommittally, Lala Kanshi Ram noticed she had especially dressed up to come to their place. She was a matronly woman with a pinched, ill-defined face, so that what you saw of it was only the chin. Her hair was combed back over her ears, from which hung two gold trinkets. She was wearing a white silk blouse and a fine white muslin sari. And she had a pair of lavish Punjabi shoes on, with gold trimmings all over their surface. He looked at Dr Chander Bhan and found he too was wearing spotlessly clean white clothes, with a black cap on his head.

This disturbed Lala Kanshi Ram. Why were they so overdressed on such a rainy day?

Prabha Rani emerged from behind the curtain that hung in one corner, adjusting her sari. They had no visitors here. Lala Kanshi Ram knew what a ritual it was for Prabha Rani to make her toilet. She had to get ready in a hurry today, and a faint blush spread on her face as she came and sat by the side of Mrs Bhan.

'It is a good day!' she said, embracing Mrs Bhan and greeting Dr Bhan.

It was the traditional sentence of approval—approval of the visitor. To this, the traditional reply was, 'It's a good day for us, too.' But Mrs Bhan remained quiet. She only leaned forward and met Prabha Rani in the embrace.

And then there fell a silence in the tent. Dr and Mrs Bhan said not a word. They did not look particularly uncomfortable. Only they did not speak and stared at Prabha Rani and Lala Kanshi Ram.

'Is anything the matter?' asked Lala Kanshi Ram, sensing danger in that silence.

'No, nothing is the matter,' said Mrs Bhan, shaking her grey head and jingling her earrings. She kept shaking her head and jingling the earrings. They surely make a good sound, she was saying to herself. And why shouldn't they? They were made of solid gold—twenty-two carat!

Again a long pause followed, when Lala Kanshi Ram fidgeted with his shirt sleeves and Prabha Rani looked at Mrs Bhan and Arun sat flurried next to his father. Arun hated Dr and Mrs Bhan.

'We've bad news for you,' said Dr Bhan finally, addressing Lala Kanshi Ram. 'I wish we weren't the messengers of this...' His tone was heavy with concern, but it was only assumed heaviness.

'Say it.'

'We've heard your daughter Madhu Bala is killed,' said Dr Bhan sonorously, almost delivering a speech.

Arun bit his lip, and Lala Kanshi Ram and Prabha Rani stared at their visitors.

'Who told you?' asked Lala Kanshi Ram, with remarkable poise and control.

'Lala Dina Nath of Gujrat.'

'How does he know?'

'He was in the train in which it happened.'

'Which train?'

'The one from Wazirabad. She was coming to Sialkot—to you. Along with her husband.'

'And her husband?'

'He too was killed.'

Arun watched his mother. She did not cry. She stared at Dr and Mrs Bhan in dismay, but she shed no tears.

But she said to Arun: 'Now you have no sister left!'

'Ma, it's only hearsay—it's not true,' said Arun.

Facing Dr Bhan, he asked crossly: 'Have you met Lala Dina Nath yourself? Where is he? I should like to ask him the details for myself.'

'Lala Dina Nath was here last night. He left for Jammu by car soon afterwards.'

'Why didn't he come and see us?'

'He said he was in a hurry.'

Prabha Rani here went behind the curtain. Arun went after her, and they could hear him whispering to her.

Said Lala Kanshi Ram: 'I wish you had first communicated the news to me alone.'

Dr and Mrs Bhan felt cheated. They loved funerals and condolence meetings. Arranging things, offering sympathy, while sitting clean and well-off themselves, there couldn't be anything more exciting in life for them! Mrs Bhan had come ready to hold Prabha Rani's arms and prevent her from beating her breasts. Dr Bhan had looked up a suitable quotation from the Gita, and was only waiting for the right moment to pass it on—with explanatory notes and comments—to Lala Kanshi Ram. But Lala Kanshi Ram and his family had acted in a most unpredictable manner. Eccentrics that they were, instead of sorrow they had displayed anger. Lala Kanshi Ram was now staring hard at their ornate dress. Dr and Mrs Bhan saw that and felt a trifle abashed and guilty.

Lala Kanshi Ram got up from the bed, indicating he wanted his visitors to leave. Arun had come back and was standing insolently by his father's side. Dr and Mrs Bhan quickly got up and left the tent, uttering incoherent apologies and words to the effect that maybe this was not true. No, they said, they would pray to God this wasn't so.

As soon as they had departed, Lala Kanshi Ram walked over to the corner of the tent and removed the curtain behind which sat Prabha Rani.

She was squatting on the ground and her eyes were fixed on the picture of Lord Krishna they had brought from home. She was still not crying. It looked as though all the blood had drained out of her face; she looked mummified. There was no movement in her lips. She did not even flicker her eyelids. After a few moments she closed the lids and kept them closed. And then she opened them and they stayed open.

'Ma, I'm sure this is only a rumour. They were idiots to have come and surprised us like this. I'm sure Madhu is alive and we'll soon hear from her.'

Without turning towards them, Prabha Rani shook her head.

'Arun's mother, give me time to check on it before you start worrying,' said Lala Kanshi Ram.

'The news is true,' said Prabha Rani quietly, looking at her husband like a somnambulist.

Hitting her chest with the flat of her palm, she said: 'I have felt it here for some weeks something very bad was about to happen. Only I didn't quite know what.'

Lala Kanshi Ram was relieved she was at least talking.

'It is unconfirmed news,' persisted Lala Kanshi Ram.

'A mother's heart needs no confirmation. I'm quite sure my daughter is gone!'

She uttered a whimper.

'It was her coming death burning me up. I just couldn't figure it out. I cooked, I washed, I cleaned—and my inside was empty, as though someone had cut a hole and my organs had slipped from my body. All along I was sad and more sad, and was for no reason bursting into tears. When did they say she was killed?'

'Yesterday.'

'Yes, she died yesterday. Today is Wednesday—she died on Tuesday, the third day of the moon. That's when the sadness reached a point. I thought I should go and drown myself.'

'You didn't say anything to me about this,' said Lala Kanshi Ram.

'What could have I said to you? I thought maybe it was the home and the shop. Now I *know*.'

And here, closing her eyes, she let out a chilling cry. It was not a wail or a moan. It was a long drawn out h-a-a-a-ai! Her mouth remained open at the end of the cry, but her eyes were closed and her features were twisted in anguish.

'Madhu—Madhu—Madhu—Madhu—Madhu—' she called, in a metallic cry, wrung from the depths of her being.

Arun leapt forward and caught hold of her arm.

'Ma, please let us verify the news, *please*!

'You do what you like. But I know—I know.'

And again she cried aloud h-a-i! And again she called out: 'Madhu—Madhu—Madhu.'

A crowd gathered outside the tent. Lala Kanshi Ram went out and dispersed them unceremoniously. He allowed Bibi Amar Vati to go in, but asked Padmini and Chandni to guard the entrance and let no one else through.

'Come, Arun. Let's go and find out more about it.'

The father and the son visited the lane in which lived Dr Chander Bhan. Alas, the news was true! Madhu and her husband, Rajiv, had been killed a few miles outside of Wazirabad. They had boarded the train to Sialkot from Wazirabad. The train was stopped beyond the second signal near the village of Nizamabad. Hindus and Sikhs in the train were singled out and mercilessly slaughtered. Lala Dina Nath was in the very compartment in which sat Madhu and Rajiv.

'How come he escaped?' asked Arun.

'By saying he was a Muslim, and by bribing a Muslim sitting next to him to vouch for it.'

Dr Bhan was still wearing the formal clothes in which he had visited Lala Kanshi Ram, but the pose, the humbug of condolence was gone. Instead he was genuinely sorry for the family. It could as well have been him. No tragedy was an isolated tragedy these days; it hurt each one of them, since the range and dimension of the blow was applicable to them all. He was relieved to see his five children sitting in safety beside him. And he was truly sad for Lala Kanshi Ram, who was left with only one.

The news about the train was all over the camp. Some survivors had reached there and Lala Kanshi Ram and Arun visited each of them. None of them knew Madhu and Rajiv, but they gave horrifying accounts of what had happened. The guards at the gate were also talking of the massacre.

It hurt Lala Kanshi Ram to think the body of Madhu should be rotting only a few miles away from him. The train had come in only last night. Maybe she was still there, piled up in a heap.

'Arun, you have to get Chaudhri Barkat Ali and go up to the station.'

'Yes, father.'

Arun's heart leaped at the thought of it. He had been longing to return to the city, but his parents wouldn't hear of it. The independence was two weeks old. Sialkot was now a part of Pakistan: it was not the same town, they said, it was a different town! For the past many weeks, refugees had been moving into the camp each day. There was such an influx—of broken men and women and silent, wide-eyed children. Prabha Rani was certain those who had stayed behind after the fifteenth of August had either been annihilated or converted to Islam; it was no city for the Hindus any longer. Arun did not share his mother's sentiments. He thought the major wave of violence had passed and the city must have returned to some kind of normalcy. But even his father, who had such hopes of living in the Muslim Pakistan, seemed afraid of letting him go. And Arun had to submit to them.

Now his father was asking him to go all by himself—and that too in the evening, when soon it would be dark. Arun suddenly felt like a man. Life, it appeared, was inviting him to take charge and work out the fantasies which previously he had only dreamt of. His imagination had only been a chain of fetters so far. It prompted him to visions that were demolished through a single phrase or a single look by his father. 'What did you say?' was all his father had to shout for him to start sweating. His mother was more indulgent, she didn't deride or reject him outright, but the way she smiled at his words, was it any different from shrugging him off? He was only a child: inexperienced, immature and lacking in strength!

Arun looked at his father with a smile, but Lala Kanshi Ram couldn't see why he was smiling. In his mind, Arun thought of the possibilities. He might see his dead sister. He might see Nur.

There were objections. 'Why are you sending your son to death?... Madhu is gone, you want Arun to go too...? He cannot bring Madhu back.'

None of that touched Lala Kanshi Ram. He was scared for Arun, he knew he wouldn't forgive himself if anything happened to him. But Madhu had been brutally murdered, and he felt he owed it to her to retrieve her body. He should go himself. Only he wanted to stay near Prabha Rani. But Arun was only an extension of him. And someone *must go.* If in the process Arun was lost too—well, well. Lala Kanshi Ram wouldn't complete his thought.

As a compromise, it was agreed Suraj Prakash should go with Arun. Sunanda offered no objection, and Bibi Amar Vati was still inside the tent with Prabha Rani. So far as Suraj Prakash was concerned, he was unmindful of personal safety to the point of stupidity. What mattered to him was excitement. The last four weeks in the camp had been the most boring weeks of his life. In the city, he had a hundred odd jobs to take care of: to collect rent, to pay the electricity and the water bills, to supervise the whitewashing and other petty repairs, to settle quarrels between two groups of tenants. Here he had nothing to do.

He jumped at the chance, and went and shook hands with Arun. Two cycles were soon procured, and they got ready. The secret of survival lay in effectively passing yourself off as a Muslim. A few of the details were easy. Muslim names were assumed by both and Arun taught Suraj Prakash the kahna, the Muslim article of faith. Suraj Prakash had a big 'Om' tattooed on the back of his left hand, and he covered it up with a handkerchief. They also tied handkerchiefs around their necks—in the fashion of scarves—like the working-class Muslim boys.

They knew none of these ruses would do in a crisis. The acid test of being a Muslim lay in one and only one sign—in circumcision. Unless you had another Muslim to vouch for you, you were rudely undressed by the mob and your vitals exposed to the curious eyes. 'Kill him—he is a kafir!' and the knife was driven at once through your stomach.

Suraj Prakash whispered something to Arun and they both laughed. Going behind the row of tents, they pushed their foreskins up.

'Does it stay like this?' asked Arun.

'See.'

Looking hurriedly right and left, Suraj Prakash lowered his pyjamas. It looked circumcised all right. Arun turned his head the other way, disconcerted.

'How is yours?' asked Suraj Prakash in a matter of fact way.

'It's all right, too,' said Arun, turning crimson.

'If the sack comes down, push it back with your fingers. They only have a quick look,' confided Suraj Prakash.

'Very well,' said Arun, wanting to change the subject.

Before they left the camp, it was late evening. They were not particular at the gate as to who left and who came in. Since the camp was in the Cantonment area, there was no fear of the Muslim population from the city invading it. Still, a few army guards were posted at the gate. Most inmates of the camp went for walks beyond the lines, and some made trips into the city as well. The policy of the two new governments was still incoherent. They were still talking of the refugees returning to their homes. No preparations were yet made to transport large numbers of them from one side to the other. In the initial stages those who went to the city did so to salvage some of their property. Now they went to loot that of other Hindus, bringing it back to the camp as their own.

Lala Kanshi Ram's instructions to Arun and Suraj Prakash were clear. They were to go straight to Chaudhri Barkat Ali's residence. They were to stay on the main road, but if they saw a crowd, they were to go into the nearest lane and either skirt the crowd or wait until it dispersed. They were to tell Chaudhri Barkat Ali of what had happened and go with him to the railway station, recover the bodies of Madhu and Rajiv, and bring them to the camp. They should depend entirely on Chaudhri Barkat Ali's judgment as to what was and what was not possible. They must return to the camp that night howsoever late it got, unless it was absolutely impossible, in which case they were to spend the night at Chaudhri Barkat Ali's place.

Lala Kanshi Ram embraced Arun and kissed him on the cheek. Much against his wishes, he was also obliged to kiss Suraj Prakash—who, seeing it as a sign of unusual affection from the otherwise stiff Lala Kanshi Ram, hugged him and said, 'Wah, chachaji, don't you worry, we'll be perfectly safe!'

The dusk was falling when they left the camp. They went over the bridge of a stream which separated the Cantonment from the city and cycled towards Mianapura.

'Wait a minute, Arun,' said Suraj Prakash.

They got off their cycles, and taking out a packet of cigarettes from his trouser pocket, Suraj Prakash lit a cigarette. He fumbled for a long while before he could find the matchbox, and heaved a deep sigh of relief when he let out the first breath of the smoke.

'Ah, this behan chode camp,' he said. 'I can't even smoke in peace there. People are ever complaining about one thing or the other and it gets on my nerves.'

Looking at Arun's distraught face, he said: 'Come on, Arun, have a smoke. You'll feel better.'

'No,' said Arun. 'Let's move on.'

They cycled fast and soon reached the first group of houses. It was the newest and the richest colony in the city, populated by industrialists, who worked in the city but preferred to live in the suburbs. The houses in this colony were big—of bungalow type, with extensive lawns in the front.

There did not seem to be much damage caused there, except that it was very quiet and there was no movement of people. Most of the people had fled. There were big locks on the gates and a couple of policemen stood there. The houses were evacuee property now and were under the charge of the government.

They met very few people on the road. Occasionally they passed a tonga, laden with goods or with people, and very often they passed other cyclists. But there were no groups of people, and no one took any notice of them.

Crossing the railway line at the level crossing, they entered the city proper, and it was then the extent of destruction became visible to them. Before they could turn off towards Mianapura from the big chowk, they had to cycle two hundred yards or so through a bazaar that went towards the chowk. The area used to have a Hindu majority and every single house in that bazaar had been burned down. Mianapura was a mixed area—Hindus and Muslims both lived there. So the mob had carefully selected the Hindu homes and set fire to them alone, with the result that much of Mianapura looked like a pair of jaws with many teeth missing. None of the houses had burned to the ground. In some cases the fire had only scorched the surface and blackened the face. In others, the house had collapsed after a part of it had burned, and while the debris had spilled on the road, the jagged portions of the house proper stood out weirdly on precarious foundations.

Yet life had resumed its play in the bazaars. Barring the Hindu shops, other shops were open. The lights had just been lit, and business in the area was brisk. Women in burqas, the traditional black or fawn Muslim veil, added variety to the colourful scene. Often people had to step over the debris on the road to get to a shop, and they did that hurriedly, with their heads down, already a little ashamed of what had happened. Vendors in the street had lit their mustard oil torches or their gas lamps, and Arun felt nostalgic to hear their shouts—'Grapes from Chaman, grapes from Chaman!' 'Take home bananas, take home bananas!' 'Fish, fried fish!' The pungent, intoxicating smell of fish followed Arun a long way. Surely these things would be there in India too, but would there be men there able to shout so lustily? The twang in their voices—like a thin pipe! And it rang in the air, reverberating, long after the words had ceased.

Arun knew Mianapura well and he could see many new traders had opened up in the area. Crudely written signboards in Urdu hung from their stores. These must be the Muslim refugees from India, he thought. They had small shops, with only a handful of articles inside: umbrellas, shoes, hosiery, or groceries. The men were nondescript, dark in their skins, thin and small in their bodies, and with ugly, reddish teeth, chewing betel leaf and throwing red spittle on the road. What were they doing here? They had nothing in common with the people where destiny had landed them. They did not even know how to write Urdu properly! Look at their sign-boards. Calligraphy was an indispensable part of Urdu, and these Muslims, from Central Provinces maybe, or from Bihar—who knows?—appeared to be foreign to its subtleties.

Arun looked at the stores again. Most of them had opened where previously there had been a Hindu shop. There was an aura of destruction and tragedy around them. And then Arun looked at those men again. They all looked unbelievably miserable. Now why in the name of Allah were they so sad? They had got what they wanted, their Pakistan. Why this gloom?

They reached Chaudhri Barkat Ali's place without any untoward happening, and placing their cycles in the vestibule below, climbed the stairs and knocked at the door on the landing.

It was Munir who opened the door. Munir and his father, Chaudhri Barkat Ali, had visited Lala Kanshi Ram's family often in the camp; Chaudhri Barkat Ali was there only two days back. Munir did not expect Arun to visit them and he was visibly surprised to see him.

He embraced him and said affectionately: 'Arun.'

He then shook hands with Suraj Prakash, and took them into a large, rectangular room, which constituted the main room of the men's quarters in the house.

The room was sparsely furnished. There was a high string cot in one corner, over which was spread a flowery bedspread. Over the bed were placed several round pillows. On one side of the room were a half dozen sturdy cane chairs. A large hookah stood close to the bed, and a whiff of smoke was coming from its clay pipe. Someone had obviously been sitting on the bed smoking—in all probability, Chaudhri Barkat Ali himself. There were also four enamel spittoons in four corners of the room. On a reading table beside the wall, an enamel vase displayed a large, single rose.

Whenever Arun came into this room, he thought it was no different in character from the room in their house where sat his father. The only distinction was instead of the family pictures or pictures of Hindu gods on the walls, they had pictures of the word Allah in Arabic. There were three of them, placed side by side, in a row. Each had the word Allah drawn with minute intricacy of patterning on a lightly coloured background. The rest of the space was taken up by a network of mosaic decorations, like those one sees on the ceilings of Muslim monuments.

But the two rooms in the two houses looked quite identical. They both indicated thrift, puritanism and hard work. A stranger would have seen at a glance the families living in them had a common background and a common ideology.

'Abba, look who is here! Arun has come,' shouted Munir.

The men's quarters were separated from the women's quarters by a large open courtyard, in which courtyard were also situated the kitchen, the toilet and the bathroom of the family. The courtyard formed a part of the women's quarters, for the women of the house moved freely there, whereas the men went in only after seeking permission.

As soon as Munir had announced Arun's presence, a utensil fell in the courtyard and went rolling loudly across the floor.

Arun heard the suppressed voice of Munir's mother: 'Take care, Nuri. You've spilled the milk all over!'

Chaudhri Barkat Ali lifted the curtain and entered from the courtyard.

'Aha, welcome, my son, welcome.'

As Arun and Suraj offered their greetings to Chaudhri Barkat Ali in the Muslim fashion, by bending a little and raising the right hand to the forehead, Chaudhri Barkat Ali said:

'May Allah bless you both.'

Dropping the formal tone, he asked Arun anxiously: 'I hope everything is all right, Arun?'

'Chacha jan, Madhu and her husband Rajiv have been killed.'

Chaudhri Barkat Ali moved not a muscle, whereas someone in the courtyard said in a voice steeped in grief, 'Hai, Allah!'

It was the voice of Begum Barkat Ali. Presently she parted the curtain and came into the room. She knew there was another person along with Arun, a stranger, but she hesitated not a moment. Only she covered her face up to her eyes with her dopatta. Advancing to the middle of the room, she caught hold of Arun's arm:

'Arun, what are you saying!'

'Chachi jan, so we hear,' said Arun, on the brink of tears.

The presence of her hand on his arm suddenly made Arun despondent—suddenly made him feel how hard it was for him to accept Madhu's death. His father, on hearing of it, had displayed superb poise; his mother had been driven into a coma. Throughout the evening, Arun had been thrown from one extreme to the other. That he could grieve over her simply, weep for her and yet maintain his dignity, they had not allowed him to feel. Now stood next to him a woman almost like his own mother, of her age, of her sturdy build, yet more like Madhu in that she was lively and was refined rather than overbearing, and like her she had a look of defiance in her eyes rather than submission, and her broad shoulders and bare arms had a smoothness closer to that of Madhu than his mother's, a woman, too, who had nursed in her womb and given birth to that marvel on earth, Nur, his beloved, so tender and delicate, and when this woman touched his arm in kindness and spoke softly to him, Arun felt like bursting into tears.

Controlling himself, Arun gave them the details. Here and there Suraj Prakash added a sentence or so.

'We must go to the station,' said Chaudhri Barkat Ali.

'Let me give them something to drink first,' said his wife and holding Arun by the hand, she led him inside, muttering to herself, 'Allah, Allah!'

Nur was bent double in the kitchen. She had heard everything. As they approached her, she clung to her mother, weeping bitterly in short, hysterical convulsions: 'Ammi, ammi, why has this happened? Why has Madhu behan been killed?'

'Patience, beti, patience. Allah alone knows.' She patted Nur's head and said: 'Get some tea ready for Arun and his friend.'

Her chest still shaking with convulsions, Nur put a saucepan on the fire. On an impulse she turned and took hold of Arun's hands and burying her head in them kept sobbing. Begum Barkat Ali stood watching, without making any attempt to separate them. Munir too had come inside and he too stood mutely by their side.

While a tumbler of tea was sent into the men's quarters for Suraj Prakash, the others sat in the vestibule on cots. Nur sat huddled next to her mother, her eyes deep red from crying. Arun sipped the tea, making as little noise as possible, so quiet they all were. When they thought no one was watching them, Arun and Nur looked at each other briefly—Nur instantly lowering her eyes and looking at her feet.

They got ready to leave. Begum Barkat Ali went into one of the inner rooms to get some money her husband wanted. Munir, Nur and Arun were alone in the courtyard. Ignoring Munir, Arun caught hold of Nur's hand and kissed her fingertips. She immediately withdrew the hand and uttered a loud, audible sigh.

A distant cousin of Munir, called Khalil Ahmad, who stayed with the family, and their old servant, Niaz Hussain, accompanied the party to the railway station. Munir and Khalil rode the two cycles the men had brought with them from the camp; the rest travelled in a tonga. Niaz Hussain had been with the family for many years. He was an old man. Arun had always seen him old; he never aged, never changed. With a white beard trimmed in the Muslim fashion around the chin, he sat in the men's quarters with a rosary in hand. All his jobs were outside jobs; mostly to handle workers of Chaudhri Barkat Ali's factory who came to the house to speak to the master. He had the look of a fakir, and the family treated him more as a holy man than as a servant. Sitting in the tonga, he was holding Arun's arm, and without saying a word to him was trying to comfort him in his own way, by repeating ayats from the Quran.

The station was deserted. It was a busy station, and usually, even when no trains were coming and going, there was much activity there. Trains were being loaded or unloaded, and a large number of coolies squatted on the platforms, gossiping. All along the platforms, small groups of families could be seen lounging—cooking food, or eating food, or just reclining. Today there were neither any passengers there, nor the coolies. Nor was there any noise of the trains shunting, or the locomotives hooting.

Many policemen were posted in different parts of the building, and a number of sweepers in blue uniforms were rushing around. Entrance to the platforms was barred by the police.

Chaudhri Barkat Ali was wondering what to do, when he saw a police officer strolling towards them.

'Assalam-o-Alaikum, Chaudhri Sahib,' the officer said, saluting Chaudhri Barkat Ali. 'What are you doing here so late in the evening?'

'Someone I know,' said Chaudhri Barkat Ali to Arun.

Chaudhri Barkat Ali made enquiries of him. Yes, a train with many dead had come in from Wazirabad last night. No, there was no way of identifying the dead. They had been cremating them since morning. They had very nearly finished. The last batch was being cremated now.

'Where?'

'In the open yard by the side of Platform three.'

Chaudhri Barkat Ali took the officer aside and spoke to him for a few minutes. The officer looked at Arun with curiosity.

Returning, the officer said to the waiting group: 'Please follow me.'

They went over the bridge that connected Platform one to Platform three. It was a heavy, iron overpass, painted in the dull, railway red. As Arun climbed its rough steps, he felt a lump in his throat. From the bridge, he could clearly see four bonfires in the area beyond the goods yard. The fires stood out like hills ablaze.

They had to get off the platform and cross a number of railway tracks before they could reach the clearing at the back. The stench was unbearable as they approached the area. The four heaps were piled high and the fires were roaring and hissing with great force, the flames climbing many feet into the air. What they saw there was only dismembered limbs, dozens of them—legs, and arms, and hands, and thighs, and feet. The fire had consumed other parts of the bodies; it was the parts which had not fully burned that stood out.

And there were the skulls. Again dozens of them. Many lay face down, the others faced the sky, or looked sideways. Bare jaws, scooped out eye-sockets, gnashing teeth. Very often a skull cracked open with a popping noise, its bones disintegrating into the heap around. Since it was a quiet night, the sound came like the crack of a rifle; it was an unnerving sound.

The dead had been removed from the train and dumped there without sentiment or concern. It so happened many of them had their arms around each other, or they were holding each other with their legs. And in the disintegration the fire brought to them, there was a constant *movement* in the heaps. Arms were climbing up or they were sliding down. Legs were yielding their hold or they were burying themselves deeper. And the eyes of one skull seemed to look into the eyes of another and send unspoken messages. For the other skull would nod, in a way saying it had quite understood.

Arun heard someone say to Chaudhri Barkat Ali: I've made further enquiries. I'm afraid they have all been cremated; there are no more bodies left.'

It was the police officer who had escorted them here.

'Are you quite sure, sir?' Arun asked him in a thick voice.

'Absolutely.' And after a pause: 'I'm sorry for you, Mister.' And then before another word could be said, one of the men who were raking the fires with long, bamboo poles, stepped up to Arun and said:

'Imagine! If it isn't Arun.'

Arun identified the voice before he saw the man. It was Abdul Ghani.

Abdul Ghani smartly saluted the police officer, and said:

'I'm one of the Khaksar volunteers, sir, helping to keep our city clean by cremating the kafir dead.'

And cynically, showing his teeth which lit up eerily in the light of the fire, he said to Arun: 'Who told you your sister was killed, my boy ? But don't worry. I put her and her husband into the fire with my own hands, and they're now on their way to dozakh, to hell—where I hope they rot for ever!' He made no effort to disguise his venom.

Chaudhri Barkat Ali was a tall, powerfully built man. He was over six feet two, with wide shoulders and strong, muscular arms. His voice, heavy and forceful, even now showed the physical strength locked up in him. But Mahatma Gandhi and non-violence had made a lamb of him and he went round in home-spun cotton shirts and loose pyjamas, his head bowed in humility.

At the words of Abdul Ghani a current shot through him. Swiftly, the moment Ghani had finished speaking he caught hold of Ghani by the neck with both his hands, Ghani only came up to his shoulders and Chaudhri Barkat Ali shook him as if he were a reed. His powerful head was bent low on Ghani's face and one could see the anger flashing in his eyes.

'You shaitan—you shaitan—you blot on the name of Islam!'

For a few seconds there was total disorder. Munir shouted, 'Abba, please!' Niaz Hussain said, 'Master, be careful you don't kill him,' and the police officer said several times, 'Chaudhri Sahib! Chaudhri Sahib!'

Chaudhri Barkat Ali paid no heed. He further squeezed Abdul Ghani's neck and shook him violently. 'You shaitan, you shaitan. What a tongue you have!'

On hearing the fray, a few other volunteers rushed over from the fires. They held their long poles threateningly in their hands. Munir, Khalil and Niaz Hussain also raised their hockey sticks, which they had taken with them as weapons. With a shout the police officer summoned other constables.

Chaudhri Barkat Ali stood staring remorsefully at his hands, when the officer succeeded in separating them. The officer gave Abdul Ghani a push and said. 'Get away, you dog, get back to your work! All the rest too, get back to your work.' The police constables pushed the men back with their sticks, repeating the words of their officer: 'Get back to work, get back to work!'

'I'm sorry,' said Chaudhri Barkat Ali to the police officer. 'I just couldn't take that. The boy is already in misery.'

The officer did not remonstrate.

'Come, children, let's get back home,' said Chaudhri Barkat Ali.

Before they left, Arun swung back and walked towards the burning fires. For the few seconds he stood there, his eyes desperately wandered over the mounds—searching for Madhu. Identical pairs of eyes and skulls gazed back at him, and frightened by the anonymity of the dead, he turned and rejoined the others.

Said Chaudhri Barkat Ali to Arun, when they were outside the station: 'Arun, son, I don't think I will be able to face your parents tonight. Munir and Khalil will see you safely to the camp. I'll come tomorrow morning.'

He took Arun in his arms and embraced him.

While Chaudhri Barkat Ali and Niaz Hussain returned home in a tonga, the four boys rode double on the bicycles to the camp. They parted outside.

Suraj Prakash had been smoking incessantly the whole evening. Lighting yet another cigarette, he stopped Arun before they entered their lane.

'Listen Arun, I haven't said much. But believe me, I'm as sad at Madhu's death.'

When he said this, Suraj Prakash was smiling. That was because he did not know how to offer sympathy, he had only learnt fooling around in life. Yet his voice was shaking with emotion.

'Here—take this.' And he offered Arun the cigarette he had lit.

Arun declined but he pressed Suraj's hand.

His mother still sat dazed, her face a blank mask, and she displayed no emotion when she heard Arun had been to the station. The kerosene lantern burnt low, and the tent was packed with mourners. His mother sat on one side in a group of women. His father sat on the other in a group of men. There was no weeping, but there was ceaseless chatter. For a while all talk died out. And all of a sudden it was resumed again. Arun did not know how long it went on. People kept coming in and going out. Someone said: 'Arun, come into the next tent and eat a little.' It was a woman's voice, but Arun couldn't make out who she was. He remembered declining. Someone else said, 'Arun, lie down and sleep a little.' This too was a woman. Arun remembered stretching himself in one corner. As he dozed, the noise in the tent, now distinct and clear, now vague, continued in his ears. And then abruptly he was fully awake, his mind alert, his eyes open, and he found himself looking at the ceiling of the tent.

He sat up. He looked around. They were lying down—his father, his mother, Padmini and Chandni. The others had left. Arun looked at his watch. It was three a.m. He could hear the faint, rhythmic breathing of Padmini and Chandni and he knew they were asleep. But he knew both his parents were awake. It was unusually still in their corner.

He stretched his legs and closed his eyes, and his mind was instantly a blank. Once again he woke up with a start and sat up. It was four a.m. This time they were all asleep. Up and down went the four chests. The breath came out softly and was as softly sucked back. This gave the tent a deceptively peaceful look. A breeze had come along, as it always did on summer mornings, and the flaps of the tent were lightly fluttering in the wind.

But something had happened, hadn't it? Arun searched his mind. Oh yes! And with searing, blinding pain, it came back to him. Madhu. Madhu, his sister. His earliest friend and companion. The one who had put him on the threshold of adult life.

He thought he would go for a walk and in the partially lit tent, he searched for his shoes. As he groped for them he saw the exposed bosom of Chandni. The girl was lying on her back, her mouth slightly open. Her being quivered ever so gently as the breasts heaved up and settled down, like waves ebbing and flowing against the shore. He forgot his shoes and stared at her for a long while, at her warmth and her tenderness. She was sleeping soundly and he could see the outline of her legs beneath her sari. She was all limp and, insouciant, and seemed so filled, so saturated with ripeness. Abandoning the walk, he crawled back to bed. Stretching himself prone, he continued to look at the girl. And as he lay there and looked, he realized completely and fully, without the shadow of a doubt, that Madhu was really dead and gone. For he would never see those slim legs of *hers* again nor *her* soft breasts.

Early in life Madhu was struck with smallpox and the disease had left deep marks on her face. Her parents often brooded over it; they felt the girl was disfigured. Madhu herself worried not in the least. It was an indifference to the small obstacles of life she had inherited from her mother. Nothing could easily beat her down. When girls in the school teased her about her face, or when someone made a tactless reference to it, she would stand before the mirror and look at herself with a scowl. The marks were quite deep in places and they had crinkled the surface on both the cheeks. She pushed her hair back with her hand and turned her face this way and that. Taking her face very close to the mirror, she pressed the dimpled skin with her finger. And then she took it away and lifting her chin upwards, looked at it from the line of her nose.

'Hunh!' she said in contempt of those who thought her ugly. She had a close look at herself and she could see how *pretty she* was.

'Eh, Arun,' she called out. 'You think I am ugly?'

Arun came and stood by her side in the big, long room, where Madhu slept, and where she had a dressing mirror.

'No, you're very beautiful.'

Arun did not say this to please her. He knew the marks had taken not a bit of her charm away. She had a skin a shade fairer than the rest, her eyes were huge and deep, and her nose was straighter and more pointed than that of anyone else. More than anything, she had an intelligence which outran others' like a prize race horse. There were infinite facets to her wit. She prodded, she bullied, she made fun. And all the time she was irreverent, all the time coming out with surprises. And she spoke not with her face alone, but with her whole body. Her limbs flashed and quivered, and she held her listeners spellbound. No, she took her face to be no handicap at all.

'You're very beautiful,' said Arun.

'Look at my nose,' she said playfully.

'True.'

'And my eyes.'

Arun was suspicious she was making fun of him; he was ever a little afraid of her.

He looked at her apprehensively. But he said: 'True.'

'And then there are no marks on your body,' said he seriously.

Madhu was amused by the tone of gravity in Arun's voice. Why did he have to sound so tragic in everything? He, poor boy, was only trying to reassure her. But as she heard his grave tone, and as she saw the earnest, pious look on his face, the devil was up in her and she forgot her anxiety about her looks.

'Aren't there any?' She watched him, full of mischief.

She went and lay on her bed and with utter casualness lifted her shirt and examined her stomach. Then she sat up, lifted the shirt further up in the rear and turning her body the other way said:

'See if there are any at the back?'

Her shirt was pulled up to her neck and Arun could see where her pearlike breasts sloped forward. He blushed, but said:

'No, there aren't.'

Turning her head, she smiled.

'Not one—anywhere?'

'No, nowhere.'

Madhu knew how blemishless her body was; she had gone over every inch of it carefully. The only havoc the disease had done was to the face. It was as if a storm had changed bearings midcourse and gone in a different direction.

'Run your hand down my back.'

Awkwardly, Arun ran his hand across parts of her back. She said: 'All the way, all the way—and slowly. From the neck downwards.'

Her face upwards and her eyes blankly open, she tried to give Arun the impression she was feeling for his hand to run over welts and wedges that might be pock marks. But she was smiling to herself.

'I'm telling you, there are no marks anywhere. Your skin is smooth like marble.'

Fed up with the joke, she quickly pulled the shirt down and facing Arun she caught hold of him in an embrace and gave him a big kiss on the mouth. 'Oh, I love you, Arun,' she said, breaking into a giggle. 'What are you laughing at?' asked Arun, confused.

One morning Arun saw she was wearing a kind of bandage over her groin and she did not remove it while she had her bath. Was she ill or something? Why the bandage?

He caught hold of her in the evening.

'Madhu, is something wrong with you these days?

'No!' She was surprised. 'Why?'

'Why are you wearing a bandage around your loins?'

'Eh—how do *you* know that?'

'I caught a glimpse of you while you were changing clothes in your room. It looked like it was a bandage—but maybe I was wrong.'

'No, it is a bandage.'

She burst into a loud, uncontrollable giggle. It was quite a while before she was able to calm down.

'All women wear such a bandage once a month.'

'Why?' Arun looked perplexed.

'You're very simple, aren't you?' she said,' continuing to giggle.

'Does it hurt?' Arun asked with much concern.

'No—look.' She caught hold of his hand and pressed it on her loins. Arun felt a wad of padded material coming in touch with his fingers. 'It doesn't hurt at all,' she was saying.

'But why wear it?'

'You will find out.' And with one bound she was running away from him, humming a popular tune.

One evening Arun found her looking at the stars. It was full moon, and the roof was bathed with the emerald light of the moon. No one knew where she was. Prabha Rani had spoiled her in her love. If she helped her with household work, it was fine, but if she stayed away, Prabha Rani did not summon her. She had matriculated from the local Arya Samaj girls' school a few years back and Lala Kanshi Ram did not suggest college for her. She did not ask for it, either. She was rather glad when the last of her exams was over. What she wanted was to run around wild. She had received no formal training in dance. But her body vibrated sensitively to any tune or word sung aloud. Taking an ordinary poem, she would cut it up into rhythmic word patterns, and was so excited by it she got up and swung her arms wide and with a swirl danced round and round on the floor as she chanted the lines.

It was late and Prabha Rani asked Arun to go and see if Madhu was in the next building.

Instead Arun found her on the roof—looking at the stars.

'Arun, what do you think those stars are?'

'They are burning gasses.' Arun was in the last year of school and reading physical sciences.

'Hunh, that's all you know! They are lovers, you silly.'

'Of whom?'

'Of the moon, of course.' And looking at the shining bright moon she stretched her body, locking her hands behind her back.

'So many?' asked Arun, laughing.

'Why not?' And she looked at Arun with a smile. 'A beloved as mysterious as the moon will always have many lovers.'

She came to Arun with a rush and dragging him by the arm took him to one of the cots.

'Arun, do you know any love songs?'

Arun fidgeted in nervousness at this abrupt change of the subject.

'Any popular film songs?' she prompted.

'You know I don't sing.'

'You must know some songs. Sing me one of those songs.'

'You know I don't sing.'

'Don't keep harping on that. Sing anything.'

Arun made contradictory gestures. He smiled and cleared his throat to sing, and then smiled again and remained quiet.

'I can't, Madhu.'

'Oh, come on—do you know the song by Sehgal where he says,

My love has run away with my heart
The spring is here but my love is not—?

Sing that to me.'

Before Arun could protest, she said:

'All right, let's sing it together.'

Holding his hand, she burst into the tune of the song and started singing. 'Come on—' she urged him, and Arun also sang a line. She slowly pulled Arun to herself and as they sang the lines:

'A great pain rises in my being
When I hear the koel in the garden cooing,'

she was singing with her cheek pressed close to his cheek.

They were rocking to the rhythm of the song. When she placed her cheek on his, Arun drew back from her nonplussed. He found her flesh burning hot and her breath blowing on his cheek like steam.

She took no notice when he had stopped. She continued on her own, as if possessed. With soft steps she danced away in a circle and then came back to where Arun stood. Now and then she looked at the moon, but for the most part her eyes were closed. Her face lit with the languor of desire—her eyes drooping, her lips pouting, her voice tremulous—she went on:

'What a face you have
What slender waist, what young age—
A new universe surely lies
In the confines of your two eyes.'

Arun was disturbed by the intensity of her feelings. He was also angry with her for singing love songs so unashamedly. He had grown up in a hierarchy where what counted was your duty, not emotions. This girl should be making chapatis downstairs with her mother. And here she was swaying dreamily, bewitched by some supernal power.

'It is a song sung by a *man* in praise of his woman friend.'

He tried to be as bitter and scathing as he could. He wanted to hurt her.

Madhu had finished the song but was still in the throes of its impact. She swung round briskly and opened her eyes as she heard Arun.

'What's the difference—I like it. Oh, you *are* a prude!'

'Go and help mother in cooking.'

'I won't. Who are you to command me? Take yourself away from here—begone!'

Prabha Rani heard their quarrel and shouted from below:

'Arun, leave her alone. I only wanted to know where she was. You come on down.'

Madhu loved collecting her girl friends in the house. They were mostly from Fort Street, but once in a while a girl came all the way from Mohalla Dharowal or from Kanak Mandi. They sat in a corner of the long room, or they sat on the roof. And what they mostly did was giggle. Arun would be straining his ears in his room to hear what they were saying, but all he caught was periodic outbursts of laughter. He made several trips from his room, pretending to be busy and rushing to get something from his father's room. They took very little notice of him. They looked up, and some of them flickered their eyelids and a few turned crimson to see a youth so near them, but they did not suspend their conversation. What irritated Arun was it was a conversation carried on in the lowest possible key. Even when he was passing through the room where they sat, he heard not a word. But suddenly they burst into a loud laugh. Mixed with the laughter he heard— 'That's right,' 'You don't say,' 'Believe me.' And then he heard nothing again until the next outburst.

The girls sat huddled closely. Madhu invariably sat in the centre. A few of the girls would have their arms around her neck, the others sat half leaning against her. They also were leaning on each other, to get their mouths close enough to each other to whisper. If Madhu decided to take them to the roof, they scrambled up the stairs in a rush. They came down the stairs in a rush too, their feet thudding. And they giggled and prodded each other in the side, until they were seated and the secret conversation was resumed.

Madhu did not sit there for long. It was impossible for her to be inactive or stationary. On the day they were coming she would be excited all morning, and would tell her mother what she should prepare for them. She rattled off a long list: pakoras, sweets, fresh apricots, cashew nuts, mango chutney. 'Why don't you prepare them yourself?' shouted Arun from his room. 'You mind your own business,' she shouted back. Going to her mother she hugged her hard. 'You will do this for me, ma, won't you?' Prabha Rani smiled and nodded.

When the friends arrived, she shrieked with joy each time. 'Malti!' 'Aren't you late, Kamini?' 'Neelam, Rekha, Kamlesh—oh, how nice!' Bubbling with enthusiasm she led them inside, and deluged them with questions. Her rippling voice could be heard all over the house. Having eaten, the group was quiet and the mysterious conversation, when you heard nothing but the giggles, would begin. But so vivacious was she, such a compulsive need there was in her to move, she repeatedly left them for brief moments. What was this strange noise in the street? And off she went to the balcony to see if anything was wrong. Or she darted into the kitchen and told her mother: 'Now, ma, don't call me when I'm sitting with my friends.' Or she came to Arun's door, and parting the curtains peeped inside. 'What is it?' asked Arun in irritation. 'Nothing—just wanted to see how you were doing,' she said with her sweetest smile, feeling immensely good towards the world. In a second she frisked back to her friends, where she bodily threw herself in their midst, often falling on purpose on top of some of them and shrieking the loudest in laughter along with the rest.

'Why don't you introduce me to some of your friends?' Arun asked her.

'You?'

'Yes. Me.'

She broke into a breezy laughter, covering her mouth with the palm of her hand.

'Why, what's wrong with me?' Arun was much hurt.

'Well, you're only a *boy*. You don't have to be introduced. You just come along when they are here and talk to them.

'But I want you to introduce me properly. You tell them who I am.'

Madhu looked at Arun. There was sweat on his forehead and he was blushing. Impulsively, she put her arms around him and kissed him on the cheek.

'All right, my sweet, don't blush. Next time I'll lead you up to them as the Prince Charming of the family.'

'Who's blushing?'

And Madhu it was who first presented Arun to girls as a suitor. One close look at him and she knew what he wanted. She had taken his presence for granted, and thought of him as nothing more than a small lad. She saw the boy had grown up. He had a mustache and the shadow of a beard on his face; there were pimples of youth on his nose and cheeks. 'Which one would you like to meet especially?' she asked, winking at him like an expert courtesan. And she laughed mischievously and said 'Aha, aha!' when he wanted to switch from one girl to another. He tortured himself to no end. He wanted to be constant in his love, he wanted to love one of these girls for *life*. And yet his fancy hardly let him stay with any single one for more than a few weeks. Now it was the girl with the long pigtail, now the one with pimples, now the plump one, now the one who had such black eyes. Madhu laughed, her red tongue flickering in her mouth like the tongue of a snake. 'Why not?' she said.

Arun was not attracted to Nur in those days. She was a regular visitor at their house. But she was much younger than he, and

Madhu treated her as a little girl. It was the older girls—older than he—that haunted him then. What worried him was he could not be constant. Was he an evil boy?

'On the contrary, you're too naive,' said Madhu, when he confided his fears to her.

She wouldn't take him seriously, this sister of his, for even now she was laughing.

'What do you mean?' His eyes had sunk in their sockets in his anxiety.

'You worry too much. Meet anyone you like. But at least say something to her when you are with her.'

'I do say something.'

'Oh, you know what I mean. Don't talk only of your course subjects and your teachers. Say something else.'

Once again she winked at him in her most lascivious manner, and raising her hand, with the forefinger and the thumb closed in a circle and the other three fingers straight up, she shook it at him as a gesture of solidarity with him.

No, Arun too, like his father, could not understand her. She was so sure of herself, so imperious, so animated, also so very frivolous. It was difficult to hold her attention for long, and when she was listening to you her eyes would be wandering all over. She had so light a step you could not hear her walk. She would suddenly descend on you, and then as suddenly depart. Her hands, her limbs, her shoulders or her hips were in constant motion when she was pretending to be standing. She seemed ever calling out to someone or ever being summoned. Frequently she raised her eyes to look in different directions. There was hope in them and expectation. 'The girl is too impulsive,' Arun heard his father say disparagingly. 'She's also so rare, so intuitive!' said Prabha Rani.

One night Madhu went and lay with Arun in his bed. In the past she used often to do that, though she had not come for a long while. It was after a fight she had stopped. She persisted in treating Arun as a little boy, and while she came to him and holding him in her arms talked to him of all kinds of subjects, she expected him only to listen. She got annoyed with him at the slightest interruption. At times she snubbed him if he as much as moved in the bed. 'Stay still, will you?' she demanded. 'Can't I get a word in, too?' asked Arun, when he was old enough to insist. 'No.' 'Why?' 'Because you don't know a thing about life, that's why.' 'In that case I won't let you come to my bed.' 'Aha!' she sniggered, throwing the cover off and getting out of the bed in one bound. 'You should feel grateful I come and enlighten your dull mind.' 'Keep your enlightenment to yourself,' Arun shouted after her as she marched out of the room.

That was the last time. No peace offers were made from either side and this pleasant pastime of brother and sister had ceased. They had indulged in it from early days, from the days when Arun couldn't sleep at night. When he called to his mother, she either did not come, or came only briefly to pat him. With tears in his eyes he approached Madhu one night, who agreed to lie with him until he was asleep. Years passed and Arun no longer needed her to go to sleep. But she now came to keep him *awake*—and to talk. And the crazy being she was, she talked of such unconnected things! Why people got old? What was death? Pleasure of love was obvious, but did he know what the pain of love was? And if once—if ever as much as once—Arun offered a reply, she shut him up right away. Now he must not interrupt her. He must only listen. What did he know about life, anyway?

It was a cold December night. It was amavas—the night of the new moon—and you couldn't see a thing. Arun knew before she entered the bed that she was in his room.

'All right, you can talk too. Now move over.'

The appeasement was unnecessary. Two years had passed since the quarrel. Arun may have been a child at fourteen. But at sixteen he was seven inches taller, his voice had lost its squeaky tenor and had become heavier, and hadn't Madhu herself introduced him to several of her girl friends? He was a man now, and he had to be listened to.

'It's cold, isn't it? Come closer.' As she shivered, she pressed the quilt hard on her side.

Madhu was lying on her back. Arun was on his side, facing her. He had his arm around her belly, exactly the way he had had it for years in the past. There was a difference of four years between them. Arun was four, when he first became conscious of fear at night, and when he persuaded Madhu to go and sleep with him. Madhu was then eight. It remained a wonder for his young brain he couldn't catch up with her in years; she ever remained a little ahead of him. He tried hard but when he became eight, she was twelve; when he became ten, she was fourteen; when he became fourteen, she was eighteen.

Today too he was four years younger than she, but for the first time he was bigger in size and physically more powerful. In former years they used to wrestle, she always throwing him to the ground—once smashing his head against the floor so hard the blood came. She also openly boxed his ears. There was no doubt who would win if they were to fight today. He was tall and strong and she lay in his arms like a delicate vine.

'Arun,' she asked as soon they were comfortably settled. 'You still want to know why women wear a bandage once a month?'

Arun did not speak.

'I'm sure you know the answer by now.'

'I don't,' said Arun, blushing in the dark and hiding his head inside the quilt.

'You don't?'

'No, I don't.'

'Eh, you're an absolute budhu.'

Arun laughed self-consciously.

'Women are very dirty for these days.' She extended her hand in the dark and boxed his ears as she used to when he was a boy of twelve.

'Why?'

'Don't know. But they bleed profusely.'

'From where?'

'From their private parts, from where else? Now don't ask me dirty questions!'

Arun had a sensation of his inside going hot.

'You shouldn't go near a woman in such days.'

Arun had not thought of that.

'I've no pains, but some women pain horribly.'

'Why?'

'Oh, shut up, why, why, why, all the time!'

Realizing she was reverting to her old moody self, she relented and kissed Arun on the forehead. 'Sorry, I'm awful.'

And she restlessly turned to the side away from Arun. Looking up through the window, she said:

'It's so dark. But how bright the stars are!'

'Where is their beloved, the moon?' asked Arun gallantly, reminding himself of their old conversation.

Madhu heaved a sigh, as if to say she did not know where she was. Then she laughed all of a sudden and said:

'She has run away with her brother!'

Arun pretended to laugh with her, but the subject was dropped. After a while she turned towards him again. They were now facing each other and Madhu's breasts were touching Arun and her small foot was lying on top of his foot. It sent wild tremors through Arun's body, but Madhu appeared to be indifferent.

'Arun,' she asked after a while. 'Do you know what a man and a woman do to each other when they get married?'

'Somewhat.'

'What somewhat? How much?'

She did not pursue this either. In her restlessness, with much fuss and flutter, she moved away from Arun to the other side, and then, before she was settled in that position, as restlessly moved back to where she was before—facing Arun.

'Arun, let's rub noses.'

'Noses?'

Arun was getting muddled. He ever mistrusted her, but today she was absolutely wild.

'Yes, you silly, this fat dumpling you have on your face. Rub it against my nose.'

And before he knew it, Madhu was gently rubbing the tip of her nose against his. Arun felt very hot in the face and strange currents ran through his groin. A drowsiness seemed to be creeping over him, when the rest of his surroundings, the house, the room, the bed on which they were lying, fell apart and sank into oblivion. The only reality of which he remained aware was Madhu. Of the warmth of her flesh, the softness of her breath, the musk of her skin as she rubbed his nose. And of a gentle pressure of her hand at his back.

'Let's touch tongues.'

By now Arun was inundated with emotions, and he found himself too weak to speak. Indeed, to his alarm, he discovered his tongue had already slipped out of his mouth and was lying on the hot and wet tongue of Madhu.

The next instant, Madhu shot out of bed like a bolt. 'Arai, baba, I must go! It's getting late,' she said with a heavy voice which did not seem to come from her larynx, and ran out of the room.

Arun was nervous to look at her the following day. What labyrinth was she leading him through last night? After all, she was his sister, his *real* sister. Or was she only making a fool of him, still treating him as an urchin?

Madhu had already forgotten the night, when she met him in the day. It was as though she had never visited him in his bed—or if she had, there was nothing sinister in it. She was bursting with energy. She had been up for a while, for she had been to the toilet, had brushed her teeth, and was looking for her jump rope to exercise with. When Arun tried to slip past her, without looking at her and without saying hello to her, she stopped him. 'Arun, are you ill?' 'No.' 'But you look ill! Anyway have you seen my jump rope?' It always went like that. She would say the most cutting things occasionally to her mother or to Isher Kaur or to Arun, but when she met them next she had already shed that memory. She would be smiling and she put her arms around you in an overflow of affection. Of all the persons Arun had known, she had the least sense of remorse. Also she was the most impetuous, the most animated, the most spontaneous. 'Oh, where is my jump rope?' she yelled at the top of her voice, wanting her parents in the other room to hear her. 'She's a thing of the wild; she should have been born in a forest,' Lala Kanshi Ram said disapprovingly to Prabha Rani. Meanwhile Madhu yelled again—'I've got it! Out of my way,' she waved to Arun impatiently. And removing her headgear, she started skipping, making neat little circles with the rope and deftly stepping over it. And she counted: 'One, two, three, four, five...'

She was married in March of the same winter. Her husband was a reader in the civil court at Wazirabad and for days before the wedding she talked of nothing else but that. Of her parents she asked, what is a reader? How many men has he under him? Does he have a government house? How big is the house? And later, bit by bit she passed this information on to her friends, savouring every single word she spoke.

Arun felt the house very empty after Madhu left. For days he carried the image of her clad in red bridal clothes in his mind. He had at no time questioned her beauty—in spite of the pock marks. On the wedding day, with all that gold and the jewels on her and the cowrie shells around her wrists, she looked radiant. Most of her facial marks were submerged under the make-up, and the rest added maturity to her girlish bearing. For once in her life she was looking shy—no, not shy—she was looking apprehensive, and walked with downcast eyes. But the longing in her for the unknown, for the new life awaiting her, was too pronounced and her movements were brisk and sprightly. Arun had seen young brides weep profusely when they got into the carriage which took them away from their parents' house. Madhu too wept—and fairly loudly—but soon she dried her tears, and after embracing her mother and father, resolutely closed the curtains of the carriage on them all.

Arun never saw his sister happy after that. Her body rounded and she put on weight, and her face, in place of the raw, rough look of an unwedded girl, acquired the seasoned look of a woman who has known physical passion. But her laughter deserted her, and she lost the lilt in her voice. She visited with them at Sialkot only infrequently. And when she came, she refused to see her friends and sat idly the whole day long on her bed, speaking to no one.

Arun's memories of those years were hazy. He was making his way through college. Each time he met her, she looked more wilted and weary. Her husband was a reserved, thinnish man, with a toothbrush mustache, and he wore heavy-rimmed glasses. Arun found it difficult to establish any communication with him. Lala Kanshi Ram and Prabha Rani did no better. Arun saw his mother often comforting Madhu. He also saw his father, who used to be so impatient with her, sitting meditatively for long periods next to her.

Two years must have passed since her marriage, when Arun said to her:

'Madhu, I didn't think you would quit smiling.'

'I haven't,' she smiled. It was a faint voice and the smile remained faded.

'What is it, Madhu?'

Arun knew what would force her to answer, a frontal attack on her personality.

'Does your husband nag you for those pock marks?'

'No!' And she was really smiling. 'The women in his household sometimes have. But not he. He finds them exciting!'

'What is it, then?'

'I don't seem to bear a child,' she said sadly.

'Have you taken medical advice?'

'We have.'

'Does it matter so much?'

'It seems to, to my husband. And to his family.'

Arun went into a mock fighting pose, his fist held in front of his face.

'Fight them back, Madhu.'

'I've tried. But for my husband's family it's a grave want in me, Arun—I'm barren!'

She was running her fingers through his hair, but there was no force in those fingers.

Only very recently, since February last, was there a revival of Madhu's spirits. It transpired they had decided to adopt a child, and this brightened the whole atmosphere. It was such a simple solution. Arun wondered why they had not thought of it earlier. Prabha Rani claimed the credit for suggesting it to them, but Arun believed it was Madhu's own idea. One of her husband's married sisters was expecting a child in November. They had several other children, and promises were made this child would be handed over to Madhu and Rajiv. That appeased the husband's family considerably. And it transformed Madhu's life altogether.

And she became exceedingly superstitious—she who was such a sceptic. She went to temple every day and observed all types of religious fasts. She was last in Sialkot in April, and she defended herself when Arun made fun of her. How come the sun stood stationary with nothing to hold it up? Were the earth and the moon and the stars made out of nothing? And who fed the sparrow in the nest or the worm in the mud? Now there *had to* be a maker of this vast drama, and surely there was nothing beyond the power of this maker. Maybe she could have had a child of her own if she had been devotional enough. And anyway, Arun had only read books. What did he know about life?

It was in this mood Madhu and her husband had agreed to go to the Vaishno Devi temple in Kashmir state in the coming September. It was a famed temple and people came to it from afar. The mother, the goddess Vaishno Devi, offered benedictions in a mysterious way, and many barren women who had adopted children were later blessed by her with children of their own. Even if that didn't happen, it was necessary to seek the mother's blessings for the child they were going to adopt. The argument was sound and Rajiv had agreed to it.

When the communal situation became serious, Lala Kanshi Ram wrote to them to join him in Sialkot. They were going on the pilgrimage in September. Why not come right now and stay on until after the pilgrimage? Wazirabad was only a small town and what protection did they have there? And then Lala Kanshi Ram saw how defenceless he himself was, with all his 'connections'—with his friends in the Muslim community and in the police. So he stopped urging. They had received no letters from her since the beginning of August. They had waited every day for some news. They wrote repeatedly. They made enquiries through Muslim friends of Chaudhri Barkat Ali. They made enquiries from people who came from Wazirabad. But no, there was no news at all. And now the news had come.

Arun looked at Chandni as she slept peacefully through the night. Her small breasts were gently moving up and down. Up they went, down they came. Attracted by an irresistible force, Arun crawled up to her and lay next to her. The tent was divided into two halves. On one side, slept Lala Kanshi Ram, Prabha Rani and Arun. In the middle were the two poles. On the other side slept Padmini and Chandni. On that side was also the kitchen, where they cooked their food.

Arun knew how foolhardy he was being. There had been a death in the family. There were other persons in the tent. But he was for the moment oblivious of everything. What he saw was the inimitable, slender figure of Chandni, stretched out lightly in front of him. She made no movement where she lay, as if someone had put her there after she had gone to sleep. Only her breasts moved up and down. Up and down, up and down. Without a pause. Up they went. Down they came. Her breath escaped through her nostrils ever so softly. Up and down went the breasts. In went the rustling breath, out came the soft rustle. Her collar bones shone dimly under her yellow skin, but that made the breathing all the more palpable. Outside, in the dark of the pre-dawn, no one was moving about in the lane, and far above, the sky too had a vibrating, pulsating quality about it. It was dark but it was getting on to be grey. And there was an unmistakable tremor in the change of that shade, as if the sky too were breathing. No, Madhu had gone, but life was continuous. The sky and the earth as ever were throbbing with possibilities. Right now, this minute. Death had hit them, and yet all around him was the flow of a force which would not be brought to an end. It was the continuity of life. It was the continuity of the will in the being of things. And never had this urge for survival, for self-assertion, manifested itself in Arun so powerfully as at this time of death. It was as if he would himself perish otherwise. He suddenly felt he needed a meal; he felt enormously hungry. Squirm though he did at the thought of it, the feeling of hunger grew upon him. The cells of his body were asserting their own reflex want, made more pronounced in the face of death. And there came upon him another kind of overwhelming desire. Again he felt mortified, again he felt guilty. He had been taught to deny himself. In renunciation alone, was he told, lay the key to man's happiness. Yet this minute he did not want to deny himself, he wanted to do no renouncing. Instead his entire being, body and soul, longed for fulfilment. In perpetuation alone lay his redemption, he seemed to think. In spite of Madhu. Or maybe because of her.

He lay next to Chandni and he wanted to hold her in his arms. He was certain now. Within the confines of that breathing body lay the antidote to Madhu. No, not antidote. That was only forgetfulness. And he didn't want forgetfulness, he wanted continuity. Yes, that was it. In the confines of her tender form lay the secret to the eternity of living. He had to enter it somehow and get hold of it. Perhaps Nur held that secret, too. But Nur—she seemed so far beyond his reach. No, she was only a chimera. What was certainty was Chandni, lying only a few inches away from him.

Raising himself on his elbows, he placed a hand firmly on one of Chandni's breasts and planted a kiss on her open lips.

Chandni woke with a start and sat up. It took her some seconds to know where she was. Even then she didn't quite know she had been kissed or touched on the breast. What she knew was there had been an intrusion. She was sleeping peacefully, her inner self was coiled up on its centre and was holding a spirited dialogue with her other self, the physical self, when there had been an interruption. It was something in the nature of violation, for she had immediately recoiled against it. What *was* it?

In panic her eyes wandered about the tent. She found Arun reclining next to her—and in alarm she shrank away from him. Her lips moved and she said: 'Thou.' But no sound came out of the lips.

Arun put his finger to his lips to silence her. At the same time he took hold of her hand.

So unexpected was this gesture of his she at once looked around to see if the others were watching them. She also attempted to withdraw her hand.

Arun held tight to her. He found his heart welling up, his emotions totally engulfing him. Now was the moment and should he let it slip? For years he had tortured himself about it. Now, now he was close enough to unravelling the mystery. His eyes were fixed on her breasts, which were this minute heaving fast in frenzy. Yes, it was right there. Somewhere inside. The entry might be denied to him but shouldn't he make himself clear? The time, the place and the loved one might not come together in a similar configuration again!

Trying not to alarm her, he looked into her eyes and said feebly:

'I love you, Chandni.'

'You must be mad,' she said, her eyes going wide in surprise.

CHAPTER 2

MADHU's death crushed Lala Kanshi Ram's will and he now insisted they leave for India at the earliest possible occasion. Arun had a unique opportunity of knowing his father these months. He had always dreaded him a little. He thought he was a bully; exceedingly intelligent and resourceful, he got his way in the end, no matter what the opposition. But one after the other many adverse things befell him these three months; circumstances in which he was a loser. And yet not once did Lala Kanshi Ram acknowledge defeat. He was benumbed by the event, he fretted, but in the next instant Arun could see him pulling his shoulders up. And there was something lofty in the tenacity with which he clung to the hope of staying on in Sialkot. Like the cornered Oedipus, he followed lead after lead. He put his faith in the local administration. He trusted the police. He trusted the army. He trusted the leaders, when they said don't leave your homes.

For the past month, since their arrival in the refugee camp, he had put his trust in General Rees. General Rees was the Commander-in-Chief of the Punjab Boundary Force which was set up in August to protect the minorities in the Punjab. It was drawn from men of the Indian army, coming from all the three communities, Muslim, Sikh and Hindu. What impressed Lala Kanshi Ram about it was that its commander was an Englishman—as were some of its officers. Now surely the white sahibs knew what they were about. An Indian had a woolly mind, he said one thing and did another. But General Rees had declared categorically no harm would be allowed to come to the minorities. Unless the world was coming to an end, an Englishman could not be taken lightly. He had to be obeyed.

And yet, one after the other, all of Lala Kanshi Ram's trusts had come to nothing. Each passing day narrowed further his chances of living in the land he loved so much. What the leaders of India were offering the people of the Punjab was an enormous bluff, he felt. They had neither the power nor the intention of maintaining the minorities in their homes; they had not the power of saving their lives. They should have devised means of mass migration to begin with, before rushing to partition. Now they should at least keep their mouths shut and not mislead the poor, credulous people. Jinnah and Nehru were villains enough. This President of the Indian National Congress—and adjusting his spectacles, Lala Kanshi Ram, checked his name in the newspaper—Kripalani, was the worst offender. More than the others, it was he who was so loud about the minorities staying where they were.

What in the end broke Lala Kanshi Ram's heart was the inability of the Boundary Force under General Rees to maintain peace in the province. An Englishman unable to keep law and order! Lala Kanshi Ram reeled when he thought of it. It was like the sun rising in the West. He soon saw how helpless Rees Sahib was, though. Most of his men and officers were Indians, and they had their separate communal loyalties. These loyalties were openly and unashamedly expressed, and Lala Kanshi Ram heard innumerable accounts of how the minorities in East Punjab and West Punjab were slaughtered while men of the Boundary Force looked on. In such a vicious atmosphere, what could one or a few Englishmen do?

That brought Lala Kanshi Ram to the end of his hopes. Desperately he looked around, desperately he searched his mind, if there was something else he might hang on to. There was nothing. The two new governments were parties to the fratricidal war, and how could unarmed men and women withstand organized slaughter? The death of Madhu was the last blow to his shattered psyche. He now did not want to consider the possibility of staying.

What stirred Arun was the nobility with which his father took his defeat. Prabha Rani, for days after the news of Madhu's death, refused to speak with anyone. Lala Kanshi Ram gave no external expression to his grief. There were many other families which had been hit in the camp, and a new kind of caste system had grown up. Everyone had lost property. That was nothing. But if you had lost a limb, or if a member of your family had been killed or raped or forcibly abducted, you won a medal for yourself. Your neighbours in the camp spoke to you deferentially, the Camp Commandant was ready to receive you in a personal interview, and in the matter of dry rations or other physical facilities you straightway received a preferential treatment. Not that the others were out to atone for what fate had done to you. Only you wouldn't let them forget for a second that while everyone had suffered, you had suffered the most. You stopped people on the road, you descended on them while they were about to have their meals, you wept your way through to officers' quarters. And you demanded—and willy nilly were given—a slightly superior status.

Lala Kanshi Ram went nowhere near this exclusive club of sufferers. He was not an introvert. He liked meeting people and talking to them. But after Madhu's death, he withdrew himself into a shell. Even to members of his own group he spoke in monosyllables. The only thing he did not give up was his prayer. Morning and evening, he still sat diligently before the picture of Lord Krishna and saw to it that Prabha Rani and Arun joined him each time; nay, Padmini and Chandni too, since they lived in the same tent with them. And he omitted not a single hymn, not a single line of any hymn, as he sang before the Lord. If anything, Arun observed, he became more engrossed in the 'silent' prayer which followed the singing. Once the hymns were over, they were supposed to close their eyes, spread out their arms in supplication, and quietly pray. Arun yawned all the way through the singing, but this part was a real ordeal to him. With his hands uplifted, his eyes closed, his father kept muttering for a much longer time, and Arun saw on his face, like a caravan passing, a whole fleet of emotions. Yes—that, certainly. But Arun did not see him ask a single favour of a mortal being because his daughter had died in the riots. Rather, he found him become indifferent to the generosity of others, even suspicious of that generosity.

When he wanted company, he sought Arun out, and the two of them went for long walks. Even here Lala Kanshi Ram did not use the opportunity to talk about Madhu. If Arun talked of her, Lala Kanshi Ram closed the subject. 'It is a question of one's karmas,' he said calmly. And then minutes later, while they would be talking of something else, something totally unrelated, Arun saw him stop in the walk and turn his face furtively aside. Surreptitiously, furtively, like a thief he lifted a corner of his shirt and wiped his eyes. Before Arun, he displayed nothing.

Yet something in him was extinguished, and he insisted they leave for India at once. It was the end of August. The authorities had at last awakened to the necessity of shifting the minorities. After the Boundary Commission's award was announced on the seventeenth of August, everyone knew where he stood—on a part of Pakistan, or of India. Violence in the Punjab reached an unprecedented pitch after the announcement of the award. Both sides felt they had been shabbily treated. The Sikhs were angry to lose fertile lands in the Montgomery area: much to their surprise, the boundary line, but for a small sector along the river Ravi, was drawn along the Sutlej river. The Muslims were aggrieved over the award of sections of Gurdaspur district to India, which gave India a contiguous border with Kashmir state. Sir Cyril Radcliffe, the British chairman of the Boundary Commission, had taken the first plane out of India on the fifteenth of August—two days before the award was announced. It was an impossible assignment; to cut a country in two in five weeks' time, especially when your fellow Indian judges on the Commission were warring with each other on communal grounds. He had ignored their rival claims, and as impartially as he could divided the country—and then left, leaving it to the communal parties to fight it out among themselves.

Eventually the two governments made arrangements to transport the minorities from one side to the other. People cornered in way out areas like Peshawar or other parts of the North West Frontier Province were airlifted to cities in East Punjab. The rest were moved by train. Or they were moved in convoys on foot.

The chaos was so absolute neither of the governments knew what rights and privileges it had in the area of the other. In most refugee camps, dry rations, like flour or lentils, were given out free to the refugees for their daily use by the authorities. After the fifteenth of August, the two governments argued about the cost. During the month of August, armed escorts for the refugees were provided by the Boundary Force. Now they were made the responsibility of each government, and units of the army were sent from one side to the other to cover their respective refugees. In case no troops arrived from the other side by the time a convoy or a train was ready to pull out, the local troops provided halfhearted protection. If the troops of the other government did arrive, every impediment was placed in their way by the local authorities to prevent them from functioning effectively.

The shortest route out of Sialkot was through the state of Kashmir. The Kashmir border was only ten miles away, but that particular exit was closed to the refugees. India and Pakistan were quarrelling over Kashmir and Pakistan had moved troops up to the border. The entire stretch of ten miles to the border was in the hands of the army and civilians were not allowed there. Refugee trains off and on ran from Sialkot to Wazirabad, and from there to Amritsar by way of Lahore. Prabha Rani said she could not face passing through Wazirabad, after Madhu's death there. That left them the direct route from Sialkot to Amritsar. Amritsar was eighty-two miles from Sialkot by that route, and the India-Pakistan border fell at about forty-four miles along the way, near a town called Dera Baba Nanak.

For some reason, which Lala Kanshi Ram could not understand, the Pakistani authorities ran no refugee trains from Sialkot to Dera Baba Nanak. There was talk of foot convoys, and Lala Kanshi Ram made enquiries every day as to when the first convoy would leave. He wanted to be in that convoy along with his family.

One evening Lala Kanshi Ram and Arun were returning to the camp after their walk, when Arun was struck by a familiar military figure inspecting the guard at the camp gate.

It was a tall, lean man, with a hawk-like nose and heavy, bristling mustache, neatly waxed and twirled at the corners. He was wearing the usual olive green of the army, and had a revolver strapped to his belt. The man was thin, but his long arms were sinewy and his hands were big and bony.

As he went round looking at the group of soldiers who were lined up at attention, Arun found something familiar in his bearing.

'Rahmat-Ullah!' Arun said to himself.

It certainly was Rahmat-Ullah Khan, an old classmate of Arun's at Murray College, who had accepted a temporary commission in the Second World War, in 1944. While the Congress urged the students to boycott the war, the youngsters considered it attractive enough to join as officers. Temporary commissions in the three arms of the service, the navy, the army, and the air force, were widely advertised. Rahmat-Ullah was one of those who were selected for the army. It was useless for the national-minded students like Arun and Munir to berate him. When he returned to the college on his first leave, he was wearing a well-cut uniform and looked so smart all the girls in the college had their eyes on him.

Rahmat-Ullah Khan too recognized Arun.

'Now, now, hello, Arun,' he said, dismissing the squad and walking towards Arun.

Arun took Rahmat-Ullah Khan's hand and embraced him in a gush of feelings.

'You seem to be a big officer now, Rahmat-Ullah.'

Rahmat-Ullah Khan winced somewhat at the familiarity.

'Yes, I'm a captain. Actually, I have just been posted as Camp Commandant of this camp.'

'But have you opted for the Pakistani army or the Indian army?'

Captain Rahmat-Ullah smiled. To him it was an unnecessary question.

'For the Pakistani, to be sure,' he said with some emphasis.

'How long have you been in this camp?' asked Captain Rahmat-Ullah Khan.

'Since the beginning of August.'

Turning towards his father, Arun said: 'This is my father.'

Captain Rahmat-Ullah Khan smiled at him and gave him an army salute.

There was an unquiet pause. Arun and Rahmat-Ullah knew each other at college, but they were not particularly intimate. Now they were on the opposite sides of a fence.

'Are you comfortable here?' asked Captain Rahmat-Ullah Khan. Realizing how facetious the question was, he added without giving Arun a chance to speak: 'Is there anything I can do for you?'

Arun looked at his father.

'We should like to leave for Dera Baba Nanak in the first convoy that is organized.'

A crowd of camp inmates had collected around them, but Captain Rahmat-Ullah Khan did not show uneasiness. Relaxed, tall, with a slight stoop in his back, as though a part of his body were resting on another part of it, he stood looking at Arun and Lala Kanshi Ram in a leisurely manner.

'You see, I took charge of the camp only this morning and know nothing about it. Is there talk of a convoy? Look, why don't you come and see me in my office. You see that building'—and he pointed to a row of army barracks a few hundreds yards away. 'That's where I am. Come and see me, and I'll be glad to help.'

'All right,' said Arun.

'What lane are you in?'

'In lane twenty-five. We're half way down the lane.'

'Come and see me.'

Captain Rahmat-Ullah Khan gave a general salute to the whole group, and bringing his long, flowing body out of its lazy stoop, smartly walked away to a jeep which stood nearby. The guards at the gate presented arms to him and in contrast to his earlier relaxed pose, he returned the salute with lightning alertness. Arun saw a part of his mustache quiver and a strange shine in his eyes.

'He is the new Commandant Sahib,' said several voices after the jeep had left.

A number of people came forward to ask Arun to intercede on their behalf. Some wanted extra rations of sugar. Some had no kerosene for the lamps. Some complained against the rudeness of their neighbours and wanted to move into different tents. All at once Arun found himself a minor celebrity.

Lala Kanshi Ram could not resist the temptation of playing his old role as a spokesman of others. First he looked at the group with a beaming face, almost saying though they were possibly not aware of it, the young man they were talking to was his *son*. And then he told Arun, with a flourish:

'See if you can help them, son.'

It was a short-lived flourish. They knew they had troubles enough of their own, and Lala Kanshi Ram lapsed into gloomy silence as they walked back to their tent.

Arun went and saw Captain Rahmat-Ullah Khan early the next morning. For a while he was afraid the Captain might take out his revolver on some pretext and shoot him. That would be one Hindu less for Pakistan. Then he laughed at his fears.

For the few minutes Arun was with Captain Rahmat-Ullah Khan, he saw men walking swiftly, turning and saluting smartly, and observing a decorum even while a file was being placed on the table or when it was being removed. Rahmat-Ullah Khan received Arun with courtesy. He offered him a chair and asked his orderly to get a cup of tea for him. He then sent for his Subedar Major who gave him details of the refugee movements.

It seemed there would be no convoy for Dera Baba Nanak before the end of September. They had to wait for the arrival of Indian troops to escort the convoy, and they were only hoping to get a contingent large enough by then. A small batch was coming next week, which would escort a train to Wazirabad. Why not go that way? Arun explained his family's objections. In the conversation it came out that Arun had lost his sister. Arun was surprised Captain Rahmat-Ullah Khan expressed no special sympathy. He said he was sorry, in English—but that was routine. He did not condemn the communal killings. Rather, he sat stonily in his chair staring at the wall above Arun's head, as if he saw on that blank wall explicitly spelled out a justification for what was happening. He assured Arun, though, that he and his parents and other members of their group would be included in the foot convoy to Dera Baba Nanak. He also promised to give them every other assistance they might need.

Two days later, on a sunny afternoon, Captain Rahmat-Ullah Khan appeared at Lala Kanshi Ram's tent. He had several members of his staff with him. He told Arun he was inspecting the camp.

Captain Khan was in his olive green uniform. Arun and Lala Kanshi Ram came out of the tent and stood by his side. Suraj Prakash came from the adjacent tent and joined them.

While answering questions, Arun saw Captain Rahmat-Ullah Khan's glance fall on Sunanda. She was sitting outside the tent on a seat improvised out of wooden boxes, and was combing the hair of her daughter, Bhavna.

Arun saw the Captain halt in the middle of a sentence.

Suraj Prakash had asked him: 'Sir, we hear Muslim refugees from Bihar have moved into our houses in Fort Street. Who is going to collect the rent for us from them?'

For a second Arun thought Suraj Prakash was being insolent. Any talk of ownership of property or rent was ridiculous in the present conditions.

Arun thought maybe Suraj was letting steam off by being rude.

When he looked at Suraj he had his usual idiotic grin on his face, and he knew it was beyond him to be intelligently critical. He was not the least concerned with property or with money. Life for him was a tamasha, a showplace, and it wouldn't matter to him if they lost the little Bibi Amar Vati had been able to salvage. While earlier he spent freely, these days he was happy if he could have a few rupees for his cigarettes.

No, Arun saw he wasn't being flippant. In his own way he was trying to flatter the Camp Commandant—by showing him how important he considered him. He had his eyes on the shining stars on the shoulders of the Captain, and he seemed to be filled with wonder.

Captain Rahmat-Ullah was amused at the question. He saw the man looked foolishly happy, and this added to his amusement.

'It will be for the government of Pakistan to decide—' he began, gesturing with his bony hand towards the horizon.

It was then he saw Sunanda. His eyes remained rivetted on her for several seconds.

Collecting himself, he continued: 'It will be for the government of Pakistan to decide that. Surely there must be property left by Muslims in India. There will have to be adjustments made. Frankly this is not my Province—I'm a soldier.'

While he spoke to Suraj Prakash, his eyes drifted again towards Sunanda, who, with her shoulders bent back a little, was pulling her girl towards herself and doing her hair into a pigtail.

Suraj Prakash wouldn't have understood Captain Rahmat-Ullah's argument. He was paying absolutely no attention to what he was saying. He was happy the Camp Commandant was talking to him. And while the Captain spoke, he continued saying, 'Yes—yes—I see—' as if he was following every single word of the Captain. He still had the stupid grin on his face.

Arun received a note from the Captain that evening, asking him to come and have tea with him at his residence. He wrote he was sending his jeep to pick him up.

Prabha Rani was against his going. What business had he to mix with a Muslim? They had killed her daughter. They might kill him too. And above all this man looked too hedonistic—Arun should stay away from him.

Arun laughed at what his mother said. He remembered how in Murray College Rahmat-Ullah was known as an 'Ashiq'—an eternal lover. He was the most gaudily dressed man in the whole college. He came in fancy sports jackets and brightly polished shoes, and instead of a tie he usually wore a scarf, always an expensive silk one and in screaming colours and patterns. Even then he sported a bristling mustache. And the number of romances he boasted of! He said he had a sweetheart in each nook and corner of the city. He was certainly seen with a few girls once or twice, but usually he was seen on his own, sighing with his hand on his heart and quoting from Mirza Ghalib. He was extremely intelligent and came from a well-connected family of skin merchants. He was also at least five years older than the average student in the class. After high school he joined his family business, but finding it uninspiring left it for the exciting life of a college, leaving that in turn for the more exciting life of the army. His classmates were afraid to make fun of him in his presence; they were inhibited by his age and intelligence. But behind his back they referred to him only as Ashiq Sahib, and they winked at each other with much glee.

'Don't worry, ma, I won't let him corrupt me,' said Arun laughing.

'As if you know the ways of such men,' said she, adjusting her sari around her head.

'Let him go. Press for an early convoy, Arun,' said Lala Kanshi Ram.

Captain Rahmat-Ullah Khan lived in a small bungalow next to the barracks where his office was. The jeep took Arun over there in a few minutes, and as it came to a neat halt by the porch, Captain Rahmat-Ullah Khan came out on to the verandah.

'Come on in, Arun,' said he as he shook his hand. He was dressed in civvies: a raw silk half-sleeved shirt, white trousers, neatly polished moccasins. He was also wearing a scarf—a light green one—in spite of the heat.

Arun liked him better in this dress; he looked less formidable. Warmly he took his hand and walked through the door the orderly was holding open for them.

'You don't live with your parents in the city?'

'Not practical. I have to be on the spot twenty-four hours a day, and this is more convenient.'

'When were you posted here?'

'I've been in the Cantonment since independence. But I took charge of the camp the day I met you.'

'Are you now married?'

'No, still single. Or so they think,' he winked at Arun. 'And you?'

'You have seen. Not yet.'

'It is better to love than to wed...'

And smiling, Rahmat-Ullah Khan quoted from Mirza Ghalib:

'The fire of love ever burns me, O Ghalib
I light it not on my own, nor can I put it out.'

The drawing room was tastefully furnished. In the middle of the room was a settee, and a number of deepset, reclining chairs. On one side there was a writing desk, on which stood a portrait of Jinnah. A large fan, of the type one sees in railway waiting rooms, more functional than beautiful, whirled overhead.

Arun saw Captain Rahmat-Ullah Khan was drinking, for his glass of whisky was on the centre table.

'Will you have a whisky?'

'I thought we were going to drink tea.'

Captain Rahmat-Ullah Khan laughed.

'Well, that's only a term of convenience. You remember when we went to eat boiled beans in the college tuck-shop, we called that "tea" as well.'

Arun joined him in laughing.

'You know I don't drink.'

'Oh, come on, it'll do you no harm. Fuck this damn India-Pakistan business and let's relax for the evening.'

'I'm sorry I can't.'

'Have beer then.'

'I don't drink beer, either.'

'That's no drink. But then what the hell!—why not? Says Ghalib:

Say not no to wine, Opious one
It's an elixir sweeter than your honey.'

'You must forgive me, but I can't drink.'

'All right, you win. Have tea.'

Picking up his glass, he finished his drink, and shouted for the bearer. He asked for another drink for himself, and tea and pastry for Arun.

The drink came soon, but the tea took some time. Ensconcing himself in the chair, Captain Rahmat-Ullah Khan played with his glass and looked at Arun through half closed eyes. His cheeks were flushed, but otherwise he was a picture of affability—courteous and deferential. When the tea arrived, he prepared the cup for Arun.

'I say, who is this woman who was sitting outside the tent next to yours?'

Arun knew who he meant.

'Who do you mean?' Arun's voice was steady, but he found his hand was trembling as he tried to lift the cup to drink the tea.

'Oh, you know who. The one who was doing the hair of a child.' Rahmat-Ullah Khan crossed his legs and took a big sip out of his drink. He tried to sound casual and carefree.

'That's her child.'

'Ah, she is married then? Who is her husband?'

Arun tried not to look at him, but he knew Captain Rahmat-Ullah Khan's eyes were on him, eager and inquisitive. Stretching his hand, Arun filled his mouth with a pastry, and Rahmat-Ullah Khan waited in impatience while the other munched and ate.

'You remember the man who was asking you about his property?' said Arun, swallowing the pastry with a mouth which was totally dry.

'You mean she is married to that idiot?'

'What's wrong with him?'

Captain Rahmat-Ullah Khan saw he was being tactless.

Leaning back in his chair, he laughed aloud. 'Come, come, no reason to take offence.'

He sent for his bearer and asked him to fill his glass.

'What I meant was she is such a beauty and the man looks an imbecile.'

'They seem to be happy with each other.'

Captain Khan did not contest that. He had become serious and was thoughtfully rubbing the glass with his lips.

Sipping the drink, he said momentarily: 'Look, I might as well be frank with you. I like this woman.'

Arun knew what was coming. Yet he did not expect himself to be as shocked as he was. He was still sipping his tea, and to hide his anger he leaned forward and placed the cup on the table.

Captain Rahmat-Ullah Khan waited artfully. He played with the glass with his lips, and hiding his face behind its shining surface, he scrutinized Arun closely.

Arun sat absolutely rigid, seemingly turned into stone, his hands folded in front of him in his lap.

'You better watch yourself—that woman is my sister.'

'Stuff and nonsense,' said Rahmat-Ullah, getting up from the chair and pacing the room. 'You damn well know she is not. Why must you Hindu boys go round making a sister of every woman?'

'It is the same thing. I've known her for many years.'

'It is *not* the same thing. A sister is a sister and other women are other women. That's the trouble with your religion, it turns everything into a metaphysical riddle—even a simple social relationship.'

To Arun's own surprise, he did not feel afraid.

'You will soon be rid of us all.'

'Oh, I wasn't speaking politically,' said Rahmat-Ullah, gesturing wildly. 'Here again you're twisting my words, making a simple thing look complicated—another remarkable feature of your remarkable religion!'

Captain Rahmat-Ullah Khan stopped and looked at Arun. He sensed he wasn't going the right way about it. Sarcasm would only antagonize Arun, and he wanted his cooperation.

Coming round to Arun's chair, he sat on the side of the chair and put his arm around Arun's shoulder.

'I'm sorry. Maybe you people are wiser than us. You see, if you were to say you also like this woman and would rather not discuss her with me, I can understand. But don't bring this sister mumbo-jumbo into it.'

Arun was obliged to defend himself.

'I don't like her that way.'

'But I do,' said Rahmat-Ullah Khan, slapping him jovially on his shoulder and laughing, as though he had cracked a witticism.

Riding the crest of his laughter, he added: 'Couldn't you arrange for me to meet her?—

I wish I could perish before her doorstep
But she would kill me not, nor sheath her dagger!'

As he recited from Ghalib and as he sighed, Arun saw the veins on his neck throbbing hard.

'If you are so fond of her why don't you go and meet her?'

'I want you to handle this for me.'

Arun found himself unwinding. Worse things were happening these days, and Rahmat-Ullah Khan was only showing his fondness for a woman who undoubtedly was exceedingly beautiful.

'How?' he tried to laugh.

Captain Rahmat-Ullah Khan was still sitting on the arm of his chair. Arun's countenance was blank. Leaning over to one side of the chair, he was looking at Captain Rahmat-Ullah Khan with a thin smile on his lips.

Captain Rahmat-Ullah Khan got up and started pacing the room. Going to the writing desk, he picked up the picture of Jinnah that stood on it, and looked at it intently for some time. Placing the picture back on the table, he turned and stood leaning against the table.

'By bringing her here one evening,' he said, staring at Arun.

There was a lisp in his voice, and Arun wasn't sure whether he was drunk or nervous. It had been plain enough to Arun what he wanted. There was no room left for doubt after these words.

Arun got up from his chair. 'Can I leave? The camp is near and I can easily walk.'

'Sit down, will you?'

Captain Rahmat-Ullah Khan was not precisely harsh, but there was authority in his voice and Arun stayed where he was. Arun was not afraid for himself. He used to be afraid, in the past. But things had been happening too fast. He had been growing up too fast, shedding his past too fast. One thing which had become clearer to him was that asking too many sureties from life didn't help. This had made him unduly bold. Particularly since the night he went into town looking for Madhu's body. And he had been learning to love, at last—learning to *live.* No, he was not afraid of Rahmat-Ullah Khan. And yet he could not take himself out of the room. The authority of his voice, and beyond that the authority of his establishment, the tidy bungalow, the smart orderlies with their clicking heels, the glittering jeep on the gravel outside, were too intimidating. And Arun stood still in uncertainty.

Rahmat-Ullah Khan drained his glass. He then wiped the picture of Jinnah with his pocket handkerchief.

'You forget I can be of much help to you,' said he, continuing to clean the picture. There was no smile on his face, and his voice was emotionless.

'If you promise to bring that woman here—'

He stopped and steadied himself.

'By the way, what's her name?'

'I don't know.'

'You expect me to believe that?'

'No.'

'All right, we'll let that pass. But as I was saying, if you promise to bring her here of an evening, I'll personally take you and your parents to the Jammu border in my jeep. You people will reach safety in less than half an hour.'

So demoralizing, so physically and mentally tiring, had been the strain of the riots, the chance of a quick escape from this living inferno held limitless attraction. Arun's face went mottled, and then soon after it went brick-red with indignation.

'I'm afraid I must leave,' he said curtly, and walked out of the room.

Captain Rahmat-Ullah Khan did not give up the pretext to civility. He lurched behind him and escorted him out. 'The jeep is there,' he mumbled.

Arun took no notice of him and walked off into the darkness, the Captain shouting behind him:

'Think it over and let me know.'

During the coming days Captain Rahmat-Ullah Khan made repeated trips to lane twenty-five of the camp. He came on various excuses. At times he drove right up to the tent where lived Arun, the wheels of his jeep bouncing up and down over the rough surface. He was most courteous to Lala Kanshi Ram and Prabha Rani and always greeted them with a military salute. Arun asked him no questions, but he had many details about the foot convoy and he found an eager listener in Lala Kanshi Ram.

Prabha Rani paid no attention to him. Indeed after each visit she said he had the eyes of a loafer, and the moment he arrived she sent Chandni out of the tent.

He came repeatedly. And he stood there feverishly like an animal on must. He was so keyed up, so intense in his desire, each cell of his body seemed to vibrate with his want. Time and again he looked towards the tent of Suraj Prakash. There was no privacy in those tents, the flaps were open, and one could see everything inside. Sunanda was there most of the time. As soon as he saw her, his whole face took on a shine. And he was like a moth—for the time he stayed there. Feverishly moving on his feet, feverishly gesturing with his hands, feverishly talking to Lala Kanshi Ram in a nervous, high-pitched, staccato voice. There was only one wish his taut body seemed to proclaim. And it was to go and burn himself in the fire of Sunanda.

And he became bolder—and grosser—by stages. He would saunter up to their tent, and ask for Suraj Prakash. He did that when he knew the man was not there. For many days, Gangu Mull, the husband of Bibi Amar Vati, had not been seen. He had disappeared one day, and worried though Bibi Amar Vati looked, to Lala Kanshi Ram she said: 'Good riddance, he was only a liability.' When Suraj Prakash was also away from the tent, only the women were left to answer Rahmat-Ullah Khan's enquiries. Sunanda turned her head away when she saw him come. Bibi Amar Vati gave brief replies as to where her son was or to the other queries of the Captain, and the conversation was soon over, and yet he lingered on. He could only see Sunanda's back, she resolutely refused to turn when he stood there. But the back was more than enough for Rahmat-Ullah Khan, nay those ribs of that softly curved back he found an even finer cradle of sensuality than her front and he was just about ready to die.

The night of the full moon came—purnamashi. Arun was sitting outside the tent, looking at the moon and listening to the camp sounds filtering through to his ears. He felt a gentle touch on his shoulder. It was Sunanda. She had a bucket in her hand, and she said: 'Come with me to the water taps.'

The taps were located at various places in the camp. The nearest group of fountains was in an open space about fifty yards away. Beyond that space was the side boundary of the camp, beyond which ran the small stream that separated the Cantonment from the city.

There was no rush at the taps, but Sunanda did not go there. She took Arun to where the fence was.

Placing the bucket on the ground, she leaned against the fence, facing Arun. She was also facing the moon. Her complexion looked like amber in that light, and her heavy breasts stood out so conspicuously they cast a shadow on her belly. Behind her the stream and the town of Sialkot also glittered in the dream light. Was she the sleeping princess come awake to talk to him? What did she want to say to him?

'Arun, this friend of yours, the army officer, why does he come to visit you so often?'

Arun missed a heartbeat. He said nothing.

Sunanda seemed to be glowering, for plainly even the moon could not soothe away the creases on her face.

How much does she know? thought Arun. How much does she guess?

'Will you tell him one thing when you see him next?' She was looking at the moon, and her lithe body shook with contempt.

'What?' Arun was relieved she was not looking at him.

'Tell him I'll kill him, if he ever tries to touch me.'

CHAPTER 3

After that day, Arun was spoiling for a quarrel with Captain Rahmat-Ullah Khan, but the Captain did not give him a chance. Arun did not want it in the form of an open brawl. That would have ruined Sunanda's name. Besides, in a physical fight with the strong and experienced Captain he had no illusions of winning. What he wanted was to corner him alone, and make him aware of his anger through reprobation. Captain Rahmat-Ullah Khan maybe suspected his mood and refused to see him when no one else was there. Arun went up to his office twice, but he was sent away by the Subedar Major on the excuse the Captain was in conference. On other occasions, he had Arun's kinsmen—the other refugees—around him to shield him from his censure.

And then Arun was in any case too deeply in love with Chandni to worry himself much about Sunanda. Other people now existed only at the periphery of his consciousness. It was true Captain Rahmat-Ullah Khan was unpardonably vulgar. It was true Sunanda was hurt. It also was true that Madhu—*Madhu,* of all people, who was made for life—had died. But it was true too how a girl had the smell of olives in her skin and she had opened herself out to him.

Their love did not grow by stages; it came upon them with a rush. Chandni's protests were silenced by Arun when the following night he held her hand near the water taps and dragged her to a far-off corner. Firmly holding her against the fence, he kissed her hard on the mouth and her throat. The girl struggled and pushed her face away from his lips. And then she ceased struggling. A shiver ran through her body and she felt overcome. Soon she swooned on his shoulder, as he continued to kiss.

'What will your parents say?' she whispered, recovering.

'What will they say?'

'They will not approve of this.'

'I love you, Chandni.'

'Do you know what you are saying?'

'Yes, I do. I'm going to marry you.' Arun had not planned to say that but it came out.

'You're mad.'

'Don't ever say that again. I'm going to marry you and soon. Will you be my wife?'

'I can't think of the possibility.'

'I'm telling you.'

'Your parents will never agree to that.'

'Who are they to object?'

'My caste.'

He lifted up her chin with his hand and placed a slow, deliberate kiss on her lips.

'We're living in a different India. No one can talk of caste today.'

'And we are so poor.'

'All that has no relevance now. After the partition, we're in a different phase.'

Arun had no basis for the conclusion, but he seemed so convinced of it. The appalling misery they were going through had to have some meaning. They had to emerge different, modified, reborn. Otherwise one might as well shut up about being a man. His young mind saw no impediments which could restrain him. The shape of things to come was altogether in his hands. He was so firm and sure of himself.

Chandni was clinging to Arun.

'I don't know,' she murmured, sighing, and pulling his face nearer and passionately kissing him, biting him with her teeth.

'Believe me,' he cried into her ear.

Chandni and her mother Padmini had appeared in their household years back. She would be two years younger than he—of the age of Nur. Arun was touched by the care with which her mother chaperoned her. She would not leave the girl alone for a moment. If Prabha Rani wanted her to stay and do some needlework for her, the mother refused. Tactfully, she said the girl was not well. Or the girl had to go to the temple. Or the girl had to go shopping. If she could not get out of the situation, she came back with her herself and hung around while Chandni took care of the additional chores.

The mother, Padmini, was a strikingly graceful woman. She walked with a native poise, and not in the least felt repressed by her position as a domestic servant. Admittedly she was poor, but she kept herself and Chandni scrupulously clean. As far as Arun knew, Chandni could not read or write—she had never been sent to school.

None of these things, her education, her status, her breeding, her poverty, mattered to Arun in his present disposition. He had found a new identity for himself, an identity which had partly been thrust on him by the surge of events, and which partly he had worked out for himself metaphysically. He did not want to give that identity up.

Unfastening her blouse, Arun put his hand inside and her nude breasts went hard under his touch, her nipples rising like tulip buds.

'Please don't.'

'Not yet you mean?'

'Yes.' Her head hung low and she was looking at the ground.

'Oh, my beloved!' He did not remove his hand.

Chandni was rather dark of complexion, but otherwise she was a winsome girl. When had he seen a Punjabi girl who was not beautiful? thought Arun wistfully. Chandni was of a medium height. Her body was very compact and she had the alertness of a pigeon. Her features—her nose, her chin—were rounded rather than sharp, but the roundness was of a soft, smooth quality, and it made her look quite desirable, if a little defenceless.

Only her complexion was not like that of the other Punjabi girls in the household and Chandni was clearly self-conscious about it. Perhaps this was why she did not mingle with the other girls and hung close to her mother. Most of the time Arun saw her squatting on her haunches near the kitchen sink. She had shapely arms and thighs, and as she scrubbed the dishes, her thighs shook in rhythm with her arms. Arun did not ever see her running around through the house freely. If she happened to cross his path, she was in a welter of confusion. He knew she was blushing, even though the blush could not be seen on her dark face. The hue of her skin acquired a heavy coppery look and her hands would be needlessly twirling her dopatta or her sari round and round. It must be her father who gave her that complexion, for her mother was so fair. Only compared to the calm of her mother, the girl was a nervous wreck, thought Arun.

'I'm so dark,' she said tearfully, raising her head and trying to look into his eyes in the dark of the night.

'I love you!'

It became customary for the two of them to meet at the fence near the water taps. Mostly they met under the cover of the evening, but they also met in the afternoons, when Lala Kanshi Ram would be having a nap. At night, inside the tent, Arun sneaked up to her, though Chandni shivered with nervousness and would urge him to get back. Arun himself was jumpy, he knew how critical his parents and Padmini would be if they found out. But the experience of holding Chandni as they lay with his naked feet touching hers in an embrace and the front of his legs touching her front, was so satisfying for him, so deeply gratifying, no risk for its sake was too great. She lay quiescent in his arms, once she had made her protests. He dug into her flesh all over, finding limitless delight in that voyage of discovery; and she responded to him vibrantly, like a highly sensitive instrument. She finally turned the other way with a huge sigh. 'Go back,' she whispered through her panting breath. He lingered a while before he acquiesced.

Chandni flowered strangely under the impact of Arun's love. Physically she did not change much, she continued to be compact and pigeon-breasted, and rather circumscribed and quiet in her manners, yet she ceased to be self-conscious and a glow of happiness spread on her face. Words like 'I love you', or 'My love', which Arun said unendingly to her, meant nothing to her. She had not been to school as he had. But she knew truth from untruth instinctively, and she believed Arun really wanted her. The thought of marrying into their family was so staggering, so fanciful for her, she turned her head away from it in fear. It was not caste alone. Their whole life-pattern was different. Only Arun said he would marry her, come what may, and she wanted to believe in him—without reservations. Which she did.

Her eyes followed him all day long, and it seemed she now lived for him alone. They said nothing to each other in the presence of others, but it was not necessary. A gentle smile played on her lips when he was near, and her face was indescribably and instantaneously lit up each time their eyes met. And they touched each other tenderly, lingeringly, with the tips of their fingers when the girl brought him his food or his tea. Her simple mind struggled with the difficulties of their situation, but she knew there was much pride in it for her too, much personal elevation.

So bare had been her existence she clung to the new possibility with touching, almost pathetic longing. She had always been respectful to Lala Kanshi Ram and Prabha Rani; like the rest, she called them chachaji and chachiji—uncle and auntie. She now became extra concerned for them and tried to anticipate their demands. 'What, chachiji?' she said eagerly, when Prabha Rani raised her head to summon her. 'You want anything, chachaji?' she said to Lala Kanshi Ram. So eager was she in her soul to align herself with them that when she felt threatened on some count, she ran to *their side* for shelter rather than to her mother's. Her mother still tried to chaperone her, but Chandni learned how to dodge her, and like a doe she nudged closer to Prabha Rani in moments of danger than to her.

And she turned extraordinarily beautiful in her happiness—even her complexion became lighter, as though the pigments in her skin had dissolved under a magic potion. Through all her waking moments she thought of what her life would be as a bride. With a smile on her face, she went into a prolonged reverie. She would be good, she said to herself; she would make Arun happy, plenty happy. She thought of the marriage ceremony. She thought of the ornaments Arun's parents would give her. She thought of the new clothes she would have. Her daydreams did not run according to a sequence. Like real dreams they suddenly dissolved into nothingness and a new reverie appeared instead. Only unlike real dreams, they were always pleasant dreams. At times she even thought of herself as a middle-aged woman—on the day of the wedding of their son—hers and Arun's first son.

All these dreams gave a quiver to her heart. She felt a warm feeling come over her, and lowering her eyes she smiled genially to herself. But the reverie which sent her pulsing fast so she felt the blood rushing to her face was when she thought of Arun's first entry into her body. Local myths had created a terror in her mind of that event; her mother herself had hinted at its painful nature. Yet in her reverie it was an event of limitless pleasure. If there was pain in it, she longed for that pain too. Repeatedly all her other reveries dissolved and came back to the moment when she would be lying on a flower-bedecked bed, that part of her which she had watched over with such care for these eighteen years fully exposed to Arun's eyes, and when he would be entering her. In her unabating yearning for the moment of contact, her dream registered no other details. She thought not of her clothes, whether she would be dressed or undressed. She thought not of the position Arun would take. She thought not of the other parts of her body or the role they would play in the splendour of that night. She only saw herself on the bed, with lights dimmed, and she saw the sunflower of her body exposed to Arun, exposed from end to end, all along the line of the piquant cleavage, and she saw Arun coming on her in a hurry, piercing through the sunflower, and going inside of her—hurting her in the process if necessary.

She wanted to cry out when she thought of the consummation and invariably she uttered a deep-throated groan. She did not see anything wrong in thinking about it. Her mother had chaperoned her and preserved her for this day and moment. It was the inevitable summit of man and woman; in its own time, in its own season. That time and season had now arrived, and Arun was her destiny. Why fear then, or why feel guilty? At least in dreaming about it?

'You must call me Arun.' Arun was holding her by the waist and they were looking out over the fence towards the city.

'Nay.' She said the longer no of Punjabi, hiding her head on his shoulder.

'Say Arun.'

'Nay.'

'Say it!'

'Thou.' She used the second person plural, customary for addressing people you adore or hold in esteem.

'Arun.'

'Thou!'

These were such new things for her, so unfamiliar, and she felt utterly bewildered. She liked it when Arun talked in this fashion. Half closing her eyes, with her lips half open, she drank his words like a wholesome draught. Often she did not quite hear his words. She only caught the drift of them, and that was enough. When she was by herself, she practised calling him by his name—'Arun'. The day's chores were done, her mother was with Bibi Amar Vati in the next tent, Prabha Rani was lying down, the men were to be seen nowhere, and slowly, sounding each letter separately, she said distinctly A-r-u-n. It sounded so musical and she said it over and over again. She liked the name, particularly the run of the last syllable, ending on a nasal tone. And she made out as if she was trying to summon him. And she shouted silently, without uttering any sound, Arun, Arun. And getting bold, she really shouted out aloud, A-r-u-n. Then immediately, getting shy, she ducked her head and chuckled to herself. She then quickly looked around to see if someone had watched her.

In Arun's presence, she was tongue-tied. She wanted to say that name, she wanted to say it with her lips touching Arun's cheek, but all she could bring out was 'Thou'. At times, Arun felt angry. The girl was primitive, she was slow, she couldn't move a few steps away from what she had been drilled to do—in so small a thing, like calling him by his first name, when it mattered so much to him, she wouldn't satisfy him. But he looked at her and he found her nostrils dilated with passion and his anger was washed away.

'All right, say it in my ear.'

'Nay,' she whispered deep into one of his lobes.

In a fit of enthusiasm, Arun told his mother late one afternoon, 'Ma, I want to marry Chandni.'

It was only a couple of weeks after Madhu's death. Prabha Rani was still prostrated with grief. It was as if she had entered a different cognitive region. She stopped bothering about some of the dearest things to her heart—like the welfare of her husband. She did not ask whether there was enough cream in his milk, or whether his two pillows were properly placed under his head at night. Vaguely she was aware Chandni was taking care of him, but she did not fret about it. Life was going on, and if it could do without Madhu it could do without her. Mechanically, as if in deep sleep, she attended to her physical needs—but just about. She ate her food, she went to the taps to wash herself, and the rest of the time she stared at the sky gloomily, or she stared at other people, still remotely hopeful of stumbling upon her daughter amongst them.

It took her some seconds to absorb what Arun was saying.

'What are you saying?' she said without much interest.

'I'm telling you I want to marry Chandni.'

'Which Chandni?'

'Our Chandni. Who else!'

'Are you crazy?'

She said that without anger or cynicism. A few words had entered her consciousness and brought a reaction, in which the active participation of her mind seemed to be absent.

'I'm *not* crazy. I like Chandni and want to marry her,' Arun said a little loudly.

They were alone in the tent. Lala Kanshi Ram was standing outside and talking with Suraj Prakash, but he was far away and he could not hear them.

This time Prabha Rani looked up, and she saw before her her pimply, shy boy speaking to her of marriage. As in the past, he was a little nervous, he was a little unsure of himself. He was not looking her straight in the eye, which was how he looked at people. In spite of his loud voice she knew he was afraid of what she might say. She wanted to laugh at him. Chandni! His father would give him a beating if he heard of it. She was also amused. This was the same boy who hid in his room when Madhu's friends visited with her. Nur, she knew he liked. But Nur was like a member of the family, like Madhu, and she did not feel threatened at the idea of losing him to her. Now there was an adult longing in his voice, which in spite of his nervousness had a steely, decisive ring about it, and this upset Prabha Rani.

'This is not the time to talk of marriages,' she said.

'I don't mean right now. When we reach India.'

'There has been a death in the family.'

'Yes.' Arun had the feeling his mother was trying to blackmail him. 'In a year's time, then.'

'Why with Chandni?'

'Why not?'

'Wouldn't you rather have an educated wife?'

'I like her.'

'You may like someone else better.'

'That is beside the point. I'm determined to marry her, mother.'

Prabha Rani had not known Arun speak so forcefully. And she saw how wrong she was when she had surmised Arun was afraid of her. If the boy did not look her in the eye, it was only out of regard. His entire posture otherwise exuded confidence.

'You will have to ask your father.'

'I'll go ahead even if he doesn't agree.'

'Not in this house.'

'Why not?'

'We have to respect his wishes.'

'He must respect ours. I see nothing wrong in marrying Chandni. She may be poor, but I don't need anybody's money.

And as far as caste is concerned, I don't subscribe to it. My whole being revolts against it.'

Prabha Rani saw her son had become a man, he was ready to fight for himself. And she felt for him in her heart.

She said, though:

'The girl can't even read and write.'

She herself couldn't do that, she knew, but she wanted it different for Arun.

'I'll teach her. These are such unimportant things, mother. What matters is we should love each other.'

A smile came on Prabha Rani's face. Arun speaking of love! She saw he was blushing. He blushed like a girl and at once she was reminded of Madhu. What mattered was not even love, she thought. What mattered was to live. Arun at least was alive.

She took his hand in hers and patted it lightly.

'You will have to bring your father round.'

'I'll do that when we get to India. But you are with me, mother, aren't you? Please.'

'I'm saying nothing.'

Arun saw she was smiling and the glint in her eyes was not unfriendly.

Hugging her hard, he said: 'Oh, ma, I love you so much.' He lifted her off her feet. 'Oh, I love you! I knew you wouldn't say no to me.'

'Take care, take care,' said Prabha Rani, disengaging herself from his embrace. 'I'm saying nothing.'

'Oh, I knew you'd agree,' Arun said again impetuously, dancing with delight.

Before Prabha Rani could recover from his smothering embrace, Arun had marched out of the tent.

In a little while he reappeared, dragging Chandni along with him. He had found her near the camp dispensary.

Lala Kanshi Ram could see something unusual was going on. But he was too engrossed in what Suraj Prakash was telling him about Niranjan Singh to make enquiries.

'Touch mother's feet,' said Arun to Chandni theatrically, as soon as they were inside the tent. 'I have told her everything.'

This was most unexpected. Prabha Rani had not thought Arun would go so far with her passive approval. And besides, it was all so in the future—so uncertain. Why make premature declarations?

She pulled herself away as Chandni tried to fall at her feet. Catching her by the shoulder she raised her and steadied her.

'I don't know what Arun has been telling you. Please know I have made no promises. Be good, both of you, and let time take its course.'

They accepted this as an assertion of her support, and Chandni once again leaped forward and fell at her feet. In her mind Prabha Rani was annoyed with Arun for creating such a scene, and her lips were pursed. Yet now she did not pull herself back.

Life in the camp, in spite of the hard times, had settled to a not too unpleasant routine. People woke up around six, went to the toilet in the community latrines, bathed in the community bathrooms, collected dry rations of wheat and rice from the government store, ate lunch-cum-breakfast around eleven, spent the afternoon visiting fellow refugees in the camp, had the night meal around seven, and went to sleep soon after. No marriages were performed in the month and a half Arun's family was there, but children were born each day and a number of people closed the chapters of their lives and passed away. There was a dispensary, where a doctor was in attendance morning and evening for a couple of hours. But the people took their illnesses stoically. The right to consideration and sympathy had been so conclusively appropriated by those who had suffered in the riots, the others felt silly in talking about commonplace ailments. And where the sick person was an old man and he died, the consensus was that was a blessing rather than a tragedy. The old bones would not have felt happy in new surroundings. It was better the land which gave them birth should receive them back. It was indeed a deliverance in their case.

So when Sardar Jodha Singh died after a brief illness of diarrhoea, the family quietly cremated him by the side of the stream close to the camp. His ashes too were immersed in the same stream, no one thought of saving them and carrying them to the distant Ganges. His reaction to the partition had been typical of the men of his age: he had gone utterly mute. During the last few months, he had hardly spoken a few sentences to his son, Sardar Teja Singh, or to his granddaughter, Isher Kaur. Prabha Rani was sad on the day of his death, for he would tell her such stories of what passed at his store. With healthy ribaldry he singled out the women for his criticism. This one had such a face, that one had hefty arms, that one spoke through the nose. And did you think they came to the store to buy things? They came to display themselves! They even made passes at him, he would add mischievously.

As his thin and wasted body burned on the pyre in their midst, the flames cast portent shadows on their faces. They were all there—that is, those of them who were still in the camp. Lala Bihari Lal and his son, Phool Chand, had left for India in one of the refugee trains by way of Wazirabad. So had Mangat Ram, the revenue officer, along with his wife. No news of them was received, and no one knew whether they had reached India or were languishing in another refugee camp. If no connecting train for Amritsar was available at Wazirabad, the entire load of refugees from Sialkot was transferred to the camp in Wazirabad, until an onward train was ready. Very often the refugees had to wait at Lahore, the final connecting point for Amritsar. If a train was attacked on the way—as many were—the surviving refugees were transferred to the nearest camp close to the scene of the attack.

Lala Kanshi Ram had suggested to Niranjan Singh they leave by train on account of Isher Kaur. They made ready to go, but the day the train was to leave Isher Kaur felt so ill they had to cancel their departure. Now they wanted to walk. They had heard of such violence shown to the Sikhs they were afraid to take the route which involved changing trains. To journey on foot would be more hazardous, they knew. Yet they felt safety in the mass of people who would be along with them on foot. In a train, people were divided into sections, into separate compartments, and they were butchered before they had the time to offer resistance or receive help. And then they wanted to be with Lala Kanshi Ram and his family, with whom they had spent so many years. Ishero had wanted this from the start.

But the tragedy which awaited that Sikh family was reflected nowhere in the red and yellow flames of Sardar Jodha Singh's funeral pyre. For many weeks Sikhs in the refugee camp had been going through the worst kind of ordeal. Sudden death at the hands of Muslims was nothing compared to the ordeal they were being asked to accept by choice. It was being widely reported the only way for a Sikh to get safely through Pakistan was by shaving off his hair. The Sikh faith enjoined strictly against it. It was one of the tenets of the faith the hair of the head and the beard be not cut. It was a kind of badge of courage, which in olden days distinguished you as a warrior. In these times it was like shouting your identity from the housetop—which meant speedy death for you at the hands of the Muslims.

When Sardar Jodha Singh's family was getting ready to leave by train, the subject came up for discussion amongst them.

Sardar Jodha Singh was then alive.

'I'm too old and even if someone kills me, it doesn't matter. But I urge you both to cut your hair,' he said to Teja Singh and Niranjan Singh.

For months Niranjan Singh had been boiling at the insults they were being asked to accept. His wife was expecting his child, and while he wanted her to have that child and he wanted that child to live, he wanted him to live honourably. How many compromises could a man make with his conscience just to survive? Today a venerated Sikh—the grandfather of his wife—was trying to deflect him from the path of dharma. He did not hold this against Sardar Jodha Singh. He was old, he was afraid, and at the moment he was not concerned with dharma, he was concerned with them, his children. And yet was life so precious as that?

'I'll not cut my hair,' he said.

Said Sardar Teja Singh: 'Safety demands we agree.'

'You cut yours. I won't.'

'Think of me,' said Isher Kaur.

'You know what our dharma says:

Lose your head, if need be
Don't lose your Sikh faith!'

'You won't be losing your faith,' said old Jodha Singh. He knew how upset Niranjan Singh had been these months. He was young and very strong; each morning he gave himself an oil massage and did a hundred sit ups and a hundred bend stretches before he went and had his bath. Often, while Lala Kanshi Ram and the rest debated the safest course to follow, he had seen Niranjan Singh looking at his arms and flexing his biceps. It was of no avail. Circumstances gave him no chance of equal fight, and he could only fret and nag himself. 'The moment you reach India, you can grow your hair again. And if you like, you can do penance at the Golden Temple in Amritsar.'

Niranjan Singh brooded silently. His face was grim with the sense of humiliation involved. He looked at his arms and one by one flexed the biceps. Absent-mindedly, he also twirled his mustache.

While the others looked at his face, Niranjan Singh shook his head.

'No, I can't do it. I have a promise to keep with Guru Maharaj.'

'Ishero, why do you worry?' he said to his wife. 'Guru Maharaj will protect me for your sake.'

Ishero started crying. Fears of many kinds had been gnawing and kicking at her inside all through the riots. Now the child too had started kicking her, and she went mad with confusion. What was happening inside of her? What were these forces that were bent on destroying her? This was her first child, and the early months of pregnancy were months of anticipation for her. She was no longer sure what the child was fated to do to her, the way it kicked her and discomforted her. And on top of everything, her husband was bent on adding to her worries. She was so afraid of being murdered, the thought was a perpetual nightmare for her, for she wouldn't know what would happen to the child in that case. The child would die too in all probability, she thought. If only the child could survive, at any cost. But how was he to survive when this pig-headed husband of hers was being so stupid about a few trivial hairs? He would not only destroy himself, he would be the death of them all—including the poor child.

She covered her face with her dopatta, in her effort to control herself, but her sobs broke through the veil and the others looked at each other silently.

Niranjan Singh felt Sardar Jodha Singh and Sardar Teja Singh were holding him responsible for Isher Kaur's crying.

He went forward and fell at Jodha Singh's feet. 'Please, grandfather, I'll give my life for your sake. Only please don't ask me to cut my hair.'

They did not go by the train they were scheduled to take, and then Sardar Jodha Singh died and the matter was dropped. From time to time they reverted to it, especially when fresh reports of atrocities committed on the Sikhs reached the camp. Niranjan Singh remained adamant. His life was entirely in Guru Maharaj's keeping, and cutting the hair would be denying the power of the Guru. He was certain Guru Maharaj would protect him from harm.

'Guru Maharaj couldn't protect his own birth place—how will he protect you?' said Lala Kanshi Ram to him.

He was referring to Nankana Sahib, the town where Guru Nanak, the founder of the Sikh faith, was born and which was the holiest of holies for the Sikhs. It was situated in West Punjab and after the partition it had fallen inside of Pakistan. Reports had it all the Sikhs were massacred there and the shrine was closed.

When Lala Kanshi Ram said this to Niranjan Singh, he was at his most expansive philosophical self.

This mood off and on came on Lala Kanshi Ram. He suddenly felt he had touched the heart of the human enigma. He did not have too pronounced a metaphysical bent of mind. That is, he did not drive himself to misery concerning his beginnings and his ends. He said his prayers, he offered his worship, and for the rest he lived on faith. Arya Samaj forbade him to kneel before idols. Yet Prabha Rani was fond of Hindu gods, especially of Lord Krishna, and he accepted them with few reservations. What difference did it make? It was necessary to form a personal equation with God, and any type of equation would do. Having done that, he did not bother himself further with esoteric problems. He conserved his energies for his business and for human relationships.

All the same, on certain days he felt a strange calm descend on him. He might be in the process of supervising the unloading of a new consignment of goods. Or maybe he was sitting down to urinate beside the narrow drain at the back of his shop, and was mentally working out yet another manoeuvre to outdo Seth Ruldu Ram, his nearest rival in the grain business. And all of a sudden the competitions and the small lies of his business sank into the background and his mind became absolutely still. It seemed to him as though he were seeing *through* everything—beyond and away from the mesh of immediate pettiness. It was like seeing a vision. All doors were open, and the vistas were imbued with rich, glorious colours. And life shimmered through those vistas like a perennial, sun-drenched river, a river at whose golden waters he had just slaked his thirst.

Lala Kanshi Ram retained that mood for two to three days, on occasion for a full week. He became supremely himself in those days. His face had not many wrinkles on it, but his cheeks hung somewhat loosely, as if suspended insecurely from the bones on which they rested. Come the feeling of revelation, his flesh became firm and the cheeks were pulled up and inward. He insisted on dhobi washed clothes on such days, and he examined them carefully before he went in for his bath. He cut his already thin mustache thinner, meticulously weeding out the white hairs, and spent a long time before the mirror cutting the hair in his nostrils. After the bath he looked flushed and happy and seemed to take inordinate delight in the sheer act of getting into his clothes. Repeatedly he looked at himself in the mirror and smoothed out the shirt and the tight pyjamas on his body. When it came the turn of the turban, he pulled it hard so that it sat like a skull cap, fitting his head neatly and tightly. He also got his shoes cleaned by the shoeshine boy.

Armed like this, he issued forth from his house and contended with the world in those days of illumination in a state of mild delirium. He looked shrunken, but more solid, more pithy, as though he had discarded his flaccid, external self and the kernel alone remained. His glasses perched at the bridge of his nose, he peered at others from a distance which was no distance—or so he thought. The good humour did not stay with him for many days; he was soon fussing and fuming as of old. Yet so long as it lasted, he was most indulgent not only to his immediate family but to everyone. Yes, he had seen the vision. The only problem was to put it in words and say it properly. But then why put it in words and say it?

Lala Kanshi Ram was passing through one such phase. He was looking prim, and strangely self-satisfied. Prabha Rani sneered at him as she saw him bathe and dress up. He had lost his daughter, didn't he remember? Why must he have these spells of insanity? He surely was getting worse, if he couldn't contain himself in times such as these.

Lala Kanshi Ram put his hand on the shoulder of Niranjan Singh and said gently: 'Come, sit with me.'

'Yes, chachaji.'

'So you won't cut your hair?' He looked at him through his glasses, which were balanced right at the tip of his nose.

'No, chachaji.'

Lala Kanshi Ram removed his glasses, and folding them carefully, he held them in his hand. He chuckled to himself, as though on a profound thought.

'Why?'

'You know my reason.'

'Tell me.'

'My faith.'

'Faith in what?'

'In my religion.'

'What does the religion say.'

'Not to cut my hair.'

'Is it in the Granth?'

'Yes it is.'

'And you would rather lose your life than cut your hair.'

'That's so.'

Lala Kanshi Ram was impressed. Deep faith was ever so much more convincing and binding than cold logic, and Lala Kanshi

Ram respected faith, in himself and in others. Yet this did not shatter his other perception and, like the Kundalini serpent, he remained solidly coiled on his secret knowledge.

He opened his glasses once again. They were his accessories to argument in heightened moments of awareness. Slowly he placed them on his nose and looked benevolently at Niranjan Singh.

'Listen, son, I admire your faith. Only don't forget for a moment the religions of man are the inventions of man himself.'

'What do you mean?'

'They are the creation of men with inspiration so that we may lead inspired lives.'

'Not of men. Of avatars—of reincarnations of God.'

'The same thing. They are only men more inspired than the rest of us.'

Niranjan Singh remained silent.

'These religions are meant to be practised only where human life exists. You can't practise them when beastly times prevail. And even among humans, they must be accepted with a pinch of salt.'

Niranjan Singh remained quiet.

Lala Kanshi Ram searched his face, and he could see how agitated he was under his bushy beard.

'These are not normal times. I have not known of or heard of worse days. You may safely cut your hair under these circumstances and you'll be denying no religion.'

'It is making religion a matter of convenience.'

That's what it is, Lala Kanshi Ram wanted to say, but he held his tongue. He was coming too close to formulating a creed. No, he did not know anything for certain. He had an obscure kind of comprehension and he felt good about it momentarily, but beyond that he knew nothing.

'No, it is not a matter of convenience,' he said, after a long pause. 'It is giving religion chance to work again through you and do good on earth. If you perish, your religion will perish with you.'

Lala Kanshi Ram got up. He had an impish look on his face, which was tinged with humility.

'I suggest you accept what the late Jodha Singh told you,' he said, before he walked on.

Suraj Prakash had a different approach to the whole subject. He had heard of the fuss Niranjan Singh was creating, and he felt he was a bloody fool.

'He is after all a Sikh,' he said to Sunanda, who did not laugh at his joke.

'Now, don't say any such thing in his hearing,' said Bibi Amar Vati.

'Rest assured,' said Suraj, throwing out a jet of smoke and dropping the ash of his cigarette with a snap of his fingers. 'I will say something else.' He was smiling.

'Why must you interfere at all?' said Sunanda. There was a sedate look on her face. She was thinking of her parents of whom she had no news since partition. They had asked her to come to them in Kashmir. Once or twice she suggested this to Bibi Amar Vati, but did not insist when she showed no interest. Now she knew it might be a long time before she met them again. She was feeling sad about it and her eyes were watery. She sat there like a picture—immobile, rooted in her own consciousness, her sanguine skin looking pale and the two patches of natural red on her cheeks a shade faded.

'I rather like his stand. Leave him alone to sort this out in his mind.'

'But he is a Sikh—he has no mind!'

'I know of someone else who doesn't have one either.'

A roguish smile appeared on Sunanda's face as she said this, and she looked at her husband coquettishly. She wanted to play with him, mock him and excite him, for she loved Suraj Prakash in spite of his handicaps. But Bibi Amar Vati was sitting in the tent, staring at them.

Sunanda's mere presence was enough to inflame Suraj Prakash physically. For the first few years of their married life, he had gone round in a state of perpetual must, desiring her every hour of the day. And when she added playfulness to her nearness, Suraj was up in no time.

He looked at her as she leaned against a wall of the tent, her legs crossed in front of her. Well, maybe he had no mind, but he was very good at one thing, said Suraj to himself. He saw the slight bulge of her crotch, and he wanted to gather her with his thighs and crush her.

He smiled and said: 'I'll get even with you later.'

Just then their children came in, the tempo in the tent altered, passion was replaced by motherly worries, Sunanda busied herself with the children and Suraj Prakash walked out.

Suraj got hold of Niranjan Singh at last. They had gone to the government store to collect the dry rations for the week, when Suraj stopped him.

'I say, Niranjan, what is all this noise you are making?'

Niranjan shrugged his shoulders and kept quiet. Suraj was no longer his landlord and he was not obliged to explain himself to him.

'Listen, brother, don't you want to sleep with a Muslim girl?'

'What?'

'Don't you want to live long enough to lay a Muslim girl?'

'What are you talking about?'

'You have no idea. Muslim girls are so good in bed.'

'How do you know?'

'You have only to look at them. They exercise, they eat meat—they keep themselves fit. Hindu girls give up so soon!'

Niranjan Singh felt like laughing. It was difficult to take offence at anything Suraj said. It was only a part of the bravado that constituted his mental make-up. What he wanted was approval, a pat on the shoulder. If the chance to sleep with a Muslim girl came his way, he would probably run away from the scene in discomfort. Yet he enjoyed strutting around and talking big. With his cheeks burning not with passion but with the excitement of causing a sensation, he held his cigarette in his trembling fingers and looked at Niranjan with a fatuous smile on his face. If only Niranjan Singh would laugh heartily and be intrigued by what he said. That would be satisfaction enough for him.

'We both have such beautiful wives,' said Niranjan.

'Ah, what has that got to do with it?' Suraj shook his head, deeply dissatisfied with Niranjan's level of intelligence.

'And what has this got to do with my hair?'

'Bhai, you can only lay a Muslim girl in East Punjab—provided the Hindu and Sikh bastards there leave a few for us. And you must survive to get there.'

'If you don't cut the hair,' he said, emphasizing his words, 'the chances are you will be killed by the Muslims.'

'The chances are I will live,' said Niranjan, pushing him aside.

The date for the foot convoy to Dera Baba Nanak was fixed and massive preparations were under way to organize the convoy. A large body of Gurkha troops arrived from India to escort it. They were commanded by a young Gurkha major, who had two captains and several lieutenants with him. They drove up one afternoon in a small convoy of olive green jeeps and three-ton trucks. Bren guns were mounted on top of each truck, and there was excitement in the camp as the convoy arrived there. A part of the field adjacent to the camp was assigned to them, where by the evening they had pitched their tents. The men from the camp cheered, as they saw the troops unload their equipment—bren and sten guns, many rifles, many wooden cases of ammunition. These troops were their deliverers, and the men inside the camp cheered repeatedly, many shouting 'Jai Hind', the warrior cry Subhas Chandra Bose had given to India.

The entire camp had come to their side of the fence, and men, women and children were packed tight behind the barbed wire. The Gurkha Major, flanked by some of his officers, watched the people from the outside. Captain Rahmat-Ullah Khan stood by his side, his mustache twitching a little. He was in command here, he was standing on his own soil—the Pakistani soil—and he had not the slightest fear of the situation getting out of control. Usually the inmates were allowed to move in and out of the camp freely. Today the big gate was closed and was securely guarded by Pakistani troops. In the past, when the Indian troops came to escort refugee trains, they came in small batches. They were quartered inside the barracks of Pakistani soldiers, and few people were aware of their presence. This time they had come in numbers, like an avalanche.

Captain Rahmat-Ullah Khan knew of their pending arrival and had made preparations to receive them. He did not expect, though, this demonstration of feeling by the camp inmates. Pakistani soldiers and subalterns stood by the gate of the camp, and Captain Khan knew he could send for more at short notice. He let the men cheer and shout, without interfering to stop them. The sound of 'Jai Hind' was repugnant to his ears, yet short of firing at the crowd he did not know how else he could silence it. So he bore with it.

The Gurkha officers were short-statured by comparison with Captain Rahmat-Ullah Khan, but they stood solid and firm on their stocky legs as they watched the Indian refugees. Rana Jang Bahadur Singh, the Gurkha Major, was a sturdy man of forty, with very broad and thick shoulders. As he looked at the excited crowd through his mongoloid eyes, the tip of his sharp but sunken nose quivered and the veins on the side of his closely cropped head stood out in anger. Only a few minutes back, he had had an argument with Captain Rahmat-Ullah Khan, when the Captain refused him permission to hoist the Indian tricolour by the side of their tents. Before him fluttered the green and white flag of Pakistan at the mast near the gate, and his brow was clouded. Though he was from Nepal, he had served in the Indian army for the last twenty years, and shared the ties of religion with these refugees. This was the first escort duty he had come on, having driven straight from Dehradun with his men (with an overnight halt at Amritsar). He knew he shouldn't antagonize Captain Khan, since the safety of his men and the refugees depended on the goodwill of Pakistani soldiers. Yet he wanted to inspire the refugees, too, who lined the fence with scared, grief-stricken faces. He let them shout for some time. Meanwhile he exchanged glances with his subordinates. He then quickly looked at Captain Rahmat-Ullah Khan with a smile, and raised his hand and shouted back to the refugees—'Jai Hind'. He also marched forward to the fence where the men and the women were at their densest and said to them in Hindi: 'Have no fears. We'll take you to safety.' Captain Rahmat-Ullah Khan angrily rocked back and forth on his feet but said nothing.

The Indian officers were not allowed to inspect the camp from inside, but from that day they were permitted to meet selected inmates to settle the details of the convoy. At a rough tally, they discovered there would be over twenty thousand people in the convoy. This meant a column over ten miles in length. That wasn't unusual. Convoys of ten miles were common in both directions, one convoy from Rawalpindi, slowly wending its way towards the Indian border, was reported to be seventy-five miles long. Virtually the entire five hundred and fifty miles of the border between East and West Punjab was used by the minorities to cross from one side to the other, the people heading for the point nearest to their own homes. But organized convoys, whether foot convoys or convoys of trains, were passed through two main checkpoints;

convoys from the northern parts of the Punjab passed through the Wagha checkpost near Amritsar; those coming from the southern part used the route through Bahawalpur state and passed through Macleodganj. This convoy was taking a shorter and more direct route to Amritsar and would not touch Wagha. Along the route, there were two more refugee camps; one at Pasrur, the other at Narowal, both tehsils, sub-district headquarters of the district Sialkot. Refugees from those camps were to join this very convoy. Those who wanted to go with the convoy were split up into ten large units. To save army personnel for security jobs, each unit was placed for all organizational matters under the leadership of a camp inmate. The job of this leader was to keep people together while on the march and to report their problems to the army officials. Each unit was also assigned vehicles to carry the arms and equipment needed for the defence of the unit. While officers would be driving up and down the marching column, inspecting things, men of the Indian army, carrying loaded rifles, were to march on foot with the refugees.

Dera Baba Nanak, the border town on the Indian side, was forty-seven miles from Sialkot. It was decided the convoy would do at least six miles a day, more if possible. They could not move faster because of the large number of women and children. Room was made available in one truck per unit for those who were extremely old or those who couldn't walk for some other reason. The convoy was to avoid all towns, they were to camp only in open fields. Only a night's stop was scheduled at each place, except for Pasrur and Narowal, where other refugees were to join the convoy. Detachments of Major Jang Bahadur Singh's unit had been left behind in those two camps, and they would have everything lined up when the convoy reached there. Major Jang Bahadur Singh set aside two nights each at these places.

Making allowance for emergencies, the Major was hopeful of taking these people to India in fifteen days' time.

Lala Kanshi Ram was appointed the leader of one unit, and he felt quite elated when Major Jang Bahadur Singh asked him to agree.

'I'm not much good, sir, but I will be proud to assist. Anything in the cause of the motherland!' he said, rubbing his hands happily together.

Donning his turban tightly on his head, and trimming his mustache thin, the first thing he did as the leader was to assign a place to Isher Kaur in the truck which was to carry the old and the disabled. She was in the advanced stages of pregnancy, and it was obvious she could not walk. Lala Kanshi Ram brooded over whether or not he could squeeze Prabha Rani and Arun in. For his own self he did not bother; he wanted to walk and stretch his legs (as he said to himself). But Prabha Rani had waned after Madhu's death and Arun was so frail. Arun said he wouldn't hear of it and began lecturing to him on duty and responsibility, when Lala Kanshi Ram cut him short by saying: 'I was only joking.' He was obliged to leave them out in any case, when he saw before him a long line of the truly old and sick. It was with some difficulty he was able to save room for Isher Kaur.

Each day he spent several hours with Major Jang Bahadur Singh in his tent, going over the details. Lists of those who were going were prepared and Lala Kanshi Ram was asked to familiarize himself with the two thousand included in his unit. He visited each of the families in their tents and tried to memorize the names of the principal persons of that family. Major Jang Bahadur Singh had only given him a list of names. He subdivided them into various categories: men, women, children, the sick in the family and the old. He had Arun prepare for him several separate lists. Before each name, he also entered the age of the person. As always, he wanted to be thorough.

Major Jang Bahadur Singh told the camp leaders the army would provide no vehicles for their luggage. They did not expect it, either. They knew it was going to be a hard subsistence-level march. They were to sleep in the open, since there would be no tents. They were to carry their own rations with them, or buy stuff locally if they could. Many starvation deaths in other convoys were reported, and it was common knowledge that only about half the number of any convoy got through safely. They perished of hunger, or disease, or exposure, or they were killed by violence. The escorting army had barely vehicles enough for its own logistics, and they couldn't spare any to carry tents or rations for the people. So Major Jang Bahadur's announcement came as no surprise to the refugees. Indeed they had already made arrangements for their luggage. A number of people had carts with them, pulled by buffaloes or bullocks. Their services were hired by others, amongst them Lala Kanshi Ram and his group. Many more had bicycles. The rest planned to carry things themselves.

The convoy was to leave on the twenty-fourth of September. It would be the first day of the lunar month. The Major would have liked to have a bigger moon, to take advantage of its light. But it could not be helped and he wasn't going to put off the departure date for that.

And only then, only a couple of days before the convoy was to set out, the wheel of fate closed in on the family of Sardar Teja Singh. Niranjan Singh became increasingly morose as the days went by. The subject of their hair came up each night, and he maintained as strongly he would not cut it. Sardar Teja Singh remained neutral. He said if Niranjan cut his, he would go ahead and do it too. Isher Kaur cried each night. At times she felt like agreeing with her husband. At others she thought he was a headstrong brute. It was her tears which ultimately moved Niranjan Singh. He said one night he would after all cut his hair, if their safety depended on that alone. He would do it a day before they were to set out, he said.

For the first time in weeks, Isher Kaur slept peacefully that night. There was a reasonable chance they would get to India safely now. And she said to herself she would join Niranjan Singh in the penance at the Golden Temple in Amritsar. Surely, Guru Maharaj was there to forgive them for their follies and not to punish them. She slept peacefully and in her sleep she saw dreams of her child suckling at her breast. Unlike other Indian women, she wanted her first child to be a girl. The boys were trouble-makers, the girls were so gentle and meek. And they suckled at the breast so softly, so noiselessly—and so gratefully, happy to belong to the mother. Whereas the boys tugged and pulled at them like monsters, wanting to tear the source of their birth apart.

She saw in her dream her little girl holding her white breast with her pinkish little hands and nibbling at her nipple with her pinkish mouth. The dark nipple, dripping with milk, slipped in and out of her little mouth and the rub of toothless gums on her sensitive skin was giving Isher Kaur the most delicious feeling. She saw the child still attached to her through the umbilical cord, though she was lying next to her in the bed. She liked the sight of that thin cord, starting out from the girl's small but swollen navel and disappearing into her interior. No, please don't cut the cord, she muttered to a fat ugly midwife she saw advancing towards them with a huge pair of scissors in her hand. The dazzling light of the scissors blinded Isher Kaur in the dream. No, please don't, she shouted out aloud—please, *don't*!

Isher Kaur woke up and found herself drenched with sweat. She heard a number of voices outside and saw Bibi Amar Vati advancing into the tent. Her arms were raised in the air like two scissor blades, and her white, terror-filled eyes shone bright in the early morning light. She was saying: 'Ni, Isher Kaurai, get up. A terrible thing has happened, a very terrible thing!'

Isher Kaur was instantly awake. She also saw her father, Teja Singh, getting up bewildered and going for his turban. Her husband she did not see on his bed.

'Ni, come, you unfortunate one, your husband has set fire to himself!'

Isher Kaur clutched her big belly, as if someone had given her a blow there. She said, 'Hai,' and in an instant she was outside the tent, running behind Bibi Amar Vati. Sardar Teja Singh ran alongside her. While running, he asked incoherently of the crowd: 'What's happened?'

When they reached the fence near the water taps, they saw in the distance a mass of burning wood. In the middle of the fire they saw a hunched up, drooping figure—all aflame. It was Niranjan Singh.

'Hai, hai; hai,' shouted Isher Kaur and she wanted to run straight into that fire.

Lala Kanshi Ram held her firmly and said:

'No. No, beti, it's too late.'

'Hai, hai, hai,' shouted Isher Kaur, and she bit at Lala Kanshi Ram's hands to get free.

The fire was roaring and burning with great force. There was chaos among the hundred odd people who were gathered there. Some were vainly throwing earth at the fire, some were throwing water. So strong were the flames it was impossible for anyone to get too close to them. A cry went up from the flames. Niranjan Singh was still alive. And he shouted in agony but distinctly and clearly: 'I belong to Waheguru, Waheguru is great.'

At this Teja Singh started sobbing. He too wanted to rush into the flames, but he was being held back by Arun and Suraj Prakash. He sobbed and wailed: 'Oh, my son, what have you done?'

Isher Kaur beat at Lala Kanshi Ram's chest with her fists, and said: 'Leave me, chachaji, leave me.'

Lala Kanshi Ram held her firmly. Prabha Rani also caught hold of her.

Another cry of pain went up from the flames: 'Life I'll gladly lose, my Sikh dharma I won't!'

'Hai, hai, hai!' howled Isher Kaur.

In the same instant, the sitting figure slumped forward and Niranjan Singh's head and his hair were seen catching fire. That was the end.

A solemn quiet descended on the audience as Niranjan Singh burned before their eyes. His views concerning his hair were known to many in the camp, and it was clear to them he had instead chosen to kill himself. This—martyrdom—was something they had heard of but not seen it happen. And such a supreme sacrifice had a singularly humbling effect. Sardar Teja Singh said briefly, 'Only last night he had agreed to go along with us,' but after that he only watched wide-eyed. Isher Kaur too became quiet before the enormity of the event. Her stomach had expanded vastly, and her arms, her breasts, her face, had all considerably swollen. In the early morning light she looked positively hideous, as she stood with her stomach almost falling over her legs. But there was also a calm on her face, a calm not much different from the one that came on her when she thought of the baby inside of her and its mysteries. She had stopped crying and was staring at the flames. They were all staring at the flames.

In that silence, the noise and the crackling of the fire seemed out of place. No, it did not seem out of place, it belonged with the sanctity of the moment. Soon the burned out pieces of wood crumpled into ash and only a smouldering heap remained there. And then someone picked up the chant, 'Waheguru, Waheguru, Waheguru.' It was the voice of someone unconnected with the family, but it was a weeping, trembling voice. The others joined in and it became a gentle, steady, roll. 'Waheguru, Waheguru, Waheguru!' 'Waheguru, Waheguru, Waheguru!' And slowly they started going round the fire. With hands folded in obeisance, they made a circle, and bowed deep before the heap of bones and cinders. They also kept up the chant.

The news spread, and a steady stream of men, women and children kept circling the ashes throughout the day; in no time the ashes had become a samadhi, a place of religious veneration. Captain Rahmat-Ullah Khan arrived at the scene along with a few soldiers, and he said he wanted to investigate. The other Sikhs in the camp had posted a guard of five men with sword in hand around the ashes. When Rahmat-Ullah Khan saw this he abstained and standing silently for a while went back to his office. So loud was the protest from the crowd he also took his men back with him.

It was easy for Niranjan Singh to have picked up the wood from the huge store that was kept in the camp for the use of the inmates. No one knew how he had obtained the tin of kerosene which was found lying next to the fire, or when he had got out of his tent and made all these preparations. The first notice of the event was taken only when he had already set fire to himself and was loudly proclaiming, 'My life I may lose, my Sikh dharma I won't.' There were many early risers in the camp, and many now claimed to be the first who saw him burning. These details were of no meaning to Isher Kaur and Teja Singh, who were led back to their tent in a daze. They were torn with sorrow, but everyone said Niranjan was a martyr and they felt they shouldn't cry. Isher Kaur also felt a state of amnesia come over her. Who was this Niranjan Singh they were talking about? Was he really dead? Was it true she was carrying his child in her womb? Was he her husband?

Niranjan's ashes were collected the day after, placed in a red cotton bag, and the bag handed to Isher Kaur. It was her express wish the ashes be carried to the Ganges, and everyone agreed. ('Besides, I'll have company on the way,' she said.) Without a break, inmates of the camp were still filing past the ashes twenty-six hours later. They came throughout the day; they came throughout the night. Many placed a mark of the ash on their foreheads; many others carried it back with them, tying it up in a part of their dopattas or turbans. So sharp was the desire for a memento the volunteers were afraid nothing of the ashes would be left; in the end, they would not allow anyone to touch them. No garlands and flowers were available, but tree leaves were placed in the bag, before Lala Kanshi Ram and Sardar Teja Singh picked up each piece of bone, washed it with water, and lowered it into the bag. Soon Niranjan, reduced to a handful of bones, was in the lap of his wife once again. And she kissed him and took him home into the tent.

These nights Chandni was terribly frightened and she fiercely clung to Arun. This was the first unnatural death she had seen and she was all shaken up.

'I'm so afraid,' she whispered into Arun's ears.

'Why? I'm there to take care of you,' whispered Arun, lifting her shirt and pressing her naked belly to his own.

'I'm afraid for you too.'

'Nothing will happen to me.'

'Do you really love me?'

'I do.'

'Truly?'

'Truly.'

'And you'll marry me?'

'I will.'

'Make me your wife?'

'I will.'

'Truly?'

'Truly.'

'Say "wife" to me.'

'Wife!'

'Say again.'

'Wife—beloved!'

'Oh!'

She hugged him hard in the dark, her belly twitching involuntarily against his skin.

CHAPTER 4

ON the first day of the march, most people in the convoy repeatedly stopped and looked at the distant landmarks of the city of Sialkot. Its houses, its temples and its mosques, its church spires, its factories, stood out sharply in the blazing sun, and the men vied with each other in identifying them and pointing them out to others. It was a warm day, and the fields stretched clean and wide, ready for the winter sowing. There was no activity in the fields, though; they were deserted. The sowing would have to be postponed this year, thought Lala Kanshi Ram.

Their friends in the city had come to see them off. Chaudhri Barkat Ali and Munir had reached the camp before dawn. Muslim friends of other inmates came, too. Munir handed a letter to Arun from Nur. There were only a few lines in Urdu on a piece of paper taken from a college exercise book, with several smudges where the ink had trailed down to the next line. 'I'm weeping when I write this to you,' wrote Nur. 'Will I ever see you again? God alone knows why people are so full of hate. I wish they were not to part souls that love each other. But I'll think of you till the day of my death. May Allah protect you. Khuda hafiz.'

There was no rhetoric in the letter. No grandiose promises were made, no pledges offered, no pledges demanded. It was clear Nur saw no hope of meeting Arun again. It was also clear how hurt she was to be losing him. The letter was not only smudgy with her tears; the whole paper seemed to have been dipped in the sadness of her heart. As Arun held it in his hand and read it, it rustled ominously and it looked as though any minute it would fall apart.

A surge of pain came over Arun as he read the letter. Quickly, hurriedly, he glanced through it and put it in his trouser pocket. Quickly, he also looked at Munir. Chandni had seeped so deeply into his consciousness Nur now seemed only a milestone—a milestone which he remembered, but had left far back on his path. And yet he felt an acute pain rise in him, and he gasped for breath.

A large crowd of spectators from the city had assembled outside the gate of the camp. They were held back by the Pakistani guards; only those who could identify themselves were allowed to enter the camp. But as the convoy moved out in batches, they jeered at the men and women and shouted insults.

Lala Kanshi Ram's unit was fourth in the order of the march. To maintain discipline, the Indian Major had decided on moving people line by line. First one line of the tents was cleared out, then the next. The army vehicles forming part of each unit rolled forward precisely as the men of that unit marched out.

Lala Kanshi Ram was too restless to stay with his family, and since early morning was touring the lanes, supervising the preparations of various families. Now, well before the turn of his unit came to move out, he went up to the main gate to see how things were going.

There was nothing much to see. Since the army was handling the arrangements, there was clock-like regularity in everything. Last evening Captain Rahmat-Ullah Khan had formally handed over to Major Jang Bahadur Singh the list of people who were to go in the convoy. The Major signed a paper in Captain Rahmat-Ullah Khan's office saying he had taken charge of them. The two commandants then shook hands, and moved to take tea with the other Indian and Pakistani officers. The Indian soldiers too were entertained at a formal tea by the Pakistani soldiers. The idea was to part in a spirit of goodwill. Some of these men had known each other in regimental centres in the prepartition days, and two officers with Major Jang Bahadur Singh, a captain and a lieutenant, were contemporaries of Captain Rahmat-Ullah Khan in the Indian Military Academy at Dehradun. No attempts at conviviality amongst these men had so far been made. The Indians had stayed in their enclosure; the Pakistanis had stayed in their quarters. But the Indians were leaving tomorrow and an effort was made to establish the fellowship which the different communities had in the pre-1947 days. The tea did not succeed, though. The officers and men remained cold towards each other, and their smiles did not spread beyond their lips.

Lala Kanshi Ram stood at the gate and looked at the refugees departing from the camp. The bullock carts creaked unsteadily. Most men carried bags on their backs, or on bicycles. The women marched along with their men, holding their children not by the finger but by the wrist, afraid someone would come and snatch them away at this last moment. A squad of armed Pakistani soldiers was lined up near the gate. Two machine guns were mounted on raised platforms, both commanding a clear view of the gate. The machine guns were also manned by Pakistani soldiers. The safety of the refugees, until they had moved out of the camp limits, was still the business of the Pakistani army.

The Indian officers moved around with confidence. Their badges glittered in the sun and they looked cool and self-possessed. All of them carried revolvers. Many had sten guns slung over their backs. They smiled at the refugees encouragingly. They also urged them along in a friendly way: 'Hurry up. Get a move on.'

As he stood and watched the flow of the convoy, Lala Kanshi Ram became aware of someone trying to attract his attention among the crowd of Muslim spectators. It was a familiar face, yet it was also somewhat unfamiliar. A haggard pair of eyes; red, paan-smeared, charred lips; a vulgar, commonplace smile. That was familiar. A Muslim fez on the head. That was quite unfamiliar. Why, it was Gangu Mull!

Gangu Mull had not been seen for many days, and it was taken he had been killed by the Muslims or he had deserted Bibi Amar Vati and gone off to India in one of the refugee trains. Bibi Amar Vati wasted no tears on him. She even looked glad to be rid of him. When Lala Kanshi Ram found her too sombre and chid her for missing Gangu Mull, she said: 'That loafer? Never!' This was not quite true. Lala Kanshi Ram knew when she took him into her household, she had surrendered a part of herself to that vagabond for good. Maybe she needed him for her quarrels, but need him she did. For often she sat vacuously now and would be unusually peevish.

It had not remotely occurred to Lala Kanshi Ram that Gangu Mull might have become a Muslim.

He saw him trying to draw his attention, and couldn't believe his eyes.

Lala Kanshi Ram walked up to him in utter disbelief, his hands raised in surprise.

Gangu Mull was surrounded by a throng. He caught hold of Lala Kanshi Ram's hands and took him to a quiet corner.

'What's the meaning of this, Gangu Mull?'

'I'm Gangu Mull no more, I am Ghulam Muhammad.'

The man was laughing, but his voice was unsteady, embarrassed at the admission.

'So I see. But how awful! What will Bibi Amar Vati say?'

'You don't have to tell her, Lala Kanshi Ram. You know what a bitch she is—foul mouthed and always quarrelling. I was sick of her, as it was.'

'But turning a Muslim?'

'Why not? What would India have given me?'

'And now?'

'Now I own our two buildings in Fort Street.'

'You don't say.'

'Well, they were my property, and I have decided to stay on here as a Muslim. They will continue to remain my property.'

There was something absurdly comic in that claim. Lala Kanshi Ram would have liked to see Bibi Amar Vati handle him herself on this!

'I'm also thinking of taking a Muslim wife.'

Lala Kanshi Ram was so intrigued he could not help laughing out aloud. And suddenly, in a flash, the rare sensation of seeing through the humbug of existence flooded him once again, and he saw before him clearly the bare, basic meaning of living, shorn of trimmings and embellishments. He at once squirmed a little, shrugged his shoulders and pulled himself together. His chin stiffened, his chest expanded, his nose acquired a firmer footing on his face—and he felt utterly perceptive, utterly knowledgeable. He took out one of the ends of his turban and pulling it tight tucked it back in giving the turban a trimmer look and a more solid, square hold on his head.

'If you will be any happier that way,' he murmured.

'I'm sure I will be. Can't you see?'

'Yes, I think I can,' he said looking at him searchingly.

Lala Kanshi Ram heard a sound behind him.

'Now who could have thought it!' came the taut, sharp voice of Bibi Amar Vati over his shoulder.

Lala Kanshi Ram did not know who had informed Bibi Amar Vati, but there she was standing at his elbow, her head tilted back, and staring at Gangu Mull.

Bibi Amar Vati neither abused nor kicked at her husband. She only kept staring at him with that brazen look in her eyes. And then she went into a paroxysm of laughter. Peels and peels of it spurted out of her throat as she looked at him and continued to laugh. And much to Lala Kanshi Ram's surprise, Gangu Mull did not run away from the scene, nor become violent. While Bibi Amar Vati laughed, he stood his ground and stared back at her. And lo, soon he joined her in the laughter, and he too was laughing. Not loudly and madly like her. He was laughing self-consciously, surreptitiously. But he was laughing all right.

Gangu Mull spoke first.

'Couldn't let you go from here without seeing you.'

He looked at Bibi Amar Vati with an odd longing.

'Ah, ha, ha! Without seeing you!' said Bibi Amar Vati, speaking incoherently through her spurts of laughter.

She stared at him with unending curiosity, especially at the red fez on his head.

'You know it's true.'

'Ah, ha, ha!'

'Don't laugh.'

'What else?'

'I'm only protecting your interests—your property. I thought this was the best way of doing it.'

'Ah, ha, ha!'

'I'll only be acting as your agent.'

'Ah, ha, ha!'

Right off Lala Kanshi Ram had the unmistakable feeling he was not wanted there; they wanted to be left alone.

Neither of them looked particularly impressive physically. Bibi Amar Vati was thin and straight like a pole. Her breasts were flattened like pancakes and hung low to her navel. Her neck stood out because of the swollen veins of her throat, but it was a parched and emaciated neck. Her cheeks were sunken permanently, and nothing, no amount of pleasure or excitement, could liven them up. Gangu Mull was equally repulsive to look at.

And yet they were staring at each other in some dire want, and this made them look imposing.

Bibi Amar Vati was no longer laughing. Lala Kanshi Ram was certain at this precise moment she had lost all consciousness of his presence near her. Her eyes were fixed on Gangu Mull and she seemed to be hardly breathing.

'Come with us! I want you to.' Bibi Amar Vati seemed to; be reciting an incantation, to be casting a spell on him. She said each word slowly.

'No.' Gangu Mull was evasive.

'So what you wanted out of me was my money?' The fire was back in her voice.

'No.'

'Come with us!' She returned to the slow chant.

'No.'

They were quiet after that.

'Come, brother Kanshi Ram,' said Bibi Amar Vati turning away.

Even at this stage, when all hope of reclaiming Gangu Mull was gone, she did not get wild or abusive. She looked crestfallen, confirmed as she was in her knowledge that the piece of charcoal she had been trying to pass off as a jewel all these years was nothing but a piece of coal. A greyishness came in her eyes, but beyond that and beyond a slight trembling of her lips, she gave no indication of her inner turmoil. When she met Suraj Prakash coming her way and when Suraj wanted to know whether or not the news about his father was true, she sent him back, saying: 'You are not going to see him.' To Lala Kanshi Ram she said: 'It's better this way. At least the property will remain in the family!' She tried to laugh but only a harsh sound came out of her throat. Yet she did not flinch for a second. By the time their unit left the camp gate, Gangu Mull had disappeared. In the meantime, many others had gone up to the gate to see him, but she allowed no one to discuss him with her. Sullenly she sat on a discarded oil drum near her tent, and continued to supervise Sunanda's packing.

Throughout the first day's march Bibi Amar Vati remained taciturn. In his long association with her, Lala Kanshi Ram had always seen her imperious. She missed no occasion of scoring a point over her adversary, and was dreaded in the whole street. Today she was like a beaten warrior; her armour was down and she was looking a shrivelled, old woman, who could not even walk straight. Of the many things that had recently grieved Lala Kanshi Ram, this in some ways cut the deepest. He had known Bibi Amar Vati as a lioness, fierce and unyielding. While he himself fought her on occasion, he was also attracted by the intensity and determination with which she single-handed held her ground. He saw her now as a scarecrow and this hurt. He wanted her to be a lioness once more.

She walked on dejectedly, avoiding all conversation. For Bhavna and Nava Kant, the children of Suraj Prakash, the march was much fun. They were so excited and talkative, and were running from person to person. Bibi Amar Vati rebuked them and sent them away, when they tried to talk to her. She walked on alone.

She asked Lala Kanshi Ram briefly:

'Did you find out about Mukanda's mother?'

'She was killed, he told me.'

'Any news of Mukanda?'

'None. Maybe killed. I hear a mass killing of Hindu prisoners did take place inside of the city prison.'

'He might have become a Muslim!' she said in bitterness.

Soon after they had passed the Ramlila ground by the side of Murray College, the city was hidden from their sight. Like the rest, Lala Kanshi Ram in his mind was busy adding up his losses. They were numerous. As the city vanished from his sight, he became more concerned about what lay ahead. The problems that loomed in the future were a thousand fold more complex and bewildering than what he had gone through. Hitherto he had only died—in various ways. It involved no act of the will on his part; the death came suddenly and swiftly and offered no alternatives. The act of creation on the other hand demanded a slow nursing, a careful watch, which in spite of the long effort might or might not blossom into fruit. Many parts of him had died but there were others still alive, forcefully and affirmatively alive, and he knew he was not defeated. But the tasks ahead of him were multitudinous and he faltered and fumbled in his steps.

For the first night, the convoy halted at Gunna Kalan, a village six miles out of Sialkot. The front columns of the convoy reached there three hours after they left the camp in Sialkot Cantonment. Small groups of inquisitive men were collected at a few intersections of the Cantonment, but on the whole these six miles lay in the open countryside and the refugees met with no hostility. They walked on the main highway, which was paved and which had large shisham trees on both sides of it. The dust kicked up by their feet rose like thin haze. Between whiles they passed dumps of refuse, consisting of discarded clothes, a few shoes, battered steel trunks and walking sticks. These were remains of the groups that had been attacked by hostile mobs. But because of the nearness of the Cantonment, there had not been much violence here. At least they saw nothing compared to the reports they had heard in the camp.

The convoy stopped for the night in open fields outside of Gunna Kalan. Like a swarm of locusts, the units arrived and spread themselves out in the fields. The army suggested they stay in neat lanes. Yet they spread more in clusters and groups, several families staying close to each other. Every available foot of space in several large fields was taken up, and improvised beds, mostly jute mats or sheets, were rolled out on the ground. The food was cooked jointly by many families together, and no one complained.

Facilities for water existed in the form of wells nearby. For toilet, the other fields served the purpose.

Chaudhri Barkat Ali and Munir had walked these six miles along with Lala Kanshi Ram's family. By the time they had found a place to camp, it was three o'clock, and the shadows in the fields had started to lengthen.

'We must return,' said Chaudhri Barkat Ali, his giant frame shaking.

'Khuda hafiz, brother Kanshi Ram,' he said, folding his hands.

'These have been good years,' said Lala Kanshi Ram, taking Chaudhri Barkat Ali's hands in his own.

There were tears in the eyes of both men.

They had nothing more to say, having exhausted themselves of emotion in all these weeks.

'You took a lot of trouble for us.'

'Now, brother Kanshi Ram!'

Facing Prabha Rani, Chaudhri Barkat Ali said: 'Sister, khuda hafiz.'

'If not in our life-time, Insha-Allah in the life-time of our children this folly will surely be undone,' said Chaudhri Barkat Ali, looking at Lala Kanshi Ram. 'We are one people and religion cannot separate us from each other.'

'I hope you are right.'

Munir was tongue-tied throughout the day and Arun wondered why he had come. He gave no signs of boredom either and seemed most reluctant to leave.

'I'll write to you, Munir.'

'You must. Send your address, wherever you are.'

'Tell Nur I'll think of her.'

There was no essential lie in this, thought Arun. He did miss Nur and was unlikely to forget her ever. The loves of a man come and go, but the memory of the first love is always a little more tender than that of the other passions. And then the thought that the moment Munir left, it would be the end of whatever link he still possessed with Nur, saddened Arun considerably.

'I shall,' said Munir.

'Tell her I love her,' said Arun in a rush of sentiment.

Munir looked closely at his eyes.

'I shall.'

Arun embraced Munir and Munir returned the embrace.

When Chaudhari Barkat Ali and Munir left, for a long while Lala Kanshi Ram and Arun stood looking in the direction they had gone. They had bicycles with them, and soon they were out of sight. Lala Kanshi Ram and Arun looked in that direction and they did not speak to each other. Lala Kanshi Ram was thinking of Chaudhri Barkat Ali, but Arun was thinking neither of Munir nor of Nur. This minute; he was thinking of Sergeant Bill Davidson. He had see him in his barracks once since he helped them to get to the refugee camp. Munir had told him he had been transferred back home and had already left for England, to be demobilized. Arun was surprised he had not come and said goodbye to him. Maybe he was feeling embarrassed, Arun was saying to himself. On account of what? he asked himself.

That evening Arun was exposed to a wondrous new beauty he had never dreamt of before, never dreamt it existed. As the evening fell, a stillness seemed to envelop the whole camp. Arun was a city boy, for whom days and nights were only signs to measure time; he did not invest them with abstruse qualities. He opened his eyes in the morning and the sun was out, shining on the world. And he did not know it was night, until all at once he saw the shopkeepers switching on lights and he looked up at the sky and found it had got dark. The sun, the moon, and the stars were only so many objects of convenience. That they possessed a life of their own, a viable, independent existence, and could influence his moods the same way a human being did, he had never considered.

The sun went down the broad horizon as if it were literally walking down a flight of stairs, taking each step with the majesty of a king. Arun had been told not to look straight at it. It might damage his eyes. But so harmless was that storehouse of energy today, so mildly reddish, he stared at it unblinking. Its solidity shook Arun. He had read in books it was so much bigger than the earth. He now felt its size, as he saw its gigantic bulk sink lower and lower. The shrubs in the fields were silhouetted against it, and it seemed to be pulling the whole earth behind it—so powerful it looked.

The dusk came on and it was silent as in an empty classroom. There were no dusks in town. Until it became dark, it was an extension of the day. When darkness fell, it was night. Here the half light held a distinct sway on the land. Arun couldn't say for certain whence that light came. The sun was gone, and the hairline of the moon seemed too weak to be any good. And yet the earth was lit up. Oh, yes! It came out from the earth itself—through small pores along its surface. Now wasn't he lucky! For the first time in his life he was seeing the light—the only true light—shed by his own planet.

And the silence. It was *pure* silence, unadulterated. Not that there were no noises. There were the birds that flew overhead in groups, chirping. There was the noise from the camp. There were the crickets, so loud in the fields. There was the hoot of a water-mill near the village. There was the occasional noise of a car or a truck speeding on the highway. But over and above these noises, shrouding them all, was the blanket of silence. Rather, it was a noise in itself, that silence. Suspended from the sky by invisible hands, it fell gently on everything below like a waterfall. It had not only sound, it had mass and substance to it. Arun could feel, he could touch that silence.

It was getting darker by degrees and he wanted to walk deep into the fields—away from the camp.

A guard stopped him.

'Where're you going?'

'Only for the toilet.'

'See you don't wander too far. It's dangerous.'

'Don't worry about me.'

He walked with heavy steps, feeling strange and newly fashioned. This particular field had been tilled and his feet sank into the soft, upturned earth. The feeling of communion grew on him, as he walked; he was establishing new contacts, growing new roots. As he saw the dusky emptiness of the air above the fields, he was convinced emptiness had volume, it had a shape. For it seemed to be hugging him—the ephemeral nothingness that lay between the sky and the earth. He breathed deep and felt satiated, lifting his head high into the sky and exposing his neck to the caress of the spirit roaming there. Some distance away, he could see the guards pacing up and down. He also saw the innumerable little fires over which the refugees were cooking. A little to the right, the army had pitched its tents and the army vehicles stood parked by their side. The lowing of the bullocks which pulled the carts came to him, too. But he thought himself in no danger and looked upon them all as an intrusion.

The stars came out and still he did not return to the camp; he lingered. It was now totally dark; even the thin crescent had vanished. High above, countless lights twinkled in the sky. He knew of some names. The Big Bear. The Little Bear. Cassiopeia. But there were formations he had not seen before. The noise of the crickets had increased and they seemed to be shrieking from every bush and tree. The other noises had dimmed. The mill had stopped altogether. There were no cars or trucks. The noise from the camp continued, but only in the background, like the noise of a distant fair you might be hearing in your room. There was only he there and the crickets and the peace of the star-studded night. And right then he wanted Chandni to be with him. And he wanted to make love to her. The odour of growing vegetables assailed his nostrils from the fields and acted as a strong aphrodisiac. Yes, he wanted to hold Chandni in his arms and make love to her. On the damp, upturned field—sinking into the earth and smelling of it. It was a need of the moment driven hard unto him, and he longed for it as he had never longed before. He could feel the blood racing fast in him and he pounded his chest with his fists to quiet it down. And he suddenly felt frightened to be standing there alone. The wild was only a wilderness if the beloved was not there with you. He started walking back towards the camp.

The ground under his mat was hard, but it was cool and Arun slept well through the night. Indistinct noises of children weeping, men coughing, the guards hailing each other, kept coming to him, yet they did not disturb him; in the context of the vast openness, they were soothing noises. Off and on he awoke and saw the stars overhead, each time a different figure confronting his eyes. Some time in the night he also heard the honking of wild geese. In half sleep, he raised himself and looked around. Chandni was asleep a long way from him. He saw a heap, and he saw others, so many of them, who lay between him and her. Yes, he must take her out into the fields with him, he said to himself, before he dropped off to sleep again.

Chandni did not agree to go, until they had reached Narowal some days later. They were obliged to spend an additional night at Gunna Kalan, and could not leave the next day as scheduled. It was for the first time in their lives many people had walked six miles on foot, and there were many casualties. Many had blisters on their feet, many complained of stomach ailments, the others just appeared fatigued. Much against his wishes, Major Jang Bahadur Singh sanctioned another day's halt at Gunna Kalan, making up for it the day after when, instead of stopping at Badiana or

Chawinda, they marched straight through to Pasrur—a distance of ten miles from Gunna Kalan and sixteen from Sialkot.

Arun spoke to Chandni on their second day at Gunna Kalan.

'I want you to go out with me to the fields this evening.'

'Which fields?'

'Over there.' He pointed towards the horizon.

'Why?' She looked surprised.

'To look at the wilderness.'

'To look at the wilderness?'

'Yes.' He was becoming clumsy.

'What's so special about it?'

'It is so beautiful!' He tried to smile.

She seemed to consider it.

'No, I won't.' She shook her head.

'Why not?'

'It is too dangerous.'

'How?'

'There are Muslims all around.'

'We'll be close enough to the camp.'

His voice was hoarse and she looked up at him. He was blushing.

'No.' She too blushed.

'I want to be alone with you!'

The blush on her face spread to her neck and she shook her head.

'We're alone a good deal.'

'It is not the same thing.'

She looked at the ground and said nothing.

'And besides it's a different world out there.'

She said nothing.

'You will come, won't you?' He seemed surer now.

She shook her head and kicked the earth around with her foot.

'I feel afraid!'

'Of me?'

'No!—just afraid.'

'What of?'

'I don't know.'

Her eyes lowered, she kept scraping at the earth with her foot.

It was a shapely foot, the ankle was strong, the instep was fatty and arched smoothly, the toes he could see through the sandal small and rounded.

'You don't trust me.' The longing in his voice gave him away, though.

'I do.'

'You must come then. For a few minutes.'

A crimson hue appeared in her eyes and they became moist with desire. She shook her head and continued to scrape the earth.

'I cannot.'

The convoy moved very slowly. At Pasrur, the tehsil headquarters, they were obliged to spend four days. The arrangements for the departure of refugees from the local camp had not yet been completed. The liaison officer Major Jang Bahadur Singh had left behind in Pasrur said the Pakistani authorities were creating obstructions on purpose. He warned the Major the convoy might be attacked by the local Muslims. He had seen large concentrations of them in the city. He feared it was to help the mob that the Pakistani authorities were not letting them depart.

The Pasrur camp was located in a large school building on the outskirts of the town. While a few thousand refugees from the convoy were accommodated in the building, the rest stayed in the grounds and the fields adjacent to the school. There were only two thousand refugees in the camp, and it was decided to distribute them amongst the ten units of the convoy; no extra unit was formed for them. Men and women in the convoy had heard of the threatened attack and each night they waited breathlessly. The Indian officers were extra vigilant. For all the four nights, Arun kept awake. So did Suraj Prakash. So did hundreds of other men. The women kept awake half the night, gossiping of domestic things but with their ears alert for the Muslim war cry of 'Allah-o-Akbar', and then, exhausted, dozed off to sleep.

No attack came and the convoy set out on the fifth day after its arrival in Pasrur.

It was a weary convoy which pulled out of Pasrur. Men's nerves were taut from four sleepless nights. Major Jang Bahadur Singh tried to cheer them up, but they had seen with their own eyes the extent of the havoc. In each village they passed, they found the remains of parties that had been attacked and butchered. In many cases, the dismembered human limbs and skeletons were still lying there, and the stench was intolerable. And they saw only bearded Muslim faces in these villages. The Hindu population had been completely driven out—or completely exterminated. Hindu and Sikh places of worship had obviously been defiled, because outside of them there were obscene words written in Urdu. When at a few of the places, the Indian officers enquired if there were Hindu families there, the bearded Muslims smiled insolently and said: 'Look for yourself.' In some villages Major Jang Bahadur Singh went round in his jeep shouting through a loud-speaker, asking the Hindus and the Sikhs to come out. His words were greeted with silence from empty houses. In one small village of twenty houses, every single house had been destroyed and there was not a soul in sight. It looked a phantom village, the men were gone, the collapsed mud walls revealed broken charpoys and household goods in disarray, even the stray dogs had vanished from its only street. The refugees in the convoy had seen all that for themselves and the officers of the Indian army failed to hearten them.

Paradoxically enough, Lala Kanshi Ram was feeling fine that day. These fields around him running up to the limit of the sky, the large mango orchards, the unpaved village roads crisscrossing the highway, the big shisham trees beside all the roads, the robust men you ran into, the village rainwater tanks with the buffaloes bathing in them, the innumerable wells and the bullocks and the Persian wheels of those wells, the titilating breeze that blew, they were reminders enough he had not left his beloved Punjab behind yet. He thought of his childhood in rural Sambrhial and back to him came identical fields and orchards, identical roads, identical tanks, identical wells, to confirm his feelings. He too had passed the last four nights in tension, but he did not feel at all exhausted. Rather, the landscape immediately after Pasrur had taken on such an intensely Punjabi character Lala Kanshi Ram was feeling curiously invigorated. The morning breeze was scintillating, it was so refreshing. And the soft rumbling sound of the Persian wheel coming from a well sounded most melodious to his ears. And Lala Kanshi Ram stepped ahead with alacrity, sad but cheerful.

The first attack on the convoy came soon afterwards. Lala Kanshi Ram was shaken out of his feeling of wellbeing by the noise of machine-gun firing and the men of the Indian army shouting: 'Stop where you are. Sit down, sit down on the road. Don't panic!' Before Lala Kanshi Ram knew what was happening, he caught hold of Prabha Rai and was squatted on the ground. He shouted for Arun, who ran to him, holding Chandni by the arm. They too sat down near them. Padmini, Bibi Amar Vati, Sunanda, Suraj Prakash and Sardar Teja Singh were squatting a few feet away. Instinctively, each one sat down where he was.

The firing lay somewhere ahead but they saw nothing. They heard tumultous shouting and cries of 'Allah-o-Akbar'. Human shrieks and loud cries were clearly audible in that uproar. The Indian soldiers near Lala Kanshi Ram had taken positions on both sides of the road, and a jeep went whirling by with a few officers in it. One of the officers was shouting: 'Remain seated. Don't panic.'

There were several bursts of machine-gun fire. Many single shots were also heard. And a fresh uproar went into the air, now from a little to the left of the road.

The countryside was flat like a table top. There were some mango orchards ahead of them, and they could not see what lay beyond. The attack was coming from somewhere ahead of those orchards.

The Indian soldiers had orders to protect the special section of the convoy to which they were assigned and not to rush ahead or backward unless they were summoned. So the soldiers attached to unit four stayed with that unit. They looked nervously ahead and waited for developments. Rifles and sten guns at the ready, they scanned the horizon. The noise and the tumult remained confined to the section ahead of them.

The convoy was halted there for over two hours. People looked wan with fear and tension. Many were shivering, and murmuring prayers. Some of the women were weeping. After the initial burst of firing was over, Sardar Teja Singh got up and walked back to where the trucks were to see Isher Kaur. Suraj Prakash went with him. Arun still held Chandni, who seemed frightened to death, by the arm. The girl leaned against him and her eyes were wide open! Padmini saw her from where she sat and she did not like Arun's hand on her arm, his fingers going deep into her flesh. Then she saw her terror-stricken eyes. While Prabha Rani remained squatting, Lala Kanshi Ram had raised himself on his knees and was asking the soldiers: 'What's up?' 'We don't know,' said one of them.

It was only after they had reached Qila Sobha Singh in the afternoon they got to know the details. The convoy had been ambushed, and the sword had fallen on parts of unit two and unit three. The first unit had reached Qila Sobha Singh, a distance of seven miles from Pasrur, and they were unpacking. Some of the rear units had not yet left the Pasrur refugee camp. As soon as the second unit had passed the mango gardens that cut off one half of the valley from the other, they heard gun shots and shouts of 'Allah-o-Akbar' and 'Ya Ali' and saw a group of armed men on horseback to their right. The Indian army opened fire at the group, but the people in the convoy panicked and seeing the attack coming on them from the right of the road, they ran into the big mango gardens on their left. And that's where the ambush awaited them. The attack from the right was a ruse, to frighten them and make them run to the left. A large number of Muslims armed with rifles and swords were concealed in the gardens. That's when the second shout had gone up. In the close, hand to hand, slaughter that followed, the Indian army was not of much help. The soldiers couldn't fire on a crowd so mixed up, where they were afraid of hitting their own people. They fixed bayonets and attacked into the gardens, but many of them were killed, along with hundreds of refugees. The attack was broken off after some time, when the Muslim mob disappeared on horses, carrying away a number of young refugee girls with them and raising a storm of dust in the air.

So many villages dotted the fields. The marauders disappeared into these villages, and it was for Major Jang Bahadur Singh to decide whether or not to pursue them there. Considering the cover given to the enemy by the foliage in the valley and the trees, he decided against it. He was worried about the security of the rest of the convoy. Tragic as the attack was, it had hit only a small section. He wanted the rest to reach safety.

When Lala Kanshi Ram's party passed the spot where the ambush had been organized, they found the road littered with articles, discarded turbans and female headgear, shoes, umbrellas, sticks, and cans of food. The things were strewn diagonally—from the road to the orchards—as though a wind coming from the right had carried them over to the left. In the gardens, which ran for over a mile by the side of the road, dead bodies were lying all over; there were bodies on the road as well. When people died of illness or exhaustion, as many did, they were cremated by the roadside and the family moved on. It was decided to leave these bodies where they were; they were far too numerous to be attended to. A party might return in the evening to collect them and cremate them, but first Major Jang Bahadur Singh wanted the convoy safely settled in Qila Sobha Singh.

The men in the convoy stepped over the bodies in their way and hurried along. The women covered up their faces with their dopattas, though as yet there was no stench. Most of the dead lay fully dressed. Only a few women lay with their breasts exposed, with a dead child next to the breast. Most of the children lay with their faces downward. The men lay on their backs or on their sides, their mouths open. Some women lay doubled up like bundles. While there were splashes of blood on the ground, and in a few cases on the tree trunks, the bodies themselves were relatively clean. Only their unnatural postures gave out they were dead.

As they were coming to the end of the orchards, Lala Kanshi Ram saw the body of Dr Chander Bhan. He lay with one of his legs over the fallen branch of a tree and both his arms were spread wide. His eyes were open and he seemed to be staring at the men on the road.

Lala Kanshi Ram shuddered when he looked at the body. He tried to turn Prabha Rani's face, but she had seen him.

'I wonder what's become of his wife,' said Lala Kanshi Ram.

'And his children.'

When they reached Qila Sobha Singh they learned that while Mrs Chander Bhan and three children had survived the attack, two of their daughters, aged nineteen and seventeen, had been carried away by the mob. Other people had similar shocking stories awaiting them, about their acquaintances.

The following day, while the convoy was moving from Qila Sobha Singh to Narowal, they were ambushed again in an identical manner. Only this time, it was the rear of the convoy that was attacked, and none of the other units actually saw what befell the last unit. The attacking mob suffered many casualties. There were additional army men at the rear and they took a heavy toll of the attackers. Still over two hundred Hindus and Sikhs were killed, many women abducted and the number of wounded climbed to several hundred.

The second attack took place near a notorious Muslim stronghold, called Alipur Saiyidian. The front sections of the convoy had already arrived at Manjoke, a village seven miles distance from Qila Sobha Singh. That was the most restless night the refugees spent along the route. Manjoke was a small village of forty to fifty houses, and they felt no threat from those quarters. But there was Alipur Saiyidian in the vicinity, and they had been attacked from there once that day. Little unpacking was done that night and most people slept with their shoes on. No fires were lit and they ate the left-over food of yesterday. Throughout the night the wounded kept trickling in. With the first light of the next day, men were on their feet once again. Narowal, a major district town, was only six miles away. There was a regular refugee camp there, and they saw safety only in reaching it as quickly as possible.

It was at ten in the morning, on the ninth day and thirty-six miles away from Sialkot, that the advance sections of the convoy entered the premises of the camp at Narowal. The refugees there lined up to see them come in. They had lost over fifteen hundred of their number. No one had shaved for the last few days, none had had a bath since they left Pasrur. Food had run short and many had not eaten for a couple of days. And to the last person they looked demoralized. The refugees in the camp waved to them but hardly anyone waved back. They stared wearily and went straight to where their tents were pitched. The news of the two attacks on them had reached here and they had hot tea waiting for them. The tea was served to them in mugs and tumblers, and they hungrily drank it down. And then they, slumped down, lay on their luggage, and went to sleep. It was only later in the evening they unpacked.

Narowal was a sub-district headquarters. There was electricity in the town, and they had also electrified the camp. There were sufficient tents for the entire convoy. There was a hospital there. There were many other facilities, too. Major Jang Bahadur Singh ordered a halt of a week, for the convoy to recoup and recover its strength.

CHAPTER 5

Two things happened to Arun at Narowal. He killed a man. And he lost Chandni for good.

Narowal was a town of a sizable population, with a heavy concentration of Muslim zamindars. Another town nearby, Zafarwal, which was connected with Narowal by a highway, had an equally strong concentration of these landlords.

The Dera Baba Nanak border with India was only eight miles from Narowal. There ran one of the five rivers of the Punjab, the river Ravi, which formed the boundary between the two new nations in the upper regions of the province. Most Hindus and Sikhs from the area had trekked to the river and crossed into India. About a thousand still languished in the Narowal refugee camp and they were to go with the convoy. Apparently the camp at one time sheltered many thousands more. There were rows upon rows of empty tents which had not yet been taken down. The men from Sialkot were first asked to occupy these tents. Only then were more put up for them.

With his usual adroitness, Lala Kanshi Ram managed to move into the already pitched tents. They were smaller in size than those erected later, and they were closer to the various camp conveniences. He got two of those tents. Into one of them, he moved himself along with Padmini and Chandni. Into the other went the remainder of their group—Bibi Amar Vati, Sunanda,

Suraj Prakash, and Teja Singh and Isher Kaur. Padmini was afraid for Chandni after she had seen Arun's hand closed intimately on her arm, and the way her daughter was leaning against him. She tried to switch places with Teja Singh and Isher Kaur. Artfully she suggested maybe Lala Kanshi Ram would like to have the unfortunate girl under his personal care. Lala Kanshi Ram wouldn't hear of it. He and Prabha Rani had come to depend on Chandni, and he insisted they should stay with him. Arun was never more happy with his father than when he asserted himself that day.

They were so exhausted in the evening that soon after they had eaten, they fell asleep. While the beds were being spread, Arun's head swam with his fancy. He would have Chandni in his arms again after all these days. He would be cautious but he wouldn't wait too long. He knew Padmini was suspicious. But how long could Padmini keep awake? She was sure to fall asleep some time. She thought she was clever but she did not know him. He would throw a rock or something, or make a sound, and if she moved he would know she was awake. The best thing would be to make no movement at all for the first hour. Only then test her out. Then the slow crawl towards Chandni. The nights were beginning to be cool and they used heavy chaders of blankets now. And then—and then, he sighed to himself—a gentle rustle and he would be lying next to Chandni's warm body. Supposing he made a mistake in the dark and went next to Padmini? He smiled at his own naughtiness and said to himself, no, he wouldn't make that mistake; he would make sure. He felt so amused at what he was thinking he started humming in English, he would make sure, he would make sure, he would make sure. Prabha Rani looked up and Arun smiled at her, but he continued to hum. Chandni was straightening the beds out and her slender, compact figure was alluringly seductive in her movements. He must have that figure in his arms tonight. He would make sure, he would make sure, he hummed with a smile on his lips.

But the moment his head was on the pillow—and while to his satisfaction he was cleverly giving time for Padmini to fall asleep—he tumbled into oblivion. When he opened his eyes next morning, it suddenly occurred to him he had overslept. He sat up in a huff, throwing off his blanket, and looked about him. The sun was shining and its first rays were already inside the tent. His father, his mother, Chandni, were still asleep. He found Padmini sitting up in her bed and staring at him. Had she sat up the whole night to find him out? Or had she only now got up? She had covered up her head with the chader, but her face was peeping out of an opening at the top. She appeared to be muttering something, reciting the morning prayer. But her eyes were fixed on Arun, and on her face there was a scowl. Arun groaned and to hide his disappointment stretched his arms and yawned, muttered, 'It's r-a-t-h-e-r-e-a-r-l-y', and fell back on the bed. He did not stir from it until he was quite sure others were awake in the tent and he wouldn't have to face Padmini alone.

Suraj Prakash said to Arun later in the day: 'You know they are going to parade naked women in the town this afternoon. Wouldn't you like to go and see?'

Arun had just finished reassuring himself. Padmini had taken no notice of him after he got up. Maybe he was imagining things. Chandni as usual had served him his breakfast, and Padmini was sitting in the tent and she had not intervened. She could have brought him his food herself. She stared hard, but she said nothing. He had gone on to touch Chandni's fingers as he took his tumbler of tea from her. She had seen that too, and no frown had appeared on her face.

Arun was feeling happy, when Suraj came with that explosive piece of information.

He immediately became tense.

'Who is parading what naked women?'

The cigarette in Suraj Prakash's hand was dancing in his excitement—his unsteady fingers trying hard to keep control over it—and there was a coarse look on his face.

'The Muslims in Narowal will be parading naked Hindu women.'

The whole camp had heard of it. The Muslims in the town were incensed at the arrival of so many thousands of Hindus and Sikhs at the refugee camp. Overnight, this had changed the character of the camp. It was a dying camp till yesterday. There were a thousand Hindus, but they were the invalids and the sick who could not make it to the border on their own. Now there was a noisy, bubbling township of tents, and once more the communal ire had raised its head in the city. And one way of overawing the Hindus was to do something really stunning. They could have attacked the camp, but that required time, and they wanted to do something quick, something *today.* A number of abducted Hindu and Sikh women were in their custody. Many of the kidnapped women disappeared into private homes. A lone Muslim dragged a woman away, and kept her for his own exclusive use. Or he took her with the consent of other Muslims, converted her to Islam, and got married to her. The rest were subjected to mass rape, at times in public places and in the presence of large gatherings. The rape was followed by other atrocities, chopping off the breasts and even death. Many of the pregnant women had their wombs torn open. The survivors were retained for repeated rapes and humiliations, until they were parceled out to decrepit wrecks—the aged, the left-overs who couldn't find a wife, or those Muslims who wanted an additional wife. In the meantime more women were abducted and the cycle was repeated all over again.

It was some of these women, recently brought to Narowal, that the Muslims of the town decided to parade through the streets.

The local authorities, the police and the military, did not interfere when such gatherings were organized. The only restriction they placed this time was that the procession should not be taken to the refugee camp; they did not want an outright clash. This did not upset the leaders. At least they would be able to give vent to their rage. And the news of the procession was sure to reach the camp and hurt.

'I hope they don't parade the girls they took away from our convoy,' said Lala Kanshi Ram, after he had heard of what was to happen.

Suraj Prakash was not concerned with that.

'Wouldn't you like to go and see?' he asked Arun, lowering his voice.

He prevailed upon Arun and the two of them, without telling anyone, disappeared from the camp after the midday meal.

As when they had gone into Sialkot, Suraj Prakash was galvanized and looked upon it as a great adventure. The promise of what he was likely to see when he got to the city, further whetted his excitement. They thought out new Muslim names for themselves, dressed more or less to look like Muslims, with their shirts sticking out of their trousers and handkerchiefs around their necks, and once again Suraj ran through the farce of making himself and Arun look circumcised.

Before the convoy started from Sialkot, Suraj had bought a second-hand cycle from another camp inmate. He had carried his children on that bicycle during the march. He suggested to Arun they ride into town on it. On second thoughts, they decided to walk. The town was only a half mile away, and they felt they would have greater mobility in the bazaars without the bicycle.

They knew no street names, and they need not have. There were only two big bazaars in Narowal, which intersected each other in the heart of the town. The road from the refugee camp led straight into one of these bazaars. As soon as they reached the intersection, they knew the procession would be along the other bazaar. Thick crowds lined the other bazaar as far as they could see, and the intersection was jammed with people.

It was the most unwholesome gathering Arun had ever seen. Not only did the men there look unclean and vulgar there was an indecorous thickness in the air and the whole atmosphere was smeared over with smut, as if a brush of some grisly substance had been run over the men, the buildings, and the bazaar. Most of the men wore crescent-shaped Muslim beards, but many were clean-shaven. Most had paan in their mouths, and the road was splattered with the red betel leaf spittle. (Arun and Suraj bought paan, too.) All windows and blinds of the houses above were shut, but all shops at the ground level were open. Many men from the crowd were squatting or standing on the shop-platforms; the rest were lined up on the road, four rows deep. The road was cleared of vendors, but the vendors (selling sweets, or toilet goods) had pushed their carts to the sides, where they formed small islands in the dense crowd—wherever the carts were. It was only three in the afternoon, but the vendors had lit their mustard oil torches which smoked in the sunlight. Whiffs of smoke were also rising from the paan and cigarette shops, where small lamps or ropes burned on shop-fronts as cigarette lighters. While Arun saw a few Central Indian Muslims there, it was by and large a Punjabi crowd. Not a single woman was around; only men. And they were strong and muscular men, their hair cropped close, their skulls heavily oiled, their eyes black with kohl. Most of them wore plain shirts and lungis or tehmads—garments they frequently would lift with their hands to cool their legs. Most of them were also wearing charms and amulets. Studded in silver or copper, and tied to the body with a black thread, there were amulets around their necks, amulets around their upper arms, and amulets around their wrists. But what unified the crowd and soldered them into a single mass was the look on their faces. It was the look of extreme sensuality.

And it was the look of hate. And furthermore, as an additional sign of their oneness, all eyes were turned east; the side from which the procession was to come.

The procession arrived. Arun counted them. There were, forty women, marching two abreast. Their ages varied from sixteen to thirty, although, to add to the grotesqueness of the display, there were two women, marching right at the end of the column, who must have been over sixty. They were all stark naked. Their heads were completely shaven; so were their armpits. So were their pubic regions. Shorne of their body hair and clothes, they looked like baby girls, or like the bald embryos one sees preserved in methylated spirit. Only the breasts and the hips gave away the age. The women walked awkwardly, looking only at the ground. They were all crying, though their eyes shed no tears. Their faces were formed into grimaces and they were sobbing. Their arms were free, but so badly had they been used, so wholly their spirits crushed, their morale shattered, none of them made any attempt to cover themselves with their hands. They swung their arms clumsily, often out of coordination with their legs. The bruises on their bodies showed they had been beaten and manhandled. Their masters walked beside them and if any of the women sagged or hung behind, they prodded her along with the whips they carried. At the head of the procession marched a single drummer with a flat drum, thumping heavily on it and announcing their arrival.

There seemed a tacit understanding between the crowd and the leaders of the procession. No one from the crowd jumped forward to molest the women or interfere with the progress of the procession. Barring that, not a single shred of decency was left. It no longer remained a lewd scene; it became evil incarnate. Darkness was added to darkness and a strange terror was let loose on earth.

The procession moved through the bazaar, and along with the procession moved a river of obscenities—foul abuses, crude personal gestures, spurts of sputum, odd articles like small coins, faded flowers, cigarette butts and bidis that were thrown at the women. As soon as the women came near, that section of the crowd became hysterical. 'Rape them.' 'Put it inside of them.' 'The filthy Hindu bitches.' 'The kafir women.' Some said worse things. Then came the shower of spittle. Almost everyone spat, and hundreds of tongues were pushed forward inside of their teeth and hundreds of uplifted faces canon-like fired the saliva. Bits of the saliva fell on the crowd ahead, but no one minded, so long as the main salvo hit the women. Many men in the front rows of the crowd lifted their lungis to display their genitals to them. Others aimed small articles at them and tried to hit them. Again, by some arrangement, no one threw a rock. Injury to the women would have brought the procession to an end and they wanted the women to parade. And almost to the last man, whether they spat or shouted or threw things or just stood with their mouths open, they stared at the pubic regions of the women. Through indelicate exposure those areas had lost their glory, lost all magic, and there was only a small, slippery aperture you saw there. But men's eyes were settled on these apertures. And the moment the women had passed ahead, the eyes were settled on the bruised buttocks.

For a while, as the women neared, Suraj Prakash hit Arun in the ribs with his elbow. Later he became too engrossed to pass on his excitement to Arun and stood staring, forgetting Arun. Arun felt his legs giving way and he could watch no more. Weakly, he sat down on the shop-front where he and Suraj were standing and he wanted to throw up. It was the shop of a hakim, a doctor practising an indigenous system of medicine. The hakim sahib was a man of forty, with a brown, dyed beard and he sat on his carpeted seat in the middle of the shop, surrounded by medicine bottles, a wooden chest in front of him. The procession was now before the shop, and sitting on the shop-front Arun was hemmed-in from all sides by excited legs which jerked up and down as the owners of those legs jeered and shouted. Arun turned his head away—and from an opening through the legs he saw the hakim sahib. He almost revived and his eyes opened wide, as he looked. The hakim sahib had covered his face with his hands and was rocking a little and he was saying, 'Allah, Allah, Allah!' And then he knelt on his knees, raised his arms and spread his hands before him as while saying namaaz. There was the look of infinite pain on his face. His thin, frail eyelids rested on his eyes as if they would never open again. And moving his outstretched hands, like begging alms, he murmured in Punjabi, 'Rabbul-Alamin, forgive these cruel men. And, oh, my Allah, oh Rabbah, protect these women!'

And then Arun heard a different kind of shout, a more frivolous and noisy shout, with a lot of jeering and whistling. He looked towards the bazaar, but he couldn't make out what it was about. The women had gone ahead, where the crowd now was getting hysterical. What were the men near him laughing at? He looked at Suraj and he too was laughing. What had happened? Unable to find anything new, he looked back into the shop. The hakim sahib was still in deep prayer. This unhinged Arun. It was better if the day had ended on an unmixed note. He could have then hated freely, without feeling guilty. He had seen the very core of evil, and he wanted to see nothing else. But the bearded Muslim weeping for Hindu women made no sense to him. He made his task too difficult.

'Why was there a general shout at the end of the procession?' Arun asked Suraj, while on their way back to the camp.

'They were laughing at the last two women, who were nothing but wrinkles.'

'Oh, that!'

Suraj looked at Arun.

'What's the matter, Arun? Didn't you enjoy the show?'

'Yeah, I enjoyed it.'

'Why don't we stop off at a wine shop and have a drink? No one would know who we are.'

'You know I touch no such things.'

'I don't, either—mostly. But why not today?'

'What's today?'

'It is such a day!'

Arun watched Suraj's face. It looked ecstatic. They kept walking towards the camp.

Arun and Suraj were not the only ones who had been up there; there were others. That evening they talked of nothing else in the camp. Some of the men had identified one of Dr Chander Bhan's daughters amongst the marchers. They wondered where the other one was. Groups formed in each lane and the men spoke in whispers. The women stood with their fingers on their lips, utterly astounded. Rama, Rama, Rama, said most.

'Why didn't you come last night?' asked Chandni, as soon as Arun was by her side at night.

She sounded frightened. Also irritated.

Instead of answering, Arun folded her in his arms and put his mouth on her lips.

He shivered because of the cold and held her with his mouth and his legs until he was warm against her.

He was extremely tender with her as she snuggled up to him. There was no passion in him today, only softness. She buried her nails into his flesh, and he held her and kissed her, but made no advances himself.

'Why didn't you come last night?'

'Your mother was awake,' he whispered, close to her ear.

'I wouldn't care.'

Gently he passed his fingers over her face. He touched her nostrils with the tip of a finger and ran the finger up and down her nose. He took hold of her ears, one by one, and rubbed them with his thumb and his forefinger. He passed his hand over her throat.

'I want to go out with you to the fields,' she said.

Arun's heart jumped.

'Yes. Soon as we can.'

'When?'

'There are no open fields here. It's a town.'

'When then?'

He held her hard and could feel her ribs below his hold. Softly he kissed her lips, over and over again, assimilating their nectar into his being.

'At Dera Baba Nanak.'

'And when do we get married?'

'They will hear us.'

'Say when?'

'Soon after.'

'I'm so scared.'

The faces of women in the camp had fallen, after they heard of the procession.

'I know.'

She pressed him to herself and put her tongue inside of his mouth.

'Shall I say something?' she whispered.

'All right.'

She buried her face next to him.

'I'm all yours.'

Arun stroked her bare back with his hand.

'I let no one ever touch me before.'

Arun held her hard.

'Now I want you to take me.'

Arun had longed for this all these days, and yet when it came his way he was not keen on it. He saw before his eyes the nude spectres of the afternoon, and he felt dead inside. But he melted where he lay, as he heard her speak. It was like consummation itself and his tortured mind relaxed. Must have cost her a good deal, though, he thought. To say it. In as many words. She was an orthodox Hindu girl. Was it only despair?

'Make me yours fully,' she was saying, her hand on the quick of his body. 'Now—here!'

'At Dera Baba Nanak,' he whispered, and slid deep onto her middle and kissed her there.

And like a child, she suddenly fell asleep in his arms. One moment she was whispering to him. And the next Arun heard her soft, rhythmic breathing. She lay with her face close to his and her warm breath fell on his cheek. She had a strong, heavy body, but in sleep she became exceedingly light, and Arun felt he was holding a bird next to him. He was afraid of falling asleep himself. Gently he lifted her head from his arm and put it on the ground. Gently he tucked the chader around her. Leaning forward he kissed her on the forehead. He then returned to his bed and lay awake a long time pondering in the night.

The following night, the third of their stay at Narowal, there was a massive attack on the camp. It was a complete surprise. No one expected it, there was not the least rumour about it during the day. The procession of women, instead of pacifying the communal venom, had plainly fanned it further. A large number of Muslims had arrived from Zafarwal, and this might have further tipped the balance in favour of the attack. But the camp population had no warning of it until the moment it actually took place—around eight in the night.

Arun had gone to the lavatory at one end of the camp. Suddenly he heard cries of 'Nara-e-Takbir, Allah-o-Akbar'. The assailants had achieved a surprise even over the army, for it appeared they were already inside the camp. He also heard repeated bursts of machine-gun fire. And as though the camp had wakened from a bad dream to a worse reality, a deafening clamour rose from the camp.

Arun was seized by panic before he quite knew what was happening. Hurriedly he got up from the lavatory seat and buttoned up his trousers. His legs were trembling as leaning against a wall of the lavatory outside, he steadied himself and looked ahead. Utter chaos raged before him. The electric wires had been cut, but because of the moon, the lanes were not in total darkness. He saw figures screaming, and running—he didn't know whither. Skirting the lanes, he ran towards their tent. He stumbled several times, and at times bumped into other people. He did not know who they were. Steadying himself he kept running, avoiding the lanes where there was too much confusion and noise. He found no one inside their tent; it was empty. He felt cold in his limbs and ran out. There was no one in the adjoining tent either. They had all disappeared. In the distance he saw people he thought he knew, but the lane was practically deserted. He ran. The uproar was deafening, and there were cries all over of 'Help', 'Save us', 'Bachao'. Arun ran for the fence and passed an Indian machine-gun position. They were firing in the direction of the city. Two men running ahead of him fell down and Arun didn't know who had hit them. Instinctively he ducked and ran on. He passed another gun position, this time firing in the direction of the Narowal railway station. A soldier ahead was firing in the same direction with a bren gun. He was propped up against the fence and his gun was resting on a wooden post. Arun saw him violently jerk up, spin and slump to the ground. Now he knew. They were being fired at. He ducked and ran. He stayed by the fence but ran towards the back of the camp. On his left he passed many fields. They were not large fields as in Gunna Kalan; there were houses on them. Many people were vaulting over the fence and running for the fields. He found that side too exposed and ran for the left wing, where there was the railway yard and a number of railway buildings.

To his dismay, he heard cries of 'Ya Ali' coming from the railway yard too. He saw a crowd gathered there in the moonlight. They were being held back by the Indian troops.

Arun turned round and ran back to where the fields were. Ducking low, afraid of being hurt, he climbed over the fence and jumped outside. He slipped and fell down. Rising, he ran again. He found himself in a field of sugar cane. There was activity in the other fields but this one was quiet. He was exhausted. Parting the thick sugar cane stumps, he fell on the ground, facing the camp. He could hear his heart beating fast against the dry ground.

The camp faced the city, and between the two ran the Sialkot-Dera Baba Nanak railway line. The Narowal railway station was on the eastern wing of the camp; on the west were the railway sheds. It was at the rear of the camp the fields lay.

The attack came in waves and Arun watched it for several hours. There was heavy firing for some time and once an Indian position was silenced, a crowd of Muslims, brandishing guns, sticks and knives surged into the camp. Arun only heard the shouts of 'Allah-o-Akbar' and he knew when a fresh wave had attacked. The firing was intermittently resumed, and from different directions, as though the Indian soldiers were constantly rearranging themselves. There was firing from the city at the camp. There was also firing—very heavy firing—from the direction of the railway station at the camp. And from both places, it was the machine-gun firing that came.

It seemed there was perfect coordination between the assailants and those who were giving them the covering fire. For soon as the shouts of 'Allah-o-Akbar' started, the firing from the city and the railway station ceased. And soon as one wave of slaughter had finished its work, the firing was resumed.

People from the camp ran in all directions. Under the cover of darkness, many disappeared into the town. Some dodged their assailants and disappeared in the railway yard or went round and hid themselves behind the station. Many ran into the fields, pursued by their assailants. Even the sugar cane field in which Arun was lying was not safe. He heard groups of people passing within yards of him.

Arun was in agony about his parents and Chandni. The pandemonium was coming nearer. He got up and ran further away. Clearing the sugar cane field, he went over an irrigation ditch. He did not see it at first and stepped into it and wet his shoes and trousers; it was with some difficulty he saved himself from falling headlong into it. There was a small dam on the other side and he slid down the dam. Two houses stood on his right, and there was light in the windows. He avoided them and ran on. He was in yet another sugar cane field. Beyond that he came on a dirt road. There were many scattered houses there, but he was, afraid to seek help. He was no longer running; he was running and walking. It was cold in the open, but he was sweating. With his handkerchief he wiped his forehead. He also buttoned up his shirt because of the chill.

He was now in a long field, where nothing was growing. The tumult of the camp still came to him, though he was over a mile away from it. Behind a group of trees in the field he saw a barn. It was a long shed with a tin roof. He couldn't see the barn until he was very close to it; it was hidden behind large peepal trees. Arun saw no light there and he walked towards it. To his surprise, he saw an army jeep standing in a dark corner of the ground. He stopped where he was. What was the jeep doing there? There was no sign of life near the shed or inside the shed. He looked in every direction. The nearest house was four to five hundred yards away. Stealthily he took a few steps forward. An owl fluttered and went hooting from one tree to another. Arun stopped instantly, his heart palpitating against his ribs. He was not sure what to do. He was tired. He was hungry too, since he had not yet eaten his dinner. Stealthily he took a few more steps. He decided to go and see if the door was open. There was no lock outside. He pushed at the door slowly but found it locked from inside. Slowly he went round the barn, smelling hay and cow dung. He passed a window and he thought he heard movement inside. He ran and sank down behind a tree. Hastening from one tree trunk to the next, he moved towards the other side of the barn. As he neared the window at the rear, he was frozen in his tracks. A woman was crying inside: 'Leave me, you brute. Have pity on me.' It was the voice of Sunanda.

For the next few minutes, Arun acted like a man in a dream. He was hardly aware of what he was doing. Later he wondered at his own daring. But at the moment he was hardly conscious of himself. Swiftly he stepped forward, moving on his toes like a cat, and put his face next to the glass pane of the window. His heart was beating fast, it was thumping, and his mouth was open with fear as he pressed his cheek against the pane and looked. He could see nothing. He was surprised, for there was sufficient moonlight. Yet as he searched with his eyes and pressed himself harder against the pane, he saw only darkness. The barn was quite long, but he felt he was looking at a very small place. And then he saw. There was a wall directly ahead of him, obstructing his vision. Apparently there was a partition in the barn, and this was a small room at the back. Looking closer, he saw hay stacked in the small room. He heard Sunanda again: 'Let go of me, let me go, you brute.' It seemed someone's hand was on her mouth, for her words came out in muffled gasps. Arun's cheek was cold from pressing against the glass. He turned his head and put the other cheek against it. He also wiped the glass with his handkerchief; it had become frosted with his breath. He tried to push the window open. It was locked from inside. His fingertips resting on the cold glass, he looked at the different glass panes. All the panes were intact. He felt the sweat running down his armpits. Bracing himself against the window, he pushed it several times with his shoulder. And unbelievably for him, the window shot open. Maybe it was not bolted, only the shutters had got jammed. He shot forward and caught the shutters with his hands, to prevent them from banging against the frame. Opening them gently, making no sound, the next minute he was inside the room.

He was standing on dry hay. He saw there was a passage between the two rooms, but there was no door fixed to it. He took off his wet shoes and slowly tiptoed forward. He had heard nothing for the past some minutes. There was no movement either in the other room. Arun's heart was beating very fast and he could hear it thumping in his head. Then he heard Sunanda weeping. But it was the weeping of a person drained of all strength, a completely subdued weeping.

Standing behind the wall, leaning against it with his hands, Arun looked through the passage. First he saw the hay stacked ceiling high in one corner, then he saw a number of farm implements, including a wooden plough, and in the far distance he saw the large, iron door of the barn. It was only then he saw Sunanda or what must be Sunanda. She was lying on the ground on an improvised bed of hay, in the far corner. Her head was away from Arun and he saw her legs. Between her legs and on top of her, was lying a man.

The moonlight was coming through the window in the larger room and Arun could see clearly. She was still weeping. Softly and tamely. Her breath was choked with convulsions. 'Get off me now,' she said in a tired voice. The man did not move. Instead he started laughing. He laughed smugly, a high-pitched, shrill laughter. The sound reverberated in the barn and the iron door rattled slightly. 'I knew I'd have you one day,' he said conceitedly. And he laughed again in triumph and satisfaction. 'You're a beauty,' he was saying. 'But you made me wait a long time.'

Arun knew who he was before he had spoken. The strong slender back. The tall frame. The familiar sound of the laughter. The shock of it singed him, as recognition shot into him like a leaping flame. He did not stop to think. He did not even know what he was doing. Quietly, step by step, he walked into the other room and picked up a sharp wooden spike from among the farm implements. Step by step, holding the spike firmly in his hands and raising it above his head, he walked to the distant corner. He walked gingerly, as though he were sleep-walking at the top of a precipice. He still did not know what he was doing. The spike was raised above his head and his hands were trying to get a firmer hold on it. He made no sound whatsoever but somehow he did not worry about sound. And yet he walked step by step, very carefully. And going near them, while he still heard the sobs and the laughter somewhere, he brought the spike down with all his force on the man's head.

He had seen the mass of black hair and he had taken a careful aim. Lying atop her, the man was still holding her in his arms. With the blow his arms slackened and he rolled off to the side. His body twitched but the man did not move after that. Arun hit him repeatedly on the head, as though he had gone mad. Sunanda uttered a scream and sat up. 'It's me—Arun,' he heard himself saying. But he was looking at the collapsed heap of the man and he was hitting him repeatedly on his head. He swung the spike high above and brought it down with his full force. Again he swung it high and brought it down. And again. He continued hitting.

He stopped and found himself panting. Holding the spike in one hand, he bent low and looked at the man. He lay with his face to the side, but the top of his skull was smashed and there was blood over his face and his shoulder. There was also blood on the ground, under his head. Arun turned him on his back. He leaned on his knees and put his hand on his chest and felt his heart. He then put his ear to his chest. He listened for a long while. He lifted one of his arms and let go of it. He lifted the other arm and let go of it. They both slumped down. Once again he put his ear on his chest and listened. No, there was no doubt. Captain Rahmat-Ullah Khan was really dead.

Getting up, Arun looked at the wooden spike. It was an unevenly fashioned spike, in the rural manner, but it was strong and heavy. One end of it was dark with Rahmat-Ullah Khan's blood. Arun looked at it with disgust. He felt confused and tried to sort things out, but his head reeled. He discovered he was sweating profusely. He wiped his brow with one of his arms. Alternately, he looked at the body of Rahmat-Ullah Khan and the spike. It seemed certain to him he had killed a man. He shuddered at the thought of it. And he threw the spike away in a corner of the barn, where the hay was. And shaking his head, he went and sat next to Sunanda.

'I have killed him,' said Arun, trying as much to strengthen himself as her.

Sunanda leaned against him and started sobbing. This was outright weeping; loud and pitiful. Arun had not been trained to console people older than himself. He felt nervous, as Sunanda rested her delicate arms heavily on him and wept. He was also feeling cold, as his trousers were still wet. So he sat shivering, raking the hay with his hand, until she finished crying.

'How long have you been here?' Sunanda asked.

'A few minutes.'

Silence.

'How did you get here?' asked Arun.

'He dragged me.'

'From the camp?'

She nodded her head and blew her nose.

Arun wanted to ask what had happened at the camp, where his parents were, where Chandni was.

Instead she asked:

'Have you seen Bhavna and Nava Kant?

'No, bhabhi. Where are they?'

In reply she broke into yet another burst of weeping. She also slapped the ground with her closed fists.

'How do I know? How do I know? He snatched me from them and dragged me here.'

She sounded as if she was suffocating.

'I can't bear to sit here, with him lying there.'

They moved into the smaller room, Arun bending low to look at Captain Rahmat-Ullah Khan's body and kicking it as he left.

'We should get away from here. There is his jeep outside. We may be discovered any minute.'

'He had a gun on him. Go get it.'

'I wouldn't know how to use it.'

'Get it all the same.'

Arun returned to the bigger room. In his mind he was wondering how to make their escape. The border was still a long way; they would never be able to make it on their own. Where was Chandni? And his parents? Had they fled to the border perchance? Were they alive? What was happening at the camp? Maybe the army had been able to restore order. He had to go back and find out. But how? Where to leave Sunanda? How to take her with him?

Captain Rahmat-Ullah Khan was dressed only in a shirt. His trousers and a light jersey were lying near his corpse. They were civilian clothes, he was not wearing his uniform. Arun searched his trousers. There was no gun there. Feeling afraid of the dead man, he reluctantly went near to the body and searched around it. No, he couldn't find the gun. Hastily he turned and made for the other room. Remembering something, he turned back and picked up the trousers and the jersey.

Sunanda was leaning against a stack of hay.

'We have to get out of here. I suggest you change into these clothes.'

'What clothes?'

Arun was sorry for Sunanda. He should be sympathizing with her and saying words of comfort—he who had loved her so dearly for so many years. But they were in grave danger and there was no time to talk.

'You must dress up as a man. You can't move through the countryside in a sari.'

'What is there left of me to lose.'

She was sobbing.

'Oh, come on, bhabhi. Do as I say—please.'

She wiped her tears.

'Not in *his* clothes—no!'

'Take mine then. Only my trousers are wet. You better wear these.'

One is all the time making concessions to the moment and she agreed. While Arun looked aside, she changed into Captain Rahmat-Ullah Khan's trousers. Arun was restive to get away, and he turned and looked at her before she had quite finished. She had rolled up the bottoms to suit her height and she had stuck her blouse inside the trousers. In a spite of the tragedy of the situation, Arun couldn't fail to observe what a ravishing figure she had—tiny, but sumptuous. He was glad they had the jersey with them; no one would have taken her for a man otherwise. Only when she had donned the loose jersey was her heavy femininity somewhat hidden from the eye. Arun also made a turban for her out of her sari—in the Muslim fashion, with one end of the turban hanging low at the back.

'But where are we going?'

That stalled Arun. He didn't quite know.

'The best thing would be to return to the camp.' Now that he had said it he believed that was what they should do.

'To get killed?'

'To find out what's happening.'

Yes, to find out. With a pang she remembered her children and moaned. They had to find out.

'What time is it now?'

Arun looked at the luminous hands of his watch.

'Three o'clock.'

'It is almost day.'

Arun put his shoes on and slowly stepped out of the window. He stood there for a while, feeling afraid. The moon had nearly set and it was darker than in the early part of the night. Arun listened with one ear pushed forward. Some noises in the distance could be heard, but there was no sound of firing. He gave Sunanda his hand and helped her out of the window. They took a few steps. Both looked apprehensively around. Sunanda held on to his hand. They came to the jeep, which stood like a wild beast in the night. Arun found a bag in the jeep, and in the bag he found Captain Rahmat-Ullah Khan's gun. Also in the bag were his uniform, several handkerchiefs, sleeping pyjamas, another civilian shirt, and a number of other things. There was a blanket lying in the jeep too, and another pair of shoes. Arun wondered when he had driven up to Narowal from Sialkot. He had clearly come prepared.

Arun took out the gun and put it in his pocket. They walked a few more steps and came to the clearing beyond the trees. They stood and listened. The moon was dying in the sky, the moon was dead. The stars dazzled and frightened Arun with their brilliance, like so many eyes watching him. All kinds of sounds came to them from afar, but they couldn't distinguish them. No light burned in any of the houses in the neighbourhood. They stood whispering; they were afraid to move on. In the end they decided to spend another hour in the barn. It was unsafe both ways. But there was greater immediate safety where they were.

Reluctantly they returned to the little room in the barn. Arun picked up the blanket from the jeep, and reclining on the hay they covered themselves with it. Sunanda talked. Like Arun, she was not in the tent at the time of the attack. She had gone to see a friend a few tents removed from theirs. With the first wave of rioters surging in, they had all panicked. She ran back to her tent, but the moment she stepped into the lane, she was caught hold of by Captain Rahmat-Ullah Khan by the arm. He threatened to shoot her if she did not go with him.

Sunanda stopped and started sobbing.

'I should have let him shoot me.'

Arun said nothing. His trousers were drying and he was beginning to feel warm under the blanket. He wanted no further details from Sunanda.

'In the jeep he swore he won't touch me. He said his men would take care of my children. He only wanted to be with me for some time. He would take me back to the children, he said.'

Arun was beginning to doze off. He woke with a start, realizing that his stomach was groaning with hunger. Sunanda was quiet now. Arun peered in the dark to see if she was sleeping. She lay with her eyes open, looking at the ceiling. And then he remembered there was a man lying dead in the next room. And he could sleep no more.

They heard the sound of a car engine. Both of them instantly sat up. The vehicle was drawing nearer. They had closed the window, and they stood up next to it. Sunanda asked, 'What will we do?' but Arun sealed her lips with his hand. The vehicle had now stopped. It was still some way from the barn—at the dirt road next to the field.

They waited breathlessly. The vehicle did not draw any nearer. And then they heard loud and clear someone speaking through a loudspeaker. It said: 'The situation at the camp is under control. If there are any refugees hiding here, come out and return to the camp with us.' The announcement was repeated after a few seconds.

Arun sprang out of the window and helped Sunanda out. Holding her hand, he ran towards the dirt road. It was only a furlong away, but they had to clear the trees first. While they were still in the cluster of trees, they heard the vehicle starting up. The lonely resident of those trees, the owl, started hooting. Arun shouted and his voice echoed through the tree grove. He shouted again, asking them to wait. But the vehicle drove away, and they saw its tail lights disappearing in the distance.

When they reached the road, they were not sure whether they had heard any announcement—they doubted their ears. Then they heard the vehicle making the same announcement somewhere else. They cursed their luck, but they knew they could now go back to the camp.

With some enthusiasm, but moving extremely cautiously, they trudged back. Arun knew the way and every few yards stopped to see if they were going right. Sunanda said it could be a trick. Arun said in that case they would kill themselves—and he thought of Niranjan Singh. They could hear noises in other fields, but they met no one on the way. Dawn was breaking when they neared the camp. Going behind a bush, Sunanda changed back into her sari, blood-soaked though it was—trampling ruthlessly on the trousers and the jersey before she left them behind. At the irrigation ditch, they washed the blood off their hands and faces, but they were too shaken to be mindful of it. Here they ran into streams of other refugees who like them were returning to the camp. Many of those people too had blood on their clothes and their bodies. They all looked worn out, dishevelled and sleepy, and there was concern on their faces. No one knew what had happened to the others and they seemed anxious to find out.

There was much movement ahead of them; they saw many jeeps moving in and out of the main gate. Sunanda pulled Arun by the sleeve and they stopped.

'Arun, don't say a word about what you saw.'

'I saw nothing, bhabhi. You and I have together spent the night with a number of other refugees.'

And to show his dismissal of the ugly, corroding night, Arun took out the gun of Captain Rahmat-Ullah Khan from his pocket and hurled it deep into the fields.

Sunanda searched his eyes, her body trembling in her need for reassurance. Raising herself on her toes, she gently kissed him on the lips.

They moved forward and crossing the gate entered the camp.

They were received with mixed feelings by their families. All were sitting together—in one tent. Prabha Rani immediately got up and embraced Arun. Sunanda's children ran to her and hugged her legs; the boy started crying and asked, 'Where were you, mummy?' Bibi Amar Vati did not stir from her place and stared at Sunanda incredulously, even with hostility. 'Suraj Prakash is missing... And where were *you*?' A twinge of pain shot through Sunanda's limbs. 'I was with Arun,' she mumbled. 'Yes,' said Arun, 'We took shelter in a barn, along with many other refugees.'

'Where's father?' asked Arun, his heart in his mouth.

'He is all right,' said his mother. 'He's gone up to the camp office.'

They were unduly quiet and their faces were expressionless.

Arun looked around.

'Where're Padmini and Chandni?' he asked his mother.

Both Prabha Rani and Bibi Amar Vati rocked and moaned.

Prabha Rani stared hard at Arun.

'Beta, how to tell you?'

'What is it, mother?'

There was a pause and everyone looked expressionlessly ahead. Isher Kaur started crying.

'The Muslims have kidnapped Chandni. We've no idea where she is.'

Arun was struck dumb. His mother was a great one for springing surprises but must she be so heartless? The others knew nothing about it, but *she* knew. Couldn't she have cushioned it—said what she had to say a little differently?

Prabha Rani was nodding, as though to say she understood how he felt, but there was no other way of saying it, none at all. Chandni had been kidnapped and taken away. Chandni was gone.

'Where is Padmini?'

'At the camp office, along with your father. They have been trying to get news of you four.'

Arun heard Sunanda's girl Bhavna whimpering and saying: 'Where is daddy, mother?' and he saw in a blurred way Sunanda patting her and saying something to her. He turned and walked towards the camp office.

No, there was no news of Chandni and Suraj Prakash. There was no news of hundreds of others besides, whose relations were lined up outside the office.

Padmini's eyes were swollen from crying, and she had bruises on her face. Lala Kanshi Ram came forward and embraced Arun, all but bursting into tears. Briefly Arun told him where he was in the night.

Arun pointed towards Padmini.

'Was she beaten up by them?'

'No, she has done this herself. She has been hitting herself all the while.'

Padmini started beating her face again with both her hands. She had taken no notice of Arun and was staring into space. Lala Kanshi Ram held her hands, but she wriggled and tried to free herself. Simultaneously, she moaned like an animal.

Suraj Prakash's body was found later in the day. He was stabbed through the abdomen; his face was also mutilated—both his eyes were taken out. More than two thousand bodies were discovered that day. So savage had been the vengeance, every single body had been badly mutilated.

But many were never found again, amongst them Chandni. When the tally was completed, over three thousand were dead or missing, amongst them many women.

Major Jang Bahadur Singh was certain the night's attack was made with the support of the Pakistani army. There was the return machine-gun firing, and the bands of hooligans were led by men who were fully trained in the art of killing. He had himself shot some of them dead, and he was sure they were regular soldiers. Many of his own men and six of his officers were killed. He said he would lodge a stiff report as soon as he got to Dera Baba Nanak.

'Where did you pass the night, father?' Arun asked.

'In Major Jang Bahadur Singh's tents. We ran with the first noise and the Major gave us shelter. We looked for you everywhere.'

Only his father could have thought of that! Major Jang Bahadur Singh and the Indian soldiers were quartered in two special lanes of the camp. While everyone else ran for the fields or the town, Lala Kanshi Ram had taken his group to the Indian army tents.

'When did you lose sight of Suraj Prakash?'

'That's a mystery. He was with us as we ran. And then he was nowhere.'

'And Padmini and Chandni?'

'They had gone to fetch water from the taps. We didn't see Padmini until this morning. She says three men caught hold of Chandni and dragged her away.'

Arun swallowed.

'Why did they leave Padmini? She is not bad to look at herself.'

Lala Kanshi Ram stared at the ground and there was that familiar see-through look on his face of utter comprehension, of utter wisdom. He seemed conscious of his own sagacity, of what he had perceived beyond the snares of the world, and as usual he was looking a little stupid too.

'She offered herself to them if they would spare her daughter. But they hit her with a stick and left her unconscious. She also thinks she was dishonoured, while she lay unconscious.'

Arun felt sick. He felt so utterly sick. Overnight all his dreams had been wiped out. He looked at Padmini and his father, and he loathed them both. It was they who had prevented their coming together—in the name of one damned godly good or the other. The fruit on the tree was ripe and ready for renewal. But they had stood guard on it like serpents. And now that fruit had been plucked and crushed mercilessly under the foot.

Throughout the day the sound of wailing and weeping came from different parts of the camp, as more and more people learned of the fate of their relations. To Arun that wailing was nothing. If the whole world were to go up in flames, he would forgive—if he could have Chandni back. He went round and round the grounds, examined each dead body, gave details of Chandni's appearance to others and asked them if they had seen her anywhere. The Pakistani authorities were now making a show of friendliness. They said they had arrested a number of ring-leaders of the rioters. They also went round the city in jeeps along with the Indian soldiers, trying to recover the abducted women. Arun jumped on one of those jeeps and made repeated trips into the town, eating nothing, drinking nothing. Some women were found—abandoned in the streets. Some men also showed up. But no trace was found of Chandni and many others.

That night Arun ate after twenty-four hours. He grabbed the chapatis and stuffed them into his mouth—recklessly, indifferently.

'There is nothing anyone can do,' said his mother softly to him, as she placed a tumbler of tea beside him.

Arun drank the tea in one gulp and he was glad it burned his gullet and chest as it went down; he wanted it to crumble him up as acid does, when it falls on something. Later, he went to the camp office again and waited there till midnight, his face worn thin with emotion. He lifted his head each time a jeep arrived. The women that were discovered were led away silently by their families. None showed joy at the reunion; some seemed sorry the girls had come back at all, soiled and dishonoured.

They waited another day, searching and looking. But two days after the attack, Major Jang Bahadur Singh gave up. The recovery of the remaining persons would have to be left to the civilian authorities, and he marched the refugees out to the border.

The convoy from Narowal to Dera Baba Nanak was a great contrast to the orderly sections in which they had set out from Sialkot. There was hardly any discipline. There was not a family which had not been hit in some manner, and the refugees were totally dispirited. They did not march in units now, but in large hordes. In places big gaps appeared in the column, when the groups were separated from each other by long stretches. The border was only eight miles away, and the word was speed: get to the border and get it over with. There were many wounded, but there were no stretchers for them. They just limped along, using stopgap bandages on their wounds. Those who could not walk, were carried by their relatives on their backs.

Between the border and Narowal lay one more Muslim village, Jassar. The refugees were scared. But so pitiable was the sight of this demoralized mass of humanity, which moved on its way accompanied by a swarm of flies, the Muslims in Jassar only stood and stared. Even anti-Hindu or anti-Sikh slogans were not shouted by them. The men stood astounded, as group after group of disabled, wounded, or weeping and lamenting men and women turned the bend, came before them, and trudged on to whatever lay ahead of them. The children were not crying but they looked dazed. The most pathetic sight was of the very old weeping hysterically. Instead of attacking the convoy, some of the inhabitants of Jassar ran inside their homes and brought water for the thirsty. Some waved and said, 'Khuda hafiz.' Most only looked on.

Arun had often thought of the time when he would be actually standing on the soil of free India. Now that he had crossed the bridge over the Ravi and was out of danger, he experienced no strong emotions. He saw many kissing the Indian soil, and he saw many others bathing in the Ravi to mark their deliverance. He saw his own father yielding to similar sentiments. Throughout the journey he never tired of talking of Sialkot. Now Arun saw him bend low, pick up a little earth and rub it with his fingers. He saw tears in his eyes and found he was breathing heavily. The father and the son looked at each other, and Lala Kanshi Ram nodded in satisfaction and smiled. Arun couldn't share his feelings and looked away as he continued to nod. In an unusual gush of feelings, Lala Kanshi Ram raised his hand and shouted 'Vande Mataram'—salute to the motherland. Arun only looked at the passive flow of the river.

Padmini refused to leave the Narowal camp that morning. She wanted to stay back until Chandni was recovered. It was with great difficulty Lala Kanshi Ram prevailed upon her to come. The camp was being closed down. Where would she stay? How would she know where Chandni was? Would Chandni at all want to return—after what she had gone through?

'And who would now take her as a wife, even if she did come back?' he asked, raising his nose and looking at her through his glasses.

'I will.'

They were sitting in their tent. There was no one else there beside Prabha Rani. Lala Kanshi Ram was trying his best (as he thought) to put some solid sense into the head of that charwoman. He could understand her sorrow, but one had to be practical in this world.

There was dead silence as Arun spoke up. Lala Kanshi Ram looked at him sternly; he couldn't believe that he had heard him right.

Arun found himself faltering.

'I mean someone *has to* accept these women back,' he said, as firmly as he could. 'We cannot disown them for something that was no fault of theirs.'

Lala Kanshi Ram quite agreed with Arun in his mind. But he wasn't going to let this piddling slip of a boy confront him with a discomfiting truth, when he was taking another line.

He said harshly: 'You've yet to live in the world to know what the world is like.' He shook his head, grunted uncomfortably, said, 'Quoting books to me!' and once more turned towards Padmini.

That was the end of Arun's venture on behalf of Chandni. She was gone, her recovery a remote possibility, so why make an issue of her?

He took no interest in the movement of the convoy after it left Narowal. A list of the abducted women was prepared, and arrangements were made with the local authorities for their repatriation to India if they were recovered. A list of the dead and the missing was also prepared. And then the refugees started walking the last eight miles of their march.

Arun was seized by a strange frenzy on this march, an unhealthy, sickly, demented frenzy. He did not stay with his family, but walked up fast and then walked way back to the rear. Once again they were on the threshold of an arrival, and his mind went back to the day when they had left their home in Sialkot. How long was the journey and when and where was it likely to end? He felt extremely agitated and fidgety. Communal or mass destiny ceased to worry him. Where was he heading—he, Arun? Nur and Chandni he was leaving behind. Nur was only the beginning, he had walked only the foothills with her. But Chandni had taken him up the slopes to the summit. What would he be without her, without his hamrahi?

Restlessly he ran back and forth, a storm raging within his young frame. Needlessly he urged others along. 'Step out, hurry up!' he shouted. Needlessly he offered help to others—carried a bag or a child and then suddenly dumped it on the ground and departed abruptly. To and fro he went in his fury, not knowing what to do. With his hands on his hips he stood watching the long line of the convoy and burst into laughter. 'You bloody fools,' he said, not knowing what he meant by that. As he walked, he kicked the stones in his way and sent them flying into the fields. 'You bloody fool, you bloody fool,' he said. He was cursing himself.

He saw the approach to the river. The land was becoming sandy, and huge, bamboo-type weeds were becoming increasingly visible. So they were getting near safety. And freedom. There was something in that. Maybe love would be there too. Impetuously he rushed forward and stood staring at the vast bed of the river. Ravi. Chenab. Jhelum. Beas. Sutlej. Slowly he whispeted the names to himself, in no special order, but as he remembered them. These were the rivers which in a way flowed in his veins too; his blood owed as much to them as to the earth under his feet. Crossing the Ravi, he would be leaving three of these great rivers behind him for ever. Not for a minute was he sorry for it. He was sorry for that other river he was leaving behind, a nameless, subterranean river, brisker than them all, more sparkling than them, sweeter than them, more exhilarating. But no, he was not leaving that river behind. He was going to carry it along with him to wherever he went. For it was a moveable river, the river of love.

'Vande Mataram,' repeated his father, crushing the earth in his hand and letting it slowly fall to the ground.

Arun saw his mother fold her hands and bow to the earth.

'One moment,' said Arun, and ran back.

'Eh, come back, come back,' shouted Lala Kanshi Ram after him.

But Arun bounded back over the bridge that was the boundary and disappeared from sight. He ran a good way before he stopped. Picking up a branch he made a stick of it and waved it wildly in the air. 'Come on, hurry up,' he shouted at the refugees. 'Get a move on—quick,' he shouted, trying to rip the air apart with his stick. 'Hurry, hurry,' he shouted at young children, who ran away from him in fear. 'Get to your mother India—quick!' he waved the stick over them like a whip. 'Hurry up! Be quick!'i

'The boy's lost his mind,' said one elderly refugee to another, while they ducked their heads as Arun kept lashing with the stick.

CHAPTER 6

FROM Dera Baba Nanak, Lala Kanshi Ram's family moved swiftly to Amritsar, and from there as swiftly to Delhi.

They had a few relations at Amritsar. They knocked at their doors, but discovered they were not welcome. The relations smiled. They said they were happy they had safely got out. Some offered them tea. Some offered food. Yet none offered them shelter. They offered apologies; they were already overcrowded, they said. Each family they visited had dependents from West Punjab staying with them. Only now did Lala Kanshi Ram discover the meaning of a blood relation. If you were a blood relation, you could shout and force your way in. But, as was the case with them, if you were a distant relation, you could only whine and wait by the outer door.

Prabha Rani suggested they go to Kanpur. Her parents had died when she was young. She was brought up by her two brothers, both of whom had moved to Kanpur years back in search for a better living. But Kanpur seemed so far away to Lala Kanshi Ram and he point blank refused. There were other alternatives. There was Jullundur. There was Ludhiana. There was Ambala. All big towns in East Punjab. Only none of them appealed to Lala Kanshi Ram. 'What's wrong with them?' asked Prabha Rani. Fumbling for a reply, said Lala Kanshi Ram: 'I don't like the sound of them.' There was only one worthwhile town for him in the Punjab—and that was Sialkot. On the off chance Arun suggested Delhi, and to his surprise Lala Kanshi Ram agreed. He thought his father was going to turn them into wandering gypsies!

At Amritsar they spent a couple of weeks in another refugee camp—this time for the incoming refugees. If they had imagined their troubles would be over the moment they reached Indian territory, they were sadly disillusioned. Not only were the arrangements to house and feed the refugees inadequate, their very presence was resented by the local people. Their number had exceeded all expectations and the food was running short. The winter was approaching and there were not sufficient blankets. There was a noisy show of sympathy but that's all there was to it. At Dera Baba Nanak, they were put into trucks and rushed to Amritsar; the Dera Baba Nanak people wanted to get them off their hands. Now at Amritsar, they were being again advised to push ahead. They weren't told where they should go, only, move on, find a town you like and settle down. Whatever practical help they did receive was from private, charitable trusts. The government itself was ill-prepared and ill-equipped to handle them. Nearly two months after independence, it still had not come to grips with the situation.

'We're at least free,' said Arun to himself, as he walked through the streets of Amritsar.

The city looked as if it had been bombed from the air. Not a building in Hall Bazaar, the main throughfare of the city, stood intact; they were in total ruin. The roofs were gone, the window frames burned out, the walls collapsed. And this continued block after block, and bazaar after bazaar; charred and blackened walls, and heaps of rubbish of what must have been impressive, many-storeyed buildings. These were the houses of the Muslims, who had now been driven out. Many Hindu and Sikh houses were damaged, too.

Padmini elected to stay on in Amritsar, in the hope Chandni might be recovered one day and brought there. Bibi Amar Vati and Sunanda, and Isher Kaur and Teja Singh, accompanied Lala Kanshi Ram's family to Delhi.

Their journey to Delhi was marked by one overriding feature: constant halts and stops. The authorities, to be sure, were eager they should depart. Only at each step delays occurred and they were obliged to wait.

Their tongas were stranded for over an hour in a side lane of the city, while they were on their way from the refugee camp to the Amritsar railway station.

Lala Kanshi Ram got restless and wanted to know why the tongas had stopped. Both the tonga drivers had disappeared, and Lala Kanshi Ram asked one of the passers-by. 'They are taking out a procession of Muslim women through the bazaar,' was the saucy reply. He spoke as if this was routine here; he showed neither surprise, nor curiosity. The women in the tongas coloured and looked down. They knew what kind of a procession it must be. Lala Kanshi Ram stared at the man. Arun thought of the afternoon in Narowal when Suraj and he were together. He saw the dome of the Golden Temple in the background and wondered if any Sikh out there was weeping for these women.

The shouts and the insults hurled at the women came right through to where they were sitting in the tongas, and Lala Kanshi Ram closed his ears with his hands. The tonga drivers returned mystified and happy. Arun dared not look at them.

Then, at the railway station, the train by which they were to travel to Delhi was not yet ready. A train with hundreds of slaughtered Muslims had pulled in and they were cleaning up the platform. It was a train carrying Muslim refugees to Pakistan; it had been stopped at the signals outside of Amritsar, when the Muslims were massacred. Lala Kanshi Ram and the other Hindu refugees waited in the waiting room, hearing the wailing of the survivors. The wailing had a familiar ring, and while many refugees joyfully shouted, 'Serves them right,' Lala Kanshi Ram looked at the ground in humiliation. It was hours before the refugee train with whatever Muslims were left in it steamed out to Lahore. The dead had been shunted to a siding, and the Delhi train came alongside the platform. The platform was recently washed, but patches of blood were on its floor everywhere. Indian soldiers stood guard with machine guns, but they were only a facade—like their counterparts in Pakistan. They had failed to protect the Muslims.

For some minutes there was a stampede as hundreds of Hindu and Sikh refugees tried to board the Delhi train. Hot words were exchanged and there were also scuffles as they struggled with each other to be the first to get in. They threw their belongings in and climbed in through the windows and the doors. The others climbed over the top of them, through the same windows and doors.

Then a police official came along into each compartment making an inventory. Refugees were required to tell their names, the place in Pakistan they had come from, the city they were heading for and their purpose in going there. Similar lists had already been prepared at different points—at Dera Baba Nanak, at the camp in Amritsar, at the municipal store from which they received the dry rations—and yet each separate organization began from scratch. Lala Kanshi Ram was highly peeved at the last question. What the hell did they think he was going to Delhi for? 'I'm going there to have a meal with Jawaharlal Nehru—to celebrate azadi!' he said to the official tartly.

No tickets were required to travel in the refugee train, and some of the men found that thrilling. 'After all, we're now free. Why should we pay to travel on our own railways?' said a young Sikh, wearing a lungi. When the train at last was ready to leave, there were people on its rooftop, people on its footboards, people hanging from the windows, people sitting on the engine, people on the guard's van. Inside the compartments, there was not standing room left. Arun squeezed out of the window to see how it looked, and he almost missed the train—that very minute it started pulling out. He ran back and jumped through the window and Lala Kanshi Ram glared at him. 'There are men everywhere,' said Arun, raising his eyebrows. Lala Kanshi Ram was not appeased. 'You fool, you would have been left behind,' he said.

He need have had no apprehensions. The train stopped several times before it was really under way. No one knew why it stopped. The engine roared for a while, the bogies dragged for a few yards, and then came to a screeching halt. Once again the engine roared, the bogies moved, and came to a screeching, clanging halt. People put their heads out of the windows and looked back towards the guard's cabin. They saw railway officials rushing about. And again the train moved. And again it stopped. When it did get out of Amritsar, it shook unevenly on its wheels under the heavy load.

It stopped for *hours* at the wayside stations. Bands of suspicious-looking Sikhs and Hindus stood at those stations, with the loose ends of their turbans wrapped over their faces like masks, and Lala Kanshi Ram had no doubt they were marauders waiting to fall upon Muslim refugees. They saw no Muslim foot convoys from the train, but they knew some must be crawling their way towards Pakistan. Many people got off the train at these points. Many more got in—struggling and fighting with those who were already on the train. At Jullundur railway station, the train halted for over seven hours. At Ludhiana for five hours. At Ambala, it stopped outside of the outer signals and it looked as though it would never move.

Twenty-eight hours had already passed since the train had left Amritsar. It normally took four to cover this distance. It was night now—the second the refugees were passing in the train—and it was halted way outside of the station. There were only open fields around them, but the city buildings could be seen in the background. People from the roof of the train got off and gossiped beside the double tracks. Many went into the fields and urinated or emptied their bowels. Food had been scarce along the way, but people munched what little they had with them. They were hoping to buy a hot meal at the Ambala station, but the train did not budge. Even the guard and the engine driver didn't know what the matter was. There was a red light ahead of them and the signal wouldn't turn green. Hours passed. It was seven in the evening when the train stopped. It was now ten o'clock.

It was around that time when Isher Kaur clumsily got up from her seat, leaned over to Prabha Rani, and whispered into her ear.

Isher Kaur had become extremely ungainly these days. Her hips stuck out, as she got up from her seat and leaned over to speak with Prabha Rani.

Prabha Raini lifted her eyes in surprise.

'Are you sure?'

Isher Kaur nodded her head.

Sunanda looked at them, while Bibi Amar Vati asked: 'What's the matter?'

'She says her pains have started.'

The three women stared at Isher Kaur. A spasm passed through her body and holding on tight to the handrail above, she struggled to control her pain.

'Sit down, don't stand there—sit down,' said Sunanda, feeling for the girl.

The men in the family stared at the women. For a few seconds Prabha Rani said nothing to them, and her husband looked at her with annoyance.

'What is it?' he asked irritably.

'She says her pains have started,' Prabha Rani repeated.

A feeling of compassion came on Lala Kanshi Ram and he felt small for having yielded to anger. He looked at Isher Kaur. She was like a daughter to him and he thought back to the day when she was married; it was only the other day. How many things had happened since then! The girl sat stupefied under the yellow, pale light of the electric bulb overhead, and she looked abashed. Perspiration spread along the line of her upper lip and her strong, heavy arms were hanging loosely by her sides. Her belly was swollen right to the base of her chest and she seemed to be breathing with difficulty—she was almost panting. Her terrified eyes flitted from person to person. She looked out into the dark, she looked closely at her father, she looked closely at Lala Kanshi Ram. And then she was in the grip of another spasm and beads of perspiration appeared all over her face. The spasm passed, she went utterly limp, and covering up her face with her hands, she started crying. Her whole inside had been taken over by her child and it was hard for her to do anything properly. Even her panting was difficult, and she had to open her mouth to gulp for air. But she covered her face with her swollen, fleshy hands and wept. Then, as suddenly, she wiped her tears and closely covered her head with her dopatta.

They made room for her next to Prabha Rani. She said, almost apologetically: 'It has been going on for many hours.'

'Why didn't you tell us? We would have got off at Ludhiana.'

She shrugged her shoulders.

'I thought it would pass.'

Her eyes again filled with tears. She had a comely face, and a skin which sparkled like lilacs. Now the skin had gone pale and the face was disfigured. The flesh around the eyes was swollen, the nose looked thicker around the tip, the cheeks bulged and spread out as though falling over a ridge. Yet she looked touchingly beautiful, as with her eyes lowered, her lips quivering with emotion, and with an aura of primeval innocence around her, she tried to come to terms with what was happening to her. At first she wiped the perspiration off her forehead. Then she ignored it. And bathed with sweat, she sat shyly in their midst and even tried to smile through her teary eyes.

The briskness with which the women in the family took charge of the situation was to remain alive in Lala Kanshi Ram's mind for a long time to come. He himself felt uneasy. He said to Isher Kaur, 'Don't worry, beti. Everything will be all right.' But even if the train were standing at the railway station, he wouldn't have known what to do. Prabha Rani saw his predicament and said: 'So what? She'll have the child here!'

A section of the compartment was cleared, and a sheet was hung to seal that section off. Everyone was eager to help. A few men ran up to the engine and brought a bucketfull of hot water from the boiler. The women in the compartment took out clean towels and linen from their bundles and gave them to Prabha Rani. Arun offered to go and look for a lady doctor on the train. 'What do we need a lady doctor for?' sneered Bibi Amar Vati, taking it as an insult to her skill as a midwife.

The news came they might have to spend the whole night there. A train of Muslim refugees had been derailed at the Ambala railway station and that's what the delay was about. It was on its way to Lahore and was running through Ambala, without stopping here. Someone had thrown the switch at the station and sent it hurtling into a shunting line, where it had crashed against a fence. It now lay sprawled partly on the Delhi track and they were clearing the wreckage. Many were reported to be dead.

Isher Kaur's severe labour started only after midnight. She could no longer suppress her screams. People in the compartment looked at each other silently. Some of the older men folded their hands in prayer. For a while a crowd collected outside. They were curious. What was happening in here? Lala Kanshi Ram drove them away, and they now clustered a little away from the compartment.

The screams were heart-rending. It sounded like someone being slowly slaughtered. Starting on a low note, they burst the air with piercing sharpness. The women behind the curtain comforted Ishero. 'Take heart.' 'Won't be long.' 'Say Waheguru.' And while she was taking heart and saying Waheguru—for she would be quiet—and while some woman would yet be saying the soothing words, in the middle of a sentence, she would break into a loud and sharp scream. She continued to pant and grunt for some time afterwards. Then there was quiet again.

The news spread and a lady doctor from somewhere materialized and she too was now behind the curtain. Hours passed. Scream after scream rent the air. There was dead silence in the compartment and the men felt shy to look at each other. Scream after scream. Scream after scream.

Around four in the morning, the Muslim train that was derailed at Ambala passed on the other track on its way to Pakistan. All kinds of rumours were rife. Hundreds had died. The four front bogies of the train and the engine were completely destroyed. The Hindu engine driver had also been killed. No, the Hindu driver had been forewarned and he had jumped off the train. Seven hundred people had died. Four hundred had died. Only twenty had died. The Pakistani soldiers escorting the train had machine-gunned the Hindu station staff. The Indian army at the station had machine-gunned and killed all the Pakistani soldiers. The cranes had taken hours to remove the telescoped bogies from the tracks. The cranes had been specially brought from Delhi. A new engine had also come from Delhi.

It was difficult to decide what to believe and what not. But when the Muslim train passed the halted train, there were no shouts from any direction. Cries of bewailing came from each compartment of the other train, but before you had paid any attention to it the compartment had passed ahead and cries of a different tenor emerged before you. Like the Hindu refugee train on the way to Delhi, the other train was fully packed and there were families sitting on the roof. The train was just gathering momentum, and the two communities of refugees looked sullenly at each other.

At five in the morning, ten hours after it had stopped there, the signals finally turned green, and the Delhi-bound train began pulling ahead. It moved very slowly, very very slowly. It passed the outer signals and entered a network of lines; it was getting into the main station yard. It passed the inner signals. They were still some distance from the platforms. And now it was they saw the smashed up bogies to their right. The cranes were still working on them. They passed them very slowly, almost at walking pace. And then they saw a long line of the dead. They were laid out beside the track, one dead next to another, and they were covered with sheets. It was clear from certain sheets there was only a child below; the corpse was so small. Lala Kanshi Ram counted ninety-four bodies. Maybe more were lined up elsewhere, he muttered to himself.

At the precise moment the Delhi train passed the dead, another kind of scream went up into the air—a thin, squealing scream. Isher Kaur had delivered her child and a new life had arrived in the world. There was peace behind the curtain, but for the thin cries of the baby. The men looked at each other with relief. Some of the women said, 'Thank God!' The train slowly inched forward, and while they all mutely looked at the dead outside, the exuberant and powerful screams of the baby repeatedly asserted that it was alive, it was very *much* alive. You better pay attention to me, it seemed to be screaming. *Pay attention to me*!

'It's a girl,' said Prabha Rani, coming out of the enclosure.

'That's what Ishero wanted,' she added, when no one cheered.

The train stayed at Ambala railway station for twenty-four hours. It was shunted to a side platform, and it became like a home on wheels for those who were in it. Many got off and decided to stay at Ambala, to look for fortunes there. Many more came on board. The women washed clothes, shampooed hair, gave baths to their children. The men too bathed and washed themselves. The platform soon came to look like a camping ground. Many vendors appeared there. Many local social organizations too appeared with free tea for the refugees and packages of food. Since it was formally announced the train would not leave for Delhi until the following morning, many people went to have a look at the town. The train was stopping at Ambala Cantonment and they got into tongas and drove to the city. Lala Kanshi Ram and Arun also went. 'How was the town?' Prabha Rani asked them in the evening. 'Disgusting,' said Lala Kanshi Ram.

The train was moving again and they were on the last leg of their journey hoping to reach Delhi in the evening.

'Arun's mother,' said Lala Kanshi Ram, pensively.

It was many months since Prabha Rani found this tenderness in her husband's voice. He had not asked her to come to him in as many words, but she knew he wanted to talk. She went to his side and changed places with Arun. The makeshift curtain still hung in the compartment, behind which Isher Kaur and her daughter were sound asleep. Sunanda's children were also sleeping inside that enclosure. Everyone else sat outside, wherever they could find place.

Lala Kanshi Ram and Prabha Rani were sitting near the door. From the window, they saw a vast expanse of land spread before them. It was fertile land, and Lala Kanshi Ram saw it had been tilled. Heavy trees dotted the countryside. Lala Kanshi Ram did not see many orchards, otherwise it was not much different from the land he had left behind.

'You know what land that is?' he asked Prabha Rani.

His finger was pompously pointed outside and his glasses were at the tip of his nose.

Prabha Rani had an urge to hold that old, furrowed face in her hands and press it to her heart. It was so like the old days! He had not asked her a single question since they left home—a question of this type, when he might want to educate her. He looked so much thinner now, the face especially. She knew he had suffered for Madhu. He had said not a word. But she knew how excruciating had been his pain. A slow, silent, eroding pain that had torn him asunder.

'No,' she answered shaking her head, her eyes filling with water. 'What land is it?'

For a second Lala Kanshi Ram felt she knew the answer and was only putting on an act to humour him, and he dropped his chin and looked at her closely.

But she was all right; she was not being clever. She was only crying, he didn't know why.

Raising his chin, he said lavishly: 'It is *Kurukshetra*.' 'Kurukshetra!'

Prabha Rani was genuinely impressed.

'Quite right. This is where the Kauravas and the Pandavas fought the battle of Mahabharata.'

Prabha Rani leaned over and looked through the window, with reverence on her face.

'Where is the sacred tank?'

'You can't see it. You can't see the town of Kurukshetra either; it's some distance from here. But these are the fields.'

Prabha Rani watched wide-eyed. Stories of the Mahabharata she had heard in her life flashed through her mind. 'Arun, come over here.' And she told him what she had just learned. Arun seemed only mildly interested and she was hurt at that. Turning towards her husband, she said to him: 'Take me to the tank for a bath one day.'

'I shall. Soon as we're settled somewhere,' he answered.

They looked on in silence. They passed a village. They passed another village. Mud and brick houses, irregular lanes, and ponds with buffaloes near them, and many many trees, and herds of cows grazing. And for a few moments they had a brief glimpse of the city of Kurukshetra out on the horizon. All this was hallowed land, where mighty stalwarts centuries back had fallen in the cause of duty. 'I certainly shall,' said Lala Kanshi Ram again.

'Arun's mother, you know what?'

'What?'

Feeling happy, she prepared herself for more about Kurukshetra.

'I have ceased to hate.'

Prabha Rani looked at him.

Lala Kanshi Ram was staring at the fields. The excitement had vanished from his face and he looked inordinately serene, even sad.

'Hate?'

'Yes. I can't hate the Muslims any more.'

This was unexpected. At no time had Lala Kanshi Ram openly said anything against the Muslims. In spite of his hurt, he had been most circumspect. And yet Prabha Rani knew how he felt. And she understood him only too well. Why shouldn't he feel bitter? Why shouldn't he nurse resentment? Their whole mode of life had been changed—nay, destroyed. She herself was so bitter, she could kill a Muslim with her bare hands.

'Hating won't bring anything back,' she said conventionally enough, striking the pose of a pious Hindu. But her heart was filled with rage.

'I don't mean that. Nothing can bring back anything, my Madhu particularly.'

He sounded so desolate and it was with difficulty he completed the sentence. Prabha Rani watched him uncertainly.

'What I mean is, whatever the Muslims did to us in Pakistan, we're doing it to them here!'

Prabha Rani watched him, trying to solve in her mind the complexities of his argument. She wanted to nod in agreement but she couldn't.

'Every single horror.'

'But they killed thousands of us without reason, raped our women, drove us out of our homes.'

'We're doing the same—*exactly the* same.'

'I don't know what you are talking about.'

'You have seen for yourself.'

'Seen what?'

'What we're doing to the Muslims in India.'

Prabha Rani was getting impatient with him.

'All right, don't hate them then,' she said, adjusting her sari, but making it clear through the toss of her head she was not with him in this. 'I'll hate and curse them as long as I live.'

'No, you won't.'

'I will.'

'No, you won't.'

He was very mild in his persuasion. He wanted to take her hand in his own, but there were people in the compartment. He leaned towards her and his arm was pressing against her arm and his head was falling on her ample bosom. She saw the thinness of his hair and the balding skull below and she saw his nose and his eyes semi-closed in concentration, and yet again she felt deeply for that parched, weather-beaten face. She could see he was not trying to browbeat her. He was not even looking at her.

'We are all equally guilty,' he said, spacing his words apart. 'Each of those girls in that procession at Amritsar was someone's Madhu, and there must have been many amongst the dead you saw at Ambala.'

Without knowing it, Prabha Rani was weeping. Softly, she called, 'Madhu, Madhu, Madhu...' And she repeatedly shook her head, for she did not agree with her husband.

'Forgive. That way alone can you make peace with yourself.'

She shook her head in slow motion and continued to weep.

'There's no other way,' he said.

'As a last resort—yes. But I don't believe in it.'

'You have to. To forgive fully.'

She said nothing and kept weeping. Forgetful of others, she placed her head on his shoulder and their two heads were now touching. Arun saw them and couldn't say what they were up to. It must be his father! He was ever springing surprises and dragging the poor woman along. But he didn't like the way they were nestling up to each other in public. He felt quite disconcerted.

Lala Kanshi Ram was saying: 'We have sinned as much. We need *their* forgiveness!'

A drizzle started as they got off the train at Delhi. They had been lucky with weather so far. It had not rained at all during their two-week march on foot, and only once while they were at Amritsar. But the sky at Delhi was overcast and looked iron grey, as a slight drizzle fell.

'It's a bad beginning,' said Lala Kanshi Ram.

'Since when have you become superstitious?' asked his wife.

Lala Kanshi Ram had agreed to come to Delhi as it was the seat of the government. All the leaders lived here and he found the thought exciting. He also felt there would be greater business opportunities for him here. But his welcome was bleak: he saw only unfriendly faces on the platform. It was difficult for him to find a porter to carry his luggage. The porters knew these refugees did not have much money on them and in any case these Punjabis haggled a lot. So they did not go near them. Arun had to make two trips in the rain, to ferry what little they had to a waiting room.

The station was big, the waiting halls spacious. There were crowds everywhere.

It took Lala Kanshi Ram and Teja Singh several hours in the line to reach the officials who sat at one end behind large tables receiving the incoming refugees. Everyone referred to them with awe as the Rehabilitation Officers. And the first words of the swarthy Rehabilitation Officer before whom Lala Kanshi Ram ended up were severe and abrupt.

'Why have you come to Delhi?'

Lala Kanshi Ram looked up at him in surprise.

'I am from Pakistan,' he said, feeling certain this was identity enough.

The officer scoffed.

'I know, I know. But why to Delhi?'

Lala Kanshi Ram was at a loss for reply. He had not thought for a moment he would have to justify his presence anywhere in India.

'Why to Delhi?' The officer was harsh and overbearing.

'I hope to settle here,' he said.

'Why not in East Punjab? Why do you Punjabis lift your faces and march on to Delhi?'

The man was at least ten years younger than Lala Kanshi Ram in age, but he was scolding him as though Lala Kanshi Ram were only an infant. He was chewing paan and was continually spitting at the wall behind him.

Lala Kanshi Ram held his tongue and said nothing.

'It's the *capital* of the country, do you realize? We can't let you people swarm here and disfigure it'

'Do you have a relation here?' he asked.

'No.'

'Do you have a job in hand?'

'No.'

'What do you do?'

'I'm a grain merchant.'

The man looked at the form Lala Kanshi Ram had filled in.

'Who are these Amar Vati and Sunanda Bala? You haven't mentioned their relationship with you.'

'They lost their menfolk in Pakistan. Now they're part of my family.'

'What a large family! And your son is only a student. Who's going to feed you?'

'I will, sir. All I want is a roof over my head.'

Teja Singh pushed up before the officer.

'I'm also with Lalaji, sir.'

'And why have you come to Delhi?'

He grilled Sardar Teja Singh as he had Lala Kanshi Ram.

'Sir, I lost my son-in-law in Pakistan.'

Sardar Teja Singh thought that was a point in his favour.

'Sir, I lost my daughter,' said Lala Kanshi Ram.

'Ah, yes. Ah, yes,' the officer said impatiently. 'You have all lost someone!'

Lala Kanshi Ram could see the interview was not going in their favour. The officer was needlessly cutting and sharp. He saw before him visions of being forced to return to cities like Ambala and Jullundur—cities that he detested. His heart sank and he saw darkness before his eyes.

Swallowing his pride, he pleaded meekly: 'Sir, I'll be ruined if you don't come to my rescue. I only want a small flat and a small little shop to be allotted to me.'

The officer's eyes popped out of his head.

'What? A shop and a flat? What shop and flat?'

'Why, from those the Muslims left behind. Refugee property, I mean.'

Lala Kanshi Ram had heard that much. There were three hundred thousand Muslims in Delhi and most of them had gone.

'We too have left property back in Pakistan. Maybe an adjustment could be made,' he added hopefully.

The officer had leaned back in his chair and he was doubling up with laughter.

'Do you hear?' he shouted to the officer on his left, who was baring his teeth at an old woman in rags before his desk. 'This old man wants a house and a shop. Refugee property, he says.'

The other officer bared the teeth a little more and his scowl became a grin, before he narrowed the gap and started glowering at the woman again.

'We should really do this screening at Ambala or somewhere else in East Punjab,' said the first officer. 'It is silly to let them come here without appropriate means.'

The other officer nodded his head approvingly, and resumed his glaring.

Lala Kanshi Ram swallowed several times while this dialogue was going on. He felt small and debased. He did not want to move away from the table empty-handed.

The officer leaned forward and said: 'Lalaji, what fool's paradise are you living in? It is the middle of November. Six hundred thousand Hindu and Sikh refugees are already in the capital. Do you think there is a house and a shop left waiting for you? They've all been allotted to refugees, or forcibly occupied by them.'

He seemed to think as he looked at the humble figure of Lala Kanshi Ram. There was a dignity in that humility he couldn't ignore.

'I should really put you on a train back to East Punjab, or leave you to fend for yourself. But you are old'—the officer faltered. 'All right, I'll find room for you both in one of the camps, though they're full, too.'

Taking his pen, he scribbled something on the forms of Lala Kanshi Ram and Sardar Teja Singh. While he was writing, Lala Kanshi Ram thought with a shudder, what another camp? No!

'Sir, give us a *single* room in some house,' he implored.

'I've told you. Kingsway Camp!' The slight deference he might have felt for him was gone, and curtly he waved him and Sardar Teja Singh along.

Lala Kanshi Ram would have felt it beneath him to let his disappointment be seen by his family. He gave out he was happy. They had at least a place to live. They would soon find something better.

He did not move to the camp right away. They spent the night at the station. Meanwhile he diligently worked out plans in his busy head. He thought and thought. When the others in his group wanted to go and look at the famed Chandni Chowk, only a few hundred yards away from the station, he refused. 'You go, I'll stay with Isher Kaur.' They had spread their beds in one corner of the waiting hall, where Isher Kaur was sleeping the sleep of exhaustion. Her shirt was lifted and the little child, red and pink like a piglet, lying with eyes shut tight, was sucking fast at her breast. Ishero did not know about it; she lay in the arms of forgetfulness. 'Someone has to stay with her,' Lala Kanshi Ram justified himself.

It was still drizzling, and the sky was raw and formidable. But Chandni Chowk or Red Fort were fabulous names for them—names associated with unearthly splendour. And all of them, including Sardar Teja Singh, walked across the Town Hall gardens in front of the station to see the bazaar.

'You should have seen the way it glitters. Millions of lights,' said Prabha Rani on their return.

Lala Kanshi Ram paid no attention. He was busy thinking. They had lost everything—everything. The three thousand rupees in his pocket had dwindled down to two. How much longer would that hold out? Surely everyone here couldn't be so unsympathetic. But who, who as the last, the *final* resort, should he go to? He brooded and he brooded, and paid little attention to what went on around him.

The sky was still overcast in the morning, but it was not raining. Lala Kanshi Ram by then knew of his course of action and he wondered it hadn't come to him earlier. That was the thing to do! The others might shirk and back out, but *he* had a moral responsibility. They had been pushed into this partition, they didn't ask for it, didn't sanction it in any form whatsoever. And no arrangements had been made to meet the consequences. They could take their camps and free blankets back, if that's all the arrangements they had made. No, he would go and confront the man who had accepted this settlement in their name.

Making enquiries, changing buses, fumbling for change in his pockets and apologizing for his slowness to the conductors, hearing other people's tales and telling a few of his own, staring unbelievingly at the dense traffic, looking at the regal structures of what someone in the bus said was the 'Big Office' and the Lok Sabha, looking at the national flag that flew atop many buildings (he bent low and looked high above), he reached the residence of Nehru. Let the others go and rot in camps. They were not ingenious enough. He had to get a shop and a house. He knew for sure he would be able to convince the Prime Minister.

To his astonishment, he discovered the same idea had come to hundreds of others as well. There was a huge crowd outside Nehru's residence. The police would allow no one in. He waited for hours. Many in the crowd were shouting slogans. It was no organized demonstration; each man stood only for himself. It was easy for the police to resist such a crowd, and they did not open the gate. Later, it transpired Nehru was out of Delhi that day. 'Don't you read the newspaper? Panditji has gone to Bombay on tour,' said one police official. They're liars, said Lala Kanshi Ram to himself, for he saw cars going in and out of the gate constantly. A shining limousine would draw up to the gate, the gate was swung open, the stray refugees who tried to rush inside were caught and brought back, and the gate was closed once again.

Lala Kanshi Ram knew it was hopeless. Some in the crowd bellowed, 'Go to the Rehabilitation Minister.' Some said, 'Find a sympathetic MP.' Or: 'Bribe the Rehabilitation Officer.' Or: 'Go to the Area Custodians.' A wag said: 'Go to the Hanuman Temple near Connaught Circus and pray.'

Lala Kanshi Ram knew how hopeless it was. Who would travel such distances and who would seek out the Rehabilitation Minister or an MP? It was in any case beyond him, and he felt tired. Maybe he would return another day and meet with Nehru. But he couldn't sit and let events catch up with him. He would go and look for a house on his own—a house he could rent.

With this resolve, he returned to the railway station. He found that Sardar Teja Singh and Isher Kaur were not there.

'Where are they?' he asked.

'Oh, they met an acquaintance of theirs, who lives in Shahdara, a suburb of Delhi. He took them home. They'll stay with him.'

It was good, they had after all found shelter, a decent shelter, better than a refugee camp where life was so uncertain, and Prabha Rani seemed happy as she passed the news to Lala Kanshi Ram. Lala Kanshi Ram felt inordinately hurt. It was another bond that had snapped. One by one, he was losing his limbs, and he touched his two arms reminiscently.

'They could have waited until my return,' he said, offended.

Bibi Amar Vati and Sunanda and Arun looked up at him.

Prabha Rani said: 'The man met us accidentally. If they had not gone with him, they wouldn't know how to get to his house. At least that luckless girl will have some comfort! Teja Singh will come and see you this evening.'

Lala Kanshi Ram stood there vexed.

'Both of them were weeping when they left.' Prabha Rani was soft and tender, for she knew how he felt. 'Ishero spoke of you and said you were dearer to her than her own father.'

'Who was the man anyway?' he asked, still contentious.

Arun said, 'He was a Sikh official of a kind. Sardar Teja Singh said he was related to him through his wife. He seemed to be well off.'

Lala Kanshi Ram took a deep breath and went and sat near the group.

Bibi Amar Vati tried to console him: 'It was good they went.'

'We have been together for so many years,' he said sadly, turning towards her.

For the next three days Lala Kanshi Ram took Arun with him and they searched every single locality of Delhi to find a house. Daryagunj, Chandni Chowk, Lal Kuan, Khari Bauli, Sadar, Pahari Dhiraj, Rooi Mandi, Bara Tuti, Batha, Subzi Mandi. They dared not to go to 'New' Delhi—its extravagant name seemed to scare them away. But they visited each of the areas in Old Delhi, while the family lived and made do at the railway station.

They followed the same pattern everywhere. They first went into the office of the Area Custodian of evacuee property. Many of these officers were Punjabis, who had themselves migrated from West Punjab. But they looked a different breed from the refugees who came and lined up before them. Drunk with the power of their office, they were impatient and intolerant—at least with most of the refugees. 'It takes a thousand rupees to put the sahib in good mood,' whispered one of the clerks at the Bara Tuti office to Lala Kanshi Ram. Lala Kanshi Ram recoiled at the information. That would leave him with only a thousand. At each different office, some clerk of the government passed the same information on to him.

'They're servants of the people, they're supposed to serve us!' Lala Kanshi Ram was feeling scandalized only because the bribe demanded was beyond his means.

'They do,' said the clerk with a dull smile. 'For a thousand rupees you get a refugee flat, with a nominal rent of rupees fifteen per month. What more do you want?'

But the initial investment—Lala Kanshi Ram swayed when he thought of the amount involved.

'And a shop?'

'Maybe another thousand,' said the clerk nonchalantly.

The clerk had almost dismissed him, for while Lala Kanshi Ram sat before him, he took out a sandwich from his drawer and started munching it. But he had not dismissed him, he was watching him.

'Have you got the money?' he asked, munching the sandwich.

'No.'

After that the clerk didn't look at him. He took out a file and started reading through it, while continuing to munch.

At none of the offices did the officer himself deign to talk with them. He sat in a small room, surrounded by people who by turns went up to his ear and whispered into it. Most of the time Lala Kanshi Ram found him shaking his head. It was early winter and Lala Kanshi Ram and Arun were wearing flimsy pullovers they had bought in cheap stores. But the Custodians sat snug in tweeds and their shoes were immaculately polished. Many of them had woollen scarfs around their necks, and when they glared at the crowds they glared from bright, shining eyes across well-fed cheeks.

'Is it true these officers too are refugees like ourselves?' Lala Kanshi Ram asked of another refugee.

'They *were*. They're no longer.'

Crowds and crowds everywhere. Very few people in there with the sahib, but outside, in the room where the clerks sat, a vast throng. Tall men in tehmads, flowing robes, and with loosely wrapped turbans on their heads. Men with the funniest haircuts he had ever seen, with their hair falling over like wigs—

unclean, unkempt, shaggy wigs. Men speaking strange brands of Punjabi, which sounded more like words hurled at you through a popgun. Then there were men with faces red like pathans. They wore shalwars like women, thick, wide-bottomed shalwars, but they were a head taller than the other men in the crowd. Their turbans were wrapped tightly—not directly on the head but on hard skull caps. All these were men from parts of the Punjab Lala Kanshi Ram had not visited. Men from Multan and Jhang and Naushehra and Dera Ismail Khan or from the North West Frontier Province—from Peshawar and beyond.

A large majority of them were from Central Punjab, though, the area from which came Lala Kanshi Ram, and he did not feel out of place with them. They were physically fit and strong like him and in spite of their sorrow they had a healthy laughter. There were very few women in those crowds. It was the men who went and advanced their claims.

They had just visited one of these offices. It was the third day of their search. With each day, with each visit to a separate area, Lala Kanshi Ram's face was becoming more and more pallid. At each office they were told the same thing. The refugee property had already been allotted. They were too late. It was the middle of November. There were six hundred thousand refugees already in Delhi. No, there was absolutely no flat left, nor a shop. And like the final act of a ritual, they were also asked in the end if they had any money on them. Maybe then. Maybe then. But did they have the money?

Lala Kanshi Ram became pale by degrees and now it seemed there was no blood left in him. He positively did not want to go to another refugee camp. Four months of that had shrunk his heart. Never before in his life had he felt so exposed, so naked, so defenceless. He was not born to riches and it was not the material comforts he missed. Yet he was used to, he had got used to, warmth. Out of the dark cave that life was, Prabha Rani had carved a sunny patch for him and then sealed it off. Prabha Rani was still with him but the seal had been smashed. There were too many eyes peering in on them at these camps, too many ears listening. Each was a curiosity to the other, but no one had any identity. He wanted no more of that. He wanted a name for himself once again—not fame, just a name. And the wind that blew nonstop through those tents, it had driven holes through his body. He wanted walls around himself and doors and he wanted a bed to lie on and clean sheets and he wanted Prabha Rani to be alone with him. The only time he now had the feeling of Madhu's presence near him was when he was alone with his wife. In a few months' time it had become difficult for him to recall and rebuild her from memory! What kind of a nose did she have, what kind of eyes? He remembered, to be sure he remembered, but the images overlapped and then it was so difficult for him to give them life even if he did succeed in putting the features together. The vision hardly ever moved, it gave out no fragrance, held no sense of being. But when he was alone with his wife, be it only for brief moments, Madhu came back to him in person; he would suddenly become aware of her. It didn't happen each time they were alone, but they had to be alone for it to happen; even Arun had to be absent from the scene. He couldn't say what magic it was, what charisma. Maybe it was only a similarity in features, or something in her eyes. Yet his pain was lessened somewhat at such moments. And when the presence was lost—as it was, soon enough—he still stayed happy for hours. No, he wanted to live in no camp now, amongst strangers. He wanted a home, where he could be alone with Prabha and see his two children.

In each of these areas, they also enquired for a flat in a private home. The native people in Delhi seemed so afraid of the Punjabis. The moment they gave out their identity, the door was shut on them. 'Punjabis? Never! You're too quarrelsome.' As an Arya Samaji, Lala Kanshi Ram loved academic debates. He very much wanted to have a heart to heart talk with some of these people. What more about life did they know than chewing betel leaf? Did they know what they, the Punjabis, had gone through? But the door was shut tight and even when he pounded hard on it, it was not opened again. Only in one instance the man reappeared at a window on the first floor and said: 'Now didn't I tell you, you people are too quarrelsome! What are you breaking my door for?' In odd cases, where the flat was offered to them, they demanded too high a rent. In addition, they demanded paghri—black money, to the tune of several hundred rupees.

The Bara Tuti officer had curtly dismissed them and turned them out of his room. Lala Kanshi Ram looked extremely despondent. Arun stood quietly by his side in the Bara Tuti chowk, looking at the traffic. He wanted to cheer him up, but he himself was feeling low. They had tried everything and failed. The traffic moved unconcerned in the big chowk, the tongas and the tram cars. Looking at Delhi, one wouldn't know something like partition had taken place and towns in the Punjab and Bengal lay in total ruin. Muslims from some part of Delhi had been driven out, but there had been little damage done to property and all the buildings stood intact. The exuberance of the town was undiminished and there was a press of shoppers in Bara Tuti. The father and the son stood lost in the middle of it. It was afternoon. They had left the railway station in the morning with only a glassful of tea and some buns and had had no lunch. There was a restaurant directly ahead of them, a dilapidated place, with a newly painted sign-board saying 'Master Hotel'. Arun suggested they go and eat there. Lala Kanshi Ram nodded his head, but did not move.

'Wait here a second, Arun, I'll be right back,' he said looking lost and hurt and confused.

'Where are you going?'

'I'll be back.'

'Let me come with you.'

'No, you stay here. I'm only going back up to the Refugee Office.'

'But the officer has already said no.'

'I know—I know—'

Soon Lala Kanshi Ram had disappeared into the lane where the Refugee Office was. Arun did not know what to make of it. He stood uncertainly, watching a Chandni Chowk bound tram roll through the chowk with a tolling noise of its warning bell. He was feeling uneasy about his father, he had looked so unhappy. After waiting for a while, he too walked back to the Refugee Office.

The office doors were screened, and from the road you couldn't see what was happening inside. Moving past the groups of people sitting in the clerks' outer office, Arun went through a narrow passage and was outside of the Custodian's room. Arun intuitively felt his father had gone there. Surprisingly, he was allowed in. His father was stunned to find him there, and he tried to conceal his tears. Had he been weeping? *His* father, weeping openly?

The officer looked relieved to see Arun.

'Here,' he said with forced heartiness. 'Take care of your father. He has been weeping. I've told you people. There is nothing that I can do! There simply aren't any more houses.'

His speech was meant to be sympathetic, but he sounded crude. He tried to laugh, seemingly at his inability to help them, but his laughter was harsh and presumptuous. Arun led his father out.

As they walked towards the chowk, Arun had his arm around his father's shoulder like a friend. Arun had not ever touched his father intimately like this, and he was cut to the quick to feel his thin shoulder blades.

Master Hotel was a small place, but stairs led up to a second floor where there were more seats. They sat in the main hall upstairs. Arun ordered naan and mutton curry for himself, but Lala Kanshi Ram said he would only have tea and biscuits. His lips just wouldn't cease quivering. He would break a biscuit and put it into his mouth, but his lips quivered and he wasn't able to eat it. He was not weeping, it was worse. Tears floated through the ducts of his eyes and went back, but they did not leave the eyes. He looked utterly distraught. He tried to drink his tea but his hand shook so, he left the cup on the table. His lips quivered, his cheeks became pouchy in his attempts to take hold of himself, and his watery eyes looked through space at nothing. Arun felt guilty for ordering a big meal for himself. He now quietly ate it, without talking. Through the large glass window, they could see the traffic in the chowk; but it was Arun only who looked at it—Lala Kanshi Ram was looking elsewhere.

Arun was at a loss. So much sorrow for a house! Such prostration! Such weariness of the spirit!

'We'll find a house, father. Don't worry so.'

Lala Kanshi Ram nodded his head, slowly and heavily.

'Father!—'

Arun's morsel stayed in his hand.

'Father, what is it?'

Lala Kanshi Ram made a mild attempt to reassure Arun. He looked at him and tried to smile. But it was a ghost smile and it never came on. Arun would have accepted even that but soon afterwards, he saw his face tighten, as though a spasm had hit him

'What is it, father?'

Lala Kanshi Ram did not answer for some seconds. Instead he lowered his head and looked at his feet. He again tried to bite the biscuit and his lips quivered violently. He then sat back and withdrew his hand from the food.

'Father?'

'Well, if you must know, it's Madhu.'

'Father! I had no idea.'

That evening they moved to Kingsway Camp on Alipur Road. A pleasant surprise awaited them. They were not housed in tents but in brick hutments. These were hastily got ready barracks, but they were a lot cozier than tents. They were given two adjacent rooms. They were small rooms, twelve feet by twelve, but they had a covered verandah in front where they could set up a kitchen. And the floor of the rooms was paved. After about four months of irregular living under canvas, they found this a luxury. Lala Kanshi Ram went tapping with his stick to see how thick the walls were. They were thin, but they would do. That very evening he bought cots for each member of the family, and he bought fresh sheets. 'You are my responsibility now,' he told Bibi Amar Vati loudly. She smiled sadly. 'Sunanda will find work,' she said. 'There's no hurry,' said Lala Kanshi Ram.

It rained again that night. It had been cloudy all these days, and now it was pouring. But they were well protected under a corrugated roof. 'Let it rain real hard,' muttered Lala Kanshi Ram with some satisfaction. And it did.

PART III
The Aftermath

CHAPTER 1

Lala Kanshi Ram had to wait for more than an hour at the bus stop before he got the bus. His one grievance against Kingsway Camp was it was situated at one end of the city, while the government office where he had to file petitions for refugee compensation was situated at the other. He was standing outside 'P' Block in New Delhi. That's what the main Rehabilitation Office—an ugly building next to the imposing Lok Sabha—was called in the jargon of the government. It was a little before five in the evening; he had been standing here since four. Bus after bus would come, but none stopped at the request stop where he was standing. He put out his hand, but the bus went roaring by. In his early days in Delhi, these buses were a great amusement for him. Nothing like that existed in Sialkot, where you either took a tonga or walked. In Old Delhi, tongas did make short runs. But if you had to go ten miles—as 'P' Block was from Kingsway Camp—there was no choice but to go by bus. And Lala Kanshi Ram liked paying a small fare and riding such a long distance. A man in uniform went round shouting, 'Tickets, please. Tickets, please,' but Lala Kanshi Ram did not wait for him. The moment he had deposited himself in a seat (he preferred it by the window), he called out: 'Eh, conductor there. One ticket to "P" Block.' And with much relish he placed the change, coin by coin, on the palm of the conductor and looked up at him smiling, almost saying, now didn't he see, what a good man he was?

Two and a half months of Delhi, and he was no longer enamoured of bus travel. At Kingsway Camp it was all right. It was the end of the route and you could find a seat easily. But, man, do you think you could get a bus at 'P' Block? These request stops were a hoax; anything by request was a hoax in Delhi. Lala Kanshi Ram put out his hand, making the 'request' to the oncoming bus, he even made a pathetic face to win the driver's sympathy. The bus went roaring past him.

Each day he told himself he wouldn't stop at the request stop; he would walk over to the regular stop four hundred yards further up, near the North Block of the Secretariat. Yet such weakness is the human flesh prey to, each day once again he first took his chance at the nearer stop.

He was disgusted today. It had been the longest wait. And now the offices had closed and there was absolutely no hope of getting a bus here. So he walked over to the North Block, and took a number nine special that started from there when the offices let out.

Standing in a line, Lala Kanshi Ram missed the first special, but got a window seat in the second one. As the long, hooded bus pushed its hulk across the roads of Delhi, Lala Kanshi Ram slowly leafed through the file in his hand. He didn't know how often he had gone to 'P' Block. In terms of numbers, this must be his twentieth or thirtieth visit. And yet what had he accomplished so far? Even the preliminaries had not been completed. It took him weeks to get the right form, and to learn the distinction between moveable and immoveable property (they had to be entered separately on the form). Then you had to find witnesses to vouch for you. They must not be members of your family. They must not be too well known to you. They must be 'independent' witnesses. Then they had to testify before an officer, whose convenience must be sought on his terms. And so on and so forth, there were endless formalities. In the end—in the end—the government might decide to give you some compensation for your losses. But surely this would have to wait until the figures of all the refugees had been put together. And this would have to wait further until the property left in India by the Muslims was added up. You saw that, didn't you? How else could you arrive at a proportionate figure? And all the while you stayed where you were and did for yourself.

The bus went slowly because of the rush hour. In Daryagunj two rickshaw drivers decided to have a chat while they were driving, and they almost blocked the road. They drove side by side and talked. The bus driver impatiently honked his horn but they paid no attention. That was another side of Delhi Lala Kanshi Ram enjoyed. There was constant excitement here, and to that extent he preferred Delhi to Sialkot. He got up from his seat and went up front to have a look at the rickshaws. And to the great annoyance of the bus driver, he laughed like a child when the rickshaw drivers wouldn't let him pass.

As he got off the bus at Kingsway Camp, it was around seven. These were winter evenings and it was dark. A small bazaar had sprung up outside the camp, where all kinds of odd thing from string cots to toiletries, were sold. Lala Kanshi Ram quickened his step to reach home; he was not properly clad and he was feeling cold. Somehow he sensed much tension in the bazaar, as he walked through it. He also saw small groups of people formed at various points, especially outside of the paan shops or tea shops where they had radio sets.

Lala Kanshi Ram noticed all this and yet he didn't think anything was wrong. Nor did he make any enquiries. Stepping out, and worrying about his financial situation, he reached his barracks and entered his room.

He saw the women of the family sitting together. Bibi Amar Vati and Sunanda had come over to their room, and they were sitting on cots.

Prabha Rani saw him and said: 'Have you heard? Gandhiji has been shot dead.'

'When?' he asked, stopping abruptly.

'This evening. We don't have the details.'

'It's good he is. He ruined us,' said Bibi Amar Vati.

Lala Kanshi Ram did not hear her. Without entering the room, he retraced his steps and went back to the bazaar.

He joined the first group he found. They were talking in whispers.

He asked of a man: 'Is it true Gandhiji has been shot?'

'Didn't you know?'

'Is he dead?'

'Yes, he's dead.'

They were playing devotional songs over the All India Radio. A news bulletin came on, and it confirmed what the man had told him. It said Gandhiji that evening had died at the hands of an assassin. He was walking to the prayer meeting from his room in Birla House, when a man approached him and fired three shots. Gandhiji's last words were 'Hey Rama' before he fell. The assassin, the announcement said, was a Hindu. To remove any misgivings, it was repeated the assassin was not a member of a minority community.

Many similar announcements were made that evening. Jawaharlal Nehru also came on the air, when he spoke of a light going out of their lives. It was no ordinary light, he said, it was a most extraordinary flame. It was now gone and India was plunged into darkness.

Lala Kanshi Ram heard all that but paid no serious attention to it, though a part of his mind said, wake up, these are good words. Gandhiji was dead—fully dead, completely dead. He found anything after that irrelevant and insignificant.

Arun heard the news at the river. He had joined Hindu College—one of the four men's colleges in Delhi—as a student. They wouldn't have him in the final year of the MA class, since the courses at Delhi were different. So he joined the lower class and was repeating a year. Beside Sialkot flowed the Aik, which was only a small stream. But beside Delhi flowed the sacred Yamuna. And Arun became a member of the College Boating Club, and every evening would cycle over to the river to row. His college was four miles from the camp. The Boat House lay midway, about two miles from either side. Often he stayed on at the college after his classes were over, and returned home only after he had done his rowing. He ate a snack in one of the shops outside of the college in Kashmiri Gate, and in the afternoon read in the college library. Then he cycled to the river and loved taking a boat out and being by himself for an hour or so. He was a lonely young man and he liked lonely, solitary games. At Sialkot he played tennis, which involved the minimum team work. Rowing involved no proximity to another human being at all.

He had brought the boat in and he was feeling happy. It was a sultry evening, but over the water there was a breeze. The porter who looked after the boats had a radio in the Boat House, and it was while Arun was returning the oars to him that he heard the news.

Taking his cycle, he blindly rushed home. He was afraid there would be a riot, even though they had announced the killer was not a Muslim. Many Muslims still lived in the Jama Masjid area; there were some in other areas too. Cutting through lanes, he reached Indraprastha College for women and from there took Alipur Road which led straight to the camp.

These had been bad months for him. He became aware of the loss of Chandni only after they had reached Delhi. When she was abducted in Narowal, they were on the move, and while he felt the hurt, he didn't have the occasion to fathom it. Now, with things more or less settled, he could open his heart to himself.

And it bled. Each night he wanted the night to extend for years. He wanted darkness in which he could drown himself—for ever. He went to bed and said, oh God, let the day never dawn. And he hugged his sleep, in which he found no peace but he found oblivion. If he woke in the middle of the night he groaned. Turning on his side, he went off to sleep again—or he lay half asleep and half awake. Chandni was gone. She was still alive, though? Hopefully. Where was she? In what shape? In what state? Turn on your side and drop off once again. Hug your sleep. Hug the darkness. Don't let the day dawn again. Look at your watch. A quarter past two. That gives you four clear hours of the night. Hold your pain. It's stealing up on you, it's coming, it's on your heart. The heart suffers a dull thud, a dull shock, and you have an unhealthy sweetness in your mouth. Hold it there. It is still dark. Turn over. Go back to sleep. Three o'clock. Four o'clock. Five o'clock. Even fifteen minutes of darkness were more welcome than the sun that was soon to rise. Oh, Chandni. Oh, Chandni. Oh, Chandni.

He got up in the morning, but only barely. Only a part of him got up. It washed itself, got dressed, took the cycle and went out into the day. The other part remained inert. No, it dragged him backwards. It pulled him back into that dark membrane where there was forgetfulness. He felt like flinging himself against a bus and destroying himself. But he stayed alive, to feel his hurt. In death he would feel nothing, he thought. He wanted to feel his pain, to sense it. In that hurt he still had a bond with the girl. Without the hurt the bond might be lost.

His father waited for a letter from Padmini; they all waited for a letter. None came. Arun thought it was better that way. What if the letter said there was no news of her? That she was dead? And if she was recovered, how *much* of her was recovered and had come back? It couldn't be *his* Chandni. He would gladly take her still but would *she* take *him*? He was afraid of what she might do or say. No, it was better this way. At least he had a memory. Day and night. Night and day. He saw girls in the college, the urban, stylish girls, and they were like marionettes to him—lifeless. He preferred his memory.

This had been his life these two and a half months, since their arrival in Delhi. Chandni had become his second self. She moved with him, ate with him, went to sleep with him. Only she ever remained a little apart. And he ached so because he couldn't shorten that distance.

Arun cycled fast, he wanted to get home before the situation got bad. He was certain a riot would break out in the city. If not the Muslims, the Punjabi refugees might be attacked.

'Did you hear the news?' he shouted, the moment he had placed the bicycle in the verandah.

'Yes,' said his father. 'What have you heard?'

'The same.'

'Where are you coming from?'

'From the river.'

'Not from Kashmiri Gate?'

'No.'

'I should like to know what's happening in the town.'

'I too.'

They looked worried.

'Well, it's a good thing he is gone. He brought nothing but misery to us,' Bibi Amar Vati said.

'Don't say that, behan.'

'Why not? Isn't that true?'

Lala Kanshi Ram was quiet.

'Look at your own lot. Compare your present "store" with what you had in Sialkot.'

In a part of the verandah, Lala Kanshi Ram had fixed up a couple of wooden crates, where each morning he set up a small shop and sold groceries. Prabha Rani helped him carry the stuff from the room to the corner of the verandah. In the evening she helped him carry it back to the room. The competition was hard. There was a bazaar outside, and there were several similar stores set up by other refugees inside the camp. But it was on the meagre earnings of this store the family now lived.

It hurt Lala Kanshi Ram no end. From the time he set up this little shop, he had stopped wearing a turban. A turban was a sign of respect, of dignity. He had no dignity left. He now wore a forage cap. Or he sat bare-headed, advertising his humble position to the world.

'I'm ruined, but look at *your* luck,' Bibi Amar Vati said.

'I agree. Yet his death hurts.'

'Hurts, hurts, hurts. You're too sentimental!'

'It does hurt, mother. Men like him come once in centuries,' said Sunanda.

After the disaster at Narowal, Sunanda's face had acquired a tragic mould which was shattering for those who had known her before. She was ever so dainty, so distant. Now she withdrew herself to the other end of the world. But with dignity, with absolute dignity. She had lost her husband, she had been defiled. Her honour remained intact, though, in her own mind. That's why she did not feel embarrassed before Arun. She joked with him and laughed at his jokes, and so innocent and dove-like did she look, as though through some miraculous process she had not only been restored to her wholeness but also to her virginity. But she looked tragic, too. Her features had mellowed further under suffering and had become confirmed in their remoteness.

'I like *you* saying that,' Bibi Amar Vati flared up. 'You lost your husband—nothing worse could have happened to you!'

Arun and Sunanda looked at each other.

'It all happened because of the partition. And it was Gandhi who sanctioned the partition.'

'That's not true.' Arun felt he had to put the record straight. 'It was the other Congress leaders, like Nehru and Patel.'

'They were his stooges.'

'No, auntie. You're wrong there. In the final days, they didn't listen to him.'

Bibi Amar Vati looked at Arun with displeasure. How ugly had he grown over the months, with those pimples on his nose!

Nava Kant came in crying and said his sister was beating him. Sunanda got up and left for the adjoining room.

'I'm sure it must be some Punjabi who has killed him and I don't blame that Punjabi,' said Bibi Amar Vati, before she also got up and left. It was Bibi Amar Vati's guess, but they felt it must be a Punjabi. Only the day after they learned the killer was a Maharashtrian, and a rank communalist.

Prabha Rani sat silent throughout. She was an uncomplicated woman, and to her Gandhi was a mahatma, a great soul. The death of any mahatma would upset her, and she felt bad about it.

'I better light the fire,' she said, for want of saying something.

'No, Arun's mother, don't light the fire today.'

She thought for a second. 'I guess you're right.'

'You may eat if you want. Arun may eat. I won't.'

'I won't eat, either,' said Arun.

They sat on their cots and no one said anything more. In the next room Arun could hear Sunanda sewing on her newly acquired sewing machine. That's how *they* made their living. They had bought a used sewing machine, and Sunanda took in odd tailoring jobs. She mostly made children's clothes. She also took in clothes for alterations.

Arun went to the bazaar several times to listen to the radio. Lala Kanshi Ram went with him. For the first time Lala Kanshi Ram became aware of a blessing azadi had brought them. The crowds in the bazaar were thick. Some shops were closed, but many were still open. Groups of people stood all over in the bazaar, and each face was blank. They were all refugees from West Punjab and there was not a man in that crowd who had not suffered in the riots. Yet they all looked crestfallen, as if this death was a personal loss. Some did speak in the vein of Bibi Amar Vati, blaming everything on Gandhi. Most stood quiet with pursed lips, afraid of bursting into tears. Those who talked, talked in hoarse asides. As soon as a news bulletin came on, all noise died down. After the news bulletin, they resumed talking in subdued tones.

What impressed Lala Kanshi Ram was the pride with which each man stood. He would be blind if he didn't see that. He thought of the pre-independence days before the nation was free. How self-conscious the people were then! An Indian leader dying and the crowd feeling openly for him? It was unthinkable. They sorrowed and they came out on the roads, but there was no dignity in it. They were afraid of persecution at the hands of the British, they were afraid of violence, they were afraid of their own people who might betray them. And in reaction to those fears, they went into excesses. They wept too loudly or they shouted too loudly. Today the men stood in pride—evenly balanced, firm, sure of themselves. Unlike the past, there was no leader urging them to demonstrate their feelings. The feelings had their own recourse. Lala Kanshi Ram raised his head with pride and stretched back his shoulders. He was unrestricted now, he was untrammelled.

But was he really? Lying on his bed late in the night, he thought of it. What of the loss of personality he had suffered? What of the material losses? What of Madhu? *That* could never be made good, never atoned for. And he saw years of bleakness before him, *years* of desolation. Queues and long waits and filing of petitions and more petitions and further bleakness. He felt himself standing before a tunnel, where he could not see the other end. How long was the tunnel? And it all looked so unnecessary, so superfluous, to him—what they were going through. Freedom was on its way and nothing could have stopped it. If only they had not given in so easily to the partition.

He lay awake and thought. He felt so tired, his legs sagging heavily—even as he lay supine on the bed. If he closed his eyes, he saw the rough corridors of 'P' Block and the harsh, rude faces of the men who were to decide his future. If he opened them, he saw the grey, unfeeling corrugated ceiling of the roof. Coldness and bleakness, close the eyes or open them. He wanted to talk about it to Prabha Rani or to Arun. That was another ruin azadi had caused. He had lost the ability to communicate with his family. He couldn't establish a contact either with his wife or with his son. The affection was there. The concern was there. Their respect for him was there, too. Yet the contact was broken. Something had driven them apart. No, he couldn't reach them. For a few moments he had succeeded in the train—with his wife. That wouldn't come again.

In their beds, Arun and Prabha Rani too were awake. Their eyes were open and they were looking at the ceiling. Arun wanted to sit up and speak to his father, but he couldn't. He too felt a wall between them, a hostility of a kind, he didn't know for what. His father had been superb throughout, he had carried his pain nobly, and Arun loved him for that. At a certain level he cared more for him than before. Yet he could not form a connection with him.

Prabha Rani knew her husband was awake, but she did not feel like calling out to him. She was caught in the same snare. She had lost the ease that was between them, and had become confined to her own single self.

The three of them lay fully awake. Not being able to fathom their minds and feeling restless about it. Not being able to talk to each other and feeling guilty about it. Not being able to go to sleep and feeling angry about it. A sadness weighed on their hearts, and each felt stifled, crushed.

In the adjoining room, Sunanda's sewing machine was still running at top speed. Occasionally it stopped. Occasionally it made only a slight noise, as when the wheel had moved only a circle or two. And then it went wheezing on at top speed, as though it would never stop.

Arun tried to imagine her. She must be biting the thread with her white teeth and with those sensuous, delicately curved lips. She must be running the wheel back and forth with her hand. Now the tender hand with its tapering fingers must be on the handle attached to the wheel, for she was running it real fast. But that did not work either. Arun had lost contact with her too.

The machine went whirring on, its wheel turning fast and its little needle moving up and down, murmuring and sewing through the cloth. The doors of both the rooms shook with its vibration.